PRAISE FOR DANIEL GONZALEZ

"Gonzalez has married Americans' childlike sense that TV characters are real people with the now-warped Horatio Alger notion that anyone can come up with the next big thing if one taps into the underbelly of fad fascinations, like celebrities' real-life downfalls and obsession with psychopathic spree killers. Around the edges flicker our common annoyances with aspects of everyday life from airline-travel protocol, to celebrity chefs, to theme restaurants, to the way failed relationships continue to affect us. With a style at once deadpan and tongue-in-cheek, Gonzalez has tweaked the definitions of representative, realistic and dystopian fiction."

— CRIS MAZZA, AUTHOR OF *IT'S NO PUZZLE: A MEMOIR IN ARTIFACT*

"In a world of tradeoffs, how do we live an authentic life? Thus wonder a pair of earnest and loveable seekers so hungry for lives without duplicity or regret that they slip down a rabbit-hole proposition: that psychopaths will show them the way. Funny, upsetting, and unique, *Death Row Restaurant* is a prison-cooked satire that hits the spot, and throws away the key."

—ALEX SHAKAR, AUTHOR OF *LUMINARIUM*

"Death and ingestion, culinary art and literary art, the act of killing and the act of cooking—*Death Row Restaurant* probes each of these and more, exploring nothing less than the violence underwritten by our present age. Gonzalez is cooking with gas. A darkly hilarious and innovative novel."

—BROOKS STERRITT, AUTHOR OF *THE HISTORY OF AMERICA IN MY LIFETIME*

DEATH ROW RESTAURANT

DANIEL GONZALEZ

Copyright © 2024 by Daniel Gonzalez

Cover by Matthew Revert

ISBN: 9781955904971

Troy, NY

CLASH Books

clashbooks.com

For Darcie

Since sex criminals do not change their MO or by nature cannot do so, I will not change mine. The code word for me will be... bind them, torture them, kill them, BTK, you see he 's at it again.

—DENNIS RADER

Serial killers do, on a small scale, what governments do on a large one. They are products of our times and these are bloodthirsty times.

—RICHARD RAMIREZ

I haven't blocked out the past. I wouldn't trade the person I am or what I've done or the people I've known for anything. So I do think about it. And at times, it's a rather mellow trip to lie back and remember.

—TED BUNDY

CONTENTS

DEATH ROW RESTAURANT

PROLOGUE

"THERE'S fried and scrambled and, uh…"

"That's not what I mean," Dave interrupted. When it came to the topic of cooking an egg, Dave had the patience of a glacier. Anyone calling himself a cook must be intimately familiar with how to prepare an egg. But how could Dave get a fifteen-year-old kid cooking on weekends in his Oklahoma diner to take this seriously? "The egg is nature's perfect food," Dave began, "but also its most vexing." The word 'vexing' caused his young assistant to wince and shift his weight from foot to foot, as if he had a fierce need to pee.

"Hard boiled?" the teenager offered. He had taken this job solely to earn enough money for a PlayStation 5. Then he would quit, hopefully without absorbing these life lessons.

Dave clutched his forehead.

In the few minutes they had been considering the neatly stacked pyramid of fresh eggs on the diner's counter, the sun had fully risen. It screamed through the diner's window, erasing the scuffs and dings in the well used diner countertop, which needed replacement. Dave snatched an egg from atop the pyramid and Billy did the same. With a quick and intuitive movement, Dave dashed the egg against the flat surface of the counter, the proper way to do it, and then pried the egg open over the griddle. It spurted and jiggled on the hot butter.

"The difficult thing about cooking an egg," Dave continued, bending over the griddle with rapt attention, "is that the whites cook at a different rate than the yolk."

Billy placed his egg back on the pyramid. This was not the kind of training where you mimic what you are told. The point, Billy understood, was deeper.

"The secret, Billy, is not to flip it." Dave tossed a pat of butter onto the griddle, then spooned the hot butter over the top of the egg to finish cooking it.

Before Dave could say anything else, the bell over the diner's entrance clanged, indicating a customer. A burst of dust and road oil blew into the diner, along with a gangly black man who ambled to the counter with a teenage gait.

"Coffee," the man stated, brushing his graying hair with his fingers. He dressed mortician chic, a thin black tie, white dress shirt, and plain black jacket and pants. Dave wordlessly reached in front of Billy and retrieved the coffee pot, revealing several raised, translucent scars snaking across Dave's forearm.

"You get those scars from cooking?" Billy asked.

Dave set a saucer and then a coffee mug in front of their lone customer.

"He got them in prison," the gangly man corrected. "In San Quentin prison, where this man cooked in the greatest, most authentic restaurant that has ever existed." The man lifted both the saucer and coffee cup to his lips with a steady hand and took a sip. "In prison," the man continued, setting the cup back down on the counter and tossing aside the saucer. "In prison, you gotta protect what's important. You gotta protect your neck. That's how you got those scars, isn't that right, Dave?"

"You gonna order something?"

"How would I know any food cooked in this place is authentic?" The man demanded.

"We got eggs, chorizo, hash browns, pancakes and grits," Dave handed the man a greasy menu. "All of it cooked with great care." Dave turned and with a flick of his wrist, pirouetted the fried egg off his spatula onto a plate. He dashed some pepper on the egg and slid the plate to their lone customer. A near perfect fried egg. It gleamed.

"I've got the gas chamber," the man declared.

"Try your egg," Dave insisted. "It's just as good as any egg we served in San Quentin."

"The gas chamber. We had it disassembled and stored after the incident — until things died down. It's in a warehouse in Lambert, Oklahoma. All we have to do is put it on a truck and take it to

Macalester, the largest maximum security prison in Oklahoma," the man said. "We assemble the gas chamber at Macalester. They have nearly seventy men on Death Row who could be our staff."

"Look, Todd. I'm done with all that. I've got a nice place here and I'm going to teach my man Billy how to cook."

The black man frowned. He hated being called Todd.

"Come on, Dave," Todd said, pushing the plate with his perfect fried egg aside with disinterest, "you have to admit, no one cooked gnocchi with burnt butter and walnuts the way Gary Ridgway did. No one," he repeated, taking a sip of coffee. "You know it. I know it. Ridgway confessed to fifty murders. He was meticulous. And he made the most delicious gnocchi the world has ever tasted."

"Forty-eight," Dave corrected. "Though he is suspected of more than seventy murders."

It was the old routine. Dave and Todd Bridges had poured over hundreds of dossiers of serial killers together, some of the worst men in the world. And Todd was right. Gary Ridgway had taken to cooking right away. From the beginning, Ridgway knew how to improvise. Like with the gnocchi, Ridgway gave the dough a short knead, shorter than Dave had thought advisable. But before Dave could correct his technique, Ridgway was popping off fluffy nuggets of gnocchi with a flick of his wrist. At San Quentin, Ridgway often paired his gnocchi with wild greens and ricotta. But once, when Death Row Restaurant hosted a contingent of NBA All Stars, Ridgway had served his gnocchi in a semolina porridge dredged in brown butter and sage.

The dish was sublime.

"Ridgway's gnocchi was delicious because Ridgway is a killer. He owns what he does as who he is," the lone customer in Dave's diner insisted, raising his coffee cup to his lips, attempting to drink from the empty cup and then setting it down again as if he had gotten a hot pull of joe.

Dave pivoted his hips, snatched the coffee pot, now more than an hour old and refilled the man's cup. "Gary Ridgway had absolutely no reason to work at *Death Row Restaurant*, Dave. Ridgway was never getting out of prison after forty eight cold blooded murders. And *Death Row Restaurant* paid him nothing for his work. Ridgway had no reason, no reason whatsoever to make gnocchi in semolina porridge in our restaurant except that he wanted to make that gnocchi," Todd asserted. "Now I know things didn't go perfectly at San Quentin," He had already finished his second cup of coffee, but once again lifted the empty coffee cup to his lips and pretended to take a satisfying swallow, which bothered Dave, "—but the principle of it, the kind of authenticity that really matters in a restaurant — that absolutely holds."

"Things didn't go perfectly?" Dave repeated, astonished, then pulled his sleeves up to show the full extent of the scarring that snaked up and down his arms. "I was one of the lucky ones that night. What about what happened to the Governor?"

"What happened to the Governor was a tragedy."

"What about Kate?" Dave insisted. "You forget about what she went through?"

"Therapy helped," Bridges shrugged. Then he slid his hips off the greasy stool and stood up before Dave could refill his cup for a third time. He locked eyes with Dave and then ceremonially adjusted his thin, black tie.

"Kate would want this, Dave. Right up to the end we were all intrigued by the idea of Death Row Restaurant. I can still feel the place," Todd said, using the soft tones of a minister.

"He's going to make an exit," Dave turned and remarked to Billy, who was still shuffling from side to side. Dave decided the boy might really need to use the restroom. "He always does this. He's a former 1980's television star. He plans his entrances and exits more carefully than NASA plans atmospheric reentries."

Todd took a few steps towards the door. The sunlight was blinding. Then he turned and tossed a rubber banded stack of manila folders onto a nearby table.

"Those are the dossiers for Macalester. We won't have the star power we had at San Quentin. But Macalester has plenty of great candidates. It's the oldest prison in Oklahoma."

"Todd," Dave called out, just as the man had opened the door, letting in another burst of road oil, only this time flush with the scent of roses. After relocating to Oklahoma from San Francisco, Dave had been surprised to learn that Oklahoma residents love their roses. Not all varieties grow in Oklahoma. No sissy roses, Dave had been informed by his neighbors. Only the heartiest of roses survive here. Todd paused in the doorway as if he had just remembered something, only he didn't turn around to ask anything. He just stood in the doorway, his silhouette accented by his mortician chic suit. Sunlight rushed past him on all sides. It looked like a movie poster. Dave knew Todd would love that. "I don't understand why you would do this. I mean, after what happened the last time at San Quentin."

Todd turned his head slightly. He shrugged and tapped his AirPods. Dave thought he heard faint applause. Then the man exited the diner, trailing his arm behind him, pulling the door fully open so that it slammed home.

PART I: KATE

KATE WOULD NEVER HAVE GOTTEN involved with Death Row Restaurant if she hadn't hated Wichita, Kansas so much.

The whole thing began in the lobby of a United Airlines' flight attendant training facility in Chicago. Kate and Tina, both in their mid-twenties, had just endured a long-winded graduation ceremony, the culmination of ten weeks of flight attendant training. When most people think of flight attendants they picture them pouring diet cokes into small cups and doling out headphones. But the reality of flight attendant training had been much more intense. At thirty thousand feet dangers proliferate. Flight attendants now get significant medical training and even hand-to-hand combat training. Fully one third of Kate's initial training class hadn't survived the regimen. And although Kate's parents did not fly in for her graduation, and Kate's friends from college and her parents' friends from her hometown of Scarsdale, New York will no doubt think of Kate as a sky waitress, Kate had bigger concerns than their misguided notions of what flight attendants do.

What mattered to Kate on the day of her graduation was her route assignment. With zero seniority, Kate knew her inaugural route assignment wouldn't be glamorous. But Kate felt strongly, perhaps for the first time in her life, that after many cancellations and mechanical delays, her life was finally ready for takeoff. She needed a route assignment that would allow her to flourish, a city she could get intimate with in all the ways her personal relationships hadn't so far been able to accomplish. The effort Kate had put into her flight attendant training reassured her. She would be assigned to an interesting route.

At this point, the only thing dampening Kate's delicious anticipation were the graduation speeches by United Airlines executives. The female executive had surprised Kate by dressing in a sleeveless boiler suit. The look combined a 'can do' femininity with a sense of authority. The male executive had followed this lead, dressing in a power suit that had been tailored, but not aggressively, producing a softer more empathetic drape across the shoulders and waist. Each had given a short speech, riffing on United Airlines' mission statement: 'Uniting the World.' The speeches were far too whimsical for Kate, with too many jokes. They refused to mention the many issues currently confronting airline travel. Only 3% of the world's citizens took a long-haul flight in any given year, but this small group generated 5% of global CO_2 emissions. And what about the teenagers United Airlines had barred from a flight out of Denver, claiming their leggings were too racy? Or the videos posted on Twitter of an elderly doctor being forcibly removed from an overbooked flight? What about the media gaffe following the violent removal, where a United Airlines spokesman had argued, "a bakery doesn't want a bunch of stale bread it can't sell at the end of the day. An unsold seat is stale bread. We have to overbook."

Kate had always been bothered by flippant positivity. At this crucial stage in her life she needed more. But unlike the idealistic college student Kate had so recently been, Kate no longer let herself get wrapped up in moral contradictions. She had started to feel her own contradictions full force as she pushed towards her late twenties. She wasn't joining United Airlines to 'unite the world' or to 'save the planet.' She was doing it for personal reasons, even if she was unable to articulate these reasons to her disappointed parents, who like most Scarsdale mothers and fathers, had expected Kate to take a job in finance after college, not to flounder around waiting tables before becoming a flight attendant. So as soon as the graduation ceremony concluded, Kate and her friend Tina shuffled into the lobby where Kate was finally handed her route assignment letter. She set the letter briefly in her lap. Her skirt had clumped from static and Kate smoothed the wrinkles before tearing open the envelope.

ORD to ICT, Kate noted. She would start her career in the Midwest.

"At least Indianapolis has a major sports team," Kate muttered to Tina. The lobby, which had felt churchlike only minutes ago, had filled with the clicking of hard heeled formal shoes and cloying perfume as newly minted flight attendants sought their route assignments. "Wasn't Michael Jackson from Indiana?" Kate asked.

"Dallas! I got Dallas!" Tina gasped, pressing her palm to her chest and fanning herself with the envelope of her assignment letter. Tina had neatly sheared her envelope open. Her excitement was palpable. Tina had always wished she'd grown up in Texas.

"Looks like I got Indianapolis," Kate tried again, shoving Tina's shoulder slightly. "ORD to ICT."

Tina's head popped up.

"ICT? That's not Indianapolis. That's Wichita."

"Wichita?"

Kate hadn't thought about Wichita since her sophomore year in college when she had faked an interest in the 'Wichita Shockers' men's basketball team during March Madness in order to spend time with her boyfriend. By the time Brad's Cinderella team ended its run for an NCAA title, providing Kate a certain satisfaction, she had accumulated a laundry list of concerns about their relationship. Before the post-game show had ended, Kate sat Brad down to discuss their issues. For instance, prior to his obsession with March Madness, Brad had presented himself as someone who valued world cultures and fighting injustices. Brad enjoyed sunsets and discussing socialism, sometimes over a bottle of wine. Yet during March Madness, Brad's tribalism became clear. He favored the Wichita Shockers to an astonishing degree.

"They're my team," Brad shrugged. He could barely understand what Kate was accusing him of, his head still lost in might-have-beens and bad calls.

Kate went down her list of grievances one at a time, and although Brad nodded and reassured Kate, although he sometimes squeezed her shoulder and once almost apologized, Kate didn't feel heard by Brad at all. In fact, the whole conversation left Kate feeling invisible. So much so, that when Brad believed that he'd smoothed things over nicely and went back to the post game show, Kate slipped out of his apartment for good. This quiet ending to Kate and Brad's relationship proved particularly difficult for Kate. She and Brad had spent months living out of backpacks at one another's apartments. They had held hands as they walked to class, as they stood in the corners of parties. They had attended each other's fraternity and sorority formals. And in Kate's mind at least, she and Brad had made plans to stand apart from the herd. They planned to travel and find their own path in life. They planned to make a pile of money without actually caring about the money. And Brad, how could he not even have noticed Kate had walked out on him for good?

Very quickly after the break up, Kate's hatred for that stupid, over-achieving 'Wichita Shockers' basketball team was replaced by something far more troubling, a bizarre news story about a Wichita serial killer who had finally been captured. Over a period of thirty years, husband, father and church president, Dennis Rader had ritually murdered ten people in Wichita, Kansas. Outwardly, Rader had been a model citizen. Even his family hadn't known about his ravenous sexual brutality. And while every aspect of Rader's story troubled Kate, one victim struck Kate the hardest. Victim number nine, Vicki Wegerle. Rader had strangled Vicki Wegerle in broad daylight on her living room floor, her two-year-old son nearby. Rader had selected Vicki because he happened to drive by her house while she was practicing piano, and Vicki's powerful music, an anomaly on the otherwise quiet, residential Wichita street, was what had drawn him to her. Simple facts from the case left Kate struggling to do even basic things for herself like floss her teeth or take out the trash. Every detail of Vicki Wegerle's murder terrified Kate. For instance, Vicki's husband, Bill, had arrived home for lunch minutes after Rader had fled the scene. In fact, Bill Wegerle believes he drove past Rader a few blocks from his house. Bill had noticed a car that looked just like his wife's car, but driven by a strange man. Although Rader bungled his escape in a dozen ways, authorities investigated Bill Wegerle for more than a decade. It wasn't until Rader sought credit for strangling Vicki, it wasn't until Rader sent media outlets Vicki's driver's license and polaroids from the killing, that Bill Wegerle was cleared as a murder suspect.

Perhaps the worst part of Vicki's story, for Kate, was how clearly all of the reports articulated Rader's pride in what he had done. Kate was unable to recover from this. She wasn't proud of anything she had done in her life and the strangeness of comparing her own deficiencies to Dennis Rader's pride in murdering poor Vicki Wegerle had left

Kate unmoored and helpless. And here Kate was, years later, sitting in the lobby of the United Airlines training facility with sound bites about 'uniting the world' still bouncing around in her head as she thought about the most horrible time in her life and the shittiest place on earth — Wichita, Kansas. The traveling Kate had once naively planned with Brad, the perpetual 'fresh start' Kate was still searching for would instead be the ORD to ICT route serviced by United Airlines — Chicago, Illinois to Wichita, Kansas.

Just the thought of visiting Wichita made Kate nauseous.

Kate tried to put things into perspective. She felt much older and more experienced than the naive college sophomore who had stumbled upon the story of Dennis Rader's arrest at a vulnerable time in her life. That was how Kate had always couched her brief fascination with Dennis Rader. But Kate realized now that even her privileged and safe encounter with Rader would have lifelong consequences.

While many who followed Rader's story reveled in the stupidity that led to his capture, Kate had been oddly devastated by the sequence of events that had led to Rader's arrest. Rader had kept hoards of souvenirs from his victims, a stash he raided in order to send proof of his crimes to police and media, to garner attention. Only Rader grew tired of the work involved. In order to send a package to police that could jolt them into responding, Rader had to shop for dolls he could use to painstakingly re-enact his murders in ways that only the killer would know. He had to scrub away fingerprints and play cat and mouse with the police to ensure his packages were received and given proper attention. And all of this took a great deal of time and labor. Aside from the packages, Rader spent whole afternoons stalking potential victims. But, Rader had a job as a compliance officer and his own family to attend to. He needed a more economical way of ensuring he got proper credit for his murders. So in a note to police, Rader asked if it was safe for him to forward floppy disks. The police of course accepted the offer and then traced the disk's metadata to Dennis Rader's church — and ultimately to serial killer Dennis Rader himself. For Kate, the fact that Rader was this stupid and impulsive, the fact that Rader had killed Vicki Wegerle and Shirley Vian in broad daylight and that he signed his notes to the police by childishly embellishing the "B" in BTK into breasts, made Rader's decades long elusiveness impossible to stomach.

Yet Kate couldn't blame the police for not catching Rader sooner.

Unlike Ted Bundy, whose victims tended to have straight hair parted down the middle and hoop earrings, Rader never had a type of victim. Rader killed men. He killed women. He killed children and grandmothers. He was very hard to catch because what mattered to Rader was the ritual, the slow strangulation of bound victims, bringing them in and out of consciousness, extending the torture while taking pleasure in the arousal their helplessness generated in him. For Dennis Rader, the identity of the victims was secondary to the act of possessing them.

"We have to celebrate," Tina said, gripping Kate's shoulder. Tina was still gushing over her Dallas route.

Still hunched over her knees on the small, marble bench they shared, Kate gave a slight nod. Her stomach was queasy. She burped quietly. She held her United Airlines route assignment in one hand and the destroyed envelope in her other hand. ORD to ICT. And Kate could still picture the moment Rader had heard Vicki Wegerle playing Mozart, his elbow dangling out the window of his truck, a sack lunch on the seat next to him. And Rader slowed down to listen.

In college, Kate had tried to evade her terror by considering how unlucky it is to encounter a serial killer. High estimates put one's chances at .00064%. Practically nonexistent. Meeting a serial killer was as unlikely as winning the Powerball. But this randomness failed to reassure Kate. After all, what was Kate's ever shifting college major if not the product of random aspects of her upbringing? And Kate had met Brad, who she once thought was the love of her life, in a bowling class she had registered for because she felt bloated one afternoon and wanted a fun way to get a little exercise. Kate had often shared the story of how she and Brad met in bowling class at parties, thinking it cute. But after learning about Dennis Rader, Kate couldn't stand her random life. The more closely Kate looked at herself, the more everything she did bothered her. She crumpled toilet paper rather than folded it, for instance. And the procedure she caught herself employing to choose fruit in a grocery store was just a series of shakes and squeezes that she had seen in movies. Kate had no idea what she was doing in even the most basic aspects of her life.

Killing, Kate realized, shifting her weight on the uncomfortable bench in the United Airlines lobby, was how someone like Dennis Rader lived the United Airlines' motto. United Airlines existed to make money. That was the central premise of all their routes and procedures. Plastering "uniting the world" on billboards and stationary transformed work done to make money into work done as an end in itself. Yet compared to BTK, the cheap parlor trick of their corporate motto had its meaning evacuated. Unlike United Airlines, whose procedures and ad campaigns were constantly updated and revised to better fit public preferences, every detail of Rader's murders was an absolute necessity. They were 'ends' not 'means.' Kate couldn't say the same thing about anything in her life. Kate didn't even want to be an airline stewardess. That was just a means to a different end. She thought travel could help sort herself out.

On a personal level, Kate saw herself as very much like Vicki Wegerle. Part of it was that like Vicki, Kate played the piano, although she had no illusions about her music being moving or beautiful. In fact, playing piano had always made Kate feel clumsy and unlovable. She had started piano at six years old, pushed by her mother. And Kate struggled in those early years, her fingers so tentative that she barely made contact with the keys when she played, making her music almost inaudible.

"You'll grow to love it," her mother always argued, no matter how much Kate cried and insisted that she hated piano. And when she finally dug in her heels at the age of nine, crying angrily and insisting that she couldn't do it, that her fingers were not good enough and never would be, her mother hugged Kate tightly and whispered in her ear that she believed in her. She believed Kate could do it. She believed this even as Kate stumbled through beginner lessons. She believed this even when Kate's piano teacher suggested she switch to a less complex instrument — like a recorder. But Kate stuck with piano, which became her proof that what we do today is a down payment on tomorrow. This was how to build a life. In middle school, Kate studied the seven habits of highly effective teens. She forced herself to practice piano, even though she hated it. She learned where to place her hands and how to touch the keys. Unable to play piano with both hands, Kate practiced playing with one. She learned the left hand, then the right. And when she couldn't play both parts at once, she cried and then tried again.

And now, as she sat in a lobby in Chicago, an inaudible hum of voices reacting to their route assignments, reacting to the start of something new, Kate clutched her ORD to ICT route assignment letter. She was once again living for the future, for a time when she would finally be where she wanted to be. She would 'puddle jump' for a few years, then get a route to Paris or London, Copenhagen or Moscow.

Kate thought about how she would sometimes watch boxing with her father, how they had their little daddy/daughter shows. Kate had liked that it was boxing and that her father didn't treat her like she was fragile or dainty. One time, her dad leaned over, digging into the popcorn bowl between them on the couch and said, "the great boxers make their opponents feel like they are actively participating in their own ass kicking." Kate hadn't understood back then. Now she did. All Kate had was her future, her habits, her routines. The very things that a serial killer preys on. And she felt a cloying sickness.

"Wichita isn't so bad," Tina assured Kate. She had put her route assignment letter into her purse, refusing to even fold it. And with a surplus of sympathy for others less fortunate, Tina added, "besides, you'll spend half your time in Chicago. And we'll only be jumping puddles for a year or two."

It was true. When Tina and Kate had started their flight attendant training ten weeks ago, Midwestern commuter routes seemed quaint. Not everyone had grown up in Scarsdale among the children of brokers and financiers. Not everyone summered in Southampton and played tennis and squash and had driveways one could land a plane on. Although Tina wasn't from Scarsdale, she had grown up in the Philadelphia suburbs in the 'Main Line,' where the railroad first connected suburban country estates to the city, one of the wealthiest areas of the country. Tina grew up around places like the Appleford Estate, a three-hundred-year-old, twenty-four-acre garden, arboretum and bird sanctuary designed by a famous architect whose name Tina constantly referenced (and Kate could never recall). 'Main Line' was home to the Devon Horse Show, one of the country's oldest and most prestigious equestrian events. So to Tina and Kate, the wholesome earnestness of states like Nebraska, Wisconsin, Iowa, Indiana, and Kansas sounded as exotic as any country in the Far East. For Kate, Kansas might as well be Kathmandu. The customs and aspirations of Kansas residents would certainly be accessible to someone with backgrounds like Kate's and Tina's only from the outside — as tourists. Ten weeks ago, all this had made Kate feel good about the idea of jumping puddles, had made her feel that this period in her life was itself an experience, a destination rather than a layover. A Midwestern commuter route, she had thought, will be sort of like a vacation. But now that it was really happening, Kate felt like she would never understand Wichita, just like she would never understand a serial killer like Dennis Rader.

And perhaps, if Kate had landed on a route to Milwaukee, WI or to Columbus, OH or even to Iowa City, IA — things would have worked out for her. But like when Kate's college boyfriend drank so much beer during the Wichita State Shockers' upset victory over number two ranked Tennessee that he woke up in the middle of the night and urinated in a wicker basket next to Kate's desk, ruining all of Kate's birthday cards from her family and friends — Kate knew that her current situation was doomed.

"I thought it was the toilet," Brad had said the next day, as if this kind of thing happens to everyone. Then he popped a frozen breakfast sandwich in Kate's microwave.

It was, Kate suspected, all of these things at once that made her assignment to the ORD to ICT route so devastating. But there was nothing she could do about it. So Kate left the United Airlines flight attendant training facility with Tina and a gaggle of other recently minted flight attendants. And after a few drinks and numerous toasts at a nearby bar, Kate resolved to maintain a positive mental attitude for the rest of the evening and for the following week, and even at the moment Kate's inaugural flight as a fully trained United Airlines flight attendant lifted from the ground at O'Hare International Airport and banked hard northwest from Chicago towards Iowa. As she steadied herself in the crew rest area, she closed her eyes and tried with all her might to feel she was embarking on an entirely new journey.

And Instead, Kate knew with absolute certainty that she just couldn't stand Wichita, Kansas.

———

Only slightly less populous than Memphis or Milwaukee, Wichita felt less deserving of its minor status as hub city. Milwaukee has its famous cheese curds, Memphis has BBQ and blues, Wichita isn't known for anything but a deranged serial killer and a modestly over-achieving college basketball team.

"People are nice here, dear," Kate was told, by a frumpy, grand-motherly type as the few passengers on her inaugural flight deplaned in Wichita. The flight had been unremarkable except for a bit of turbu-lence common on the route. The woman mumbled this Wichita truism while lightly gripping Kate's elbow for stability as she stepped from the plane to the passenger boarding bridge. And Kate, to put it mildly, had a strong reaction to this suggestion about Wichita. A stripe of nausea leapt up her throat, and Kate clenched her mouth shut and swallowed hard. When the nausea relented, she found herself fighting a sudden urge to storm the cockpit, grab the controls, turn the plane around, and immediately get the fuck out of Wichita. Kate manufactured a smile. She smiled her way through the post flight airplane check, smiled as the crew strode through Eisenhower Airport to the airport Hilton. Then Kate slammed her hotel room door on the good-looking pilot who had escorted her on her first layover in Wichita, Kansas. Had the pilot lingered, he would have heard Kate retch into the toilet.

Layovers in Wichita became a regular thing in Kate's life and she discovered that Wichita not only made her nauseous but invariably gave her a sore throat as well. Kate suspected her raw throat and crackling voice came from actively stifling her gag reflex for the sixteen hours she had to spend in Wichita. After a day or two elsewhere, her symptoms always dissipated. On top of her physical symptoms, Kate found Wichita to be psychologically demanding. Anything she had been looking forward to disappeared behind a fog of depression upon entering Wichita airspace. In Wichita, Kate's whole rationale for becoming a flight attendant — traveling the world — felt both unlikely and beside the point. The feeling was so rigid and overwhelming that after a single glance at the flat desolation of the Eisenhower airport tarmac and a porter's strangely proud declaration that the terminal had recently been renovated with led light strips, Kate threw up on her shoes. Kate knew, just knew — that no one who spends this much time in Wichita goes on to anything substantial in life.

———

When Kate was first introduced to Dave, she did not see him as a love interest. Part of it was his uneven balding and generally puffy appearance. He had to be in his forties. But part of it, Kate knew, was the effect of the men's United Airlines uniform, which suffered from the designer's attempts to distinguish it from everyday apparel (and from the uniforms of police and security personnel). The resultant flamboyant sleeves and poofy shoulders approached the idea of military tassels but then aborted the look just in time. The uniform was both tailored and baggy. It had stylish flourishes yet refuted them with a sack-like overall look common to prison jumpsuits. So it was hard to get much of a sense of Dave on their first flight together, ORD to ICT, a nauseating affair that left Kate feeling especially lonely and useless (there had been almost no passengers on the flight). Mid-flight, Kate sat herself down in the galley, burping up bile, her head pounding and her throat threatening to close. She had already acquired a reputation as a "slam and click" — a flight attendant so above spending time with pilots that she slams her hotel room door in their faces and then locks the latch. Kate didn't recall locking the latch on pilots who had escorted her to her room, only the dry heaves that consumed most of her evenings at the airport Hilton in Wichita.

Dave brought Kate a cup of Earl Grey tea. He told her not to worry about the rule that flight attendants could never be seen eating by passengers. He reserved some of the fresh chocolate chip cookies he had baked for first class passengers and gave them to Kate. They were still warm when she dunked them in the cup of milk Dave brought her. The empty flight started to make Kate feel close to Dave. She was still keenly aware that Dave lacked just about everything she considered a prerequisite in a boyfriend. Dave wasn't just a flight attendant. He was a career flight attendant. Dave wasn't just balding, but balding poorly and unevenly. And he was too old for Kate. But Dave had a kindness she could only describe as instinctual. Dave's surprisingly efficient movements in the cramped quarters of the galley and his succinct, yet polite replies to the few passengers on these pointless flights to Wichita indicated to Kate that there was more to Dave than met the eye.

Flight attendants make a habit of temporary relationships, of practiced cordiality and attentiveness. It's part of the job. Kate wanted that Teflon personality. She had observed it first in her parents' friends. Nothing stuck. Not marriages, bills, corporate failures or personal obligations. In Scarsdale, everything slid right off. Her friends' parents could run a steel mill one month and a coffee empire the next. And as crazy as it sounded, flight attendant Dave possessed this same Teflon quality. It was visible, as obvious as a square jaw or piercing blue eyes. In the cabin of an airplane, where Dave had spent twenty years, nothing could rankle him.

And Dave had something else, a quality that struck Kate as more important than everything she had long thought of as non-negotiable in a potential mate. More important than symmetrical facial features and a house in the Hamptons.

Dave made the world feel less complicated.

Dave made the world feel explainable — the opposite of Dennis Rader. Just watching Dave smoothly roll the beverage cart down the aisle and engage the foot break autonomically, made traveling the world feel possible again.

———

It was another two months before Kate managed to get together with her friend Tina. Kate had changed so much over those two months. She was tougher than she'd been. She had expanded her idea of herself and the world. Tina was exactly the same — smug about her Dallas route and already dating a Texas businessman whom she suspected harbored a huge bank account. Tina dumped her happiness on the cocktail table between them like a robber displaying a sack of cash.

"Texas is the land of sweet tea and wildflower highways," Tina whispered, dreamily. Kate downed her martini, taking care not to spill. She would need every drop to survive the evening. "How's your Wichita route?" Tina asked.

Kate set down her drink. One of the shittiest things about Wichita was that it always sounded so petty to bitch about its shortcomings.

"Well, there's this guy I work with," Kate confessed.

"Oh, no kidding. Go on," Tina coo'd.

Kate had not told anyone about Dave, yet. And she had trouble continuing.

"His name is Dave. And" — what could she tell a friend about Dave that would be interesting? "Well, you know how our high school teachers always told us how vibrant and smart we were, and how unstoppable we would be in the world?"

Tina sipped her martini. She was wearing paste on eyelashes and heavy, dark mascara which contrasted with her platinum blonde hair. The look was such a drastic change from how Tina had looked at UMass, where she was hippyish and had used hemp-based beauty products, that Kate had trouble maintaining her train of thought. "Well, what Dave has — he's been all over the world, you know. And well, Dave's really efficient at everything he does." Kate picked up her martini. It mattered to her that she got this right. But despite her efforts, each subsequent word delivered the unmistakable sense that she was embarrassing herself.

"That's great," Tina insisted blandly, holding up her champagne glass for a toast. It was a type of toast, Kate realized that she and Tina had shared countless times in the course of their friendship (since being assigned to neighboring rooms in the freshman dorm at UMass) a toast to all the great things to come, and it suddenly felt to Kate so unbelievably disingenuous that she knocked her martini over just to avoid participating in it.

Kate's parents didn't find much to like in Dave, either. He looked tired, they said.

"You're too vibrant for someone like that," Kate's mother declared while chopping scallions in her Scarsdale kitchen. It was her mother's way of addressing the age gap between Kate and Dave without resorting to straightforward ageism. But Kate knew the deeper truth. Dave wasn't just older than her. He had never been as attractive or energetic as Kate. And of course, the real problem was that Dave was a career flight attendant. He had traded in his adult life for weekends in Baja (or so Kate's parents believed). Kate was just taking a few years of travel to find herself. Her plan was certainly to move on from this job, Kate's mother believed. In fact, Kate's mother believed that moving on was every flight attendant's plan. Longevity in that industry meant failure, and Kate's mother felt this immobility almost like a physical defect, like hardening of the arteries. Dave's career complacency lent itself readily to the kind of metaphors Scarsdale parents couldn't help spinning out over dinner. "He's on his final ascent, dear and you're just leaving the hangar," Kate's mother quipped while cutting Kate's filet mignon into bite size pieces. "That guy is like a server group named after a Star Wars character," Kate's father added. And so forth.

But all this criticism of Dave had a paradoxical effect on Kate.

The more her parents and friends found ways to insult and belittle Dave (who worked four flights to and from Wichita the weekend Kate visited her parents) the greater Dave rose in Kate's estimation. Yes, Dave was graying at his temples. Yes, he had a cheap haircut. Yes, he was forever disheveled, even in his wrinkle free, synthetic United Airlines uniform. Yes, Dave wore exceedingly practical shoes. And yes, he was a career flight attendant. But when Kate strode purposefully through O'Hare airport arm in arm with Dave, she felt something. She felt lighter. She felt electrically charged and nothing made

Kate happier or delivered a wave of gut cooling assuredness (the agonist to nausea) than the double takes random O'Hare airport travelers made when they looked up from their phones to see Kate walking arm in arm with Dave, obviously in love.

Kate and Dave were not only dating — they were happy. And Dave's lack of obviously attractive qualities made her feel mysterious and interesting. Like lancing a boil, being with Dave brought Kate an immediate physical relief, not only from the sore throats and sinus pressure that she attributed to her Wichita nausea, but from the oppressiveness of her photoshoot perfect upbringing. All those weekends in Southampton. Tennis on grass courts. Her parents sipping drinks by the pool while Kate and her friends squealed as they slid down a slide. All those photos at father/daughter dinners at the club, before school dances, before prom. With Dave, she didn't have to protect or prove her vibrancy. With Dave, even the beige decor of the Wichita airport Hilton, right down to its vomity bath mats and beige frosted glass wall sconces, no longer made her burp up her lunch. With Dave, she could still imagine herself traveling the world — light and free. And Kate came to believe that only Dave could curate the kind of trip around the world that she felt would forge her into a complete human being.

———

Death Row Restaurant hadn't been Dave's idea at all.

The idea for the restaurant had come from Todd Bridges—on a flight from Chicago to Wichita, KS. The Wichita route was the kind of nondescript, zero amenities flight that everyone involved in it (from passengers to pilots to preflight cleaning crews and baggage handlers) endured as best they could. The Wichita route passed through an ecosystem on the verge of collapse. The route was prone to sudden winds, lightning, turbulence and hail, and thus, constant delays. The planes that serviced the Wichita route were holdovers from the 1970's, barely updated. Flights offered few amenities. In-flight entertainment was projected onto a single screen at the front of the main cabin and due to various licensing technicalities consisted of little more than old Anthony Bourdain episodes.

Despite this, the Wichita route proved more enjoyable than any Dave had serviced as a flight attendant during his twenty years in the sky. The Wichita route never disappointed Dave in the one way that had come to matter to him: with no reason to fly to Wichita other than genuine necessity, passengers were more authentic. Dave would often ask as he performed the beverage service, "so what takes you to Wichita?" and no matter the age or appearance of the passengers, they always had a clean, coherent answer, like a crisp twenty-dollar bill.

As a seasoned flight attendant with no disciplinary letters in his file and twenty years of seniority in a high turnover industry, Dave could easily have gotten himself scheduled on direct flights to Paris, to Rome, to Berlin, to Istanbul, to Tokyo or to Singapore — or even the serene flights to Joshua Tree State Park or Napa Valley. And Dave had worked those routes over the years. But over time, each of those routes disappointed Dave in a way that Wichita never had. There was even something serendipitous about Dave's discovery of the Wichita route, a favor he agreed to do for a colleague who was having a medical procedure performed overseas in order to save money.

"It's surprisingly charming," Jake had told Dave in those hard to fill moments after Dave had agreed to do him the favor and cover the Wichita route for the weekend.

And although Dave couldn't immediately put his finger on what it was that he liked about the Wichita route that first time he traveled it, he felt compelled to return to Wichita — and eventually, to request ORD to ICT as his permanent assignment.

Dave formally committed to Wichita in an authentic fashion — a spur of the moment decision. It was a Tuesday, a day like any other day, a day where the various tasks that constitute flight attendants' duties had left his breath acrid from dehydration. Dave was filing paperwork for a delayed flight to Amsterdam, when he spotted his boss, Dana. He had been mentally reviewing an email he was planning to send to request the Wichita route. But the route was so unpopular, so out of the ordinary for someone with Dave's seniority that requesting it sounded suspicious. So he had concocted a lie — an elderly aunt in Wichita whom he wanted to visit on a regular basis.

"Wichita is really the perfect route for me right now," Dave told Dana. Just this morning, while tossing out a Cinnabon he'd eaten only half of, Dave had decided to add those last two words, 'right now,' as if the whole thing was temporary, like a weather delay or a downturn in profitability, the kind of unforeseeable events the airline industry understood perfectly.

"Wichita?" Dana set her coffee on the stair railing of the United Airlines terminal.

"That's right," Dave agreed. "Chicago to Wichita. ORD to ICT. United Airlines gives back to the community by providing those few passengers returning to Wichita, Kansas a direct route. I want to give back to my aunt by visiting her on a regular basis." Don't overdo it, Dave chastised himself. He stood there stiffly while Dana leaned casually on the railing. Her fresh cup of coffee sent puffs of steam into the air between them.

"You're asking for ORD to ICT?" Dana again clarified. Dana had been promoted to Vice President of Personnel in the Midwest Region just six months ago, and the last thing she wanted was to be the butt of a joke. A request this bizarre threw up red flags. If it wasn't a joke by one of her colleagues, it could be an employee on the edge. It could be a warning sign of a whole slew of negative outcomes that it was her job to see coming. Dana's first instinct was to kick this upstairs for review. And Ross, President of the Midwest Region certainly enjoyed busying himself with minor details of operations. This was how he projected a deep investment in the mission of United Airlines to his employees. Ross often spoke up in their monthly meetings about "getting hands on" or "getting his hands dirty." Or at least, Ross had said such things until the sensitivity team advised him that his metaphors were a little too "handsy." Since then, he had switched to advising the entire Midwest Region of United Airlines to "lean in," as if flight schedules and FAA regulations were analogous to Olympic ski jumpers trying to keep their heads over the tips of their skis so as not to end up immortalized in 'agony of defeat' trailers on NBC. Would kicking Dave Aslin's request for the Wichita route upstairs to Ross qualify as "leaning in?" Or was it just meddling and micromanaging?

When Ross had interviewed Dana for Vice President of Personnel, Dana could tell that he was the type of President who prided himself on knowing the data which orbited at the fringes of the worldwide operation. Ross had no real interest in day-to-day operations. For instance, the first task Dana had helped him with was to get 'hands on' with the roast level of the in-flight peanuts they served. Ross purchased a small nut roaster and he and Dana spent hours toasting containers of peanuts and performing blind taste tests. Following the peanuts, he pursued a bizarre plan to automate the tossing of luggage onto conveyor belts so as to eliminate claims of baggage handler roughness. Each of these concerns, Dana knew, were concerns that Ross felt projected his total dedication to United Airlines — and each of these contained no possibility of scandal. If Ross was going to sign his name to something, it needed to be innocuous and banal. And what could be more banal than Wichita?

Dana tapped her nails on the railing, peering first at Dave's broad forehead, next at his receding hairline, and finally surveying Dave's uniform and posture. He seemed entirely earnest in his request. Nothing about Dave's body language suggested anything different. Someone has to work the Wichita route. Maybe Dave really just wants to look after his aunt? Dana glanced out the window at the O'Hare tarmac. She watched the sky for a few seconds, until a plane taxied in front of her, blocking her view. It was already four o'clock. If Dana kicked Dave's route transfer request up to Ross, the request would linger in an inbox until Monday morning and then require all sorts of quarterbacking and conference calls to re-establish the context of the request. Ross never touched anything without being advised about all the angles. For all Dana knew, she might be asked to provide a complete personnel file review. For all she knew, this minor route change request could end up involving dozens of people, each of whom would wonder why such a small matter had been pitched across their desks. Someone must be wanting to cover their ass, they'll think. Eventually, someone with real clout will ask, "why are we spending so much valuable time on the Wichita route?"

Dana couldn't come up with a single, reasonable response to that question. A headache now dug into the soft space behind Dana's eyes. There was no point in bothering anyone with the Wichita route, she decided. And immediately, she began looking forward to spending her weekend lounging in an infinity pool, perhaps in Lisboa or Barcelona.

"Sure, Dave. We can do that for you. You know our motto," Dana began, "Every day, Every Passenger, Whatever it Takes."

Dana really liked their corporate motto. It articulated United Airlines' commitment to basically anything and everything at all times. United Airlines was inclusive. United Airlines was egalitarian.

"Thanks, Dana," Dave said. Dave's eyes, she thought, appeared visibly relieved. In fact, for a second, Dana thought he was tearing up.

———

The route transfer gave Dave a new lease on life. He had grown sick of Napa Valley. And the pressure of finding an even better route, one that could bring some new and widely desirable feature into his life, exhausted him. Over the last twenty years as a flight attendant, Dave had used his free flight privileges to experience every part of the globe. He had maximized every layover, every weekend, taking in major attractions and local, out of the way streets. Wherever Dave traveled, he aspired to feel like he belonged. For instance, when on layover in Istanbul, when Dave was about to bite into a Lahmacun — a sort of Turkish style pizza, but rolled up and without cheese but with bright bursts of lemon and parsley — at such times Dave would think to himself just as his teeth penetrated the crust, that for him, eating an authentic Lahmacun in Istanbul was as normal as grabbing a cold cut combo at Subway. So even though Dave could barely stand the dryness and the pungency of Lahmacun, the authenticity of it appealed to him.

On such trips, Dave strolled through the grand bazaar, seeking a level of comfort and banality defined by barely taking notice of the colorful pottery, the rows of candles and stacks of pillows with hand embroidered Middle Eastern swirls on them. Dave wanted to be aware of the way dry desert air evaporated sweat before it could darken clothes, but not too aware of it. He just wanted to feel such things so he could reject their novelty. For years, Dave transferred from route to route, seeking these sensations, imagining that the routes he traveled on wound around the globe like his very own spider web.

And now? Now Dave preferred Wichita.

In Wichita, Kansas, he had discovered something that far flung destinations never had. For instance, Dave's favorite thing to do on a layover in Wichita was to spend a few hours at Wichita's Museum of World Treasures. With everything from dinosaur bones to WWII artifacts, the museum's 'world treasures' are unabashedly family and tourist friendly. In fact, in the lobby of the museum — a sign bragged that visitors can 'see the entire world and its most grand treasures in under two hours.' Something about this was a total relief to Dave. Unlike Paris or Istanbul or Rome, with all of their tradition and history, Wichita possessed no grand narrative. Europeans anchored their authenticity to the past. Wichita embraced the present. Or so Dave felt about it.

The twice daily flights from Chicago to Wichita were no frills, and Dave liked that the only entertainment on board was a loop of old Anthony Bourdain episodes. Anthony Bourdain was perhaps the one man Dave knew of who had, without apology, claimed to find, not just authentic food all over the world, but authentic experiences. Sitting on an overturned bucket at a roadside cafe in Vietnam, swatting mosquitoes while digging into a bowl of spicy noodles as cars and motorbikes farted leaded gasoline in his face was Bourdain's total experience. According to Bourdain, all of the great meals in his life had been eaten in this fashion.

Although Dave meticulously emulated Bourdain's travels, he never experienced that kind of immersive authenticity, the kind where you forgot yourself. Dave had sat on buckets at those same roadside cafes in Ho Chi Minh City, in Guam, in Madagascar. He had even studied Bourdain's posture and style of dress, the way Bourdain slurped bowls of noodles, dug through their vibrant ingredients with chopsticks and commented on their combination of heat and sweet. Dave drank Bia Hoi served from a plastic hose right out of the keg for twenty-five cents a glass. Yet even Ho Chi Minh City, where just crossing the street was an adventure, felt staged. And whatever Dave did on such trips, even when he focused on involuntary things like hiccups or tripping on a sidewalk, left him feeling that he was just doing what internet guidebooks and travel blogs told everyone to do or to watch out for. The stifling heat, the steering wheel sized mosquitoes, the overwhelming sense of unruly beauty — none of it felt authentic. That, Dave came to understand was the truth of Bourdain's life. Television made it seem different, but in terms of real-life experience: the Vietnamese cafes, the overturned buckets, the French Alps, the riverside cafes in Laos — even Bourdain had felt it, how scripted and mundane they were as experiences.

This revelation hadn't come easy. Dave had spent years upping the ante, searching for more and more immersive experiences until finally, while hunting through the Dilli Haat Market in New Delhi for a food stall which Bourdain had anointed as serving "the greatest curry in the world," Dave arrived at the truth. After hours searching for the food stall, Dave found the curry. It was thin but complex. Dave dug through its components: tendon, noodles, blood cake, vegetables and aromatics. Dave took an inventory of its smells, took an inventory of the sounds and sensations of the bustling market — the smoke, the disembodied legs, arms and elbows at work at the edges of his vision, the agile tongues of Tamil, Tannadu, Telugu and other dialects. The caramel skin of the locals, the camels kneeling in order to be loaded with fifty-pound sacks of lentils, the sizzle of dough slapped onto the sides of a clay oven — at every level, the experience Dave was having was perfect. And yet, it didn't feel any more immersive than anyplace else he had been.

For the first time, he understood the tragedy of Bourdain's show. Bourdain had trudged on all of those years, studying culture after culture like an anthropologist, tasting every kind of dish because even the most delicious, most perfect, most existentially demanding foods at the edge of the world had not been enough. Not even a perfect curry in the most bustling market could be truly authentic.

So by the time Dave's passport had been stamped more than the stage of Riverdance, by the time his lifetime guaranteed travel luggage had fractured a zipper, by the time he could order coffee in dozens of languages — by that time — Dave had determined that traveling was a fucking waste of time.

———

It was not long after that Dave and Kate were scheduled to work their first flight to Wichita together. He had spent so much of his time traveling to out of the way locales, that it hadn't left much room for romantic entanglements. He'd had a few flings over the years with fellow flight attendants who liked to travel to out of the way places. But those relationships expired the instant spending a holiday together stalled or grew tense. Dave could often pinpoint the exact moment that these relationships ended: the disappointment of a weak or watery cocktail, a strange smell on an otherwise gorgeous beach, or his companion's beach bag bouncing off her leg as she walked. These minor imperfections torpedoed months spent getting to know one another, as if the point of a relationship was curating it to perfection.

Dave's longest romantic relationship survived dozens of these overseas trips. Dave and Emily even bought a condo together in their home base of Los Angeles. Yet their near constant travel made nights in their own apartment feel like a crappy Airbnb. One night, Emily couldn't find their wine key. And that was it. After exhausting the places Dave and his lovers wanted to visit or return to, these relationships, like every flight, reached their final destination. What persisted after these missed connections was always the idea of the perfect route, if not the perfect traveling companion.

From the beginning, Dave's relationship with Kate had been different. Kate and Dave never left the airport. With Kate, the problem of authenticity never reared its head. There was, quite frankly, no reason for Kate to spend time with him if she didn't authentically want to. Certainly, Dave had tried to get Kate to leave the airport and check out the places he enjoyed in Wichita, like its Museum of World Treasures or Wichita's "butterfly house" or its CowTown Museum. These were places Dave could relax because they were so obviously not trying to provide any coherent experiences. You could feel however you wanted to feel there. But usually, Kate wanted to stay in. Usually, she didn't feel right, a quality Dave hated in himself and adored in Kate. And what she typically asked for, what she wanted, was to not go anywhere. When in the grip of her Wichita nausea, the thought of traveling was too much for Kate. But talking, just chatting about where they might go some day or making vague plans for actually going on these international trips — Kate loved this. And she loved to hear about all of Dave's travels, his decades gallivanting around the world. And it never occurred to him to tell her how these trips always left him feeling fake and void inside. Inside the Wichita Airport Hilton, with its excessively beige decor, Dave's stories about Cambodia, Jakarta, Johannesburg and Finland felt like complete experiences. As long as they never left the hotel room, all of these places retained their potential. Kate's desire to travel was best realized by never leaving Wichita, Dave thought, a fact driven home by their slightly drunk first kiss in her room at the Wichita airport Doubletree Hilton. And as they finished this first kiss, he noted that Kate still had her hand on the handle of her rolling carry-on luggage.

There was, Dave felt, something extraordinarily earnest in this. In the way Kate invested every ounce of her energy into world travel while never even managing to leave her hotel room. But over time, Kate developed the notion that she could in fact travel, that the headaches and nausea which kept her confined to hotel rooms in the Wichita airport region would be relieved elsewhere. That was when Kate, following an especially nauseous flight from Chicago to Wichita, a flight in which Dave insisted that she remain in the jump seat for the better part of beverage service, taking deep breaths and sipping lemon tea, asked Dave if he would plan a trip for them.

At the time Kate made this request, she and Dave were at the Air Capital Bar in Wichita's Eisenhower Airport waiting out a mechanical delay. They were supposed to turn it around to Chicago. The delay, Dave had just found out, would keep them in Wichita overnight. But he hadn't yet shared this news with Kate, whose color had only recently returned to her cheeks in anticipation of leaving Wichita.

Dave would let her have a club soda and lime before sharing the news. The weather in Wichita that day was dreary. The bar overlooked the tarmac, which had a sterile feel, its enormous window streaked with rain, the lights of several taxiing planes pulsing behind it like a heart monitor.

As if to counter this sterility, the Air Capital Bar had installed framed newspaper clippings about the Wright Brothers... "Flying Machine Soars 3 Miles in the Teeth of High Winds..." as well as a series of time lapse construction photos depicting the growth of Eisenhower airport from its humble beginnings as Wichita Municipal Airport. Dave found the triviality of it somewhat pleasing, a century of development that goes completely unremarked.

"Is the Middle East a good place for a honeymoon?" Kate asked, snatching his hands into her own, as if they were saying a prayer for a sick child. Kate's nausea, a Wichita staple, had now completely relented in anticipation of the return to Chicago, and the future trip she imagined Dave would plan for them. The cheeseburger he usually coaxed Kate into taking tiny bites of had already been devoured. "We need to get out of here," she added, peering left and right. "We need to get out of Wichita for good."

Kate let go of Dave's hands, ran her fingers up her thighs, then set her hand down on his leg. Smiling, she slid her hand towards Dave's crotch. It was then he realized what had been happening over the last few months, why this young woman had kissed him in her hotel room, had found him so much fun to strut through airports with, had wanted to share hotel rooms and stay up all night on layovers talking about world travel. The whole thing hadn't been based on Kate's illness or the way she was struggling through her mid-twenties, as so many people do. It had been based on a very real, if unallocated hatred, a hatred so pure that it simply couldn't boil down to just Wichita.

"Forget the perfectly planned trip around the world," Kate blurted out. In the throes of their various evenings in the sickly beige hotel rooms of the airport Hilton, they had discussed so many trips that an actual trip had begun to feel almost impossible. "Forget planning," she insisted. "Just make the whole thing a surprise." Kate turned away from Dave and pushed her palms forward as if to ward off an attacker. "You can decide the whole thing. You can curate it from beginning to end." She was surprised to hear herself say this. But for once, her unplanned, unhindered thoughts had come out just right.

All of a sudden, Kate felt herself ovulate. Or at least, she thought she did. Her college roommate Tina used to brag about this all the time back at UMass, that she was so in touch with her own body she could feel it the second an egg released from her ovary and traveled down her fallopian tube. Kate had always been jealous of this, and now she had felt it, now she too was in touch with herself — all because of Dave and the trip he would plan for her. The joke Kate had made about this being a honeymoon felt exactly right to her. And she was again buoyed by a sense of internal wholeness. Dave would make a good first husband, she thought — and Wichita an offbeat and intriguing engagement story. So what if Dave wasn't figuratively going places. He could literally take her places, and in a style that was even better than the luxury tour guides her parents and parents' friends always used. And besides, with their age difference and with Dave's flight attendant career, his constant travel, his utter lack of opportunity for advancement, Kate felt certain a divorce at some point would make sense to everyone. It would be like returning a defective toaster, little more. "Let's get married," Kate whispered, practically tingling from her spontaneity. "Let's get married and take a trip together. Wherever we go, it will be perfect."

"I kind of like Wichita," Dave said, bringing his empty coffee cup to his lips, tilting it up pointlessly and then setting it back down again. "I know you think Wichita has nothing to offer. But it's a good place, actually. A place I legitimately enjoy. We've hardly seen any of it. Wichita could be where we really get to know one another," he added, taking Kate's hand in his and slipping down on one knee in Eisenhower Airport.

Oh god, Kate thought, her nausea hitting her full force. She gagged a few times, then through sheer force of will, swallowed hard. She had of course assumed over all the time Dave spent nursing her through her various Wichita symptoms that he hated the place as much as she did, that he was just putting up a good front for her sake. But now Kate knew the truth. She knew that Dave had filed away their sexual encounters as a sort of bonus to a place he actually liked being in, like getting an extra chicken nugget in a McDonald's value meal. And Kate was epically unequipped to handle this realization.

"Wichita, Omaha, Sioux Falls, Boise..." Dave was still on one knee, as if proposing to her by rattling off the most mundane locations he could think of. "They are as authentic as any place in the world, Kate. Maybe even more so," he continued. "These places don't claim to have any distinct experiences. That's what I love about them. And I would like to take you to these places so you can feel complete, too."

Kate could only nod slightly and burp through her nose. These were Dave's truest feelings.

How humiliating for him.

It occurred to Kate that if she and Dave stopped seeing one another, no one would ever even ask about him. Kate certainly didn't have to explain herself to anyone. In fact, if she ended it right here and now, she would never have to think about the fact that she had been fucking a guy who was fully content with a tuna sandwich from a Wichita gas station. This final realization was so specific and horrible to Kate that she could only offer herself immediate and unconditional forgiveness. On the spot, she granted herself a "do over."

"It was nice seeing you," Kate said to Dave in a formal tone, as if they hadn't been fucking on layovers for the past six months. Then, she offered him a wooden handshake. She extended the handle of her travel suitcase and in just seconds, Kate was free of Dave and she slipped into a purposeful stride, making her way through shitty Eisenhower airport as fast as she could, and upon passing a mirror, she very much liked the professional look of her uniform and the gentle hum of the high-performance wheels of her overnight bag. She would get off this shitty route eventually and with a little lobbying she might end up on the redeye to Paris or Rome or Berlin. In one of those great cities there would be a man, or woman for that matter, who would transport her around the world in the style she clearly deserved.

For Dave, the breakup with Kate had been so swift and baffling as to be almost inexplicable. Unlike his previous relationships, he could not pinpoint the moment where things went wrong, where the illusion had been compromised. He had believed that Kate's preference for discussing trips rather than taking them revealed an uncommon maturity. Obviously, he had been wrong. In their final interaction, after so many nights of passion and (he had thought) true understanding, Kate had shaken Dave's hand as if he was a candidate at a job interview who had just performed especially poorly. Her handshake had been so firm and impersonal that it communicated: we wish you luck elsewhere. With this one gesture, Kate had transformed herself from Dave's lover to an amorphous, corporate "we." In his younger years, Dave would have been devastated by such a breakup. But he was approaching fifty and this was just one more thing that had been revealed to be a mirage, a ruse, a thirty second burst of advertising copy. He held up his coffee cup. His waitress noticed immediately and refilled his cup. By the time Dave had finished his second cup of coffee and walked to his hotel room at the Doubletree Hilton in Wichita's Eisenhower Airport, he felt relieved, relieved that he was free to like Wichita as much as he wanted to.

———

This was the first night in some time that Dave had spent alone in Wichita. He had trouble falling asleep. He was resolved not to change anything. He would settle into a routine again, ORD to ICT. Dave and Kate were professionals. Her wooden handshake assured Dave that they could quite easily ignore one another on flights to and from Wichita. This thought comforted him late into the night, until he eventually drifted off to sleep.

Dave woke up refreshed. He shaved without a single nick, his mind pleasantly blank. He'd spent most of the previous evening catching up on training videos he'd neglected while spending time with Kate. No doubt, Kate was also realizing this morning that they were better off as friends and colleagues than as lovers. He even felt flattered that someone as attractive and young as Kate could have been interested in him in the first place. So what if their relationship was just a hiatus, a vacation which like any vacation reaches its end? Now it was time to get back to work.

Kate called in sick the next day. So it was not until several days later, on a flight from ORD to ICT, the flight that Dave and Kate had first met on, that they saw one another again. And unfortunately, instead of Kate and Dave going about their flight duties with a slight awkwardness due to the formal way in which they would now treat one another, Dave found Kate openly hostile to him. She sneered and rammed him with the beverage cart whenever she had the opportunity (which was quite often). She resented not only Dave's presence, but the presence of everyone who had secret reasons to travel to Wichita.

Had it not been for one remarkable development on this normally quiet flight to Wichita, Dave and Kate might have had to seek a management resolution for their dispute. That is, had it not been for a surprise passenger on the normally nondescript flight to Wichita, Dana would have had to face the fact that she had screwed up, that her management intuition may not be as strong as she supposed, that she had a thing or two to learn from people like Ross. But as it happened, seated in row 22, seat B — was Todd Bridges.

Dave recognized him immediately.

Bridges had played the character of Willis on the hit 80's television show, Diff'rent Strokes. Although he was obviously older, a mere shell of the promising teen he'd played on television, the resemblance was unmistakable. It was enough to flood Dave's mind with memories of his favorite episodes, like when Willis starts hanging out with a classmate who's in a gang, a kid played by a young Andrew Dice Clay. In that episode, Willis begins carrying a gun and nearly shoots his adopted father, Mr. Drummond. Dave hadn't thought about Diff'rent Strokes for decades. And in that moment, the show's moral lessons struck Dave as entirely unique. Diff'rent Strokes had never tried to sort good behavior from bad or to sort good people from bad on any strict basis. The show did something else, something Dave had forgotten was a possibility.

"Fuck!" Dave rubbed his knee. Kate had rammed him with the beverage cart again.

"Are you going to help out with the beverage service or what?" she demanded, as if she had never once considered fucking him. "If not, then just take a seat with the rest of the passengers," Kate huffed.

"Do you know who that is?" Dave whispered.

"Who?" she grunted, refusing even to glance at him.

"Don't look. Row 22. Seat B."

"How am I supposed to see who it is if I don't look?" Kate demanded.

Dave didn't know why he bothered telling Kate about Willis. Not only was she being petulant, she was probably too young to have heard of the show.

"That's Todd Bridges," Dave said. Not wanting to alarm Todd Bridges, he had leaned in to whisper the name to Kate, and his proximity to her ear and to the vulnerable area of her neck made him feel a sudden intimacy with her, even though he knew how thoroughly Kate despised him now. It was weird.

For Kate, when he leaned in close to her out of excitement over whoever this person was, she felt a faint flutter in her chest, deeper and more profound than the sex they had engaged in for months. She couldn't believe it, and this fluttering feeling and the fact of once again traveling to Wichita made Kate angrier than ever. And then it happened. BTK popped into her mind. She thought about how close

Rader had to get to his victims, the horrible intimacy of strangulation. For every victim, Rader was the last person they saw. Kate got that same sense of overwhelming fear and impotent anger that she had had as a college sophomore, when she had first heard about Vicky Wegerle and her beautiful piano playing. She suddenly longed for the kind of meaningless relationships she had in her early college years, relationships full of shallow social rituals, almost like a romantic comedy on television.

"That's Willis," Dave insisted a little louder, "Willis, from Diff'rent Strokes." He was so excited that he didn't care whether Kate had the slightest interest in the news he was delivering. He simply had to tell someone about it. No one on board had recognized Todd Bridges.

"I thought he was dead?" Kate retorted.

Just about the entire cast of Diff'rent Strokes actually had died by then. Dana Plato went into a tragic tailspin after the show. Her overdose was officially ruled a suicide. Gary Coleman had made his life-long virginity public while he was still married. Then he died from a brain hemorrhage at forty-two. Such facts, Dave thought, lacked the kind of coherent narrative Diff'rent Strokes provided on a weekly basis. Yet for some reason, putting the facts into any sort of coherent narrative no longer mattered to Dave.

"Not Todd Bridges," he finally replied. "He's still alive. He's right there."

"Who?" Kate demanded. "I thought you said that guy was Willis?" She sighed, exasperated and strangely frightened at the same time. She kept thinking about how she had quit piano so suddenly, how she always made sudden, terrible decisions — like signing on to this shitty flight to Wichita and all its shitty, nice residents who were no doubt perverts, too, like BTK. And then Kate remembered that Dennis Rader had once taken the body of Marine Hedge, a neighbor he strangled, to his church to take bondage photos of her for his fantasies. She felt nauseous and lost.

"Nevermind." Dave pressed the emergency brake on the beverage cart, causing Kate to stumble over her own legs. Her sudden awkwardness made her furious. Dave took control of the cart and expertly maneuvered it towards the galley. "I'll handle the beverage service, Kate. You can do the pretzels."

"Fuck you," she spat at him, storming back to the galley and slamming a bunch of drawers.

Dave found himself suddenly angry as well, yet he felt strangely grateful for the feeling. The unexpected bitterness now surging through him was liberating. He knew that like in a vicious divorce, Kate was going to do everything in her power to get him to abandon what he loved — the Wichita route. Kate would do this, not because she wanted the route, but because she wanted to get back at him. She was from Scarsdale, after all. Instead of claiming a set of golf clubs or a country club membership she didn't want, Kate would claim Wichita. And there would be no talking her out of it.

Dave grabbed a steamed towelette and made his way to Todd Bridges.

"Towelette?" Dave used a pair of tongs to offer Todd Bridges a steamed towel. He couldn't believe Willis from Diff'rent Strokes was on his flight to Wichita. What possible reason could Todd Bridges have for traveling to Wichita? Despite the show being on the air so long ago, a remnant from his childhood, Dave had difficulty separating the actor from the role. He had to remind himself that Willis wasn't on the flight to Wichita. Todd Bridges was.

"Thank you," Bridges said, laying the towel over his face and pressing gently around his eye sockets with his thumbs.

Why did he have such strong feelings towards Todd Bridges, anyway? Dave wondered. He literally hadn't watched Diff'rent Strokes since he was ten years old. But all of a sudden, with Todd Bridges leaning his head back and massaging his eye sockets, Diff'rent Strokes seemed the most important event in Dave's life. And Dave realized that the last time he had seen Todd Bridges on television wasn't on Diff'rent Strokes. It was years after the show had ended, in fact, years after Bridges had spiraled into drug abuse, encounters with law enforcement and rehab. The last time Dave had seen Todd Bridges on television was when Bridges fought Vanilla Ice on an episode of celebrity boxing. He remembered being happy when Bridges won by unanimous decision.

"Champagne?" Dave offered, placing the champagne flute on the folding plastic tray in front of Todd Bridges. Dave frantically sought a way to introduce himself, but it was awkward. Should he just say that he loved the show thirty years ago? That for reasons he couldn't possibly explain, he remembered the episode where teenage Willis bragged about his new chest hair? Dave didn't know all the details of the intervening years between Bridges' hit show and whatever he was doing by traveling to Wichita. But he did know that just about everyone from the cast of Diff'rent Strokes had struggled to reenter normal society after the show. And that Todd Bridges was now the only living cast member.

"I'd like some champagne," insisted a middle-aged woman sitting next to Todd Bridges in torn sweatpants and a Mickey Mouse t-shirt. Dave filled a champagne flute and handed it to the woman, who guzzled it and then shoved it back across Todd Bridges' face waiting for a refill. "And how about one of them hot towels and maybe something better than Anthony Bourdain for the in flight movie? You got Cutthroat Kitchen? Or what about Beat Bobby Flay?" She chugged her second flute of champagne, then shoved the glass out for another refill, knocking Bridges' arm off the arm rest.

"Here," Dave said, handing the woman the entire bottle of champagne. "Help yourself. In fact, why don't you take a seat in row twelve, which is empty." Then, turning to Bridges, "you're Todd Bridges, aren't you?"

Dave hoped Bridges wouldn't be too taken aback. Bridges smiled politely as the woman climbed over him, wielding the bottle of champagne.

"I am Todd Bridges," he admitted.

Dave experienced a wave of nostalgia, then a flood of questions, each of which receded before he could apprehend it. So he just stood there with his mouth open. But it didn't matter because the way Bridges had admitted who he was, after all the sordid news stories and public fascination with Bridges' fall from grace — just admitting who he was felt meaningful. Dave had spent most of the last twenty years in formal, bureaucratic situations. Airports were official places with policies for every situation, with contingencies for contingencies, lists of lists. In an airport or at a customs office, official documentation replaces a deeper sense of identity. You have to account for yourself entirely through the kind of banal responses one must give when answering questions for security or customs. Business or pleasure? The stamps of approval doled out across a customs desk or at a credit kiosk were designed to conceal individuality, designed to make declarations like the one Todd Bridges had just made, declarations that take ownership not of an official identity one was born into — but of one's actions themselves, irrelevant.

"Wow. I mean, I'm Dave," he said. "This is such a surprise. I —" Dave stumbled over his words, unsure whether he wanted to talk to Todd Bridges or to the fictional character, Willis. Which of course, was ridiculous. Only an asshole would ask Todd Bridges to pretend to be Willis.

"Go ahead, Dave," Bridges said, seeming to understand Dave even better than Dave understood himself. "You can talk to Willis. He's right here." Bridges pointed to his temple, indicating that Willis still lives in his mind.

"I was sorry to hear about the death of Conrad Bain —er, Mr. Drummond," Dave corrected himself. He'd played the role of Willis and Arnold's father on Diff'rent Strokes.

"Thank you," Todd Bridges said. "Conrad Bain was more of a father to me than my real family had been," Bridges admitted out of nowhere.

Dave felt like he'd heard that line before, on Oprah, perhaps. The details of Bridges' fall from grace were coming back to him. And they were spectacular, even in the world of sordid celebrity implosions and unfathomable quantities of meth and crack cocaine. Bridges had gotten involved in pimping, too, and at one point, he was put on trial for capital murder. Yet here was Todd Bridges, riding in coach on a boring commuter flight from Chicago to Wichita. Todd Bridges had survived. He'd survived sexual abuse from a family friend. He'd survived crack and meth addiction. And no matter what horrors other people riding that flight to Wichita had endured, Todd Bridges had been America's darling. While some people had complained that in order for black people to be on television in the 1980's they had to have a rich, white savior like Mr. Drummond, the truth is Diff'rent Strokes had anticipated the rise of the billionaire as America's moral and political center.

"Have you read my memoir," Bridges said, holding up a hardcover copy of Killing Willis. A bookmark from 'Barbara's Books at O'Hare' peeked out of the top of the book. Had Bridges purchased his own book preflight?

"I've been meaning to," Dave said.

"Well here are a few tidbits. Gary Coleman had a secret will," Bridges confided. "And then there's the bus stop."

"The bus stop?" Dave could barely recall something about a bus stop from that same episode of Oprah.

"In Los Angeles," Bridges continued, looking at his fingernails, which were perfectly manicured. "Because of my history of drugs, I'm not allowed to have a driver's license," Bridges confessed. "So I have to take the bus."

"Jesus," Dave sighed. When he had been based in LA, working flights to the far east and Hawaii — and now that he thought about it, to Singapore, Hyderabad, Delhi, Beijing and Tokyo — he was rarely at the LA apartment he shared with his flight attendant girlfriend, Emily. Yet even though he was almost never actually in LA, Dave had purchased a Honda Accord and spent thousands on storage. Public transit in LA was that unbearable. "I can't imagine taking the bus in LA," Dave commiserated.

"It wasn't the bus so much," Bridges continued. "It was the bus stop." He paused, put his head in his hands briefly. "Every day I waited at bus stops so I could go about my business. I wore little disguises. Fake beards, hats, high shirt collars. But no matter what I wore, someone always slowed his car down near the bus stop and yelled, 'hey Willis. Fuck you, you fucker!'"

Dave had been anticipating the end of Bridges' story. He was leaning forward, ready to commiserate. But the end of Todd Bridges' story left Dave no room to commiserate. The end of Todd Bridges' story left Dave feeling as if he hadn't had a true feeling or committed a genuine action in years. Why would people slow down their cars just to say 'fuck you' to a fictional television character from the 1980's? It was, Dave realized, his mouth hanging open, the most authentic story he'd ever heard.

"Wow," he eventually said. "That's —"

Instinctively, Dave leapt onto Bridges' lap as Kate nearly ran him down with the beverage cart.

———

The flight to Wichita was only two hours. Yet with Kate slamming the beverage cart around (and at one point, tossing hot towels at Dave's head), it felt a lot longer. His only consolation was the time he got to spend talking with Todd Bridges. It became apparent rather quickly that the only safe place for Dave on this flight was seated as a passenger. Kate had hijacked the cabin. She controlled every aspect of the beverage service and announcements not made by the pilots. Her sole demand was that Dave no longer work the Wichita route. Not starting tomorrow or next week. Starting right now. Interestingly, Dave found that he didn't much care about his status as the senior airline steward. He didn't much care what Dana might say. And he didn't care if he worked another flight in his lifetime.

"I don't quite understand," Todd Bridges said. "Are you a flight attendant on this flight?"

"Yes and no," Dave answered, knocking back a shot of tequila.

"Sir, would you please buckle your seatbelt?" Kate said, zooming by at eighty miles an hour with the beverage cart. "Thank you for cooperating with FAA regulations," she added, tossing a hot towel over her shoulder at Dave's head.

"It's complicated," he admitted, once he was out of Kate's range. "Kate wants the Wichita route to herself and, well..." Dave thought about telling Todd Bridges about his brief relationship with Kate, about what she wanted from him and how he was simply unable to provide it for her. That was the simple version. To explain it all, the nauseous sex, the fantasies Kate and Dave had fed one another — it was too much. And oddly, he was sure it was also not enough. After all, Dave had read somewhere that Bridges had been in a romantic relationship with Dana Plato on the set of Diff'rent Strokes. He was no stranger to half-baked, short-lived relationships. But with Dana Plato's death from a drug overdose in 1999 (later ruled a suicide), and the death of Dana Plato's son a few years later (also from suicide) — and the fact that Bridges and Dana Plato had played brother and sister on the show, Dave decided not to say anything more about his relationship with Kate. Instead, he shrugged. He had a pretty pleasant tequila buzz going, and he was a little giddy about the fact that he was once again heading to Wichita, Kansas.

Yet Dave also understood that he was reneging on his legal obligations to United Airlines. This was serious. He was responsible for passenger safety and he'd already violated dozens of rules. Flight attendants weren't even allowed to be seen eating on a flight, let alone knocking back tequila shots. Although people think of flight attendants as glorified waiters, their training isn't a joke. More than a few people don't make it through the ten-week intensive course. Learning FAA regulations is only one aspect of the training. Flight attendants are instructed in a variety of other topics, from hand-to-hand combat to water rescues to how to contend with in-flight medical emergencies. And Dave was twenty years in; twenty years of raises and seniority benefits that he was throwing out the window because of a childhood television show from the 1980's.

At the same, Dave felt fine. He really did. The seats in coach were surprisingly roomy. And whenever Kate attempted to ram him with the beverage cart, Dave was able to ninja a few bottles of liquor from it. He knew that beverage cart like the back of his hand. Sitting with Todd Bridges, Dave considered the 1980's and how no one back then saw a problem with the fact that African Americans on television were all wealthy — like the family Todd Bridges and Gary Coleman were adopted into on Diff'rent Strokes. In the 1980's, people didn't bother pretending the world was an equitable place. They just teased their hair into the stratosphere, combed out their mullets, and then slipped into a pair of uber-tight parachute pants on their way to a club. In the 1980's, everyone knew society was fucked up. Dave missed that. He had thought his relationship with Kate was different, since it had been based on obvious deficiencies in both of their personalities. But in the end, this wasn't true. Maybe it was fucked up to enjoy Wichita. But Dave also knew that the alternative, the idea of the perfect experience or perfect life, the authentic bowl of noodles eaten on an overturned bucket, would always expose a hollowness inside. He had seen every episode of Anthony Bourdain's No Reservations and Parts Unknown. Why did Bourdain keep doing it? Once he had found the perfect curry in that market in Delhi, once he'd had Kao Piak Sen, Laos' version of chicken noodle soup — with slimy, thick tapioca noodles, lemongrass, fresh galangal, and charred onion — why didn't he just stay? Bourdain's episodes were littered with friends who had done just that, expats who fell in love with Vietnam or Laos or Myanmar and stayed. But Bourdain always left. Why? Why was what he loved only complete when he left it? It was questions like these that Dave hoped to understand by signing on for the Wichita route. And although that part of his life was coming to a close, Dave didn't find it sad. The Wichita route had always been a hedging of his bets. He had never fully committed to living in Wichita. The airline job had always provided an escape hatch. Maybe this was why the dozen or so FAA regulations Dave was currently disregarding were making him feel oddly good about his life.

"So what brings you to Wichita?" he finally asked Todd Bridges. A twinge of sadness welled up in Dave's throat, then dissipated. This was the question he had most enjoyed asking passengers on the many flights to Wichita he had worked.

"Prison," Todd Bridges responded, melodramatically. "I'm heading to El Dorado Correctional Facility."

Dave had read about Todd Bridges' troubles with the law. But thinking back to the last Oprah special, Bridges' legal troubles were presented as a thing of the past.

"You're giving a talk?" A pack of pretzels hit Dave in the face, slid down his cheek. Kate had pretty good aim.

"Pretzels, sir?" she offered Todd Bridges.

"No, thank you," Todd Bridges told her. Then, turning to Dave, "Part of it is a talk and part of it is a job interview."

"I didn't know you did work in prisons," Dave said. He was impressed. Maybe that was what he needed, he thought. Maybe he could find something meaningful in his life through charity work now that Kate was dead set on taking his Wichita route, now that the Wichita route had been exposed as a halfway commitment. "What's it like being a drug counselor?" Dave asked. "Are all drug counselors recovering addicts?"

"I'm not a drug counselor," Todd Bridges said, holding up a second copy of his memoir, Killing Willis. This copy also had a book-mark from Barbara's Books at O'Hare. Dave thought Bridges was going to give him the book, but apparently, Bridges had just sold a copy of his memoir to a woman across the aisle. "Do you happen to have change for a twenty?" Bridges asked Dave. Dave dug around in his wallet.

"I don't, sorry," he said quickly, then winced as Kate whipped by with a pot of hot coffee. When the transaction was complete, Bridges turned back to Dave and offered him his complete and undivided attention. It was striking. Bridges was engaging Dave more fully and completely than most of his previous sexual partners had. With a simple raising of his eyebrows, Bridges indicated an intense desire for Dave to continue his line of questioning. Bridges' command of simple but meaningful gestures was remarkable. Dave wondered if this skill was the result of Bridges' acting career or if this skill had been developed for completely different purposes. "Are you a corrections officer, then?" Dave asked.

"No," Bridges replied. He seemed very used to being misunderstood and to spending his time clarifying exactly who he was and what he was trying to do. "These days, I'm a restaurateur," Bridges said, "and I'm going to open up the most authentic restaurant the world has ever seen."

"Really?" Dave almost laughed out loud. Having been around the world and having eaten nearly every cuisine in the most authentic conditions possible, the idea of opening a restaurant in the United States and calling it "authentic" seemed ludicrous. For Dave, there had always been a disconnect — between himself and the food, between himself and the experience, between himself and himself. Everywhere Dave had gone he had felt like a tourist, even when sitting on an overturned bucket in a roadside stall in Ho Chi Minh City. Even while eating the exact same food and under precisely the same conditions as locals.

"Authentic restaurants don't exist," Dave stated, flatly.

"Agreed," Bridges said, surprisingly. "But that's why my restaurant is so sorely needed. And that's why this job interview at the El Dorado Correctional Facility is so important."

"I don't understand. What does a prison have to do with authentic restaurants?" Dave asked, dodging a sleeve of plastic cups hurled at him by Kate. She must have competed in track and field at some point in the past. She had near perfect form on her javelin throw.

"Few people understand the connection between prison and authentic restaurants," Bridges replied. "That's one of the primary reasons why it's been so hard to get Death Row Restaurant up and running. But I'm not going to give up on creating the world's first authentic restaurant," he was repeating himself now. There was literally nothing new in what he was saying. Yet Bridges' statements had gained the simple, repetitive power of a prayer. "Everyone who will work at Death Row Restaurant will be absolutely perfect for the job they do," Bridges continued. "That's why I need this interview to go well. Death Row Restaurant needs a perfect dishwasher. And no one is better for this job than Dennis Rader," he said, his voice dipping low, yet somehow growing more assertive. "But getting someone like Dennis Rader on board will be quite a task," Bridges insisted. "Dennis Rader is one of the most infamous men in all of Kansas, maybe in all of the world. Not everyone will understand what we are trying to do. And even when they do understand, the logistical hurdles of Dennis Rader's employment will be nearly insurmountable," Bridges admitted. He took a deep breath, as if he'd spent countless late nights working over the details in his mind. "But the first and perhaps biggest challenge is getting Rader to agree. It can't be forced. I have to explain it to him, to help him understand — to help Rader to see that he wants to wash dishes at Death Row Restaurant," he concluded.

Dave had heard the name Dennis Rader before. But he couldn't recall when or who Rader was. The information was there but felt just out of reach. Dave's tequila buzz had receded and a hangover had begun to assert itself, replacing the drunk's clarity of vision with the relentless critique of the morning after. In an hour or so, once Kate reported Dave's inflight behavior, his entire career, more than twenty years — would go up in smoke.

"Who is Dennis Rader?" Dave asked. Not wanting to face the prospect of his future sober, he was scanning the cabin for the beverage cart.

"He's better known as BTK, for bind, torture and kill. He's one of the most infamous serial killers in the world — and he's serving his time in a Kansas Prison," Bridges said. "Rader killed ten people in cold blood — and he will be the most authentic dishwasher the world has ever seen."

———

All of the cultures Dave had visited — from Istanbul to Nigeria, through India, across Europe, Asia and Australia, were places whose history stretched back in a way that Americans didn't understand. For a long time, he blamed his own inauthentic feelings on America's lack of cultural sensitivity. But over the decades, as he became comfortable in even the most outlandish corners of the world, he began to attribute his inauthentic feelings to the world at large. How could Dave live a true life in a false world? How could anyone? And it was this realization more than anything else that made Todd Bridges' proposal for Death Row Restaurant so striking. Dave was immediately, almost viscerally attracted to it the way a duckling must feel drawn to a pond. And on arriving at the pond, the duckling discovers she already knows how to swim. This is how Dave felt, upon hearing Bridges' explanation of Death Row Restaurant.

"There are only two types of restaurants in the world," Bridges continued. "First, those whose goal is reproducibility — that the meal should taste the same any night of the week, any month of the year. This is the promise of most American eating establishments, a promise born on the wings of Protestant ideals. The meal itself only matters as much as it (and by extension, the entire restaurant) are reproducible, perhaps even franchisable. A Big Mac in Paris is largely the same as a Big Mac in Cleveland. The second type of restaurant pursues the same, drab ideal in a different way. Rather than reproducibility, some restaurants claim that their food is authentic. It doesn't matter whether it's Indian, Mexican or even 'farm to table.' The goal for these restaurants is to find a way to transform reproducibility into authenticity."

Bridges had a tiny bit of coca cola left in his plastic cup. He swirled it, then gulped it down. "Death Row Restaurant will be entirely different," Bridges claimed. "Death Row Restaurant won't make the category error that every other restaurant in the world has made — that a restaurant's authenticity has anything to do with its food."

Dave was starting to understand the idea, but he didn't understand why Dennis Rader was the world's most perfect dishwasher. In order to fully digest the idea Bridges was laying out, Dave thought they needed an actual meal in front of them. He knew that inflight beverage service was itself a symbolic act, one which affirmed each passenger's itinerary through life. The smallest choices, even whether to have ice or not — meant something different at 30,000 feet. These choices demonstrated one's agency, that we are in fact directing our lives. In the same way, Dave felt that Dennis Rader's betrayal of society could only be understood in the context of the ultimate symbolic act of togetherness — a family style meal.

"Even in modern society," Bridges continued, as Dave scanned the cabin for Kate and her prowling beverage cart, "the first principle of the world is that you have to kill to survive. Every creature has to eat. And let's face it, whatever you are eating," Bridges held up a pretzel, then popped it into his mouth, "was recently alive."

Kate was occupied. She was busy attending to the first-class cabin. Having relegated Dave to the status of a passenger, an unruly one at that, managing the flight had become somewhat taxing for her. She no longer had time to hurl pretzels at Dave. He leaned into the aisle. He could just make out Kate's athletic calves beneath the curtain separating first class from coach. Dave was again struck by the improbable events of the last few days. Less than a week ago, he and Kate had been a couple, sharing intimacies, sharing their bodies. And now, she couldn't stand his presence and Dave was scheming to eat dinner with Todd Bridges — Willis from Diff'rent Strokes. The fact that Bridges was heading to Wichita, flying coach, was no less extraordinary. The whole thing began to feel like a progression to Dave, so much so that to hire Dennis Rader as a dishwasher, for whatever reasons Todd Bridges entertained its necessity, began to feel entirely plausible.

"All of our celebrations ultimately pay homage to this brutal first condition of life," Bridges added, chomping his last pretzel and then crumpling the bag noisily. "We all kill to survive."

Dave nodded his head, peeked towards the curtain separating Coach from First Class. Most First Class passengers choose beef or fish over chicken. He knew there would be a few leftover chicken cacciatore meals in the galley. He just needed to get them without Kate seeing him. Obviously, flight attendant Dave had every right to be in the galley and to distribute the meals as he saw fit. But he also knew that he hadn't really been honest with Kate when they had been dating. Dave hadn't actively deceived her, yet he had always known that their relationship had been built on a misunderstanding. Obviously, Kate had hated Wichita from the beginning. The very thought of Wichita made her gag. If fucking their way through a layover in Wichita hadn't been deceptive, it had at least been enabling. Dave didn't want to make any more trouble for Kate. The airline hospitality industry would prove tough enough for her.

But then, Dave heard her laugh. It was the same overzealous, high pitched and then husky laugh that he recalled from their first night together in the Doubletree Hilton in Wichita. Kate wasn't tied up with requests in First Class. She was flirting with a passenger. She had detached her fantasy of world travel from Dave and sutured it to someone else. The operation, he knew, would take little time to complete.

"In our politics," Bridges continued, "we are just as insistent on authenticity. We joke about it, but when it comes down to it, Americans insist that their politicians own what they do at the level of who they are."

"Hold that thought," Dave said over his shoulder, preparing to fling himself into the aisle and towards the galley. He knew his only chance to really understand Todd Bridges instead of seeing him as 'Willis' from Diff'rent Strokes, his only chance to ascertain exactly why anyone needed a serial killer as a dishwasher — was now. "I hope you're okay with chicken," Dave added in a solemn voice, and not waiting for a reply from Todd Bridges, Dave leapt into the aisle.

Dave kept an eye on Kate's athletic calves under the first-class curtain. She really did have attractive legs and he was struck by how such a thing as attractive calves felt intrinsic and unalterable. If a serial killer like Dennis Rader had attractive calves, for instance, his brutal murders wouldn't change that fact at all. Perhaps that was why people had been so fascinated by Ted Bundy. No matter what Bundy had done, he was quite good looking and very charismatic. Dave had seen a documentary a long time ago in which they interviewed women who showed up at Bundy's murder trial with their hair parted in the middle and wearing hoop earrings — styles that Ted Bundy's victims had worn. Bundy had even gotten married and fathered a child while on death row. It was weird, Dave thought, as he snatched a half dozen or so chicken cacciatore meals and handed them out randomly to passengers in coach. Todd Bridges was right. Being a serial killer didn't preclude a person from being an excellent — even the world's best — dishwasher.

But why did it matter? How often does a restaurant patron even see the dishwasher? Kate's luxurious calves were still in the same spot, just past the curtain separating first class from coach. She raised one of her legs slightly and emitted another high-pitched laugh. No doubt Kate's hand was parked on the side of the first-class seat, too, as if she and her no doubt good looking and successful passenger were lounging in their own living room, like lovers. Dave loaded his arms with food. He tore open the top shelf liquor and filled his pockets. Then he bounced down the aisle like a pool ball in one of those trick shot videos on YouTube. He barely made it to his seat. Dumping the stash on Bridges' tray table, Dave said, "first, we eat. Then, I want you to tell me all about Death Row Restaurant."

———

The restaurant wasn't as easy to understand as Dave thought it would be. Bridges didn't help the situation by providing a rambling account of his legal troubles, starting with the way local cops would pull him over when he was still a perfectly law-abiding citizen, for driving while black. And yet later, when Bridges was committing crimes on an hourly basis, he deserved those same cops' suspicions. Dave listened intently, especially when Bridges got to the part about being put on trial for capital murder.

"I had been America's darling teenager on Diff'rent Strokes — and they threw me in a cell on 'Murderer's Row.' I had the Menendez brothers on one side and Richard Ramirez — a serial killer nicknamed 'the night stalker' on the other," Bridges said. "Richard Ramirez was an avowed Satanist. He used to threaten to kill me just about every night. He bragged about raping old ladies, carving pentagrams into their skin. It was crazy." Bridges cut off a very small piece of chicken, a single, neat cube. "But I realized something, too," Bridges added, chewing methodically. "There's something about these serial killers. They own what they do at a level I'd never encountered before. There was absolutely no reforming them, no suggestion one should even try.

No aspect of their personality is an act, at that point. Part of why this intrigued me was my Hollywood upbringing, all that acting — and that was just my non television family. Then there was my television family and the constant push pull between the two. I was always wondering which felt more real to me. And as a drug addict, it was a different version of the same problem. At one point, I didn't believe I could be Todd Bridges without cocaine. Then once I started doing meth, not only did I believe that meth was an absolute requirement for me to be Todd Bridges, I came to believe that I needed meth just to be a person in general, any person at all." Bridges shrugged, moved some vegetables around on his plate. "Drug addicts are counseled to stop, counseled that drugs are an avoidance of the real you, not an expression or aspect of yourself," Bridges said, putting down his knife and wiping his chin with a linen napkin. He looked Dave squarely in the eye. "But Ramirez — killing was 100% who he was. He didn't just do things. He owned them — with all his being. Giving a guy like Ramirez the gas chamber wasn't about holding Ramirez accountable for his actions. It was about the fact that serial killers can't change. They can't get clean like a drug addict. What they've done really is who they are."

"That's horrifying." Dave meant it too. But when he said it, he was scooping up stray bits of roasted red pepper with his fork. Which made Dave feel terrible about himself.

"On the day Ramirez learned he was going to get the gas chamber, he told reporters, 'see you in Disneyland!' And that night, when Ramirez got put back in his cell, after all the nights he'd threatened to kill me, I got up in the middle of the night and yelled, 'hey Richard. How long can you hold your breath?'"

"No shit. What'd he say?"

"He said, 'Whatchoo talkin' bout, Willis?' I swear to god, that's what he said." Bridges threw his palm at the seat in front of him, as if to say, forget it. "Anyways, even being in prison next to Richard Ramirez wasn't as bad as rehab," Bridges confessed. "In rehab, while I was detoxing from crack cocaine and meth, they strapped me to a metal bed in a diaper. The pain was unbelievable. I spent days screaming and cursing out everyone I saw. Bridges pushed his tray of chicken cacciatore aside. "But like I said, this was very different from someone like Richard Ramirez. Most of us go around doing things that we will later plausibly claim aren't who we are. Look at the news. I'm not the only one. But when they strap you to a metal bed in a diaper, when you've shit yourself and every molecule in your body is screaming from detox — there's no avoiding facing yourself. Up until that point, I had blamed everyone else for my problems.

After the metal bed and diaper I had at least a faint understanding of what it might mean to own what I did, not taking accountability for it. Owning it. Owning it as who I am." Bridges paused. He stared out the window. The plane was passing through a cloud and there was nothing to look at but a blanket of whiteness. "That's why Death Row Restaurant is going to be so huge. It's the dinner equivalent of being strapped to a metal bed in a diaper."

It was another very bizarre point. Dave had trouble figuring out how to evaluate it.

"People go out to dinner to experience something authentic," Bridges continued. "Everyone confuses the whole thing with the food, that the food has to be authentic without being co-opted. Or that it has to at least be explainable according to some theme, reproducible night after night," Bridges said, taking a deep breath. "But it's the wrong kind of authenticity. It's easily faked. I mean, how does the average person even know how Banh Mi is supposed to taste? They don't. But prison. In prison you know shit is real. And if you're lucky enough to be around a serial killer, you get this unmistakable sense of reality. Here is someone who no longer fakes who he really is."

It made a ton of sense to Dave. The words, 'convict' and 'conviction' aren't all that different, Dave thought. Yet something in him rebelled at the idea, too.

"Aren't prisons filled with pathological liars, scam artists and violent criminals who would lie, cheat or steal at any moment?" Dave asked. "How is that authentic?"

"That's not the point," Bridges sighed, annoyed. "As frightening as it was to be threatened by Richard Ramirez, you knew he meant that shit. He didn't just talk about anything. He was willing to do it." Bridges began using his napkin to dig inside his nose. "It's a part of the place itself, prisons. You're on the clock all day, every day. The sheer reality of having no say at all in your schedule — a fucking gas chamber, man. You can't pretend anymore at that point. That's why Death Row Restaurant is going to be housed inside the gas chamber at San Quentin," Bridges added.

Hearing it out loud like that — the whole idea summed up in a single sentence… it sounded fucking bananas. To have a restaurant, an actual public restaurant inside the gas chamber at San Quentin — the logistics alone had to be outrageous. But a part of Dave wondered if it could actually be done.

"Sixty percent of restaurants fail in the first year," Bridges asserted. He was still digging in his nose with his napkin, although his nose was immaculate inside. "Eighty percent of restaurants go under in the first five years. These places are constantly opening and then closing, changing menus and decor. And they don't realize that the problem isn't the food or the atmosphere. It's the staff. There's nothing authentic about them. They just work a job for money, making the actual work — a thing more or less indifferent to them. Death Row Restaurant is going to change all that," Bridges insisted. And the sentence had the unmistakable aplomb of something recognizably true anywhere in the world, like 2+2=4.

Dave had to admit that Bridges had a point. A diner who drove all the way to San Quentin to eat a ridiculously priced meal inside their mothballed gas chamber, a diner who had to complete the kind of paperwork Bridges talked about completing just to conduct his interview with Dennis Rader just to eat a meal — paperwork in order to be placed on the prison's approved visitor list, paperwork necessary to clear a background check before physically passing through thorough security with the possibility of an additional cavity search — a diner who did all that, a diner who then let a serial killer who'd murdered people with his bare hands over and over again, who had cherished the intimacy of sharing the victim's final breath on earth, who had wanted to be the last person the victim ever sees — well, a diner who does all that must be in some kind of genuine position.

"I think I understand," Dave suggested, although it came out more noncommittal than he had intended.

"Let me put this another way," Bridges said, taking a sip of his Dom Perignon. "Conrad Bain was a better father to me than my own father had been." Bridges put his head in his hands. Clearly, this wasn't easy for him. Conrad Bain had played Bridges' father on Diff'rent Strokes. Dave recalled hearing news stories about his passing four or five years ago. In a subsequent interview, Todd Bridges appeared really broken up about his passing. But back then, Dave had wondered if Bridges' sorrowful display on news programs was genuine. Bridges was, after all, a professional actor. He was expected to feel the loss in a meaningful way. And Dave wondered for a few seconds if Bridges' whole story about Death Row Restaurant was just some kind of prank, if the story that he was traveling to El Dorado

Correctional Facility to interview a serial killer for a dishwashing job — was just a goof. "Conrad was just a terrific person," Bridges sniffled through his immaculate nostrils. "He was a very caring person, just like the character he played on Diff'rent Strokes. And Conrad visited me in rehab. He had a regular schedule about it. He was always there for me. At first, I just thought Conrad was visiting Willis, like how he would have if my stint at rehab was just the plot of an episode of Diff'rent Strokes."

Dave touched Bridges lightly on the shoulder out of sympathy. "There were visits when he pretended to be Mr. Drummond, my father on the television show — and I would pretend to be Willis. But other times, I don't think he was playing a role. At other times, Conrad Bain was just visiting me, just a man who cared about me. Those visits were real. The real Conrad Bain and the real Todd Bridges. And all of this happened in a way that made me think that my biological father's visits to me in those same places, in rehab and in prison, were actually fake. Something about the situation, the confinement, the way a prison works, it helped me to understand who my real father was." Bridges raised his hand, palm forward in a "stop" gesture, as if to ward off emotions that could go too far. "I don't mean to say that prison, by itself created this authenticity. But I've realized since then, that prison played a huge role in this." Bridges pinched his nose and eyes and lifted his cheeks, sort of like wincing but in this very calm and deliberate fashion. "My own father," he finally continued, "had reasons to visit me, had obligations to me. Conrad didn't. For Conrad to come visit me in rehab, in prison, for him to come there and go through the whole process of approval and security, and for him to understand his role as my father — to understand that our relationship was in fact, authentic — I don't know, I just realized that Conrad would only do that if he really wanted to," Bridges concluded. "And any diner willing to go through that whole process just to eat a meal would have to have a similar commitment."

The whole time Bridges was talking, the plane had been hitting severe turbulence. Some of the worst Dave had experienced in his twenty years flying. And then right when Bridges finished, the turbulence intensified even more, so much so that when Dave opened his mouth to speak, a violent jerk of the plane slammed his mouth shut. The intercom clicked on, asking flight attendants to take their seats. A few plastic cups bounced down the aisle of the plane like trash blowing through an alley. Kate dashed down the aisle checking seat belts. Dave wanted to advise her to take her seat, that the message from the captain was directed at the flight attendants specifically. He unfastened his seatbelt only to have Kate slap his hands away and fasten it again.

It gave Dave the peculiar sensation that whatever this new path he had chosen was, he was locked into it.

Bridges' story had reminded Dave of his own childhood — one of his earliest memories, in fact. Dave's parents had divorced when Dave was just one year old. Dave had lived with his mother in a one-bedroom apartment. One weekend, Dave's mother had packed him a little suitcase. Before Dave could even ask what the suitcase was for, a man showed up at the apartment. The man was funny and warm. He picked Dave up and held him to his chest. Dave's mother clearly knew this man — who had already made her laugh several times. Dave's mother helped Dave to put his coat on. She knelt down and kissed him on the forehead, running her fingers through his hair, as she always did — a habit she had picked up after Dave had a tick last summer after his day camp. Then she handed Dave his little suitcase.

The man drove them in a car for several hours. A really long time to Dave, who was already homesick. But when they arrived at the man's house, they were greeted by a fluffy, wolf-like dog.

"Touch his nose," the man instructed Dave.

Dave did. The dog's nose was wet. It made Dave giggle. He had never touched a dog's nose before. Christmas lights were slung up everywhere and they had a huge gingerbread house. It was Christmas Eve. They went to church and Dave wasn't old enough to hold a candle like he wanted to, but later that night Dave felt so warm and comfortable that he crawled into the man's lap and hugged him. The man's face was all scratchy. He was reading the paper and drinking some kind of strong liquor. But Dave didn't care. And he must have fallen asleep in the man's lap because he woke up in a bed, surrounded by darkness. It was scary and the windows and the trees outside were unfamiliar. But Dave remembered the man's lap, his hug and his little sighs. Dave fell back asleep and the next morning was Christmas. It wasn't until Dave returned home to his mother that he found out who that man was. That man was his father.

He was gone now, Dave's father. Lung cancer. And like Todd Bridges, Dave knew that the best moments, those that mean some-thing to you years later, come about when one has reason to believe that someone has brought his actions and his being into complete harmony, even if it's just for a single weekend. Dave had never forgotten that his first memory of his father was in some ways the memory of a stranger who had been kind to him. Dave hadn't known about their biological bond, his father's legal responsibilities. He just knew that the kindness, the affection — was real.

"We can't know if Dennis Rader was a good father," Bridges said, all of a sudden, referring of course to the BTK Killer. "Being a family man and being president of his church was a great cover for Dennis Rader's brutal murders." Bridges paused, then opened up the last container of food Dave had scavenged earlier and took a huge bite of chicken. "But if Dennis Rader agrees to wash dishes at Death Row Restaurant, it can only be because he wants to do it," Bridges said. "That's the kind of authenticity Death Row Restaurant will provide its customers."

———

Unfortunately, Dave didn't get to hear anything more about Death Row Restaurant. The plane's final descent into Wichita was the roughest he had ever experienced. The plane leapt and jerked and the pilots clicked onto the intercom to remind passengers to stay in their seats with their seatbelts securely fastened. In fact, the pilot misspoke and said 'fashioned' instead of 'fastened.' The error was troubling.

"Flight attendants, prepare for landing," said the voice, before clicking off, seemingly for eternity.

Dave unbuckled his seat belt. He was no longer a flight attendant, he realized. This job was over for him.

"Might be a good idea to keep your seat," Bridges suggested.

"I have to piss," Dave answered, then toasted to Bridges one last time and guzzled a split of champagne.

Dave bounced down the aisle. He was tossed into the laps of several different women and men, each of whom, Dave felt, received him in some way. Not angrily, but with a kind of genuine surprise that superseded anger. He made it to the lavatory, shut himself inside and slid the latch. Dave steadied himself with both hands and therefore peed without holding his penis. He was surprised by his ability to do this, the almost natural way that he lowered his center of gravity to maintain his position as the plane was rocked by turbulence.

An insistent knocking began at the door.

"Sir, sir, sir!" It was Kate's voice. "Passengers must be in their seats for landing!"

Dave shot open the bolt and accordioned open the lavatory door. Miraculously, he hadn't peed on the floor at all, but he also hadn't zipped up his pants. Kate lowered her eyes to his penis briefly, then said, "sir, you must be in your seat."

"Come on, Kate. You know who I am. We spent the last three months fucking in Wichita hotel rooms."

Kate visibly gagged a few times.

"No we didn't," she said. "That's not what I was doing."

"The fact that you get nauseous, that you suffered during this. It doesn't make you more honest or authentic," Dave said. But he wasn't really thinking about Kate when he said it. Dave was thinking about Dennis Rader. Had Dennis Rader finally felt true and at peace with himself when he killed? It was a horrifying thought. Dave zipped his pants and turned to wash his hands. Just the idea that murdering an innocent person could make another person feel authentic — it had sobered Dave up. Even the courts recognize that for a serial killer, what the person did matches with who they ultimately are. Serial killers do not argue that killing is only a small part of who they are. Unlike Dave who was closing out a twenty-year chapter of his life in the bathroom of a plane from Chicago to Wichita, who had only a few hours ago felt good about getting caught up on his mandatory flight training videos, who had taken a single Dramamine tablet before liftoff since the weather report called for turbulence, unlike Dave a serial killer didn't start and then end chapters in his life. Serial killers were, in this very bizarre and seemingly complete way, who they were all the time.

The airplane, a DC9, one of the smallest commercial planes in operation, hit the tarmac violently. The plane bounced off the runway like a basketball and came down again. It repeated this process several times as gasps rose from the aisles of the plane. Dave and Kate were pitched about, both scrambling for something to hold onto. And in a fashion similar to how Dave and Kate's relationship had begun in the first place, they grabbed one another in an embrace that provided neither of them with safety or even enjoyment. First, Kate fell backwards, slamming her head on the lavatory door, her body protecting Dave from harm. Then, as the plane lurched in the other direction, Kate was thrust forward. She pushed Dave backwards where Dave shielded her from harm by falling half into the toilet bowl. Finally, the plane's flaps shot up and the landing gear dug in.

Kate, separated herself from Dave. And in a symbolic gesture, with Dave still wedged halfway into the toilet bowl, she hit the flush button and stormed off.

The cabin exploded into cheers at the safe landing, followed by elaborate sighs of relief. Dave extracted himself from the toilet. His shirt had ripped. He held the ripped edges together, but as soon as he let go, they separated. Dave was too drunk to think clearly. But now that the plane had landed, his role on the Wichita route was officially over. Dave marched down the aisle, feeling both sad and purposeful. He gave Todd Bridges an inexplicable thumbs up sign, and then as the plane taxied, Dave pulled the emergency chute.

As the chute opened, stretching itself out to the ground, Dave went to the galley, unlocked the beverage cart and grabbed an armload of champagne.

"The Wichita route is yours, Kate."

And with that, Dave leapt onto the slide and deplaned. From the Air Capital bar in Eisenhower Airport, passengers waiting for their flights watched Dave cross the nearly empty tarmac struggling under an armload of champagne splits. Dave made his way into the terminal. The airport was small and intuitive. Within a few minutes, Dave had a seat at the bar. He began stacking the champagne bottles, although he also ordered a martini. When it came, Dave joined the crowd at the window, holding his drink in one hand and pointing at emergency vehicles that now surrounded the DC9, flashing their emergency lights as passengers, following Dave's lead, slid one after another down the emergency slide. Although Dave couldn't quite make out her features, he saw a woman gesturing wildly to passen gers who were lining up to deplane using the emergency slide. Dave knew it was Kate, and he briefly felt sorry for what he'd done. Though Kate at one point had blocked the slide, one after another, passengers pushed past her and slid their way to Wichita. Just before the airport police arrived to arrest him, Dave noted that Kate had given up trying to direct passengers back to their seats and was instead helping them into position on the slide and signaling when to release themselves, like a teenager at a waterpark.

Within twenty minutes, two police officers took Dave into custody at the airport bar. They took Dave's nearly full martini and set it on the window sill. Then they handcuffed him. It almost felt like they were going to return the drink to him once they had him cuffed. Dave was surprised when they didn't. Instead, the policemen escorted him out of the airport and into a waiting squad car. Each maintained a firm grip on one of his upper arms, exactly as Dave had seen it on television, right down to the way one officer palmed the top of Dave's head, making sure he didn't hit it on the roof of the squad car as he was shoved inside.

PART II: THE OYSTER

DAVE SPENT the night in a Wichita jail cell. As Dave sobered up, he worried about what he had done and what he would be charged with. He couldn't believe he'd torpedoed his career. Although Flight Attendants are often disrespected, the job itself is challenging to break into and seniority takes years, even decades to accrue. Now, no airline would possibly hire him. In fact, Dave would have to replace the emergency slide he had opened at a cost of $3000, minimum. Dave thought about that. $3000 for one six second slide and an armload of champagne (most of which had been left in the airport bar). $3000 just so he didn't have to be in the cabin with Kate for five more minutes while they taxied to the gate. Six hundred dollars per minute. And that figure didn't include any criminal charges or fines Dave might also face. But truthfully, his relationship with Kate, its inevitable implosion, only proved to Dave that he needed to commit to something once and for all. It was one thing to like Wichita for a few days on layover. It would be another to actually live in a single place for years on end, something his flight attendant career had prevented.

These concerns, as paramount as they seemed, didn't dominate all of Dave's thoughts. Instead, he found himself thinking again and again about Dennis Rader. Although Wichita had been Dave's favorite place on earth for several years, although Dave had flown in and out of Wichita at least four times per week, although Dave had considered Wichita to be his true home — he had never heard about Wichita's most famous resident, Dennis Rader. Few people will just bring up serial killers, even homegrown serial killers in general conversation. And besides, Rader had been behind bars since 2005, serving ten consecutive life sentences without parole for his brutal killings. Dave had learned those facts from his two arresting officers.

"Ever heard of Dennis Rader?" Dave had said, while handcuffed in the back of their police cruiser. At the time, Dave was leaning forward in his seat. His hands were still cuffed behind his back and leaning forward gave him a better sense of bodily control. If the car took a fast corner, Dave would not be able to brace himself with his hands.

While the arresting officers no doubt thought Dave's sudden question about Dennis Rader bizarre, they did share a few basic facts of Dennis Rader's story. Rader had taunted Wichita police for years. His victims were petite and vulnerable. Rader, Dave quickly found out, had even killed children. And the nickname BTK — he'd given that nickname to himself in a letter to police bragging about his horrid crimes. The whole story was so fucked up that Dave found himself gagging in the back of the police cruiser. How could anyone work with a man like Dennis Rader? How could anyone find such a person an absolute necessity, as Todd Bridges had told Dave when discussing the need for an authentic dishwasher at Death Row Restaurant? And yet, as Dave was being hauled out of the police cruiser like a bag of groceries, he didn't feel that what he'd done on the plane and the repercussions he would face because of it represented who he truly was. He couldn't help wondering about what it would be like to be around a person who owned what he did — as who he was.

"In the courtroom," the patrol officers escorting Dave said, "In the courtroom with Rader, your hair stood up," the detectives agreed. "You could feel the evil."

Dave wondered if the experience they were describing had anything to do with the striking experience of being around someone who was whole (albeit in this very twisted and dangerous way). Rader was a killer, through and through.

Drug addicts can go to rehab. They relapse but are consistently told that their addictions are not who they really are, Dave thought. Parents watch their children grow up and leave home. A young person is never considered static or fixed. People get into careers and even marriages and then get out of them, swap them out like a new oil filter. Todd Bridges had gone through that impermanence at an extraordinary level. He went from America's darling to a meth and crack addict on trial for murder. Yet Bridges had reformed himself.

That was the difference. A serial killer cannot be reformed. The serial killer is who he is — which was precisely why Todd Bridges wanted so desperately to get Dennis Rader to wash dishes at Death Row Restaurant.

Now that he was in a police station, getting booked, Dave understood with much greater intensity what Bridges had been talking about. Dave knew that in the court appearances he would no doubt face in the coming days, he would have to explain his self-imposed emergency exit from the ORD to ICT flight, he would have to explain his inflight drinking — and most importantly, he would be advised by an attorney to argue that those actions do not reflect who Dave really is. Any reasonably competent attorney would draw on Dave's two decades of exemplary service as a flight attendant and his lifetime of law-abiding citizenship. For Dave, this whole line of inquiry pointed out how deeply our institutions rest on the bizarre premise that people do things all the time that don't represent who they really are. And he had no trouble envisioning a courtroom and judge who would find that argument very credible. Just thinking about this left a sour taste in Dave's mouth — so much so that as he wandered in circles in the holding cell of Wichita's jail, stepping over the drunks passed out on the floor, he sincerely hoped that somehow he would be spared, that somehow, he could avoid making the case that his actions are not who he really is.

What Dave craved was wholeness, the feeling that he was more than an out-of-control bundle of emotions that led to actions which didn't properly reflect who he is. And it seemed to Dave that Americans had spent their time concerned with freedom and fairness in ways that led to exactly this sort of dilemma — the fact that our actions don't reflect who we are. Our justice system and social fabric had been built around the idea that accountability was accepting the consequences for what you've done, while arguing that these actions don't reflect who you really are. It was all quite similar to the travel industry. You travel to other countries and live like they do. And the whole trick of it, the enjoyment of it, was that you tried to act like they did, knowing you never could succeed, knowing that even locals don't succeed in feeling authentic and whole. Not unless they are serial killers, Dave thought.

Dave understood that he should probably not make life changing decisions in the holding cell of a Wichita jail. That perhaps the power of what he was feeling, which had penetrated his body, might very well be manufactured by the emotional circumstances, by the stark reality of the cramped holding cell or the giant crap one of the drunks had taken in the toilet or the steady ringing of phones throughout the police station. Part of Dave certainly wanted to dismiss the intense feelings he was having. Part of him certainly wanted to apologize to the judge, blame his emotional breakup with Kate, express remorse for his actions — and move on.

But he kept coming back to the idea of Death Row Restaurant, to the idea that even a single night in which everything diners experienced, from conversations with the driver who escorts them to the prison to the way the bartender wipes down the bar to a serial killer waiter who leans close to be certain to hear diners' orders correctly — all of it — that these actions could not be rejected as false or manufactured. That in effect, one can do things that ineluctably align with who one actually is.

Dave's musings were interrupted each time he was removed from the holding cell to be fingerprinted or interviewed. Part of him was furious at the interruption. Another part of Dave welcomed how heavy and embarrassing and real the whole experience was feeling. When he was finally handed an orange jumpsuit, a toothbrush and a packet of sugar for his morning coffee, he had to admit that Wichita jail felt exactly right to him. He felt this to be even more true when a burly prisoner in his cell block suggested that Dave might want to give him his sugar packet and toothbrush.

Eventually, Dave was allowed to make a phone call. Dave called his mother. He told her he was in jail. He told her she would need to get on a flight from New Jersey to Wichita, from EWR airport in Newark to ICT airport in Wichita. Dave told his mother that she would have to deplane in Chicago and get on a commuter flight for the last leg. He told her he could not get her a free ticket or an upgrade. Dave told her he would be arraigned in the morning on charges of 'criminal mischief' and 'reckless endangerment.' When Dave's mother asked if he was in serious trouble, he was not able to give an honest answer. The charges against him were not serious crimes. However, Dave's situation involved much more than just the charges he was facing.

Dave had difficulty sleeping in jail. He was always aware of where he was. The jail asserted itself — and he didn't know how to respond. The more Dave thought about his accidental crossing of paths with

Todd Bridges, the more he wondered if Death Row Restaurant was possible.

———

The next day, Dave met his court appointed attorney.

"Amanda Barnes, attorney at law," Amanda shook Dave's hand warmly, then sat down and began reviewing her notes. He couldn't get used to the metal table and bench, to how cold it was to lean his forearms on. Amanda's curly red hair was always falling in front of her eyes. She shook her bangs to the side doggedly whenever she went to write something, which was already making Dave feel tired. Amanda quizzed Dave about the particulars of that flight, about what drove him to deploy the emergency chute. Dave answered her questions succinctly and honestly — although he did not mention Death Row Restaurant.

"Dave," Amanda began, putting down her pencil, which rolled back and forth on the metal table, "I think we can resolve your situation with a simple fine. We'll just explain to the court that you were under duress given the termination of your romantic relationship and the aggravated hostility that had taken place."

Ms. Barnes began shoving papers into her briefcase. "You made a bad decision. You didn't think things through. With your record, the judge will understand that this isn't who you are."

"I don't want to make that argument," Dave interrupted. "I don't know what other argument I can make — but not that."

"Right. That's a good point," Ms. Barnes sat back down. "You want to be sure the judge understands that you take full responsibility for your actions. Make that clear at the start."

"No," Dave replied.

"No what?"

"Saying I take responsibility for my actions isn't the same as owning my actions as who I am. Accepting the consequences isn't the same as owning the action." Dave tried to scratch an itch on his nose. Forgetting that his hands were shackled, he punched himself in the nose. His eyes began to water.

"Look, this is just an arraignment. It will take like five minutes. You post bail and you can forget you were ever here."

"Why would I want to do that?"

"You like being in jail?"

"Not particularly," he said, his eyes still watery. Amanda raised her eyebrows quizzically, as if watching a squirrel ride a unicycle. "There is something about this side of the metal table that makes you feel it's possible to own your actions, that it's possible to be a whole human being."

Dave was cracking his knuckles for some reason, which gave him the impression of manipulating his internal structure, realigning it like a spiritual chiropractor.

"Trust me," Amanda Barnes stood up, "it's better just to post bail than whatever the hell you think you're doing." And with that, she marched to the holding cell door and signaled to the guard that they were finished. "You'll likely have your arraignment tomorrow," she said. "It has to be within forty-eight hours of your arrest. Just post bail and move on."

The guard escorted Amanda Barnes to her next client, leaving Dave alone in the room. He cracked his neck, first one side, then the other. The sound filled the room briefly.

―――

The rest of the day, Dave sat on his bunk and thought about Death Row Restaurant. How do you convince a serial killer to park cars, empty grease traps or scrub dishes? How do you convince a serial killer to care about letting the juices drain from a roast duck so as to expertly crisp its skin? How do you get a serial killer to study for years to certify as a wine sommelier so as to pair a rich roasted duck with a buttery and crisp Riesling? Will the menu be formidable? Whimsical? Postmodern? Even if the food is not the point, someone has to plan these things. Dave had eaten in restaurants all around the world — yet he hadn't the first clue what could be expected of a place like Death Row Restaurant.

Could you expect someone like the BTK killer, a man who snuck away from a Boy Scout jamboree in order to strangle his neighbor and take bondage pictures of her, could someone like that care about preparing desserts the way they do at Alinea in Chicago? Where cooks literally paint the food onto the table in the style of abstract minimalism? BTK's taunting notes to police often plagiarized children's rhymes. He couldn't possibly take an interest in the formal qualities of an upscale dinner, could he?

Dave was in a bit of a bind. Death Row Restaurant seemed to be nothing more than an abstraction. In literal terms, the restaurant was impossible. The whole thing was a gimmick, but as always, when Dave followed these thoughts to their logical conclusion, he found that Death Row Restaurant was not only possible — but absolutely necessary. After all, gimmicks aren't possible inside a gas chamber and with serial murderers. Death Row Restaurant wouldn't claim a new fusion of cuisines or a modern 'take' or a 'deconstructed take.' Although the restaurant might sound gimmicky at first, it was ultimately above such concerns. Sure, a menu had to be planned. But with serial killers at the helm, they didn't have to worry about the typical concerns restaurateurs face, like being accused of cultural appropriation. Whatever they served and whatever the circumstances, Death Row Restaurant could never face charges of exploitation. You can't exploit a serial killer. Legally, serial killers are not allowed to profit from their crimes. The only job a serial killer can take is an internship or volunteer gig. And although that sounded terribly confined, it also meant that serial killers can only do work that actually matters to them. They can't take a huge salary for work they can't stand or are indifferent to. Working at Death Row Restaurant really would be fundamentally unlike every other job in the world. No one could go viral at Death Row Restaurant for leaving a 1000% tip and scribbling 'pay it forward' on the credit card receipt. The more Dave thought about it, the more he discovered ways that Death Row Restaurant would be different.

At the same time, on a practical level, the whole idea was so ridiculous and so much trouble that it couldn't possibly be worth pursuing. A restaurant in a gas chamber? They could maybe serve two or three couples per night. And how many serial killers would sign up? As far as Dave knew, Dennis Rader was Todd Bridges' first job interview. What if he said "no. Go fuck yourself?" But then again, what if Todd Bridges could pull it off? What if Bridges and Dave could channel the serial killer's single-minded dedication, his ownership of his actions at the level of 'being' to will Death Row Restaurant into reality in the same way that Dennis Rader willed himself to leave that Boy Scout Jamboree to murder his neighbor in the middle of the night?

This is what Dave was thinking about when several security officers came to collect him for his arraignment.

———

It was immediately clear from the procedural knowledge everyone in the courtroom possessed that Dave's attorney was correct. All Dave had to do was claim he'd acted out of character, accept responsibility, show a little remorse, make bail, pay damages and he'd be released. Then he could get back in touch with Todd Bridges. And perhaps if Dave's mother hadn't been sitting in the gallery with an embarrassed look on her face, the same look she had when Dave was caught shoplifting as a teenager and utterly failed to explain why he had stolen a pack of batteries when he had money in his wallet — perhaps then Dave might just have gone along with the program. But he thought instead about how the shoplifting incident had been expunged from his official record (although Dave was banned from Kids 'R' Us, which closed in 2003). Yet Dave's punishment for stealing from Kids 'R' Us hadn't ended when the chain went bankrupt. He had spent his whole life trying to understand why he had taken those batteries (six AAA batteries, which powered virtually nothing in 1980's electronics).

As Dave stood in front of the Judge in Wichita, he realized that he could not spend his life disconnecting what he did from who he was, even if mothers and courts around the country sanctioned it.

"Mr. Aslin. You're pleading guilty to reckless endangerment and criminal mischief in the third degree?"

"I absolutely am guilty of that," Dave insisted.

"Do you have anything else to say before sentencing?"

"Only that I want to take ownership for what I did," Dave added. He was trying to marry his understanding with what his attorney had requested. But in the courtroom it just sounded like a very weird thing to say. The judge made a pinched face at hearing the phrase. Then shrugged and moved on.

"Given the defendant's admission, his record of service and the extenuating circumstances deposed by council," the judge stated, as if reading off a script, "as well as remorse, this court orders a fine of $10,000 and time served. Court is adjourned."

"You did well," Amanda Barnes said to Dave, patting him lightly on his shoulder.

Dave's mother stood up looking extraordinarily defeated. And Dave, too, felt defeated. But unlike his mother, he had a plan to set things right.

———

"All that for damaging a slide?" Dave's mother screamed at Amanda Barnes, once Dave had been processed out of Wichita jail. "You know, it's not the only time Dave interfered with someone else's property," Dave's mother told everyone in the room, making eye contact with an exhausted looking guard, badly in need of a shave. Dave steadied himself to hear about the Kids 'R' Us batteries, but instead his mother said, "Dave gave an old air conditioner I had in the garage to his girl-friend without even asking me."

Dave had forgotten all about that.

No sooner had they exited the jail when Dave spotted Todd Bridges leaning against a Chevy Malibu. He had accidentally parked in the police lot. The Malibu was surrounded by parked squad cars, as if Bridges was being taken into custody.

"Just a second, Mom. I have to go talk to someone," Dave said.

Despite all the police cars surrounding him, Bridges leaned casu-ally against his Malibu, enjoying the sunshine. He looked sort of like a limo driver waiting to pick up a client.

"I was worried about how I would contact you," Dave said as he walked up to Todd Bridges. "How did your interview with Dennis Rader go?" It was an absolutely perfect day in Wichita, crisp blue skies, abundant sunshine, low humidity. And unlimited visibility. Dave couldn't help but think like a flight attendant. Of course, it was conditions like this that enabled 9/11, Dave thought.

"You agreed to drive me to El Dorado Correctional Facility," Bridges shrugged. "My interview with Dennis Rader, for that dish-washing job. It's today."

"Couldn't you have taken a bus or an Uber or something?" Dave was happy to drive Bridges, who had no driver's license. But the idea that Bridges had been waiting around for Dave to post bail on the day of his critical interview with Dennis Rader seemed ludicrous.

"Don't you want to be the general manager at Death Row Restau-rant?" Bridges responded, tossing Dave the keys to his rented Chevy Malibu. Dave caught the keys automatically, the action serving as consent. The Malibu had a navy-blue exterior with brown leather seats. Dave found this combination attractive, even though it was parked crookedly and surrounded by cop cars.

"How can you rent a car if you have no driver's license?" Dave asked.

"Get in, Dave," Bridges suggested, popping a pair of Miami Vice shades down from his forehead and over his eyes. To Dave, Bridges suddenly appeared young, vibrant and full of promise — the way he had appeared on the television show Diff'rent Strokes. He looked like Willis.

"Mom," Dave called over his shoulder. "I'm sorry, but I have an obligation I forgot about. You remember Todd Bridges, don't you?"

"Who?" Dave's mother barked.

"Todd Bridges. From Diff'rent Strokes..." he trailed off. "Look ma, we can take you to the airport if you need me to."

But Dave's mother was already walking away, just like when security at Kids 'R' Us had let Dave and his mother leave the security hut after he was caught stealing those AAA batteries. She had walked twenty feet ahead of Dave out of embarrassment and rage.

"Thanks for bailing me out, ma," Dave called after her. And he wasn't sure if he was talking about the reckless endangerment charge here in Wichita — or about the battery theft at Kids 'R' Us, which he'd never thanked her for.

"We need to get to the prison by 1pm," Bridges said, suddenly turning serious. "Since you're not on the prison's approved visitor list, you'll have to wait in the car while I meet with Dennis Rader, the BTK Killer."

———

The drive to El Dorado Correctional Facility from Sedgwick County Jail was easy. Highway 254 took you right to the prison's doorstep. Dave and Todd Bridges drove in relative silence for about fifteen minutes. Dave hadn't been outside in at least two days. He soaked up the sunshine, the breeze. It was wonderful. Despite repeated inquiries, Bridges had never explained how he was able to rent the Chevy Malibu without a driver's license or how Bridges had gotten the rental car to Sedgwick County Jail in Wichita without driving it himself. Once they got out of town, the highway was a straight shot and the landscape so flat and unchanging that Dave had trouble maintaining a reasonable speed. He kept looking down to realize he was going ninety miles an hour. Dave was trying to soak it all in, the weather, Bridges' 1980's sunglasses — all of it. In all his years flying the friendly skies, Dave realized that he had rarely looked at the clouds. Now, he was fascinated by how the abstract shapes transformed into camels or puffy babies as he stared. At Todd's request, Dave had lowered all four of the Malibu's windows. The air whipping through the car lifted both of their moods. Ironically, driving to a federal prison was making Dave's own legal and existential troubles seem far away and inconsequential.

When Dave bonded out of jail, he got his sunglasses back, too, which was weird because he had put them on without thinking right before he pulled the emergency slide on the DC9. The two arresting officers had removed them after they had handcuffed him. The left arm of the glasses had caught on his right ear, which stuck out a little. Not having removed the glasses himself had left Dave feeling like he had a gap in his life.

"One of the first things you will notice when you visit a prison is the state seal," Bridges said. "Most state seals are ridiculously antiquated," Bridges added, and Dave had no idea if this was the entry to a longer conversation — or just a casual comment. Dave had both hands on the wheel, one at ten and the other at two, as if he'd just gotten his learner's permit. Bridges reclined his seat. He seemed very relaxed for a man heading to a maximum-security prison to interview a notorious serial killer. Why wasn't he reviewing notes or going over strategies for diffusing and overcoming any hostility to the idea? Dave had learned more about BTK while he was in the Wichita jail. Everyone knew all about it. BTK got sexual gratification from the helplessness on the faces of his victims as he strangled them. He would often tie his victims up using elaborate knots that tightened more and more as the victim struggled. Then Rader would draw out the process, strangling his victims into unconsciousness and then reviving them to repeat the experience. Rader had confessed all of this in court, trying to sound humble, as if he didn't want to brag. Just thinking about it nearly made Dave lose control of the car. He was going ninety miles an hour again and had to consciously tell himself to ease up on the throttle.

What was strange was how none of this made Dave feel like Rader couldn't be a fantastic dishwasher. The whole thing felt surreal — and nauseating. Meanwhile, Bridges dangled his elbow out of the Malibu's window. Bridges was dressed in black pants with a white shirt and a black tie. He smelled of aftershave and looked like a bible salesman.

"But what's really weird about state seals," Bridges started up again, out of nowhere, "is state seals are not advertisements for the state. They aren't like mottos on license plates or on signs that welcome you like a Walmart greeter when you cross state lines. A state seal isn't selling anything."

"So what are state seals for?" Dave demanded. He was growing impatient and irritable. A gust of wind had just swept through the car, nearly carrying Dave's sunglasses off.

"Some states, like Kansas, have Latin phrases on their seals," Bridges added, ignoring Dave's question. "Which is interesting because most people don't understand Latin. Even today, almost no one knows what the words on their state seal mean." Bridges paused and stared at his phone. "Take a left onto highway 81," he said. A second later, Bridges' phone reiterated the command in a stodgy computer voice. "But prisoners and prison employees, they see this state seal every day, everywhere they look. They all know what it means."

Bridges looked at his phone again. His finger hovered over the screen as if ready to type something but he never did. "The state seal of Kansas has the Latin phrase, ad astra per aspera on it. The words hover over a man plowing a field. Covered wagons linger in the distance."

What a weird fucking state seal, Dave thought to himself. Even for Kansas. Covered wagons?

"It means, 'to the stars, through difficulties,'" Bridges said. Dave was expecting Bridges to continue, to explain why that was relevant. But Bridges didn't say anything else and Dave turned his full attention to the road, which seemed to be flying towards them.

"You going to ask Rader about that? About the state seal?" Dave asked. He wondered what a guy like Rader — who had pointed out at trial that he gave Joseph Otero a pillow because Otero had cracked some ribs in a recent car accident, *to make him more comfortable*, before strangling his wife and two of his young children — what a guy like that, a guy who was trying not to brag and all, would think of the meaning of the state seal of Kansas.

But Bridges didn't answer him.

They drove in silence for a while, with Dave periodically waiting for instructions, until all that was left was for them to turn onto highway 54, the road that would take them right to the El Dorado Correctional Center. Dave scanned passing signs promising upcoming intersections. He had the sense that he should not fuck this up. Dave had fucked up his relationship with Kate, his entire career, maybe even his entire life. And regardless of the fines and the convictions that would end up on his permanent record, Dave had to start getting things right. At some point, he had to actually do what he wanted to do — the one thing serial killers claim to have accomplished — even if they did so in an abysmally fucked up manner. Perhaps, Dave thought, on this sunny day in Kansas as he diligently scanned passing signs, perhaps he was finally doing things right.

"Pull in here," Bridges announced suddenly.

And without thinking, Dave made a hair trigger turn, banking left into a gravelly parking lot, throwing up a plume of dust. A roar rose from the engine as they jerked to a stop in front of a squat, gray building.

"Wait in the car," Bridges said, "This will only take a minute." He slammed the Malibu's door, popped his shades up onto his head and then disappeared into the low, bunker-like building whose giant signage Dave now noticed for the first time. It read: 'The Showboat Bikini and Sports Resort." There were almost no other cars in the parking lot, which left Dave feeling suddenly adrift. He'd spent the last two nights in jail. He was minutes away from stopping at a Federal Prison. And Todd Bridges was apparently popping into a strip club to pregame his interview with Dennis Rader, the BTK Killer, a guy who hung an eleven-year-old girl from a pipe in her basement and then masturbated as she died. Was Bridges having a drink to steel himself for the interview with Rader? Was he buying drugs to smuggle into the prison inside a body cavity? Dave had no clue and everyone Dave had ever known suddenly seemed utterly unknowable.

Dave fidgeted behind the wheel of the Malibu. He'd always been a Volkswagen guy. Though he liked the look of the Malibu, the car felt foreign to him, the steering too loose, the flashes of red in the car's interior too American. Dave bit the side of his cheek, the pain and the taste of blood were achingly familiar. Bridges was taking forever. Dave couldn't remember the last time he'd eaten. His body felt empty. But within these familiarities, Dave began to wonder what it would be like to stand shoulder to shoulder with a serial killer. He tried to imagine helping Dennis Rader load a dishwasher or remove a giant rack of plates, the steam fogging up their glasses. Thinking about it in this way made the whole thing seem perfectly normal. Rader may be a cold-blooded killer whose sexual gratification hinged on a helpless victim, but they would both need to wipe steam from their glasses. They would both have to bend and position themselves to lift a heavy rack of dishes. They would both have to wring the water from their socks after a night of dishwashing.

A door slammed and Bridges emerged. He got in the car without a word of explanation and fired up Google maps on his phone. Bridges tossed a plastic sack on the back seat. It smelled like cheeseburgers and Dave's stomach grumbled. Bridges pointed towards an interchange a hundred feet away, then smacked the side of the car with his hand, to indicate they should start moving.

———

At El Dorado, prison officials brought out a drug sniffing dog to search the Malibu. Dave and Todd Bridges had to exit the vehicle. They stood around shifting their feet during the search, then Bridges took off his jacket, slung it over his shoulder and was escorted towards the entrance to El Dorado Correctional Facility. A water tower loomed in the distance. Guard towers jutted from the corners of a hardscrabble prison yard encased in razor wire, the kind of place where people get shanked in the movies leaving a small puddle of blood behind for a close up. But to Dave the towers reminded him of a church. And Dave knew the prison must also have a kitchen, hospital, locker rooms, library, and school classrooms. The prison was a small town, really. It didn't reduce to just iron bars and cement cells.

"Don't forget Rader's cheeseburgers," Dave called out to Bridges, now ten feet away. It occurred to Dave that Bridges was walking with officers on either side of him, not unlike when Dave had been escorted out of Eisenhower Airport.

"The cheeseburgers are for you," Bridges said, fumbling in his jacket pocket, pulling out a paperback and tossing it to Dave, who caught it automatically. "Make sure you read the first chapter before I get back."

"Thanks," Dave said. It came out hokey, like he was in a Western. He felt a sudden relief, too, at the prospect of a hot meal.

Dave had expected the book to be a copy of Killing Willis, Bridges' memoir. But it was a copy of Kitchen Confidential, Anthony Bourdain's memoir. Dave unwrapped a cheeseburger as Bridges disappeared into the prison, a low, squat building similar to the strip club Bridges had just left.

After taking down two sliders, Dave let out a long sigh and opened the paperback. He'd read Bourdain's memoir years ago, prompted by the endless reruns of No Reservations that were the only available cabin entertainment on his puddle jumping flights to

Wichita. And once Dave had gotten the front seat of the Malibu adjusted properly, the title of the first chapter, 'Food is Good,' brought back a clean memory of that time in his life. It felt like a horror movie where a possessed person expels a foreign entity and again takes full possession of his body. Dave felt pretty good all of a sudden.

In fact, there was a symmetry between what Dave was doing, sitting in a rented Chevy Malibu with a sack of cheeseburgers outside El Dorado Correctional Facility and the opening chapter of Bourdain's memoir. At nine years old, Bourdain had taken a trip to France with his family. By his own admission, the nine-year-old Bourdain was a bratty little bastard for almost the entire trip, complaining endlessly about everything from the weird plumbing to the way the cheese tasted "buttery." Bourdain had refused to eat anything other than hamburgers and ketchup. But then, something happened that changed everything. Something happened that made the young Bourdain realize for the first time that food — *is good*.

Dave heard a noise he couldn't identify. He looked around. Everything had gone quiet. El Dorado prison was generally quite quiet and nondescript from the outside. It didn't really look like a prison, although he wasn't sure what it looked like. All the same, Dave had that odd feeling one gets when watching someone go into a bank that clearly used to be a Pizza Hut. He had imagined that a federal prison which housed a notorious serial killer like Dennis Rader would feel somehow different. But it didn't. It made Dave wonder all over again whether Death Row Restaurant was some kind of prank. Yet Dave was simultaneously comforted by how utterly strange it had felt to be inside the Wichita jail, and he imagined that in the physical presence of a monster like Dennis Rader, you would feel something legitimate. Dave took a bite of another cheeseburger as if testing the hypothesis, then read quietly, running his tongue over his teeth now and then, and occasionally unwrapping another slider from the sack Bridges had left him.

What had changed everything for snotty, nine-year-old Bourdain was the night his parents drove to a little town in France called Vienne. Vienne was miles down twisting little roads, and when they finally stopped bouncing around tight corners in their tiny, rented Citroen, Bourdain's parents hoisted a sack of cheeseburgers into his lap and told him to wait in the car with his brother. His parents, meanwhile, beaming with anticipation, entered a restaurant named La Pyramide and had dinner for over three hours. This fact alone drove the young Bourdain mad. What could they possibly be doing in there? He knew his parents were having dinner, and he could still feel their anticipation, their insistence that this dinner was not going to be fucked up by a kid who kept bitching about the cheese being too buttery. But none of that made what they were doing understandable. And right there in his family's rental car while holding a sack of cheeseburgers, Bourdain understood for the first time that food is important, that food has secrets.

Re-reading the memoir, Dave thought over his own situation. Was the parking lot at the El Dorado Correctional Facility the beginning of a new life for him? A new self? One sparked by secrets of a different nature than those Bourdain uncovered, but secrets nonetheless? It was hard to tell. For one thing, Dave always felt lonely sitting inside parked cars. He was already resenting whatever Todd Bridges was doing inside El Dorado Prison merely because Bridges hadn't invited him along. As the minutes stretched themselves into oblivion, as Dave's questions about the relationship between serial killers and chicken cordon bleu roiled around like a pot of water, Dave thought of Kate.

Their breakup hadn't been the kind of clean and final thing that Kate seemed to want, like snapping a bread stick in an Olive Garden. Even though Kate had literally flushed Dave out of her life on their last flight together, they had never actually fought over anything or reached an acknowledged impasse. In fact, Kate and Dave had helped one another through a difficult time in both their lives. No one spends months fucking in a Wichita hotel room just to get some free vacation planning. Did she wonder about that, her hastily constructed explanation to herself? Was she thinking of him? For Dave, what had been so attractive about Kate was how ravenously she sought to understand how she fit into the world. This had been the real foundation of their relationship. He would hold Kate's hair out of her face when she vomited after especially difficult flights because she took a certain pride in forging through her life — in surviving nauseating beige hotel rooms and itchy uniforms and the route guidance systems that took her, inexorably, over and over again to Wichita.

What if Dave had taken her suggestion that they plan a honeymoon trip? What if they had gotten married? The whole thing had been so close to happening that it felt strangely likely to happen, even now. All that had torpedoed Dave and Kate getting married was Dave's flight attendant training, his habit of treating every outlying development as a procedural. But Kate had meant more than this to Dave. All of those times they had walked through airports side by side, their luggage rolling in sync. All of the meals and check-ins at hotels, the way whoever woke up first made two cups of shitty coffee in the hotel room, the way one checked with the other to see if pizza sounded good tonight. None of this was as inconsequential as it had previously seemed. At least, not to Dave, who knew that Kate would eventually make a superior flight attendant, one who chops her life into segments with the idea that it would all lead somewhere.

In a world where Dennis Rader can suddenly entertain a job interview, anything seemed possible.

———

For Bourdain, three hours in a car outside of La Pyramide aroused a spiteful vigor. The young Bourdain ate everything that came his way afterwards, from cheese that smelled like old socks to kidneys that squirted blood across his chin. But it was not until Bourdain consumed his first oyster that his transformation was complete. They were at his French Uncle's oyster farm, waiting for the tide to go out when Bourdain began grousing about being hungry. His uncle reached down, snatched an oyster from the bed below their boat and pried it open with a rusty knife. He handed the oyster to nine-year-old Anthony Bourdain, who glanced at the oyster's flesh, noted its vaguely genitalia like appearance before slurping it down. The oyster tasted like the essence of the ocean, salty and briny and life giving for billions of creatures floating through it. The moment shrank to just this one realization, the immensity of the ocean's catch, the idea of eating your world. It was, Bourdain would later recount in his memoir, the moment he became a man.

Dave's first oyster had been nothing like Bourdain's experience.

Dave ate his first oyster while he was in college. Unlike his flight attendant career, college never yielded a destination for Dave. He bounced around, taking classes in many disciplines, feeling like an outsider amongst other students who had solidified their path through the university with a clear major and a plan for employment. But there was one woman who ended up in several of his classes, a woman named Lisa. She was quiet and fidgety, which Dave grew to like immensely. During long lectures, her fidgeting, the surety of it, always made Dave feel warm and comfortable. Dave, too, often jostled his legs around Lisa, betraying his attraction to her. They rarely spoke, yet having everything between them as felt rather than spoken came to seem special.

Dave asked around. He found out Lisa had a boyfriend, which didn't change anything at all between them. And when Lisa and her boyfriend split up, it was Lisa who invited Dave out on a date. They were going to see a play, Raul Julia in Man of La Mancha. First, they would have dinner. Lisa had a coupon for a seafood restaurant in Dupont Circle. And for the first time, Dave and Lisa would have a conversation instead of kicking one another under their desks. But much like Todd Bridges' enormous all-defining past — his hit show, his spiral into drug addiction, the fact of being strapped to a metal bed in a diaper — Dave and Lisa's long flirtation proved surprisingly difficult to overcome. They didn't know each other very well and yet too much had passed between them.

Prior to their date, Dave and Lisa had spent one drunken night together. They had both turned up at a Friday night frat party. For Dave, it was of those college Fridays where he got himself drunk almost instantaneously and Lisa, equally sauced by the end of the night, wandering through the crowd, spotted Dave and then fought through the dance floor towards him. He watched her from across the room. Lisa was like a salmon fighting her way upstream. He found it rather charming. She arrived in front of Dave too winded to speak. She took his hand in hers and, well, pulled. Without a word, Lisa pulled him to her dorm room where they both passed out immediately. Neither of them even took off their shoes. When Dave woke up the next morning, fully dressed next to Lisa, their wordless night made him feel so awkward that he decided to sneak out before she woke up. His head was pounding and he had the worst breath imaginable. And of course, there was that inexplicable difference between the sober persons Lisa and Dave both were and the drunk ones who might do something like this. All of this meant that they felt compelled not just to have dinner together, not just to introduce themselves to one another formally, as if starting fresh, but also to break their paradigm. And the very first thing they did via mutual, openly discussed, sober agreement was to order two of Atlantique's oyster shooters.

The oysters arrived in a pair of champagne glasses. Celebratory flecks of ginger, buoyed by cheap champagne, rolled and tucked in the glass. The vaguely sexual oyster sat patiently at the bottom of the glass. It was the perfect metaphor for Dave and Lisa's dormant relationship. Dave, whose semester had been brutalizing in that he had yet again discovered that he simply had to change his major after taking several history courses, which had come on the heels of three semesters of physics and biology — which he had also jettisoned — raised his glass in a toast to a new beginning.

As they got ready to drink their oyster shooters, Lisa's lips parted. Her tongue emerged briefly, licked her lips, then tucked back into the mysterious darkness of her mouth. Lisa smiled, let her tongue swipe over her perfect teeth, an unconscious gesture that signaled to Dave that this moment was capable of launching a lifetime of happiness. Dave had been longing for such a moment and he rushed in, tossing the entire mixture in the champagne flute to the back of his throat. And it took everything he had not to spit that thing across the table. Lisa, meanwhile, took an exploratory sip, then set her glass down and wiped her tongue with her napkin. For the rest of the meal, the oyster sat in Lisa's glass like an aborted fetus in formaldehyde. And in that moment, the next twenty years of Dave's life had been sketched.

Dave polished off the last of the sliders Todd Bridges had left for him. He had overeaten but the heaviness in his body attested to his commitment. Death Row Restaurant was where the ship of his life had always been pointed, even if the vastness of the ocean had obscured this fact.

There was a tap at the window, which startled Dave. But it was just Todd Bridges. Dave unlocked the door, feeling sleepy and content

"Dennis Rader is in," Bridges announced, hoisting himself into the passenger seat. "And I need a drink."

PART III: HISTORY

THINGS QUICKLY GAINED SPEED. While Bridges shared comparatively little about his interview with Dennis Rader, other than Rader's acceptance of the terms of his employment at Death Row Restaurant, having Rader on board meant that Bridges' plan was viable. It was proof of concept. Death Row Restaurant had a major player on board. This meant Bridges could pursue 'buy in' at political and financial levels. Although Bridges didn't share exactly what this entailed, he suggested that the steps towards making Death Row Restaurant a reality had become concrete.

"The whole thing just seems so far-fetched," Dave said to Todd Bridges. Right as he said it, the Uber they were in, heading to Eisenhower airport for an afternoon flight to Los Angeles, hit a pothole. Although Dave had gone to bed early, he felt tired and hung over, even though he hadn't had any alcohol for several days. Factually, the last few days had been quite good. What remained of Dave's legal issues in Wichita had been settled (with surprising speed) by Todd Bridges' team of attorneys. With Dennis Rader locked in and with a facilities plan in place, Bridges could take his proposal to the governor — and get serious about attracting investors. This necessitated a move to LA — and Dave needed a fresh start.

Bridges and Dave agreed that once settled in Los Angeles, Dave would start culinary school.

"The General Manager needs to understand every aspect of Death Row Restaurant operations," Bridges had insisted. "He or she must be able to step in at a moment's notice and take over any job in the restaurant," Bridges continued. Dave wondered precisely what would come after chef training. Would he have to learn hand to hand combat? Psychoanalysis? Learning everything one needed to know about running a restaurant made up entirely of serial killers seemed like an endless proposition. He had to get up to speed on penology as well as management and culinary arts. The vastness of what still had to happen before they could open the restaurant left Dave exhausted.

"It's a good signal," Bridges added. "A well-rounded GM candidate puts us on the map with investors and state agencies." Bridges turned to Dave. He wasn't wearing his sunglasses. His eyes looked glassy and red, as if he had been partying all night. "It signals a seriousness about Death Row Restaurant that is the hardest part of the pitch," Bridges said in this very staid, sober voice. Of course, Bridges had already informed Dave that culinary school was a formality. That he would not really be working as a chef. Being capable of being a chef didn't make Dave qualified to perform the task. "Not unless you become a serial killer," Bridges had joked.

It was an example, Dave had discovered, of one of the serious problems with any conversation with Todd Bridges. Such conversations inevitably became disturbing. After all, every step forward with the project was a step closer to working with serial killers, something Dave still could not fathom. Not to mention, he could barely cook an egg. How on earth would he survive culinary school?

Despite these front and center concerns, Dave had more pressing problems. He was absolutely terrified of bumping into Kate at Eisenhower Airport. Eisenhower was probably still Kate's home airport and a small one at that. It was entirely possible they would see one another this morning, and Dave was able picture the encounter with striking clarity. Kate's hair would be stringy and thin, her face slightly green and gaunt — her Wichita look. Not at all how she looked in cafes in Chicago or New York, cities in which Kate's skin adopted a healthy glow and her cheek bones perked up, sitting high and confident on her face.

And what if Kate didn't have her "Wichita look?" Dave wondered. What if she looked great, as exes always do after a break up? What if Dave felt what he always felt upon encountering an ex-lover, a nostalgia for the time they were together —even if the time spent together was mostly awful?

But with Kate, it hadn't been awful. Yes, their sex had been a little too desperate. Yes, they'd crammed an entire lifetime of dry heaves into a three-month hotel tryst. But somehow, Dave's two nights in jail, his afternoon in a parked car eating cheeseburgers while Todd Bridges negotiated with Dennis Rader, the BTK Killer, somehow all of this granted him the perfect distance to understand his relationship with Kate. To understand that beneath the tiny sips of black coffee she would take after a bout of vomiting in a hotel toilet, something — if not authentic then at least bona fide — or at the very least, accurate, had presented itself.

"It's not far-fetched at all. You know that," Bridges said, without even turning his head to look at Dave. Bridges studied the passing landscape like a man heading into a battle that he knows he is unlikely to return from alive. Finally, Bridges turned to Dave, who realized he had been patiently waiting several minutes for Bridges to look at him, as if Dave were a dog and Bridges his owner, eating a ham sandwich. "I know what you are thinking," Bridges said. "You're thinking about Joaquin Phoenix and his documentary, I'm Still Here."

Dave nodded, although he hadn't actually been thinking about that at all. But he knew the story. Phoenix had pretended to quit acting in order to launch a career as a hip hop artist. He grew a giant beard and began dressing in the same kind of black and white, bible salesman suits that Bridges tended to wear. Meanwhile, Phoenix was secretly making a mockumentary that he wrote with Casey Affleck. Later, Phoenix claimed the project functioned as a comment on reality television, as a comment on the American inability to distinguish between what is scripted and what is real life. Jim Carrey had done largely the same thing in recent years, quitting acting and growing a huge beard. Only Carrey spends his time as a painter and metaphysical guru. And no one really knows whether he's faking it.

"Ever grow a beard?" Dave asked.

"No," Bridges said. And Dave was struck yet again by Bridges' remarkable ability to take literally any question seriously. "I'm just as boyish as Willis was in 1981," Bridges added.

"Is Death Row Restaurant some kind of reality television show?" Dave asked, spinning the question to sound more like an assertion. Whenever Dave asked a straightforward question like that, he felt a pit in his stomach and chest. The only exception he could recall was the three months he spent with Kate, in and out of Wichita hotel rooms. He'd never felt that way with her, even as he was giving the frank responses that torpedoed their relationship.

"Of course not," Bridges said. "Death Row Restaurant will be a real restaurant run entirely by serial killers. There won't be a script. Serial killers will get to act in an entirely authentic way. So will everyone involved in the restaurants."

"Restaurants?" Dave asked. "You're planning more than one Death Row Restaurant?" Signs for Dwight D. Eisenhower Airport drifted by, leaving Dave desperate to finish the conversation before they got to the airport. Like many conversations with Todd Bridges, this one felt like a once in a lifetime opportunity, a conversation that couldn't be started up again later without losing something crucial.

"I'm not entirely sure about the name each restaurant will have," Bridges said. "One thing that the general public is attuned to is how chain restaurants have no authenticity. But since San Quentin and Folsom are the two most famous prisons in California, I want to have flagship restaurants in both of them. And those two restaurants might plausibly both be named Death Row Restaurant. Plus, the list of notable inmates at Folsom is too important to overlook. Ed Kemper (the coed killer), Suge Knight, Charles Manson, Rick James. Even Timothy Leary did a stint at Folsom. If that's not a place warranting a flag ship restaurant staffed by serial killers, I don't know what is," Bridges declared. He was quiet for a moment, before turning to face Dave fully. "San Quentin is the key, though, Dave. I want you to understand that. Folsom may have hanged ninety-three men, but San Quentin houses the largest population of death row inmates in the country, nearly seven hundred and fifty men — more than twice the number of death row inmates in Texas."

It was the kind of fact that spoke for itself. Bridges knew that.

Everything Bridges said afterwards was just to elaborate. Dave wriggled in his seat, fighting against the ass indentation of the well-used Ford Fusion. Bridges sat perfectly still. He perched above the seat crater on his side of the Uber, literally above it all. Yet Dave was not above anything. In fact, he was so nervous about flying now that he could barely keep his shit together. He had bypassed check ins and security lines as a flight attendant for the last twenty years. Flying wasn't doing anything to help Dave feel grounded. Nor was Todd Bridges, who began a lengthy lecture on California's complicated relationship with Capital Punishment. The lecture continued unabated as they checked in, passed through security and approached their gate.

Bridges covered everything, ruling after ruling, amendment after amendment in California's penal history with striking detail and a narrative clarity Dave had rarely experienced before. At times, Bridges' lesson was so lucid that Dave tried to jot down notes, even as he was emptying his pockets into a plastic bin for the x-ray machine. His notes ended up sporadic. But a few key features stuck out. For instance, in 1994, six years after Bridges had himself been arrested for murder, California carried out its first execution by lethal injection — a man named William Bonin, also known as 'The Freeway Killer.'

"It's a nickname he shares with two other killers," Bridges explained.

Bridges knew a lot about this William Bonin guy. Abused by his grandfather, Bonin was in an orphanage by the time he was six. After high school he logged seven hundred hours of combat as an aerial gunner in Vietnam. Bonin's crimes were too horrific for Dave to follow while trying to get his belt back on after the security checkpoint, but Bonin's story eventually led back to Death Row Restaurant.

"The gas chamber at San Quentin should be easy to rent out," Bridges insisted. "They haven't used it since Bonin requested lethal injection in 1994."

For Dave, something about that statement was eye opening. The gas chamber at San Quentin has been just sitting there unused for the last twenty-five years. While not a proponent of capital punishment, Dave had a sudden and complete understanding of how wasteful the entire penal system was. A gas chamber mothballed for twenty-five years summed up the general state of things nicely, from the twisted necessities of serial killers to the tragic waste of the precious lives of their victims to the obligation society has to maintain order and foster justice. Prisons warehouse people, placing them on a shelf like a box of quinoa pasta no one will ever eat.

"We came up with the idea, you know," Bridges said, jabbing his finger at the air between them. "Americans. Before America got into the prison racket, prisons were where you were sent while you waited for your real punishment to be handed down by the legal system. The Puritans came up with the idea that the prison itself could be the punishment."

Dave had to admit right then and there that prisons were a first-rate failure of the imagination, and that Bridges could ultimately make a deep, structural argument about the value of Death Row Restaurant.

Despite his riveting history lessons, Bridges was a shitty flying companion. He didn't acknowledge in any way how difficult it was for Dave to return to Eisenhower airport after what had transpired on his last flight. On top of this, as Dave obsessed over bumping into Kate at the airport, Bridges hadn't a care in the world. Despite all the humiliation of Bridges' fall from grace, despite the fact that he was the last surviving cast member of Diff'rent Strokes (making a reboot impossible), Bridges maintained a movie star's knack for always doing whatever the fuck he wanted — which was very unlike Dave's SOP driven, regimented behavior in airports. This difference became apparent when, at the first boarding call for their flight to Los Angeles, Bridges stood up and walked a hundred yards away to the Eisenhower Airport smoking lounge. Dave had already gotten in line for boarding. He had to exit the line like a guy with a sudden bowel emergency.

Dave caught up to Bridges at the smoking lounge, which was this glass box with an exhaust fan mounted on top. Bridges entered the smoking lounge, lit up and took a seat in one of four folding picnic chairs. A collection of grade schoolers hung around outside the box, pointing at the smoke being produced by several people in the lounge, which was sucked up by the fan and subsequently traveled down a glass tube that terminated in a display about lung cancer. The kids ran back and forth as Bridges smoked. Meanwhile, Dave just stood there next to Bridges, freaking out that they were going to miss their flight and coughing now and again, while Bridges went right on with his lesson on the history of San Quentin.

"Four years," Bridges said in between puffs. "The four years from 1848 to 1852 set the stage for the opening of San Quentin. The Gold Rush, when thousands flocked to California dreaming of getting rich. And of course, the way to get rich back then was the same as today — you had to screw people over." Bridges went on to explain how San Francisco jails grew overwhelmed by criminals. So much so that in 1852, California began forcing convicts to build the prison that would house them, a prison nestled on 20 acres of land overlooking San Francisco Bay.

"Isn't it just perfect that San Quentin overlooks the bay?" Bridges remarked. He stabbed out his cigarette, then lit another. "It's as if California politicians in 1852 knew that a restaurant would one day operate inside San Quentin, knew that diners would want to take that scenic drive to the coast before being served a five-star meal by serial killers, even though that term wouldn't be invented for another century," Bridges said, as if simply musing to himself about it. He smoked for a while, then insisted they stop to buy a power bar. Bridges ripped open the power bar wrapper with his teeth, which was odd because Dave was wheeling both of their bags by this point, which meant that both of Bridges' hands were free. As Bridges chewed, he said, "here's to the Gold Rush."

They boarded at the absolute last second. But Todd Bridges was perfectly calm, whereas Dave kept thinking the plane would push before they reached the end of the passenger boarding bridge. Once on board, Bridges handed over his black, bible salesman blazer to a stewardess, who hung it up. Even though Dave knew it was impossible for Kate to get transferred to the LA route so quickly, he listened intently for her voice, that gravelly voice she always had from dry heaving all night in a Wichita hotel. As Dave and Todd Bridges sipped glasses of champagne and perused the complimentary medley of nuts they had been delivered, Bridges turned to Dave as if not a second had passed since their earlier conversation and said, "I'm not the first to suggest the idea of a commercial enterprise on San Quentin's land." Bridges took a sip of his champagne. "I'm just the first to suggest that they keep the prison. Most developers unimaginatively just want to sell the land. It's prime land right on the bay."

Dave waited for Bridges to continue, but he didn't. Instead, Bridges popped an eye mask over his eyes and leaned his head back for the next twenty minutes. Then Bridges sat up, removed his eye mask and continued talking as if no time had elapsed between the statement he had just started making and his remarks twenty minutes earlier. It was a weird habit he had.

"Everyone thinks of San Quentin prison as a drain. But that land is worth almost a billion dollars on the open market," Bridges explained. "Maybe more."

"A billion dollars? Holy shit." Dave exclaimed.

"Fucking 'a' right. That's a lot of money," Bridges conceded. "I used to make $30k a week on Diff'rent Strokes," he added. "Not bad for a fifteen-year-old. But selling San Quentin's land is exponentially more money. It's also a political minefield. The state will need a new prison to house many of the most notorious criminals in the country. And where do they build this new prison? What communities in the LA basin are itching to house death row inmates in their backyards?" Bridges asked. "None. Of course the answer is none. That's why Death Row Restaurant has political traction. You start commercializing this incredible property on the bay and meanwhile you avoid the hassle of arguing about where all these serial killers and hardened criminals are going to be moved to."

Bridges smiled, just like Willis used to on Diff'rent Strokes.

"I can't believe they aren't going to sell San Quentin's land if it's worth that much," Dave said.

"They won't," Bridges said in this extraordinarily patient way, as if any sane and logical person would weigh the problem carefully and naturally conclude that the best possible plan was to open a restaurant staffed by serial killers. "A lot of people would be against the sale just because they don't want any more housing in the Bay Area, which is congested enough," Bridges added. "And the people of San Quentin Village, the forty or so houses just outside the prison? They definitely don't want to see the land developed. They were able to buy nice, two-bedroom houses with spectacular views of San Pablo Bay for $265,000," Bridges said. "Imagine the taxes if that area becomes another San Francisco."

Dave thought about it. He nodded. "That's why this will work," Bridges concluded. "Californians are tired of the billion-dollar views going to the serial killers at San Quentin. They want the gorgeous sunsets on San Pablo Bay to be viewed by people who aren't murderers and sexual sadists. And you don't have to relocate the prison or contribute to overcrowding to change that," Bridges reiterated, smiling almost imperceptibly.

The rest of the flight, Bridges and Dave hardly said a word to one another. It was only when they landed at LAX, and the whole plan started to feel real that Dave wondered all over again about the impossible logistics and political ramifications of Death Row Restaurant. Wouldn't the restaurant be perceived as shameless profiteering off heinous crimes? But as they deplaned, as the gorgeous cherry-orange sunset settled over the LA basin, its fleeting rays reaching across the city, Dave let that question go. He wanted to mark the moment he had officially moved back to Los Angeles. Dave wasn't visiting or on layover. He had settled his affairs, cleared out his bank account to pay $10,000 to replace the emergency slide. And now that he was moving in with Todd Bridges, Dave wanted nothing more than to simply be who he was and to do what he wanted to do (and maybe have an occasional glass of wine as the sun set behind San Pablo Bay). All of this depended on making Death Row Restaurant a reality.

———

Dave and Todd Bridges took an Uber from LAX to Sun Valley. About forty minutes with traffic. The glowing sky diminished in stages — then went suddenly dark.

"You can stay at my place," Bridges told Dave, even though they had already discussed this days ago. "Stay as long as you like," he added. Bridges was wearing his Don Johnson shades, even though it was dark outside. But to Dave, Bridges looked more relaxed than he had ever seen him.

"LA. Feels like home to you, doesn't it?" Dave said.

"I guess," Bridges shrugged. "I was born in San Francisco. But I have no desire to live there." He shrugged again. "The house in Sun Valley is really the only thing I have left from my acting days," he confessed. "It's not as nice as my house in Northridge used to be, trust me," Bridges assured Dave. "But you'll like it just fine. And Sun Valley keeps me grounded." Bridges leaned in. "You've probably heard the story, how I stabbed my roommate in this house back in 1993," he admitted, expressionless. "It's part of a long line of shitty things that happened in my life back in the early 1990's. But the end result is that my Sun Valley house feels like a movie set to me now. Not like a real place at all."

"That makes sense," Dave said, not knowing how to respond. He had read about Bridges stabbing someone in his own house. Something about a dispute over the rent and the renter coming after Bridges with a samurai sword Bridges owned. Bridges pretty much stabbed him with a kitchen knife out of self-defense. The story was so bizarre that newspapers couldn't even write much about it. That was when Bridges was strung out on both crack and meth. He was a different person now, Dave reminded himself, which was a very bizarre thing to realize as well. Bridges had been a crackhead. Now he wasn't. In fact, right now Todd Bridges was a visionary entrepreneur, a person whose primary concern is owning his own actions at the level of 'being.' That had to count for something, Dave thought.

They were both tired by the time they got to Bridges' house in Sun Valley, which was gorgeous, despite Bridges grousing and reiterating numerous times how his house in Northridge used to be so much nicer and how he was cheated out of it by his accountant.

"The past is the past," Bridges kept saying as Dave dragged both of their bags into the foyer. "I'm sure I would've destroyed my nice house in Northridge anyway, what with all the meth and crazy people I always had over."

Bridges took Dave upstairs and told him to pick any room he wanted.

"Which one's yours?" Dave asked.

"None of them," Bridges replied. He put his hand on Dave's shoulder. "Like I said. This place makes me feel like I'm on a movie set. I can't hang out here that often." Bridges said it like he was really sorry about it. But Dave felt a strange relief. He was used to living alone. "I'm just gonna grab a shower," Bridges said. "Then I'll be off. Make yourself at home." He clapped Dave on the shoulder and Dave went downstairs into the living room and took a look around. Bridges' house was one of those modern, art deco California houses where the windows were weird geometrical shapes. He couldn't get used to looking out a trapezoidal window, though he figured he would adjust over time. Dave's entire life felt like those windows, misshapen and out of sorts. He couldn't imagine starting culinary school in just a few days.

This is a fresh start, Dave told himself several times. It's exactly what you need. Then he yawned, even though it was only like 9:00pm Wichita time.

Bridges came downstairs. He was completely naked, except that he had a towel slung over his shoulder.

"We need to talk for a minute," Bridges said. He went over to a white couch in his living room, laid the towel down on the couch and then sat on it. "I'm sorry about this, Dave," Bridges said. "But I have to be naked when I'm high. It's a thing."

"Are you high right now?" Dave asked.

"No. No. No," Bridges laughed. "I don't get high anymore. But I spent so many years ridiculously high in this house that I have to be naked whenever I'm in it, now," Bridges explained. He was perfectly relaxed and nonchalant about it. Dave rather liked that quality about Bridges. Strangely, Bridges' nakedness helped Dave to feel more at ease in the house. Plus, Dave knew Bridges was leaving soon. Dave yawned again, then sat across from Bridges in this stylish brown leather chair with super intricate bunting.

"Sorry," Dave yawned again. "I'm on Wichita time." It made no sense, but Bridges let it go.

"What I want to talk about is what has happened in this house and how it pertains to you now," Bridges said. It was a little hard to listen, what with Bridges being totally naked and all. "I did everything in this house, Dave. Everything you can imagine — and more," Bridges insisted. He was so incredibly still, almost like someone had freeze framed him and added a voiceover. It was weird. "I stabbed a guy right over there. I used to cook crack in that kitchen. Just a little water in a glass and a water bath. Cooks off all the impurities, that baby laxative they cut cocaine with. That's why crack is such an intense high," Bridges explained.

Dave couldn't tell if Bridges was confessing or just reliving his old days. "And my god, all the sex I had. I can't even begin to tell you," Bridges began. "Just understand, I was a famous movie star pulling in $30k a week back in 1980. That's more than $100k a week in today's dollars. I've looked it up," Bridges insisted.

I'm in a house with Todd Bridges, Willis from Diff'rent Strokes and he's totally, fucking butt ass naked, Dave thought to himself. "And the ass I got when I was famous and rich? When Janet Jackson was my girlfriend on Diff'rent Strokes and in real life? When Halle Berry told me how hot I was? Jesus!" Bridges sighed as if he couldn't believe his own life. Bridges uncrossed his legs, which did nothing to help Dave visually. "I just want you to understand," Bridges began, leaning forward, "that all of the cocaine and meth and money was nothing — nothing at all compared to the sex I had in this house."

Dave had no idea where this was going. So he just nodded his head a few times like he understood. He couldn't wait for Bridges to leave. He was fucking exhausted. "Hell, it's all in my memoir," Bridges bragged. "You know that."

Only Dave had never read Bridges' memoir.

He kept expecting Bridges to give him a copy. But Bridges must've wanted Dave to buy his own. "My point," Bridges continued, linking his fingers together as if about to recite a prayer. "My point, Dave is that you understand me because you grew up in the 1970's and 1980's. The era of Diff'rent Strokes, the era of latch key kids. The last generation of kids that grew up 'free range,' as they say today. And of course — this was also the golden age of serial killers. I mean, you were a latch key kid, right?" Bridges demanded.

"I was," Dave said. It was true.

"I knew it!" Bridges exclaimed, exhaling massively and slapping his bare thighs. Bridges had hairless legs. Dave wondered if he shaved them. "The 70's and 80's? Latch key kids? Gas lines? Inflation? Crack cocaine? We grew up in the most dangerous period in American history for youth. And I don't know your past," Bridges held up his hand in a Heisman gesture, "and I don't want to know. Not right now.

But you're... I could tell when I first met you, when you were sick of all that bullshit on that plane, sick of being a fraud. I could tell, this guy grew up in the 70's and 80's, this guy knows how lucky he is to just be alive and functioning somewhat normally. In other words — this is a man who will understand Death Row Restaurant."

Bridges adjusted his towel. Dave had almost forgotten Bridges was naked. Bridges' bony knees reminded him. "And you know as well as I do that the 1970's and 1980's, our childhood, was an age of sex driven murder that has never been replicated," Bridges insisted. "Experts estimate that nearly eight hundred serial killers committed their first murders in 1980. Compare that to around one hundred in 2010," Bridges concluded. "Like you, I was just a kid in the 1980's. I had no idea all this depravity was going on around me. For me, life was great," he said. "I had my TV show. I made $30k a week. But when I look back on that time now, I can see how fucked up it was, even without the serial killers. Parachute pants, AIDS, Axl Rose running around in shoulder length feathered hair and red lipstick and having actual sex in the studio to create the noises he wanted in Rocket Queen."

It was pitch black outside now. Bridges' strangely shaped window seemed like a portal back to the 1980's. Dave stifled a yawn. Bridges continued rattling off 1980's styles and trends. "Do you know how many times I've looked at old photos of myself with publicists and assured them, fucking vehemently assured them, that my acid wash jeans pegged at the ankles and baggy tank top were a very cool look in 1984? God, I think at one point my show was competing with Fraggle Rock," Bridges admitted, then scratched his armpit. Dave shivered. It was getting chilly. A window must have been open somewhere.

"Want a blanket or something?" Dave asked Todd Bridges, even though he had no idea where to find one in Bridges' house.

"You know what?" Bridges began. "I may not have known in 1974 when Dennis Rader brutally strangled four members of the Otero family, including two children. I may not have known what Charles Manson did, or the thirty-three murders John Wayne Gacy would confess to in 1978, or when Ted Bundy rampaged through a Florida sorority house in 1979, or the killing spree of 'Son of Sam' in 1976, or even the Hillside Strangler murders right here in Los Angeles in 1977."

Dave could barely sit upright, he was so tired. And it felt like Bridges might go on forever listing serial killer after serial killer. It was exhausting. Dave took a deep breath. Then another. "And then there's Jim Jones in 1978. Jonestown. The biggest mass murder/suicide in known history. Nine hundred people drank cyanide laced Kool-Aid. And I didn't know about any of it at the time. I was just a kid so I didn't know," Bridges said, sounding a bit like a teenage Willis on Diff'rent Strokes, "But I've realized in the last decade, now that my head has cleared from all the meth, coke and weed, that part of the anxiety that drove me to drugs was the sensation that something was more than a little off with the decades I loved, the 1970's and 1980's. Sure, I had a hit TV show and Janet Jackson as my girlfriend. And yes, it really was a very cool look to wear acid wash jeans and baggy tank tops. But I see now that feathered glam hair and Cabbage Patch Kids were also a sign of desperation, a sign of how out of touch with ourselves we had become." Bridges leaned in.

"Go look at a picture of Jon Bon Jovi from 1986, the year 'You Give Love a Bad Name' came out. Bon Jovi didn't just have big hair and wrap around rivet shades. He needed that hair just to feel he was a real and individual person. That hair and those shades were his banner, his family crest, if you will. Even our straight_laced athletic icons sported a version of this hair. Remember John McEnroe's bubble perm? The hint of a mullet and that uber tight headband pathetically trying to control it as he spanked tennis balls at Wimbledon? The 1980's made internal imbalances into fashion statements. Yet these attempts to own and contend with dark symptoms of self-delusion and disconnect backfired. Our world was falling apart and we cele-brated with cocaine binges," Bridges insisted.

"Yeah, I made $30k a week in the 1980's, $100k today, but did you see my pants?" Bridges asked. "And on some level, that was the glory of the 80's. We knew those fucking pants were stupid," Bridges concluded. "And what I want to find out on our first night together in Los Angeles, as we start to make Death Row Restaurant a reality, what I want to know, Dave, is what were the things that caused a lump in your throat back in the 1980's? What were the things that quietly made your skin crawl, without you understanding why? What were the things that told you even before you had the ability to process them, that underneath what we loved and aspired to, our beds were burn-ing? What did you notice as a kid that looking back on it now makes the 70's and 80's fucking full on Naked Lunch style real?"

Dave felt both a sense of relief that Bridges had finished his straw list of 1970's atrocities and hairstyles and an anxiety that he could barely follow the question he was being asked. He was going to try to change the subject, but Bridges interrupted. "You know what I was thinking about in 1977?" Bridges said. "Not Rodney Alacala, the "Dating Game Killer," who appeared on — and won — the 'Dating Game Show' in 1978 at the tail end of a decade-long killing spree with eight proven victims and between fifty and one hundred thirty suspected victims. And even later, after all the drugs I did in this fucking house, the crack cocaine I cooked and smoked, despite all the meth, the weeks long benders that left me half dead so that I would pass out for four days and no one could wake me up, what I remember with absolute clarity and what I keep revisiting is the day in 1976 when we filmed the opening sequence of Diff'rent Strokes..."

Dave didn't need to hear Bridges' description of it. He knew the opening sequence of Diff'rent Strokes. A young Todd Bridges and an adorable Gary Coleman bounding out of Mr. Drummond's black limousine as it came to a stop in the circular driveway of 900 Park Ave, New York, New York during the opening credits. In a moment of solidarity with Todd Bridges, Dave recalled with striking clarity those few seconds when Bridges and Coleman hopped out of the limo.

"That block where we filmed the opening of Diff'rent Strokes," Bridges continued. "That block was ground zero for television in the 1970's and 1980's. Right around the corner from where Willis and Arnold lived with Mr. Drummond was the building where Tony Randall and Jack Klugman shared their fictional apartment in The Odd Couple. And a few blocks east from there was where the Jeffersons had their 'deluxe apartment in the sky.' A quick trip to Queens and you'd be in Archie Bunker's living room," Bridges added. "God, in the 1980's we truly were All in the Family." Bridges declared.

"To do this day, I have a strong feeling that Mr. Drummond's apartment in New York is real, that Archie Bunker's living room is real." Bridges folded his hands neatly in his lap. "But other than the opening sequences to these shows, every scene, every season was filmed right here in California in fake studio living rooms and kitchens," Bridges admitted. "At one point after Diff'rent Strokes had ended, I rented an apartment at 900 Park Avenue. Cost me $19,000 a month, real Mr. Drummond money. And I had no idea why I was doing it. I almost never went there," he said. "In classic, 1980's fashion, I never gave a second's thought to what was really going on," Bridges trailed off, as if he still couldn't believe it.

Dave hadn't known that the shows he had watched religiously as a kid when he would let himself into his empty house after school like the classic latch key kid of the 80's, that all of those shows were filmed in a studio 2500 miles away. And this fact dislodged in Dave a memory. Perhaps the kind of thing Bridges wanted to know from him.

"Once, when I was a kid," Dave began, "a kid trying to convince his exhausted mother to buy him another Hot Wheels car at the mall, these guys in red berets and red jackets with this weird, eyeball logo started freaking me out. All they did was walk back and forth in the cold outside the mall."

Dave rubbed his nose with the back of his hand, as if he had a runny nose.

"So I asked my mother," Dave continued. "Why don't they go inside? Why do they keep walking back and forth in the cold? She explained that they were here to protect good people from bad people. And I found that terrifying. Police were not enough. Right and wrong was not enough. And the red nylon jackets and eyeball logo were creepy. And shit had happened at our local mall. Abduction. Rape. Murder. I got all the details eventually."

Decades later, Dave had looked up the group of men he'd seen at the mall, the 'Guardian Angels.' The group had been started by Curtis Sliwa, a night manager at a McDonald's in Brooklyn who got tired of all the crime on New York's subways. Sliwa started a citizen's watch group that patrolled the streets in red berets and matching nylon jackets with the Guardian Angel logo — an eye inside a pyramid with wings on either side. The logo is spiritual, meant to suggest that the guardian angels are more than utilitarian crime fighters, that they act with a spiritual kind of longing, invoking god himself.

"It's how the notion of justice includes the power to punish," Dave explained.

"The Guardian Angels still exist too. Not just in New York. They're in twenty-two states and even have international chapters, in Japan mostly," Dave added, although he was starting to wonder if he had his facts straight.

"Kids grow up differently, now," Bridges said, picking up on the thread Dave had begun. "Mostly, they hear about mass murders, spree killings, school shootings. These events feel like social problems more than individuals. And these guys kill themselves during the event. Serial killers never kill themselves when they get caught. They want the recognition. Meanwhile, guys like Stephen Paddock, who killed fifty-eight people in Las Vegas, he left no manifesto, no suicide note.

No religious, social or political agenda. But that doesn't make him an individual owning his actions like a serial killer does. Paddock was just some lunatic asshole who went on an eleven-minute rampage and then shot himself. There was no necessity in what he did. The people killed were targeted randomly, whoever happened to be in the wrong place at the wrong time. That's nothing like serial killers who have a reason for selecting every single victim. That's why no one remembers him. Fuck, even people at the craps table at the Mandalay Bay Hotel don't know Paddock's name. Meanwhile, everyone knows who John Wayne Gacy was. In the 1970's and 1980's, no one could fathom that an upstanding local businessman like John Wayne Gacy might harbor such dark secrets and twisted desires. No one imagined that if you pulled over a good-looking law student like Ted Bundy you'd find an ice pick, ski mask and rope in the trunk of his VW Beetle." That shit didn't happen by accident or by virtue of a long chain of preventable events that led up to it. It was truly who these guys were. Bridges ran out of breath. Dave hoped he was bringing this conversation to a close. But instead Bridges drew in an enormous breath and continued.

"Anthony Weiner can position himself as a champion of the middle class and then go home to his $12,000 a month apartment to sext teenagers using the alias Carlos Danger, and this kind of self-sabotage doesn't even call for serious analysis today. Unlike the serial killers of the 1980's, Anthony Weiner is just a guy who does stupid things that he can't and won't own as who he is. Even if Weiner wanted to, there's no way for him to own what he does. And that's the difference. The serial killer from the 1980's incites a dread of social unraveling because what they did was more than just an act. They felt it was their fucking duty to commit those murders in exactly they way they committed them. That's what Death Row Restaurant will be as well. It won't be just a dining experience. It'll be the start of the average diner being capable of owning his actions."

Dave was so exhausted now that he felt a strange kind of relaxation, almost like Bridges was telling a bedtime story.

"Take the case of Molly Tibbets," Bridges continued. Dave smacked his lips a few times. He was thirsty but too tired to get up for a glass of water. "What upends our world today is not the brutal murder of a young woman but the revelation that prosecutors and police concealed evidence in the case. They got all the way to the sentencing hearing of Cristhian Bahena Rivera, where everyone expected the judge to hand down life in prison without parole, and the defense attorney comes out with this claim that prosecutors failed to disclose their investigation of a sex trafficking trap house that may have involved Tibbets," Bridges put his elbows on his knees, leaned forward.

"Dennis Rader had been president of his church. Ted Bundy had worked on Nelson Rockefeller's presidential campaign, had gone to law school, and John Wayne Gacy dressed up as a clown for children. Each of these killers did things that society endorsed to cover up the devastating truth of who they were. And that's vastly different from a prosecutor concealing evidence out of a sense of duty," Bridges added. "Today, even killers are victims. Even guys like Bill Cosby, guys you know did the crimes, even they are victims of the state. There's no way to say that about Dennis Rader. He didn't even have a bad child-hood. He just did what he did because that's who he is," he shrugged.

"That's why putting these 1980's serial killers to work as sous chefs, dishwashers and back waiters in a restaurant inside a prison will be so extraordinary. People think of prisons as society's attempt to fight crime and maintain order. But prisons also discipline the labor force. They are a place where those who aren't productive have to live. Look at Rader. He was measuring the height of people's lawns in Utah for compliance with local regulations. That job doesn't even need to exist. And no one in prison has fewer opportunities to be productive than serial killers. Go look at the burgeoning market for serial killer memorabilia. The FBI hates that shit, not because killers make money selling their shitty sketches but because the whole point of putting inmates in prison is to discipline them for their lack of productivity," Bridges explained. "I don't think you realize what a big deal it is to put prisoners to work in the way I'm talking about."

Bridges stood up, buck naked.

He threw his towel over his shoulder and hopped into a pair of sweatpants and a Kobe Bryant jersey. "Get some rest, Dave. This house can be good for that," Bridges said. "After one of my fourteen day meth benders, I would sleep for five straight days in this house. That's right. I didn't piss or shit for five days, I was so zonked," Bridges boasted. "I'll pick you up Monday morning — for your first day of culinary school."

Dave yawned massively. His head was spinning from everything Bridges had told him. Every time he started to feel he had a handle on things, Bridges upended his understanding entirely. Dave desperately wanted to continue the conversation, to understand just what the hell they were doing with Death Row Restaurant, but he also desperately needed some rest. And Bridges was once again leaving without giving Dave his phone number or email, leaving Dave with no direct way to contact him. All Dave had was the phone number for Bridges' publicist. But he also couldn't stop yawning long enough to ask for Bridges' cell phone number.

And just like that, as quickly as the few seconds it took Kate to sever their months-long relationship, a relationship one consenting word away from marriage, Bridges was gone and Dave was alone in Bridges' house in Sun Valley.

———

Though Dave wasn't recovering from a bender, he spent several days mostly sleeping and ordering takeout. The haze which had settled over him like LA smog began to abate on the third day, when Dave awoke to find a package on the front porch. It was a set of brand new chef knives and a note from Todd Bridges that said, "Here's to your first day at the Henderson Institute of Culinary Arts! Pick you up Monday morning at 7:30am."

On Monday, as Dave was repacking the chef knives (having used them to slice a tomato for a grilled cheese sandwich) Dave heard two quick honks in the driveway. It was Todd Bridges. Dave hopped into Bridges' Chevy Malibu. Bridges was wearing his Don Johnson shades again. And instead of the tracksuit and Lakers jersey Dave had last seen him in, Bridges was dressed in beige slacks, a blue t-shirt and a white blazer, with the sleeves rolled up. Bridges was casting himself back into his 1980's wardrobe. Combined with being picked up for school, Dave started to feel like he had entered a time machine. Dave had even packed himself a peanut butter and jelly sandwich for lunch, just as he had done all through middle school.

But Dave had bigger things to worry about. Last night, he had reached out to Kate for the first time since their breakup. He sent her a short video of a woman feeding a cat from a can of tuna using a pair of chopsticks. Although the video didn't express everything Dave wanted to tell Kate, he hoped it would communicate the essential points: that they had in their own ways, helped one another. That despite the lack of a long term utility in their romantic relationship, Dave still valued their time together. He hoped that the patient way the cat waited for each bite of the tuna communicated how much

Dave admired Kate's willingness to make the best of what fate provided her — and so on.

But so far, Kate hadn't responded.

"There've been a few," Bridges said, as if responding to a question from Dave.

"What?" Dave asked,

"A few serial killers who were also chefs. I figured you were probably wondering."

"Oh."

"It's not typical," Bridges said. "Most serial killers who are skilled are machinists or mechanics. Semi-skilled serial killers tend to be truck drivers or arborists. Unskilled serial killers have a wider variety of vocations, but there are plenty of hotel porters and gas station attendants who were serial killers."

The weirdest thing about Todd Bridges' stories about serial killers was that no matter how bizarre or disturbing these stories were, Bridges injected something in his storytelling that made these stories seem exactly right. The idea that a serial killer would work as a gas station attendant or even that someone like Ted Bundy would volunteer at a suicide hotline, it always seemed to make sense when Bridges talked about it.

Dave's stomach fluttered. He had skipped breakfast out of nerves. Although Dave had eaten his way around the world as a flight attendant, although food had been a touchstone in his search for authenticity, Dave knew almost nothing about cooking. He had survived the last few days in Bridges' Sun Valley house by ordering takeout and by melting cheese in the microwave and then dunking cut up apples into it. Dave rolled down the window, hoping the fresh air would put him at ease. But the air outside of the car was the exact same temperature as the air inside the car. Dave looked around, tried to take in the sights and sounds of Los Angeles. But all he could hear was traffic, the steady suction of rubber on road.

Bridges pulled into the circular driveway of the Henderson Institute for Culinary Arts, which was sort of like the circular driveway at 900 Park Avenue where they had filmed the opening sequence of Diff'rent Strokes. Dave gathered up the brand new set of knives Bridges had bought him, along with his sack lunch. He felt like a grade schooler. Sure enough, Bridges stopped Dave as he was getting out of the car, to wish him a good day. Sort of.

"This is it," Bridges said. "This is the start of Death Row Restaurant."

Dave nodded. He couldn't resist when Todd Bridges flashed his innocent 'Willis' smile. Bridges drove off. Dave peered at the sky. He had hoped the smog would burn off, but so far it hadn't. A greenish, puke hue adhered to everything.

"Good luck with City Hall," Dave yelled after Bridges' Chevy Malibu. He meant it, too. It couldn't be easy to explain to a politician on a Monday the idea of renting out the gas chamber at San Quentin, let alone pitching a restaurant staffed with serial killers. Whenever Dave thought of Death Row Restaurant like that — all at once — he felt suddenly hopeless.

The main building at the Henderson School of Culinary Arts was surprisingly nondescript. Very little about it suggested food or culture. From the outside, the light gray, brick building reminded Dave of the offices he had completed his United Airlines training in more than twenty years prior. Before entering, Dave watched Bridges' Chevy Malibu disappear around a corner. He wondered if Bridges had resolved his problem with his license. Or if the whole thing about Bridges having to wait around for buses while people slowed down their cars to call Willis a "fucker" was just part of the pitch for Death Row Restaurant. Even considering Todd Bridges' naked expose in the living room of his house a few days ago, Dave felt that Bridges' story about the bus stop remained the most integral thing Dave knew about who Todd Bridges really was.

———

Once inside, Dave was fitted for a chef's jacket and hat, along with a gaggle of other students, most of them quite a bit younger than he was. Properly attired and feeling like chefs, the students filtered into the classroom kitchen, where an assistant instructor lined them up in rows, as if in boot camp. The head instructor at the Henderson Culinary Institute was chef Yiannis, a man whose beard stubble had the unmistakable harshness of razor wire. Yiannis introduced himself, immediately stressing to the class that culinary history would prove at least as important as technique to a successful career.

"Whether you are making a simple omelet or a baked Alaska, history matters," Yiannis declared, strolling through the ranks of would be chefs. Yiannis' assistant instructors stood stoically behind him. And behind them industrial stoves and polished ventilation hoods gleamed in the soft light coming through the windows. Stainless steel pots dangled eerily from hooks. To Dave's left, a pantry enclosed neat formations of ingredients, from fresh bok choy to mangos. Spices were lined up in a similarly military array. A whiff of body odor. hung in the air. Yiannis reached the end of the row for the second time, huffed to himself as if unimpressed and reversed course sharply.

Then, crossing his arms over his chest, Yiannis declared, "Chickens are the saviors of Western Civilization."

The short coughs and squeaks of rubber that had filled the room as Dave and the rest of the chefs in training shifted their weight from foot to foot, ceased. A dense, confused silence fell over the kitchen. Dave's breath turreted out of his nose. He glanced sideways. The man on his left, a short, Mexican fellow locked eyes with Dave and then shrugged. Were they supposed to respond? If so, Dave didn't have the first clue what to say Yiannis reached the end of the row. He pivoted, and reversing his trajectory like an ancient mariner who feels a fresh and favorable wind, Yiannis launched into a story about the Athenian General, Themistocles, who had been marching his army towards an invading Persian horde only to stop to watch two cocks fight on the side of road. Themistocles is supposed to have uttered, "Behold, these do not fight for their household gods, for the monuments of their ancestors, for glory, for liberty, for the safety of their children, but only because one will not give way to the other."

According to Yiannis' account, these two chickens had inspired the Greeks to repel their Persian invaders, preserving Western civilization. A few centuries later, the many ballads written to honor Themistocles led Greek commanders to erect chicken sized amphitheaters where cocks could savage one another for no discernable reason other than that Greek soldiers should learn what valor really was. Chickens, Yiannis reported, fought on even after legs had been sheared off, even after eyes had been popped like grapes by opposing beaks.

"And no matter how many cock fights a soldier observed, the mystery of this primordial conflict, as epic and crucial as anything man ever drew sword or bent a shaft over — remained."

Or so Yiannis asserted in his surprisingly riveting account.

It was at this point in Yiannis' history lesson that one of Dave's fellow chefs in training, a nonbinary platinum blonde named Chris interrupted Yiannis to ask — no demand — that they cook something.

Chris quoted an obscene tuition figure and the fact that they were a kinesthetic learner. Dave couldn't believe the tuition bill. Was Todd Bridges covering that for him? What if Dave somehow got stuck with the bill?

Yiannis didn't respond, unless pivoting in his history lesson from the Greeks to the Romans counted as a response. "It was the Romans who let actual chickens lead them into battle," Yiannis insisted. "It was the Romans who monitored their clucking and appetite as omens regarding the outcome of the impending battle. Thus," Yiannis concluded, "Each of you will learn to treat the lowly chicken, whose mild flavor and uniform texture has become the culinary world's blank canvas, with reverence. For it is very likely," Yiannis confirmed for them, "Very likely, that chickens will ultimately make or break your careers as chefs."

Dave wanted to object that Yiannis didn't know about Death Row Restaurant, whose success wouldn't depend on the food at all and would instead depend on serial killers and billion dollar real estate deals. But it seemed wise not to interrupt, as Yiannis had already started making an intricate and surprisingly lucid case that civilization as we know it hinged on a second, unexplained event involving chickens.

"Mathew 22:37," Yiannis grunted. "Where Jesus says that he cares for his people 'like a hen for her brood.'" How the metaphoric intensity of the motherly, clucking hen had failed to catch on within Christian theology (which went on to focus on the far less dynamic figure of the shepherd) was for Yiannis one of the great mysteries of Western society.

"Think of all the things that would be different if chickens hadn't taken their rightful place on the altar of civilization?" Yiannis challenged us. "Imagine prepping three hundred pounds of buffalo style goat on Super Bowl Sunday?"

A silence enshrined the kitchen.

Perhaps the chefs in training were contemplating the implications of teriyaki chicken wings and honey garlic boneless nuggets. Dave, however, was thinking about Death Row Restaurant. The food, he was starting to realize, wouldn't be entirely irrelevant.

"How, exactly," the chef next to Dave whispered to him, "do you debone a whole chicken with reverence?"

Yiannis glared at them both.

Another thing about culinary school. The answer to any question

Dave thought to ask was "you should be done with that by now." This was more or less the universal critique doled out by Yiannis' assistant instructors. Time is of the essence in the world's kitchens. And within Dave's first week of culinary school, this notion of chefs being terribly, horrifically behind in their work was reshaped and repurposed continually, until things reached a sort of metaphysical crisis. For instance, at a certain point, Yiannis set the class to the task of producing a red sauce. To do so, Dave had to blanch a basket of tomatoes. But when he hustled past Yiannis to grab a pot, Yiannis scowled so viciously at Dave that he experienced a wave of guilt similar to a time in his mid twenties when he had assured his girlfriend he would pull out during sex, but then didn't manage the maneuver.

And before Dave could even get the water boiled to blanch the tomatoes, Yiannis had demanded a halt to all kitchen activity. He lined the chefs up again, this time to deliver a lecture on the metaphysics of cooking, on the anticipatory gesture whereby a true chef actually begins preparing a meal even before the customer orders it.

Dave told Todd Bridges about all of this.

Since they had arrived in Los Angeles, Bridges had begun insisting that Dave call him Todd Bridges — not Todd or Willis. And the start of culinary school for Dave became the start of a second ritual, nightly meals shared by Dave and Todd Bridges during which they discussed the progress of Death Row Restaurant. Dave had no idea what kind of food Bridges was planning to serve at Death Row Restaurant. So they generally experimented with their restaurant choices, paying special attention to Vietnamese and high end Mexican. Oddly, Bridges had no problem with Dave's elaborate, paradoxical lessons from the kitchen. In fact, as the weeks went by, Dave concluded that Bridges didn't seem to care whether Dave was learning how to cook anything. And for his part, the question at the forefront of Dave's mind when he and Todd Bridges shared their evening meals after an entire day immersed in culinary history was: how many? How many people had taken time out of their day to call Willis a fucker? With all that had happened to Todd Bridges, he in turn seemed to Dave like a broken shell of a human being (or like a man who had been so crushed and eviscerated and betrayed by his own hand that he understood once and for all that he needn't worry too much about other people.) The broken, Todd Bridges understood, mostly survived. Even Willis.

"Any new developments regarding negotiations?" Dave asked, gently poking a hole in a Shanghai soup dumpling and letting the ginger, Shaoxing wine, and pork broth leak from the ruptured dumpling and fill his spoon. Dave wondered momentarily how a chef fills dumplings with soup? A syringe? Would Yiannis ever teach them this? Dave's hand throbbed. He had burned it during a boilover earlier in the day.

Bridges only shrugged. He either found Dave's question too idiotic to consider or else so profound as to require a lifetime of contemplation. Eventually, Bridges eked out a few details about his schedule, just enough to make it sound like progress was on the horizon. Bridges had approached several California state senators, prominent attorneys and prison wardens with the idea for Death Row Restaurant — or so he claimed.

"We might need an executive order signed by the governor," Bridges suggested. "But I won't stop until we have a fully licensed restaurant in San Quentin's gas chamber." It was statements like these that made Dave acutely aware of the fact that he had no idea what Bridges was doing all day after dropping him off at culinary school. Bridges was a professional actor, after all. For all Dave knew, he was an unwitting extra in a reality TV show. And no matter what kind of rap Bridges laid on him, Dave couldn't shake the idea that a comeback for Todd Bridges felt horribly unlikely — if not impossible. After all, Bridges was the last surviving member of the Diff'rent Strokes cast. They couldn't even do a reboot out of nostalgia.

"Do you think that the period of your life defined by Diff'rent Strokes will at some point just wink out and be gone forever?" Dave asked, dipping a pierced dumpling in fermented black vinegar and diced ginger.

"Willis never dies," Bridges replied.

This routine went on for months. By day, Dave attended culinary school, where Yiannis pressed Dave's entire cohort with a chicken-centric view of history and a metaphysical notion of kitchen work. By night, Bridges and Dave explored the LA restaurant scene, slurping on the accumulated knowledge of human culture.

———

Like a baptism, the Henderson Culinary Institute had immersed Dave in a narrative he had never considered before, a narrative that stripped away identities and sins and allowed a person to start anew — as a chef. That this narrative turned out to detail the pivotal role of the chicken in human history was surprising. But the experience fit perfectly into this period of Dave's life. In the evenings, Dave and Todd Bridges had dinner together, and Dave watched Todd Bridges in his doomed efforts to kill Willis. It was indeed a period of Dave's life that he could aptly title — Diff'rent Strokes.

As odd as it was to go from tales of the legendary exploits of poultry throughout the centuries, as passed on to Dave by his spirit guide, Yiannis, to the gruesome tales of serial killers that continued to act as a north star for Todd Bridges, there was an underlying structure to Dave's life in this period that he would never again replicate, a commitment to listening and to opening up that Dave had never experienced before. And while Dave still sometimes sent late night cat videos to Kate (who never responded to his messages), for the most part, it was chicken history and Todd Bridges that consumed Dave's daily existence.

Several weeks later, something interesting happened — the first blackout at The Henderson Institute of Culinary Arts. Dave had been so in the zone during his morning cook that he felt viscerally connected to the task, like a giant, beating heart pumping not blood but varieties of fried chicken: Nashville style with its vinegar based hot sauces and undertones of brown sugar, garlic and paprika. Japanese style, lightened almost to ethereality with ginger, sake and lime.

And in the midst of his zen productivity, a sudden darkness.

Then silence. Perhaps a moment to conquer death.

It was an opportunity that Yiannis couldn't let pass. The chefs in training were quickly lined up, and in the darkness lit only by a few flickering stove top burners Dave sensed his classmates' desperation to move on from chickens. Perhaps to steaks? Soups? Master sauces? Pastas? Yiannis had already spent a ridiculous amount of time on poultry and its central role in modern cuisine. So much so, that like an inmate staring at decades of incarceration, Dave's fellow chefs in training had begun to lose all hope of an escape from this narrative.

As Yiannis strolled the ranks, waiting for the proper moment to launch into his lecture, Dave thought about how unlike his peers, his interest in chickens had deepened since starting culinary school. In his private consultations with Yiannis, Dave peppered the man with questions about recipes from around the globe. And Yiannis would always reveal a pathway to Dave, a pathway that eventually invoked the hen, her brood, or the dynamic and brutal figure of the fighting cock. Like biblical stories that have near limitless application in the modern world, so the history of fowl found its way into everything Dave would ever cook or ask about. Even when they cooked vegan, the meal was defined by what it did not contain, by the exclusions and persecutions which have marked the histories of human and chicken alike for thousands of years.

Yiannis' assistants lit the remaining kitchen burners. And in the flickering shadows, Yiannis began the day's lesson in semi-darkness.

"The history of the world," Yiannis stated, "is a history that lives and breathes in the shadows of time. But when one looks closely, the chicken proves extraordinary."

"It's not so dark that we can't cook," someone exclaimed.

"Silence," Yiannis bellowed, holding up a grill lighter as if he would incinerate the entire building if he were interrupted again.

Part of Dave was surprised that Yiannis, for all his talk of ancient history and the elemental nature of cooking — and his general commitment to taking a long view on things — was unwilling to allow his students to try their hand at cooking in the dark. Perhaps it had to do with insurance issues, indemnity, that sort of thing. But Dave suspected that the issue ran much deeper for Yiannis. They were not ready. They were nowhere near ready for the spiritual side such cooking would involve. On top of this, no matter how many lessons Dave and his cohorts had received, history felt endless, its weight immeasurable. The best one could do was to realize that certain topics were best broached in the dark, by gathering around a flickering fire and listening to the shaman.

Yiannis went on to list a surprisingly lengthy set of accomplishments by chickens. For instance, chickens have the ability to recognize more than one hundred individuals. Chickens, like humans, have REM sleep and very likely dream. Chickens are physically unable to taste sweetness. Chickens, unlike humans, are born with a sense of object permanence. In other words, from birth, baby chicks understand that when you remove an object from its visual capacity, that object continues to exist. Dave tried diligently to find some sort of meaning in the seemingly random factoids. But it was not easy. If there was a thread of meaning, Yiannis concealed it, or perhaps like object permanence, Dave and the rest of the aspiring chefs were not ready to understand.

Precisely how the kinds of facts Yiannis was dishing out, like how the lowly chicken's claim to being the first domesticated animal to have his genome sequenced led to a discussion of the unusual love life of chickens, Dave couldn't say. As Yiannis waded into these unusual waters, Dave wondered if the darkness of the blackout would last long enough, if the moments of unbridled, illogical passion that underscore rewarding sexual embraces would be interrupted before the climax. Since arriving in Los Angeles, Dave's sex life had been on hold. Not only was Dave busy with culinary school, but he had spent nearly every evening on dinner dates with Todd Bridges. All of this passed through Dave's mind as Yiannis detailed the brutal intimacies of chickens.

"Although one thinks of the male cock as the agent of discourse in the sexual relations of fowl and one tends to think of the hen in a classic Marxist fashion, as the exploited worker who lays and cares for the critical bounty of eggs, the reality," Yiannis informed his would be chefs, "is quite different. The male may be loud, even brutal, but it is the Hen who ultimately has the final word." Stepping carefully amongst the shadows of the flickering stove burners, Yiannis elaborated on the mating of chickens — a brief and savage affair, which left Dave mildly traumatized. The male cock struts and squawks and scratches at the dirt until a female squats down enough so that he might mount her. Once on top of her, the male bites the comb at the back of hen's head with his beak, stands on her back and proceeds to deliver his sperm.

The best Yiannis could say about it was that the act was mercifully brief.

And the final word of the hen turned out to be her unique ability to entirely eject any individual cock's delivery of sperm. In other words, the hen's biology can literally transform a deposit into a withdrawal. Just as Yiannis had finished explaining the bizarre physiology of the hen, using a jar of paprika and some rice stick noodles as props, the lights came back on. The entire lesson felt much like those moments following sexual intercourse, where the intense physical and even spiritual encounter seems, after the fact, a very bizarre, almost comical thing to have engaged in.

With the lights back on, Yiannis quickly put his chefs to the task of building flavors in several varieties of cream soups, which had the inevitable effect of reminding Dave of the brutality of the male cock and the revenge of the female hen.

And for the first time, Dave wondered if he would even bother trying to explain his day to Todd Bridges over their nightly meal.

——

The following Monday at the Henderson Culinary Institute began with Yiannis dispassionately reciting a list of student chefs who had received professional infractions over the previous week. Violations included cursing, wearing facial jewelry in the kitchen, wearing logo t-shirts, excessive leather, overly long sideburns, mustaches that trended beyond the corners of the mouth, improperly cleaned or pressed attire when on campus, and failure to respect alcohol. Yiannis read the list of names in a monotone connecting each infraction to its concurrent grading penalty. He presented no judgments about ethical character. And for those like Dave who had wrangled their facial hair, their wardrobe and their drug addictions into compliance, Yiannis wanted no virtue signaling. Reading this list was, Dave realized, merely required of Yiannis.

Once class began in earnest they were presented with the problem of the egg.

"How does one cook an egg perfectly?" Yiannis asked.

Hands shot up on all sides of Dave, who looked around somewhat quizzically. Dave's eggs usually turned out rubbery and bland. He had no special technique for cooking an egg. His classmates, meanwhile, were so enthusiastic about this question their response bordered on fanaticism. Only later would Dave discover that in chefdom, how to cook an egg was a hotly debated topic indicative of a young chef's personal cooking philosophy.

"Put your hands down," Yiannis sighed, clutching at his forehead in agony. "The key to a perfectly cooked egg does not lie in your technique. It lies in understanding the problem." Yiannis whipped forward the cleaver which at all times dangled from the belt on his hip like a gunslinger's six shooter and held it briefly in front of his face in an almost prayer posture. Then, raising the cleaver above his head where it passed a glint of light from its carefully honed edge to its backbone, Yiannis brought the blade down on top of an egg in the palm of his left hand. The egg cleaved neatly into two rigid half moons. Yiannis let the shells fall to the floor while maintaining a delicate, almost loving grip on the egg's contents. The albumen glistened in his palm. The yolk was perfectly still.

Briefly, Dave considered the moment he had emerged from the lavatory on his last UA flight, the one where Kate had flushed him out of her life, for good.

"The egg is one of the few perfect things in our world," Yiannis declared. "And an improperly cooked egg is a crime."

"Sous vide it!" someone yelled to my right. "Cook it at 65 degrees for 21 minutes!"

"A hot water bath just short of shimmering! Two minutes. Don't molest the egg in any way and it will be perfect."

"Silence." Yiannis barked for the second time. His words ricocheted off the hanging pots and pans. Dave felt, all of a sudden, that he would be lucky to survive the morning without physical or psychological injury. "We are not here to debate your medieval cookery schemes. Cooking a perfect egg requires not technical skill but metaphysical understanding. To cook an egg, one must first understand the egg." So Yiannis once again began strolling amongst the ranks of chefs while he lectured them. There was a general stiffening of bodies. Dave girded himself for a long lecture, flexing his knees to reduce tension fatigue. "The egg is nature's gift to humanity," Yiannis continued. "The egg is the perfect food. The egg contains the entire panel of amino acids. The humble egg is constructed from a perfect array of fats and antioxidants. Eggs are nature's multivitamin and as every chef knows, the egg is the most versatile, most important ingredient in the world."

With that, Yiannis let the slimy egg white slip through his fingers. It hung briefly in a clump before breaking away all at once. The yolk jumped in Yiannis' palm, as if animated by a heartbeat and the albumen splattered on the floor. "The essential problem presented by the egg is that it contains two substances that cook at entirely different rates. "The whites," Yiannis said, pointing at the floor, "do not cook at the same rate as the yolk." He held his palm aloft, the yolk shimmering in the sunlight crashing through the window. "A real chef must never forget the essential nature of the dilemma the egg presents. This is why cooking a perfect egg remains the mark of a chef, for the task itself is philosophically vexing."

Yiannis bowed his head, then dismissed the young chefs with a wave of his hand. Dave retreated to his stovetop where he would spend the rest of the morning demonstrating his mettle, his fortitude, his philosophical girth — by producing a single, aptly cooked egg.

———

Dave's cohorts in training scattered in all directions and selected a startling array of cooking vessels from simple pots to computer controlled, immersible heating elements to double boilers in order to produce their exemplary egg.

Dave fetched a frying pan.

Although Dave had only considered cooking seriously since his encounter with Todd Bridges, he realized that he had been trying to cook a decent over easy egg most of his life. The result was often, as Yiannis had intimated, rubbery, slimy, generally over or undercooked and often with warring textures. But on occasion Dave had managed to succeed. In fact, Dave had cooked a perfect egg the morning after he had slept with his first real girlfriend.

Dave had met Stacey in an Intro to Political Science course in college. They bonded by griping about their professor's lisp. During an early lecture, as their professor gargled his way through Plato's dialogue on justice, Dave grew so fatigued at the level of phonemic interpretation required of him that his hand shot up almost of its own volition. Once acknowledged by his professor, Dave realized that he did not have a question. In fact, Dave hadn't even read the assigned chapter. So thinking on his feet, Dave politely requested that the professor clarify and "say more" about his last remark. The professor did so, looking Dave right in the eye and yet his words were a slippery affair that Dave found himself unable to follow at first, and a few moments later, actively avoiding.

Yet this act served as an introduction to a young poli-sci major in the class, a girl with chestnut hair and dainty feet named Stacey. Stacey was one of the most plain looking girls Dave had ever seen. Yet something about the muted earth tones of her clothing and her bony wrists proved attractive. Stacey possessed an organic wholesomeness. And as soon as Dave realized his attraction, he sensed that Stacey reciprocated. They were both too shy to admit it, but being in the same class meant they could become study buddies. And the night before the midterm exam, Stacey and Dave pulled an all-nighter. And the morning before the exam, Dave produced his first perfectly cooked egg.

Dave and Stacey had met up at the library's twenty four hour study area to prepare for their poli-sci midterm. But they quickly adjourned to Stacey's dorm room. Like Dave, Stacey would later abandon political science and cycle through majors like a calendar churning through the days of the week. Studying for their poly-sci midterm didn't go especially well that night. Instead, Dave and Stacey found via a thorough review of their previous relationships, that they had in common a series of lopsided pairings, which like an improperly cooked egg, they had partaken of so as not to waste whatever goodness or nutrition these relationships might have contained. Dave and Stacey had both dated people they had loved deeply, but unrequitedly, and they had both dated persons whom they could barely tolerate, but whose dedication to igniting a genuine romance out of sparse and inflammable kindling was so endearing that it merited hanging around to see if any sparks would take.

With Stacey on his mind, Dave returned to his stovetop and sent a flame spurting onto the bottom of the frying pan.

"I can't explain it," Stacey had confessed to Dave late that night, the two of them crammed on top of her tiny dorm mattress. They were whispering so as not to wake Stacey's roommate who had a World Religions midterm at dawn. "Ted's constant care, attention and interest in me somehow made me furious," Stacey admitted. "Once, he showed up with roses out of nowhere and I wanted to claw his eyes out."

The remark was unusually forthcoming. Whatever walls which had existed between Dave and Stacey collapsed. Dave leaned in and Stacey brushed her chestnut hair from her eyes. They kissed. Stacey's dorm room was so small that the only possibility for privacy was constructing a makeshift tent over one's mattress with a series of bed sheets hung from a rafter in the ceiling. The light filtered through tent sheets threw off Dave's depth perception. As a result, Dave misjudged the distance and the kiss ended up far more forceful than Dave had intended. Yet Stacey, still annoyed by her former lover Ted, by his excessive care, by his attempts to curate every moment with her, was pleased by this clashing of mouths and leapt on top of Dave. Stacey's bed was crooked and poorly constructed. The sheets swayed as they had sex, making Dave dizzy. Then, Stacey's roommate began to snore, puncturing Dave's confidence. Dave's assertive first kiss, which had so enamored Stacey, transitioned into a defensive posture that lasted for several years and was largely responsible for their eventual breakup.

The egg Dave cooked Stacey the next morning, however, was perfect.

Stacey was in the shower when Dave woke up. Stacey's bed, so cozy and womb-like the night before, looked positively see-through in the light of day. The sheets Stacey had hung over the mattress provided very little real privacy, perhaps a slight blurring of genitalia but little more. Dave had just met Stacey's roommate and had already forgotten her name. One of her toenails badly needed trimming and she blathered on about the violent Hindu epics she had spent most of the night studying. To escape the conversation, Dave threw himself into the task of making toast and eggs using their hotplate.

In his nervousness, Dave had shaken the egg pan lightly, almost autonomically. This movement had produced the most evenly cooked egg Dave had ever seen. The egg whites were firm and flawless, as if someone had run an egg Zamboni over them. Meanwhile, the yolk squatted inside a perch in the exact center of the egg, reveling in its position like a triumphant mountain climber. Dave slid the egg onto a plate, anointed it with a pinch of salt, removed a small, moldy spot from the bagel he had shoved into their toaster earlier and arranged the bagel around the glorious egg. In the shower, Stacey kept picking up and then dropping the soap. Each time, her feet squeaked on the porcelain and she released a curse into the shower mist. Dave pictured Stacey's naked body, already distant, foreign and mysterious. And out of embarrassment, he gave the perfect egg to Stacey's roommate — who swallowed it in one improbable bite.

―――

Dave's chances of replicating that perfect egg were slim, but that had been the essence of Yiannis' lesson. One does not begin to cook an egg with the idea of perfection in mind. What matters in egg cooking is far more ethereal and gestural. Despite social trends in chefdom, an egg, presented as a challenge to prove a chef's mettle — proved the opposite, proved the importance of invisible forces hidden beneath appearances. Stacey and Dave had followed up their first night together with six months of semi acrobatic sexual encounters on her tiny bed, and then followed that up with about a year and half of breaking up and getting back together. Dave's great failure with the first girlfriend he shared relatively equivalent feelings was that he never learned anything about the inner architecture that shaped either of them.

Dave plopped a dollop of butter onto the frying pan at the Henderson Culinary Institute, realizing that in all his subsequent visits to Stacey's dorm room he had never asked Stacey's roommate how her midterm had gone. The midterm had passed into history. Even if Dave could somehow remember the name of Stacey's roommate and track her down, he couldn't ask about the midterm without seeming like a nutjob. Dave found something sad in this, and a desire for not a perfect egg, but a decently cooked one, welled up inside him.

By this point, Dave's colleagues were already presenting their eggs to Yiannis — and Yiannis was already demolishing whatever feeble confidence they had brought to the endeavor. Some plates Yiannis dismissed on sight alone. Others by smell. Still others by a mere rocking of the plate back and forth. Noting the terrible scrutiny which could be directed at a single egg on a plate, Dave cracked two eggs carefully into a coffee mug and then slid them onto the hot frying pan. They popped and sizzled and Dave reached into the pantry of his awkward experiences, recalling the many sensuous and somewhat nauseous evenings he had spent with Kate so as to emulate the nervous jiggling that had once produced an aptly cooked egg.

One night in particular leapt out at Dave.

Dave had gone out to procure something for Kate to eat. She had been nauseous all evening and had been apologizing for hours that she didn't feel well enough to go out to dinner. Dave didn't care at all. Where Kate could see a perfect restaurant dinner, he had come to expect nothing more than mediocrity. Dave rented a car and drove it to Aldi, where he procured everything one might cook in a microwave. In their hotel room, he fixed meal after meal for her: chicken nuggets, Uncle Ben's rice in a bag, microwave burritos, vegetarian saag paneer. Kate sampled each, usually refusing the rest. In the end, it was a simple baked potato and half a microwaved scrambled egg that Kate was able to keep down.

Late that night, their room lit only by a moonlight that allowed them to forget the nauseating beige color scheme of the airport Hilton in Wichita, Kate climbed on top of Dave, their hands interlocking repeatedly as they made love in a room filled with empty frozen food boxes and a five pound bag of potatoes.

This is what Dave thought about while shaking the egg pan at the Henderson Culinary Institute.

Dave killed the flame on his stovetop. Both eggs had survived intact and while not perfect by any means, they looked appetizing. Dave slid them onto a small, unpretentious plate, threw some salt and pepper at them and then overturned a bucket and dangled his fork over the eggs.

"You call that an egg?" Yiannis grunted from the front of the room.

"While it's a miracle that you've cooked the yolk rubbery while somehow preserving a runny snot texture in the whites, that wins you no points here," Yiannis added. He handed the plate back to the young chef who slinked off in shame.

Dave pressed his fork into his eggs, recalling Kate's energetic smile when she bit into that baked potato. The bulbous yolks burst and cascaded in tearful rivulets down the sides of the whites.

Dave had just dabbed a bit of yolk onto a piece of rye toast when the door to the kitchen classroom flew open and Todd Bridges strolled in.

———

Todd Bridges went right over to Yiannis. They stood talking near the doorway. Dave's appetite deserted him. The steamy eggs began to crust and harden on the plate. Dave was vaguely embarrassed by Todd Bridges' presence in the same way the mere presence of his parents used to humiliate him in high school.

Yiannis and Todd Bridges shook hands and then Yiannis swiveled his head around, locked eyes with Dave and then waved him over.

"It appears you have pressing business to attend to," Yiannis muttered. Dave hadn't realized it, but he had brought his half eaten egg plate with him and was about to walk out the door with it when Yiannis took it and began poking and inspecting the eggs. Dave's heart sank.

"Todd, what the fuck?" Dave said, once they were in the hallway.

"Is that what all of my money is going for?" Bridges replied, indignantly. "You're literally in there learning how to boil a fucking egg?"

"It's a lot more than that," Dave replied, defensively. He was feeling strangely emotional. "What's so goddamn important, anyway?" Dave demanded.

"Investors," Bridges said. "Don't change out of your uniform. And don't call me 'Todd.' It's Todd Bridges or Willis, got it?"

"Okay, okay," Dave muttered. "You want me to walk around dressed like a chef? Why? "

"You can ditch the hat," Bridges said. "But keep the rest. And just remember, you are a representative of Death Row Restaurant."

It was striking, but when Dave heard Death Row Restaurant spoken aloud like that, he had trouble taking the idea seriously, the idea of a restaurant inside a gas chamber. It sounded ludicrous.

As they walked down the hallway of the Henderson Culinary Institute toward the front driveway, Bridges turned and slapped a sticker onto Dave's chest. It was a mockup, half stolen from the label of Death Row Records. A prison inmate strapped into a block-like chair with a black hood over his head. Literally, the only thing different between this label and the original Death Row Records label was that Bridges had put a knife and fork into the man's hands.

Dave was struck by the gulf between himself and Todd Bridges. In the abstract, when it came to the idea of Death Row Restaurant — they were on the same page. But it was becoming clear to Dave that when it came to particulars Dave had almost no idea what Bridges was planning Death Row Restaurant to entail. Dave's futility with Kate, with the eggs, these were discrete moments in a larger narrative arc. Todd Bridges' life also had an arc, of course. But for Bridges, the successes, humiliations and disappointments that had defined his life had come on suddenly and refused to relent. Bridges didn't have spurts in which formative events in his life occurred. His life was one epically long car chase filled with hairpin turns and police road blocks. This drove a wedge between Dave and Todd Bridges.

"I'll drive," Dave finally offered.

—————

Bridges and Dave drove Northeast to the Highland Park neighborhood. Traffic was light for LA and Dave felt annoyed by Todd Bridges' intrusion into his daytime life at the Henderson Culinary Institute, a place which had become a personal echo chamber for him. But as they drove, Dave realized that in terms of real progress, in terms of actually setting up a Death Row Restaurant, not much had happened since Dave had started culinary school. Bridges had made a lot of claims about imminent progress, yet few had proved actionable. This meeting with potential investors already had a different feeling.

"So how likely are we to get financing today," Dave asked, keeping his eyes glued to the road.

"Investors don't agree to a meeting unless they want to invest," Bridges stated, his gangly arms dangling out the window.

"And why are you dressed like that?"

Bridges was wearing a plaid shirt and a matching sweater vest. The colors were so perfectly aligned that it was almost disturbing. Bridges didn't answer. He just smiled behind a pair of high end aviator sunglasses. Bridges wasn't the slightest bit nervous. It was almost as if the outcome of the meeting didn't matter. The light traffic provided just enough surplus cognitive bandwidth for Dave to consider something he had not previously considered. What if Todd Bridges just enjoyed pitching Death Row Restaurant to people? After all, Bridges' television career was over. He would never again achieve the kind of success he had when he was thirteen years old. And even if he could get himself cast in the perfect role, he would likely be blacklisted for the pimping and other criminal abuses he had perpetrated. Addiction is one thing. Stringing young women out on drugs and forcing them to eat one another's asshole out when they couldn't pay — was something else. That had to weigh on Bridges' choices, didn't it?

With Todd Bridges navigating, they arrived at The Highland Park Bowl having made good time, considering LA traffic. As an airline steward based in LA, Dave had recommended The Highland Park Bowl to literally hundreds of families over the years. The place was smaller than Dave remembered, only ten bowling lanes. It had a grungy, warehouse feel, atypical for bowling alleys. The Highland Park Bowl didn't have sliding plastic seats or the 1980's alien head computer monitors Dave remembered from his childhood. Instead, the interior was appointed with luxurious Chesterfield sofas and dark stained, wooden end tables. Chandeliers lovingly crafted out of antique bowling pin racks dangled overhead, contributing to an overall vibe of steampunk. A wood burning pizza oven blazed behind a bar showcasing dozens of craft beer selections, while their menu boasted about the creativity of their modern cocktails.

Dave didn't mind hanging out in the Highland Park Bowl. The place had a certain presence, which was of course why Todd Bridges had chosen it for their pitch to investors. As great as the Highland Park Bowl's vibe was — it could never approach the profundity of presence that Death Row Restaurant would have. In fact, by comparison Death Row Restaurant would make every restaurant's ambiance feel manufactured.

Bridges began walking differently. He adopted the gangly, awkward deployment of limbs he'd had as a teenager on Diff'rent Strokes. Bridges went right to lanes four and five, where lounging on the Chesterfields and occasionally tossing balls down the two lanes was most of the cast of the 1970's television sitcom The Facts of Life — all except Tooti.

It felt good to see them. Dave had watched just about every episode of the show on a black and white television in his bedroom during the early 80's. He imagined that serial killers probably viewed their murders in a similar fashion, as if those murders had been committed on the set of some mini-series. Serial killers are massively adept at compartmentalization. Boxes within boxes, within boxes. Dave had felt this compartmentalized feeling when he first met Todd Bridges on that flight from Chicago to Wichita, when he was forced to contend with the collision between the person he was meeting and the well curated television persona he had watched as a kid. Meeting the cast of The Facts of Life in person, Dave encountered this feeling. He couldn't escape the sense that his preconceptions contained an unavoidable, almost discriminatory quality, a certain violence. Todd Bridges gave out hugs while Dave mapped the people he was seeing to his teenage memories from their show on his black and white television set. Dave hadn't known this before, but the entire cast of The Facts of Life was alive and in good health, even Charlotte Ray, who had to be in her nineties. And they had all come to hear Todd Bridges pitch his restaurant concept.

Eventually, Todd waved Dave over.

"This is my general manager, Dave Aslin," Bridges said.

"I'm a big fan. I mean, I was a fan as a kid. Still am," Dave mumbled, pumping out handshakes furiously. Charlotte Ray pinched Dave's cheeks. Nancy McKeon handed Dave a bowling ball.

"You're up, ass man," she said, riffing on Dave's last name with the trademark frankness of her character, Jo Polniaczek.

It occurred to Dave as he heaved the bowling ball down the lane, a sad effort that clipped only one pin, that The Facts of Life had been the polar opposite of Diff'rent Strokes. Unlike the troubled cast of Todd Bridges' show, which included Dana Plato's overdose suicide, Todd Bridges' pimping and rampant drug use, and Gary Coleman's lifelong celibacy and improbable, failed run for governor of California, the cast of The Facts of Life had drifted into the obscurity and silence of mainstream life without fanfare.

Once they had bowled a few games and Dave had a sheen of sweat on his forehead, Bridges sprang for a round of drinks. Drinks in hand, they retired to the Chesterfield sofas.

"Tell us about this restaurant idea," Charlotte Ray said, guzzling a mojito.

"Well, it's a restaurant. But unlike any restaurant that you've ever experienced," Bridges said, lifting his club soda and lime in a modest toast. Dave had heard this pitch so many times that he had to stifle a yawn.

"Where's this restaurant going to be?" Nancy McKeon demanded. Dave had wondered when they would get to that, how Bridges would handle it.

"San Quentin," Bridges said flatly, surprising Dave with his frankness. "Inside the gas chamber at San Quentin prison." Bridges let that sink in. Everyone just kind of froze, their glasses held halfway towards a toast that failed to materialize. Bridges sipped his club soda, shoving the lime aside with his tongue. "The restaurant will be inside the gas chamber of San Quentin," he repeated, "and diners will be served a five star, seven course meal by a team of convicted serial killers." Bridges let that sink in, too. "We won't be competing with The Olive Garden," he quipped.

"I don't get it," Edna said.

"Me either," Lisa Welchel said. She had played Blair on The Facts of Life and Dave had once read that she had appeared in every episode but one, the episode in which she was supposed to lose her virginity. A staunch Christian, Lisa Welchel had refused the role. They gave it to Mindy Cohen instead. "That's impossible," Lisa Welchel declared. "And even if it was possible, who wants to eat in a prison with a bunch of murderers?"

"Yeah, what's the point of that?" Dave blurted out, wanting to agree with his childhood crush.

"As you all know, I've been in prison," Bridges began. Despite the noise of the Highland Park Bowl, everything from screams of delight to bowling pins mixing to a bartender rattling a cocktail shaker, Bridges' voice rose up in perfect clarity. "I was wrongfully accused, of course," he continued. "But I can tell you that in prison, there's something about the place itself that cuts to the heart," he asserted. "Johnny Cash recorded an entire album in a prison. Johnny Cash understood the importance of prisons to authentic lyrics and rhythm. This importance should not be underestimated for the average American diner."

Bridges paused, as if weighing several pathways to continue.

"Look, you all know what happened to me. My uncle molested me," Bridges revealed in a soft tone, although everyone there already knew this. "My parents failed to protect me. And the family I'd had on the set of Diff'rent Strokes was worlds better than any family I might have had in real life, even if all those other terrible things had never occurred. I ended up strung out on meth, wearing a diaper and strapped to a metal bed at a rehab facility — facing charges of capital murder, pimping and distribution of crack cocaine. And when I walk the streets of LA, New York, even Chicago, there's always someone who slows down his car near the sidewalk, rolls down his window and yells, 'hey Willis, fuck you, you fucker.'"

Dave had heard all this before. The fact that strangers in LA or New York would take time out of their day to call a fictional television character from the 1970's a fucker was simultaneously the worst part of Bridges' life — and the thing he was most proud of.

"And whenever this happens," Bridges continued, "I ask myself, what can Todd Bridges even do anymore that would be authentic?"

Bridges stared off towards lane five. Dave turned and saw two technicians trying to pry a bowling pin from an automated pinsetter.

"This thing is really jammed," one of them said.

"Prison," Bridges continued. "While it was one of the worst experiences of my life, it was also the most authentic time of my life. So although I don't want to go back to prison, I do want to experience what prison brings. Prison makes you aware of forces below and beyond what can normally be seen," Bridges suggested. "I mean, if you open a restaurant, what do you want reviews to say?" He shrugged. "That the restaurant is authentic, of course."

"Isn't it the food that's supposed to be authentic?" Mindy Cohen blurted out. She had played Natalie on The Facts of Life and the only thing Dave could remember about her character was a show centered on a plot line where Natalie gets attacked while walking home alone. Her character in the show was so convinced that there was nothing at all she could have done to stop the attack that the episode had scared the crap out of Dave as a kid. Mindy sucked down the last of her cocktail, then slipped an ice cube into her mouth and crunched it.

"Not really," Todd Bridges replied. "I mean, that's what every restaurant claims, that their food is authentic or that their staff love their jobs and can't wait to welcome you while wearing a bunch of cheerful, zany buttons on their uniforms, etc.. And if that were true, you wouldn't need restaurants like these."

He nodded to Dave, their signal to break out the brochures, which Bridges had gone over with Dave ten times during the car ride over. For a second, Dave panicked, unable to find the box of brochures. Then he realized that he'd already laid them out on the coffee table. Dave handed brochures left and right. There was something comfortable, Dave thought, in the way a person usually takes a brochure when you hand it to them. Bridges pointed to the first picture, holding it up in front of his chest.

"Look at all of these restaurants whose concepts merge spectacle with food in ways that are inauthentic. At Opaque, for instance," Bridges began, his voice gaining confidence, "customers are blindfolded and have to complete a series of tasks to heighten their senses before being served their meal. It's a rite of passage, only it's inauthentic at its core," he concluded. Bridges turned the page of the brochure almost autonomically. He was entirely engrossed in what he was doing and Dave realized that he rarely saw this kind of rapt attention in real life, only on television or in street photography.

" — At Dinner in the Sky, the table and an attached bar with a loitering bartender are hoisted in the air by a crane. Guests literally strap into their seats and clip their silverware to their sleeves like little kids with their gloves. But this won't come close to what diners at Death Row Restaurant will experience. Diners at our San Quentin restaurant will be unable to forget even for a moment that they are experiencing a meal in a location and with a staff that are one hundred percent authentic."

"I've always wanted to do Dinner in the Sky — in Cambodia, though," Mindy Cohen whispered in Dave's ear. "Can you imagine slurping on a bowl of pho while swaying two hundred feet in the air?"

"What about just eating a perfectly cooked egg?" Dave replied, then shrugged.

"Oooh," Mindy coo'd, clasping his shoulder. "Like Bee Bim Bop with an egg on top served in a hot air balloon."

Bridges pointed to a picture of the actual gas chamber at San Quentin. Dave couldn't believe how small it was. Bridges turned over the brochure.

"Of course, the most famous inmate to be housed at San Quentin was Charles Manson," Bridges began. "It's really a shame that I didn't have the idea for Death Row Restaurant sooner. Charles Manson would have been a tremendous waiter." Bridges pointed to a picture of Manson in the brochure. "Manson had this ability to expand his eyes, lift his eyebrows and flair his nostrils while at the same time maintaining a relaxed forehead and an almost meditational purse of the lips and cheeks." Bridges paused again. "Imagine ordering the filet mignon and having Manson ask you how you'd like it cooked?" Bridges said, making eye contact around the group. "Why would he ask that? Why would he wait on you at all unless he authentically wanted to?" Someone on the lane next to them made a strike. Dave heard the sharp crack of a high five. "Alas, Charles Manson died in 2017. Colon Cancer," Bridges sighed. "He was probably too old to be a regular on the waitstaff anyway but he would have been perfect for special occasions. Don't you agree, Edna?"

Edna had fallen asleep. Like Dave's grandmother, Edna's nose and lips sunk to the sides of her face when she slept. Bridges turned a page in the brochure. "Ah, William Bonin," Bridges exclaimed. "The Freeway Killer. Don't you just love that mustache, the deep set eyes, the length of the ears? You know, after the fact all of these serial killers seem to be dead giveaways, don't you think, Edna?"

Mindy shook Edna a few times, who awoke again with a start. She was blinking her eyes like mad.

Dave's stomach lurched. One day he would actually have to manage staff at Death Row Restaurant. Dave hadn't even liked giving new flight attendants a basic tour of the beverage cart. He had almost no idea what it would be like to interact with employees as a supervisor, let alone supervising serial killers. But it struck Dave almost as soon as he thought it that what Bridges was doing, what Death Row Restaurant would be, was entirely different. Convicted serial killers would have no reason to work in Bridges' restaurant — except for wanting to do so.

Bridges snatched a slice of shrimp pizza that had just been set on the table and signaled the waiter for another round of drinks. The waiter brought them almost instantly.

"Edna, imagine William Bonin, 'the Freeway Killer,' a man who deployed ice picks, tire irons and car jacks to abduct and kill twenty one teenage boys along California's coastal highways, imagine him serving you a perfectly cooked snapper Veracruz and delicately deboning it tableside for you," Bridges said.

"Will all of these killers be on death row?" Nancy McKeon asked.

"Not Bonin," Dave said. "He was on death row. They executed him in 1996, right Todd?"

Bridges shot him a look. He hated being called Todd.

"That's exactly right, Dave," Bridges responded in his lilting 'Willis' voice. "Bonin had quite a last meal, though. Two pepperoni and sausage pizzas, three six packs of coca cola and an entire quart of chocolate ice cream. That's another thing we could do. We could have special menus composed solely of famous last meal requests and served by current death row inmates. Did you know that California has more inmates on death row than any other state? Imagine being served three quarts of mint chocolate chip ice cream in San Quentin — just like Timothy McVeigh had been served — for his last meal on earth. Now imagine a current death row inmate refilling your water glass, bringing you an ashtray, going over a flight of rare scotches with you, discussing potential dessert pairings while in the back of his mind he is considering what to order — for his own last meal..."

"Manson, McVeigh — all of these guys are dead," Nancy McKeon blurted out. "Who's going to actually serve this food?"

Bridges turned the page, ignoring McKeon's outburst.

"Now this guy, this guy would make a very interesting bartender, don't you think? Just imagine a man who killed sixty seven people in cold blood. Imagine him fixing you a perfect Gin Fizz and then polishing some glassware behind a low slung bar studded with rhinestones and leather bunting." Bridges paused and held up the brochure. "His name is Randy Steven Kraft, better known as the 'Scorecard Killer.' And if a guy like him agrees to be a bartender while he awaits lethal injection, you can bet that he's doing it because he wants to do it," Bridges asserted. "That makes all the difference in a restaurant. Even famous chefs who've experienced everything restaurants around the globe have to offer have never enjoyed that kind of authenticity during a meal. Anthony Bourdain searched for Death Row Restaurant his entire life," Bridges concluded.

"And what about this guy?" Nancy McKeon asked, turning the brochure sideways until a centerfold spread fell open. "What job would you offer him?

"Dennis Rader, the BTK Killer? For his first murder he killed an entire family, including two children. He left semen everywhere." Bridges paused for effect. "Dennis Rader is a dishwasher. No doubt in my mind. In fact, Dennis Rader has already signed a contract to work in Death Row Restaurant."

"Wow. You are good at this," Nancy McKeon admitted.

"We have to get Dennis Rader transferred from El Dorado Correctional Facility in Kansas. That won't be easy," Bridges said. "But Rader is a must have for Death Row Restaurant. Dennis Rader was so good at faking who he really was that he once snuck away from a cub scout jamboree where he was a scout master, took a cab back to his own neighborhood in Park City, Utah, strangled his neighbor, transported her body to the church he was president of where he took bondage photos of her — and then managed to get back in time to cook bacon and eggs for the scouts. If Dennis Rader agrees to scrub dishes at Death Row Restaurant with no compensation whatsoever — then it would have to be because he authentically wanted to do it. He's got no reason to pretend anymore."

"Wait a minute," Lisa Welchel insisted. "You're not paying them or anything? They must get free food or privileges. Something, anyway."

"No." Bridges said flatly, leaving no room for interpretation. "They get absolutely nothing for their work."

"Isn't that slavery?" Lisa asked. She had taken on a moralizing tone. It was fascinating to Dave that someone could be worried about Dennis Rader, the BTK Killer having his labor exploited by a restaurant. Dave wondered if Rader would find a way to get something out of it. Rader lived in solitary confinement. He hadn't embraced another human being in over thirteen years. Rader probably didn't even experience incidental contact, like when a checkout clerk hands you your change through a drive through window and their fingers brush your palm. For all Dave knew, Rader would insist on a daily hug from him. Just the thought of it made Dave's stomach sink into his testicles.

"Well, Lisa. The thing is, while everyone in prison understands about being involuntarily deprived of their freedom, most prisoners eventually realize that in committing themselves to tasks that are not required of them, they maintain their freedom, too. Serial killers understand this better than most because they are never getting out of prison. What Rader will be doing when he washes dishes at Death Row Restaurant is voluntarily giving up the right to dictate how he uses his time behind bars." Bridges smiled, the same goofy grin that had endeared him to America when Diff'rent Strokes first hit the airwaves in 1978 — right before the rise of the serial killer in the 1980's. Dave and Todd Bridges still had a slew of dossiers from the brochures that they had not yet covered, dossiers detailing men who were unbearably despicable. But Bridges could tell that going over them wasn't necessary. He folded the brochure he was holding for Death Row Restaurant in half and slipped it into his jacket pocket like a winning Powerball ticket.

Bridges signaled his accountant who was seated at the bar enjoying a wood fired pizza. After a brief introduction, disclosures, tax forms and their necessary riders littered the coffee table. The cast of The Facts of Life were taking a stake in Death Row Restaurant. Dave expected to note some kind of joy or satisfaction on Todd Bridges' face. He had done well. Yet Bridges' face showed nothing out of the ordinary. Not even a slight smile. Bridges had fully expected this. He was already thinking about the next big fish he would need to land to get enough capital to make Death Row Restaurant a reality.

Dave admired Bridges' dedication. No matter what hurdles he might encounter, from administrative issues to the nuts and bolts of training serial killers to be knowledgeable waitstaff or sous chefs, Bridges would figure them out. Dave wished he could say the same. He was already uneasy about having missed his culinary school lessons for the day. Tomorrow, he will be back in the kitchen wrestling with the impossible task of cooking an egg properly. Yiannis will be there as well, shaking his head, lecturing them, using words like "rubbery" and "in need of an exorcism" and "just plain boring in every way." Their eggs would represent them, would simulate their attempts at a best self that were nowhere near adequate. Dave wondered if Death Row Restaurant would actually be different.

Nancy McKeon finished signing her paperwork with a flourish of her wrist and then marched over to Dave as he slouched on an adjacent Chesterfield sofa. Before Dave could even sit up straight, Nancy McKeon grabbed Dave by the flap of his chef's coat and started making out with him.

"I want to be the first customer in Death Row Restaurant," she eventually whispered hotly in his ear.

Whether Nancy McKeon was just acting, reprising her life as the brash 'Jo' on The Facts of Life when she had grabbed Dave and started kissing him at the Highland Park Bowl was unclear to Dave. She and Dave had several drinks together afterwards, while Todd Bridges took a meeting with his financial advisors. A few times, Nancy rested her hand on Dave's thigh under the bar. Of course, Nancy was married, had two kids and had been with the same guy since 1993. As someone who had gone through the last several decades single, with occasional exceptions, Dave was curious how she sustained her long term relationship.

"With some flexibility," Nancy told Dave, squeezing his thigh. "I'm faithful to Marc, so get any notions of getting farther than this out of your head." She made a fist and held it under Dave's chin in classic "Jo" fashion.

"So making out is okay, but with boundaries?" Dave asked.

Nancy shrugged.

"The truth is that there are no boundaries in marriage," she admitted, sliding her hand towards Dave's crotch. "But then again you always find that there are." With that, she chugged her gin and tonic and left Dave alone at the bar, waiting around for Todd Bridges to finish meeting with his financial advisors.

The next day Dave returned to culinary school somewhat apprehensive. Not only had he missed a pivotal class on the perfectly cooked egg, but Dave also knew Todd Bridges had no reservations about barging into the kitchen classroom at Henderson. Although Bridges had successfully pitched his concept restaurant, extracting Dave from the Henderson Culinary Institute in the middle of a key lesson had revealed an almost terrifying naïveté. Bridges knew nothing about the core aspects of his own business. He was great at pitching the idea, but in terms of planning a menu or the ins and outs of managing an actual restaurant, Bridges didn't have a clue. When you add in the complexities of a prison and the personalities of serial killers on death row, Bridges and Dave both seemed hopelessly naive. At such moments, it occurred to Dave that Death Row Restaurant might be just another stage for Bridges to perform on. Bridges' pitch at the Highland Park Bowl was, after all, a performance. And Dave sensed that if he could, Bridges would love to live inside his Diff'rent Strokes sitcom, forever a teenager having heart to heart chats with Conrad Bain. Although Bridges had secured financing at the Highland Park Bowl, it was conceivable, maybe even likely that the whole venture would never get off the ground. That Bridges didn't even want it to get off the ground. That Bridges just liked living his life as a pitchman for an impossibly idealistic restaurant, a restaurant that sliced and diced its way through the politics of identity. At such moments, Dave felt blindsided by a wave of despair. As with his relationship with Kate, which he hadn't understood at all until it was too late, Dave felt he was flying blind.

Luckily, Dave didn't have much time to obsess about Todd Bridges or Nancy McKeon's inventive, darting tongue or her soft lips or her grip on his thighs or even the bright, refreshing gin and tonics served at the Highland Park Bowl.

Yiannis had other plans.

"There is no question," Yiannis began, wandering among the sweaty ranks of his chefs in training during their morning lineup. "The egg came first."

It was a little shocking to hear someone settle an age old question with such a cavalier statement. Dave had used the chicken or the egg debate as a punchline on so many occasions over the last four decades that a part of him winced at hearing the dilemma resolved.

"— Evolutionarily there is no debate," Yiannis clarified. "Chickens evolved from dinosaurs over hundreds of millions of years. Eventually, there was an egg which had enough genetic changes to be the first chicken."

Someone yawned. It was the worst timing imaginable. As far as Yiannis was concerned, there were no accidents. If you flexed your knees during some especially important history lesson, he took it as a rejection of his entire philosophy of history. Dave peered over his shoulder so that he could note the offender — and avoid ever interacting with him. He was baby faced, probably in his early twenties. His chef coat was wrinkled and he looked incredibly hung over, if not outright stoned. He swayed on his feet, first to the left and then back to the right. The chefs on either side of him shot fists into his ribs, propping him up and eliciting small grunts of pain.

Without acknowledging the interruption at all, Yiannis launched into what had to rank as one of the longest continuous archeological monologues in California history. He spent an hour on the Cenozoic Era alone, then followed this with a massive lecture on the Mesozoic Era. Yiannis traced what he characterized as overwhelming evidence of the evolutionary trail of the chicken to the maniraptorans so often deployed in the plot lines of Jurassic Park films. Yiannis mimicked the egg laying procedure of both the dinosaur and the chicken. He handed out diagrams comparing the shape of chicken bones to the shape of dinosaur fossils. He used a series of chili peppers to explain the striking compositional similarities between dinosaur eggs and chicken eggs. The sheer preponderance of evidence, the sheer weight of trying to prove even a single meaningless point in our world, one which had been the butt of billions of chicken and egg jokes across cultures and around the globe — made Dave dizzy.

Perhaps the most striking bit of evidence Yiannis conjured, at least for Dave, was a set of pictures he passed down the ranks of chefs. Each photo had been mounted with care on foam backing and laminated to prevent damage from kitchen accidents. Each photo was creased and bent as if Yiannis had spent decades with the photos in his back pocket as a talisman. Each photo featured a dinosaur fossil on one side and a modern day bird on the other. The posture of the dinosaur fossils was in every case uncannily similar to the everyday poses of brooding, modern birds. Dave found this unsettling. Not that birds evolved from dinosaurs. Yiannis had convinced Dave of that within the first twenty minutes of his lecture. These pictures made an even more important point — that today's birds lounge around in the death poses of their predecessors. Will the fossil record one day prove that today's hominids also spend their leisure time in an unconscious performance of their ancestral death poses? If so, Dave wondered, what the fuck does one take from that?

Had Yiannis allowed questions, this is what Dave would have asked.

But of course, Yiannis never took questions. So Dave steeled himself for the remainder of Yiannis' lecture by surreptitiously flexing and releasing his buttocks as Yiannis launched into what would prove to be his final point.

"You have undoubtedly held in your hands one of the most compelling pieces of evidence for the lineage I have described," Yiannis stated. Then from his pocket he removed a wishbone. "For much of modernity, the wishbone was considered unique to birds." Yiannis was strolling down the lineup of his sweaty, swaying chefs. He held the wishbone delicately between thumb and forefinger. "This is a very special wishbone, however. It's a dinosaur wishbone. I worked much of my life to acquire it," Yiannis said. "And like you, I have to work not to treat it like a common avian wishbone, the kind that kids snap after dinner. You must make the same effort, must keep alive a conscious awareness of the weight of history so that you treat the common chicken in your pot, the common egg in your frying pan with the same measure of respect. This is what distinguishes a chef — from a cook."

And with that, Yiannis began his demonstration of Chicken al Forno.

Having taken extensive notes on Yiannis' technique, Dave was excited to get started. He was, in fact, the very first chef to grab a roasting pan.

———

A few weeks later, Yiannis asked to speak with Dave after class. At the time, Dave was struggling to finish his coq au vin. The sauce had come out too thin and Dave was worried that reducing the sauce would overcook the chicken. He considered removing the chicken, straining the sauce and then reducing it separately. In the end, he rejected this. Not only would it look bad, but it might create a dichotomy in the dish. The sauce he strained and reduced might taste different from the sauce the chicken had already absorbed. Dave had no doubt that Yiannis would immediately detect a taste in the chicken that was unrepresented anywhere else in the dish. It was more honest, Dave felt, to maintain the integrity of the dish, even if one element of it ended up overdone. As expected, Dave's coq au vin ended up with a delectable, silky sauce paired with tasty but somewhat stringy chicken. And Dave was certain that Yiannis was going to blast him for such an uneven dish.

This was what Dave was thinking as he crept into Yiannis' office.

Yiannis' 'office' was basically a converted dishwashing area of The Henderson Culinary Institute. They had ripped out the sinks and appliances but had left behind the plumbing rough-ins, the tiled back-splashes and the rest of the functional decor of the dishwashing area. As Dave took his seat, he couldn't help but imagine that at any minute a crew of dishwashers might charge in and start re-assembling their washing stations. A damp smell permeated the room, as if it had been filled with steam in the recent past. Centered along the main wall was Yiannis' desk, a peeling, wooden affair crookedly situated above a giant floor drain. When Yiannis sat at his desk, a backwash hose dangled just behind his head. Occasionally, Yiannis moved his head in such a way that the hose appeared to be a noose and Yiannis a condemned man slouched on the platform of a gallows. The floor of the entire room, as in a shower stall, had been scrimmed and pitched towards the floor drain under Yiannis' desk. Thus, when Dave sat down in the lone chair it felt more or less like he was about to be flushed down a toilet. The idea of being flushed made Dave think of Kate, of their final moments together on that flight from Chicago to Wichita. Dave wondered what Kate was doing, if she had started a relationship with that man in first class. If she was traveling. If she was at all happy.

"Have a seat, Dave," Yiannis said, even though Dave was already sitting.

Having tasted his coq au vin sauce (which contained two full bottles of wine) a thousand times in the last hour and having also had several glasses of wine to calm his nerves over his uneven dish, Dave realized he was a little drunk. Yiannis' desk wobbled from time to time due to the pitch of the floor, and it was making Dave nauseous.

"Listen," Dave began. "I only just considered splitting the sauce. I didn't even do it. And I lost track of all the wine I was tasting. I know that was disrespectful of alcohol. It won't happen again," he pleaded.

Yiannis was stone faced. He stared at Dave numbly, wrapped in silence.

"Are you finished?" Yiannis finally asked.

"I guess so," Dave said. He stood up, began untying his apron, convinced that Yiannis was kicking him out of the program. Dave was a hell of a lot more drunk than he'd thought. He sat down again quickly.

Behind Yiannis' desk hung a framed issue of Smithsonian Magazine. The cover art featured a regal looking chicken in a Napoleonic pose wearing a French General's uniform. The headline read: 'How the Chicken Conquered the World.' That certainly made sense. On either side of Yiannis, crooked bookshelves weaved around the various pipes, plumbing rough-ins and ventilation openings in the wall. These shelves housed an array of Smithsonian Magazines going back several decades at least. Mixed in with the magazines were library bound copies of books. Some were obviously cookbooks, but others were volumes of poetry, science fiction, philosophy. Everything was heavily disorganized to the point where Dave began to wonder if Yiannis ran a used bookstore out of his office on weekends. As Dave scanned the bookshelves, he noted that above his head was a gigantic, stainless steel ventilation hood. Dave got the impression that at any second Yiannis could hit a button under his desk and have Dave sucked into the void.

"I have something to say to you," Yiannis finally grunted. But then he didn't say anything at all. He just reached into a desk drawer and brought out two potatoes. He placed them on the desk. "Both of these potatoes are on my desk," Yiannis said. "Do you agree?"

Dave nodded. His drunkenness had intensified over the last few minutes. The room had started to spin. Dave hoped to hell he could follow wherever this potato analogy was going.

"Which of these potatoes is the better tasting potato?" Yiannis leaned back in his desk chair, which let loose a horrific screech. Dave peered at the two potatoes. One of them looked a little like Todd Bridges. There was this tuft of roots at the top reminiscent of Bridges' semi-afro. Meanwhile, the rest of the Todd Bridges potato had an expansive forehead if you looked at it from just the right angle. And from that view, there were round cheeks with dimples, just like Todd Bridges had.

"This one," Dave said, pointing to the Todd Bridges potato.

"And why is that, exactly?"

"Because this potato looks like Todd Bridges," Dave said. "You met him."

"And why does that matter in terms of the taste of a potato?" Yiannis leaned forward on his elbows. Dave had been feeling a bit better, but all of a sudden the room began spinning again. The plumbing rough-ins made Dave feel like he was inside a really big washing machine.

"It doesn't," Dave admitted.

"I'm not here to debate whether a potato looks like Todd Bridges or not. My point is that a real chef would care about that question. I can always tell who is a real chef — and who isn't," Yiannis concluded.

Dave braced himself, brushed at a stain on his chef's coat, the result of an accident while spearing olives earlier in the day. "You, Dave, are a chef."

"Me?" Dave choked out, incredulous.

"Yes," Yiannis replied.

Dave was expecting something else to happen, a handshake perhaps or some explanation. But instead, Yiannis just got up and left the office. He was not one for fanfare or celebrations. In fact, Yiannis met most of society's norms with a strange disdain.

In the past, Dave had encountered teachers whom he could say had honestly tried to encourage or enlighten him. But Dave had always sensed in these moments a strategy behind their efforts. Dave had been merely a product whose reckoning was little more than quality control or inventory. The airline industry with its standard operating procedures, motivational tactics, uniform grievance policies and dime store psychology had felt similar. Everything from the steps to brewing coffee at 10,000 feet to how to hold a vomit bag during level four turbulence came with a "best practice." In eighteen years of being a flight attendant, Dave had done nothing but follow orders — at least until that last flight with Kate and his unauthorized use of the emergency slide.

But sitting alone in Yiannis' mildewy office with its preposterous angles, Dave had one clear thought — not that he had earned praise from his teacher for following all the correct procedures, but that perhaps Dave finally had done something. That he had committed an 'act' in the deep psychological sense that people like Yiannis and Todd

Bridges were always hinting at. That he, Dave Aslin had chosen chefdom and chefdom had chosen him.

The thought was sobering. Death Row Restaurant felt like much more than something Todd Bridges enjoyed pitching to has been actors, felt like much more than a stage to perform on. Death Row Restaurant would potentially be the one enterprise in the world where everyone involved was fundamentally committed to their actions rather than to doing whatever made money or defaulting to pop psychology best practices in the industry. It was the place where the structures, rules and ideologies that defined us, fell away. Death Row Restaurant would be like a lost tribe in Brazil, a place cut off from the world, from its history and from all of its incentives.

It was one of those fleeting moments where everything seemed to come together, and Dave knew the danger of overthinking it. So rather than wait for the room to stop spinning, he rose and stumbled out of Yiannis' office. Yet before doing so, Dave opened Yiannis' desk and stole the potato that looked like Todd Bridges.

———

Following their meeting in Yiannis' office, Yiannis invited Dave to meet another person that he considered a real chef, a guy named Jack Pierce. Jack Pierce was not an easy person to meet for a number of reasons, not least among them, the fact that he cooked last meals for Death Row inmates, a job that, as you might imagine, operated on a very strict timeline.

To meet Jack Pierce, Dave needed to go through the visitation approval process, a process that diners at Death Row Restaurant would also have to navigate and embrace. First, Yiannis had to contact Jack Pierce. Next, Jack had to fill out a visitation form and mail it to Dave. Jack had been instructed by Yiannis to list Dave's 'affiliation' as 'potential employer.' Next, Dave had to consent to the dress code: No leotards. No spandex. No halter tops. No clothing that looks like inmate clothing. Finally, Dave had to check a box promising to be "orderly and dignified." Once this form was in the mail, Dave had to wait for it to be processed. The prison proved surprisingly efficient. Within two weeks, Dave received an email from Jack Pierce inviting him to the prison Jack Pierced lived and worked in.

The drive from San Francisco to San Quentin takes you across the Golden Gate Bridge, through ritzy Marin County with its multimillion dollar homes and astonishing ocean views. Dave had talked about this drive with Todd Bridges on numerous occasions. Bridges wanted to curate every aspect of customers' experiences at Death Row Restaurant — including the drive to San Quentin. Unlike Dave and Todd Bridges' visit to the El Dorado Correctional Center to interview Dennis Rader, no one being seated at Death Row Restaurant would simply drive to the restaurant and ask for a table. Everyone would be picked up and everyone would take the scenic route. Dave kept this in mind as he drove to the Lancaster Correctional Facility to meet Jack Pierce. The drive to Lancaster wasn't nearly as dramatic as the drive to San Quentin. But Dave took as many back roads as possible to simulate the experience. And although the Lancaster Correctional Facility was a modern building built by a fully bonded construction crew with licenses, permits, hard hats, and degrees in engineering (and not by the prisoners themselves, as San Quentin had been built), although Lancaster didn't have anything like the famed gift shop at San Quentin, featuring items handmade by prisoners, Dave tried to feel the essence of the place, the way prisons strike at something beyond ideology. Right before Dave got to the prison, he dove past a brand new Denny's Restaurant and was comforted by the way they were still pushing their 'grand slam' breakfast on the general public.

At the prison, Dave was processed. Then a guard escorted Dave to a visiting room. Along the way, the guard shared factoids about the prison. For instance, Lancaster State Prison had been built in 1993 as a way of addressing, at least partially, the fact that Los Angeles County had no prisons but generates 40% of the overall prison population in California. Every Wednesday the Lancaster prison serves mac and cheese. Five other states have a prison with the same name. The place felt new to Dave, like that Denny's he'd passed. But it also definitely felt like a prison. Every wall, every floor tile, every door knob felt substantial and purposeful. San Quentin, Dave knew, would look very different from Lancaster, being more than one hundred and forty years older. But Dave knew that San Quentin would have the same sense of purpose, right down to its doorknobs.

At the visiting room door, the guard who had been escorting Dave handed him off to a second guard as they entered a room with white cinderblock walls and black rubber flooring like the kind in kids' playrooms, flooring that minimized impact injuries. The guard motioned for Dave to have a seat at a square, metal table with an attached metal stool. The combination of the square table with the round stools lent a kindergarten feel to the place. Since Dave had told prison officials that he was conducting a job interview, Dave had been taken to the semi-private area. But it was still packed with convicts visiting their girl-friends, wives, and family. The prison guard who had escorted Dave went back to the door and just stood there. He reminded Dave of a museum guard, just a guy standing around not really doing anything but being there. Each time an inmate arrived at the visiting room, he was handed off by the guard escorting him to the guard in the room just like Dave had been. After five minutes, the procedure felt like a canned food drive, only with human beings replacing packages of ramen noodles and cans of chicken noodle soup. When Jack Pierce arrived at the visitation room and was escorted to the square table with its round stools, the guard didn't pull Pierce along by his arm and Pierce wasn't handcuffed or anything. It was, Dave thought, more like a restaurant host escorting a customer to a table for brunch. Jack sat down. Neither he nor Dave said a word. Jack was skinny. His face had a disturbing hollowness to it, as if something were eating away at him from the inside. Jack's hair was thin and scraggly. His patchy beard needed constant scratching. Jack's teeth were crooked and yellow.

Dave should have planned what he was going to say. But because this meeting had been set up by Yiannis, Dave had assumed that a procedure or agenda for such meetings was already in place.

"It's okay, my dude," Jack finally said, clapping Dave on the shoulder. "I'm the guy you came to see. I'm the death row chef."

"I want to be able to say the same thing," Dave muttered somewhat awkwardly. "I mean, well, there may be this restaurant — in San Quentin. Maybe. I mean, it's being planned. Possibly, that is."

Dave was impressed by Jack's patience. As Dave stumbled around trying to wrangle a coherent sentence, Jack peered at him with vague interest.

"Cool, man. Cool," Jack finally said. "A lot of people don't support giving death row prisoners a last meal. Hell, at first I wasn't even sure I could cook for these dudes. But over time I really changed my mind about that. I came to think that cooking someone's last meal, honoring their final request as best I could is worth something regardless of the shit they've done. Like I told them other reporters, I support last meals not because of what they give to the condemned, but because of what this meal says about the world. The last meal, it's not like we go out shopping for it. We just do the best with what we have. And that someone, anyone tried his darndest under really shitty circumstances to give that prisoner what he requested for this one meal — well, like I said, it's a last way of affirming a different view of the world to these guys."

"The prisoner's last meal. It's like ordering off the secret menu," Dave said.

"I guess it is," Jack hooted. "I guess that's it. If you want a death row meal, just seat people and tell them to order without the menus. Then the kitchen does their best to create what they ordered with what they have. That's exactly how it works."

Dave was intrigued by the idea.

"So you're a murderer?" Dave blurted out.

"Me. Nah. I'm in for larceny, assault and battery. I just ended up getting into this last meal cooking gig and it stuck. I was surprised. Something about the process, the informal nature of it. No menus or anything. The inmate hand writes his request and then gives it to a guard who has no obligation to pass it along. Sometimes these requests come to me from a social worker or psychologist, too. There are all these different avenues. But someone gets the note to me. Sometimes in the morning, sometimes at night. They get it to me, is all. Then, I read the request. And it's not like getting email or an ad or some guy panhandling on a street corner. You read the note and there's something very final about it all. There's something there that you can't easily ignore. It's this guy's last request. And the inmate who wrote it. He knows you read it because of the food that gets sent for the final meal. And so for once at least, what they wanted mattered. These guys, they've taken everything they've wanted. And at the end, they are given something. That's their final lesson. That there's this other way of being where people give to one another rather than just take." Jack scratched viciously at his beard. "I hope you stick with that restaurant idea of yours," Jack added.

"It's not really my, well, Todd is the guy —" Dave broke off. It didn't seem worth sorting out whose restaurant it was. It was funny, even though Dave finally sat inside a prison, even though he was talking to a guy who cooked death row inmates their final meals, even though Dave could feel the grounding reality of a prison in exactly the way Todd Bridges had always described it to him — his conversation with Jack Pierce didn't seem to be about Todd Bridges or even Death Row Restaurant at all. Dave was just talking, one chef to another. "So a death row inmate," Dave began, "they can literally ask for anything?"

Jack nodded.

"Anything at all." Jack gouged at his neck beard with his fingernails. "'Course, that don't mean they will get what they ordered. That's a big misconception about the last meal. We don't send out for lobsters and steak. They just give the request to me and I do the best with whatever we got in the kitchen. If the condemned man wants lobster tails and filet mignon, well we start knocking the breading off some fish sticks and then we sculpt and plate it to look like a lobster tail. For the steak? Well, we just use hamburgers and make some gravy and try to make it look a bit like a surf and turf. And that's a powerful thing. That someone tried to get them even a shitty version of what they wanted…"

"And these inmates, they can ask for food that doesn't go together at all. Shit that's just ridiculous, right? And you give it to them anyway, right?" Dave asked. "Like a dude orders teriyaki pork served in a lemon parfait, or olives and donuts, or mint chip ice cream with habanero salsa, or…"

"Don't matter at all. Whatever they order we do our best. No one is judging."

A baby cooed. Dave turned to see a burly convict making a kid laugh. The convict's face had so many piercings that the infant was batting them around like a mobile. Dave was searching for more questions. Yiannis hadn't told Dave much about what he was supposed to find out from Jack Pierce. Yiannis had only said that Dave was 'ready' and handed him Jack Pierce's email address. At the time, Dave hadn't even known why Yiannis had wanted him to meet Jack Pierce. It occurred to Dave that he was still strikingly naive about everything he was doing. And the old fear of actually working with serial killers crept up Dave's spine. Dave shook the feeling off. He didn't know why Yiannis had sent him to Jack Piece, but Dave did know that he had not yet gotten what he had come to Lancaster Prison for.

"And once in a while," Jack added, "a guard will pass along that so and so really appreciated that last meal I had scrounged together, that the guy used a few of his final minutes on earth to tell a guard, to insist that the guard get me the message that he enjoyed that meal. Ain't no point in doing that unless you really mean it. Hell, even just eating the meal makes no sense. I mean, these guys are going to be executed two hours later, before that meal even digests. Just eating the meal says something. Anyone sending out compliments on top of that, they mean what they are saying. They ain't got no reasons to lie about liking it."

"I don't know why," Dave blurted out, "but I thought you were a murderer."

"Me? I'm no murderer. I'm in for assault and battery. And larceny. But it don't make a hell of a lotta difference, does it? You got murderers in gen-pop. And you got murderers on Death Row. I'm in the joint. Murderers are in the joint. Hell, you're in the joint sitting at this same table." Jack laughed, revealing a few holes where some teeth once had been.

"So what do you do when you're not handling last meal requests?" Dave asked. He knew executions were rare.

"I'm a cook. I cook all the time," Jack said. "But most of my cooking I do in my cell. That's why Yiannis comes out to see me. He always wants to learn the latest techniques."

"Cooking techniques?" This was surprising. Yiannis never told him he visited prison on a regular basis. "So do you have like a chicken coop or a garden in the prison yard or something?" Dave had seen such things on television, prisoners learning how to care for lettuce plants and tomatoes and whatnot.

"We don't got all that fancy stuff you have at the culinary school. For ingredients, we make do with what we got in the commissary or what we steal from the kitchen. But that ain't even the problem. The real problem is getting things cooked at all. I had to learn that, see. I had to learn how to cook food in my cell without any kind of hot plates or stoves. That's why Yiannis comes to see me."

Yiannis had instructed Dave to ask the guard for a tour of the commissary before the interview. It was packed with Ramen noodles, block cheese, tortillas, spaghetti, tuna fish, corn, beans. There was just so much food in there. Shelves of it. How could they put that much food out on display if prisoners couldn't even cook it on a hotplate?

"I don't get it?" Dave said. "All that food? You just eat it cold? Cafeteria food must be better. At least cafeteria food is hot."

"Cafeteria food! Nah, most guys can't hardly eat the stuff they serve in the cafeteria. Most guys, they eat out."

"Like Denny's?" Dave blurted out.

That had Jack Pierce dying. He slapped his thigh a few times.

"Nah, man. Nah. Not Denny's. You gotta cook your own meals in this place. You ain't far off to call prison a giant restaurant, though. A prison ain't filled with murderers. A prison is filled with cooks. I ain't calling us chefs or nothing fancy like that. But right now, about half of the dudes in here are in their cell cooking. We're all cooks in here," he repeated.

"Wait. I thought you said they eat out?"

Jack slapped his thigh again. He started hooting.

It is sort of funny, Dave thought. How most people who fancy themselves to have chef skills depended on having a big old kitchen and pantry. If you put Anthony Bourdain into a prison cell he would probably starve.

"A few of us, we banded together and formed us a little enterprise. We got some mayonnaise, see and we put it out on the windowsill in winter and everything but the oil freezes. Then we skim that off and before long we have a frying business. Depending on what the commissary has, we fry up everything. And then in the afternoon the porters come 'round and serve as waiters doling out the food. For a pack of Newports I could fix you a gourmet meal."

"Everything fried?"

"Yeah, mostly. But I can do up some rice or spaghetti for ya, no problem. You just use a garbage bag with some holes in it. Poke a few holes and you've got a boil in a bag meal."

"Amazing," Dave said. In the back of his mind he was complimenting Todd Bridges. The idea of opening a restaurant in the gas chamber wasn't as weird as it sounds. Prison was already just one big restaurant. "But where do you get the heat?" Dave added.

"All I need is some basic ingredients and a 'stinger,'" Jack mused. "I could cook for a whole wedding if I had to with just a couple of stingers," Jack scratched his beard until some crumbs fell onto the table, then pressed his finger onto the crumbs and slid them into his mouth. Jack smelled pretty strongly of fish sticks.

"A what?"

"A 'stinger,' man. That's how you cook in the joint."

In their remaining time together, Jack told Dave all about stingers. Every cell has an electrical outlet. All a prisoner has to do is hack it. "Once you get over your fear of dropping a live wire into a glass of water or oil, you can cook just about anything in your cell," Jack said. "I'm a better cook now than I ever was on the outside."

———

After meeting Jack Pierce, Dave decided to invite Todd Bridges over to his Sun Valley house for dinner. Part of it was that it was something a chef would do. And Dave was starting to feel like a chef. Another part of it was that Dave wanted to float an idea for Death Row Restaurant to Todd Bridges.

Dave stood near the oddly shaped windows in the Sun Valley house. He had gotten used to them, but not entirely. Dave didn't see Todd Bridges' car. He went over to the front door and unlocked and opened it. Then he made sure the screen door wasn't locked. Bridges had a whole procedure for how he enters his Sun Valley house. And Dave was trying to respect his wishes. He took a few deep breaths and then went back into the kitchen where Todd Bridges had once stabbed a renter with a chef's knife. There, Dave inspected the stinger he had made from the cord of his old waffle iron.

When Bridges arrived, he didn't ring the bell or anything. He just waltzed right in, went to the kitchen, opened the refrigerator and took out an apple juice. It was his house after all. Then Bridges slammed his palm against the bottom of the glass jar to pop the seal on his apple juice. It didn't work. Bridges shrugged, then smiled that big, goofy grin of his, then twisted off the cap of his apple juice. This was Bridges' entrance routine. He had told Dave about it months ago.

"I don't want you to think I'm rude or presumptive or anything," Bridges had told him. "It's not that I'm trying to make sure you know that this is my house and all that," he insisted. "It's just that when I go to someone's house, anyone's house, I just need to come right in and see what's in the refrigerator."

"Got it," Dave had said. He could care less. It was Bridges' house, after all.

"No. Look. If I tell you I'm coming over, you make sure the door is unlocked. I don't want to be ringing a doorbell or fumbling for keys. You leave the door unlocked and I just come in. It ruins my flow, my mojo, to do it any other way," Bridges had insisted.

They'd gone through the routine dozens of times over the last few months, but Dave had never quite gotten used to it.

"What do you do when you meet a woman?" Dave asked, following Bridges into the kitchen where he had once stabbed his roommate to death. "Do you tell her all this shit up front? No knocking. No doorbells. I have to be naked certain places and all that?"

"Over time, yes." Bridges said. "Look, it's how I am. I don't get on your case about your fucked up habits."

Dave had no clue what fucked up habits Bridges was referring to, although one of his roommates in college had complained about how much pubic hair seemed to fall off his body around the house. Maybe Bridges was right and he shouldn't judge.

Bridges sighed in a way that indicated he was finished with the conversation. "I'm going upstairs to grab a shower. Then I'll come down for dinner. I'll be naked, so get used to it," Bridges added.

"Fine, whatever," Dave muttered. He didn't care. He actually had something interesting to show Todd Bridges, perhaps his first real contribution to Death Row Restaurant.

Bridges disappeared upstairs.

Dave started getting his kitchen ready.

About twenty minutes later, Bridges descended the stairs buck naked, with a white towel slung over his shoulder.

"What's for dinner?" Bridges asked, his mood had completely changed. His voice had an upbeat, almost hopeful tone, as if he was sorry for being a pain in the ass to people since 1984.

Dave had wanted to give Todd Bridges the full last meal treatment, to tell him he can order anything he wants and then Dave will cook it out of whatever ingredients he has, like Jack Pierce does for his death row meals. But Dave didn't feel comfortable doing that yet. So he thought he'd start by cooking a meal the way they do in prison cells, with a stinger and some mayonnaise oil.

"Your choice," Dave said, fanning out several flavors of ramen noodles in his hand like a Vegas Blackjack dealer. "We've got Sriracha chicken or chicken mushroom," Dave said, then fanned himself a little with the noodle packages. "Or..." Dave held up a can of Sunny Sea mackerel in brine. He'd actually bought the can of mackerel in the prison commissary in Lancaster because he couldn't believe how cute the can was. The label depicted a fish that appeared to be winking at him. The background was orangish. But at both the top and the bottom of the label, a squiggly line and blue background made the briny, winking fish appear to stroll straight out of the ocean. It was corny, but Dave appreciated that even with the cheapest food imaginable, even with food whose label indicated only partial removal of gizzards and offal, someone had taken the time to make that label somewhat cute.

"I really am wasting my money on that cooking school, aren't I?" Bridges said. "All you know how to cook is a boiled egg, ramen and Jack Mack?"

"And I'm going to cook it with a stinger and with oil from frozen mayonnaise," Dave added, as if telling a diner about his locally sourced beef, where the cattle are free to roam the prairie and are massaged each evening by loving farmers who proudly proclaim that their cows have only one bad day on the farm, the day they are butchered. Dave held up an old waffle iron cord. He'd used a copper wire to affix his old nail clippers to the live wires, just as Jack Pierce had told him to do.

"Jack Mack it is," Bridges agreed. "Man," he added, chugging his apple juice.

Dave set to work cooking the Jack Mack. He had already frozen a jar of mayonnaise so that he could skim off the oil. Bridges sat around the living room, trying out different chairs, as if he didn't know how to be comfortable. At a certain point, Bridges began grooming his fingernails. Dave had always wondered whether Todd Bridges had his nails done or did them himself. His hands and fingernails were always meticulously maintained.

Cooking prison food requires many small steps. There was a Zen quality to it and Dave was already lost in the procedure. Each step required an elevated level of concentration and attention to detail. Whatever timelines one usually operated on didn't apply. Jack Pierce knew guys who would spend six or seven hours in their cell making a handful of tortillas out of ramen and other ingredients from the commissary. Dave wasn't trying for anything that complex yet. But he limited himself to only one bowl, as a real convict would have to. This meant that he had to dump the smelly mackerel out of the can and onto his palm, and that he had to be sure the water he used to clean the fish came from the tap in just a soft stream. If the water was too forceful it would break apart the fish. With one finger, Dave gently rubbed the body of the fish, removing slime and the occasional bit of gizzard.

Next, Dave laid down a small piece of a garbage bag and dumped flour, garlic powder, paprika and pepper into it. He mixed the dry ingredients using one finger and then coated each piece of fish with the mixture by gently stirring with his finger. From the couch, Willis sighed. It was not a sigh of impatience, Dave thought. In prison, everything takes time. Every moment had real heft to it. Bridges knew that.

Getting an even coating on the mackerel proved near impossible. But the toughest part was keeping the filets whole. Every time Dave nudged one of the fish it tended to fall apart. Dave peered into his bowl. The mayonnaise oil shimmered. His stinger was actually working. Dave hesitated before dropping in the filets. He didn't want them to slide down the sides of the bowl into a stack. Like a real prisoner, he was limiting his tools to what a prisoner could cook with. In prison, everything is plastic and would melt in a fryer. So Dave did what the prisoners did and used a pair of wooden chopsticks.

"Smash 'em a little with the palm of your hand first," Bridges advised from the couch. He was still doing his nails, carefully shoving slight overgrowths under his cuticles. "Trust me," Bridges added.

So Dave pressed his palm lightly onto each fillet, which solidified them a bit. Then Dave slid them, one by one into the bowl of hot oil, which began popping and sizzling instantly.

The meal didn't take all that long to cook. It was nothing like the lineups and hours long cooks Dave had endured under the scrutinizing eye of Yiannis and his assistants. But by the time Dave had finished cooking the Jack Mack, cooled his oil, put it back in the mayonnaise jar, wiped out the bowl and measured out the caraway seeds, vinegar and sugar to make the slaw, he was exhausted. His shirt was drenched with stress sweat that Dave knew contained all of the nutrients bacteria thrive on. Already, Dave could barely stand his own stench.

Dave and Todd Bridges sat down to eat. Bridges was now drinking iced tea with lemon. He tipped his glass in Dave's direction.

Dave tried not to watch Todd Bridges eat. The food was just okay, reminiscent of fish sticks and coleslaw. Prison food isn't about taste. It's about texture.

"The garlic is good in here," Bridges said. "But you need something to give it a little kick," Bridges said, chewing intently. "You need The Whole Shabang."

"The whole shebang?" Dave repeated.

"You know, the chips," Bridges elaborated. "No one who makes Jack Mack on the inside leaves out The Whole Shabang." Bridges rotated his palms slightly upward, as people often do to indicate confusion or surprise.

"I've never heard of those chips," Dave said. "The Whole Shabang?" Dave tapped the name into his phone.

"You can't get them in grocery stores," Bridges explained. "You can't even get them in the commissary a lot of times. They sell them in the prison catalogs. And man, was that ever a pain in the ass." Bridges chugged his ice tea. "I was still doing drugs in prison, at least, for a while I did. And these prison catalogs were a prime way to score. You see, you can only order from catalogs every three months. And each prisoner has to order everything he wants from the same catalog. It was a real pain in the ass," Bridges suggested.

Dave was frantically typing notes on his phone. He wanted to get all of this down. Yet he was worried that Bridges would think he wasn't listening.

"The shoes you want are in one catalog and the chips and other food you want are in another catalog. So this is where the drug addict comes in. He's the only guy willing to run around and figure out how to get his dealer all the shit he wants from different catalogs. A drug addict don't care. He'll fucking beg for a bag of The Whole Shabang chips if it means his dealer will let him cop when the catalogs deliver," Bridges said. "And what every plate of Jack Mack, or eggs or prison burritos needs is some crushed up Whole Shabang chips. They have this excessive, vinegar flavor to them. It's something none of the food you get in prison has," Bridges continued, wistfully. "And you know what?" Bridges asked. "When I was in the can right after my detox, when memories of that diaper and metal bed were still fresh in my mind and I was still kind of hating everyone, some guy who was getting out soon gave me a bag of those Whole Shabang chips. He just knew I was really struggling so he gave me those chips. And it was the first time in a really, really long time that someone had done some- thing nice for me," Bridges confessed. Then Bridges shoved his plates away and lit up a cigarette. The smoke hung in wisps in the air.

"If people are coming to a prison to eat, we should serve them legit food," Dave said. "I'm not saying we have to make the food authentic. I know that's not what Death Row Restaurant is about. But like you just were explaining, we could cook like this for other reasons," Dave suggested. Bridges was lounging around on the couch, his back to Dave. He hadn't put the towel down under his bare ass like he usually did. "You never told me that prisons were practically restaurants already," Dave said. It felt like they were having a lover's spat. "I mean, the idea of Death Row Restaurant isn't all that strange when you consider how central cooking in cells is to prison life," Dave continued.

"Listen," Bridges interrupted. "I appreciate you trying to learn about prison food. And from a marketing perspective, stingers and Jack Mack would be a popular thing to do. But there's no way I'm

serving Jack Mack in Death Row Restaurant," Bridges stated unequiv-
ocally. "We want the food to taste great, sure. But the restaurant isn't
about the food. It's about the wholeness of these serial killers. There
isn't anything romantic in Jack Mack. Jack Mack is necessity. If you
were starving, you'd eat moldy bread out of some guy's sweaty ass
crack," Bridges added. "It doesn't make your meal more authentic."

"But that's not what I'm proposing we do," Dave insisted. He was
still sweating for some reason, even though the stinger didn't put out
much heat. Meanwhile, Bridges wasn't sweating at all. Dave didn't
understand why it mattered so much that he could cook Jack Mack if
he wanted to or use a stinger. Dave tried again to explain. "Death Row
Restaurant is more than just finally getting an authentic meal. It's
more than just ambience. Our customers are spending time in the
prison. And in a prison you've got cooks, a lot of cooks. It doesn't
seem right to keep that a secret. It has to be part of the experience,"
Dave argued.

"Call them 'clients,'" Bridges interrupted. "We will call our diners
clients, not customers."

"What's the difference?"

"A customer buys goods and services," Bridges said. "A client," he
continued, "a client has an ongoing relationship for professional
services. Death Row Restaurant isn't just a place you eat dinner at on a
Saturday night and then go about your business per usual, Dave. It's
an ongoing thing, a service that keeps on serving. We don't just cook
food and have a serial killer deliver it. From beginning to end, from
the moment a client makes a reservation, we are going to steward
every aspect of their experience so that they understand what it means
to have authentic service providers, people who want to do what they
are doing at every single moment. The car clients take to Death Row
Restaurant will be chosen by us. Will be deliberately chosen. A
customer may pull up to the restaurant in a Toyota or a Honda. But
our clients will cede that to us. We will choose how they get to the
prison. Maybe a Rolls Royce. Maybe a Subaru. Maybe a converted
coach bus with leather seats and a stripper pole. The point is, while
I'm glad you've gone inside a prison and I'm glad you understand
some things about prisoners and how they may spend seven hours
making one burrito — well, that's only one part of the experience. One
part. We are going to choose the route customers take to get to the
restaurant. We are going to choose which killer makes their appetizer,
which killer reviews the dessert tray. Which killer tells a client where

the restroom is. We are going to choose with the utmost care which murderer will greet them at the door with total deference and respect."

Bridges took a puff off his cigarette, but he didn't inhale. This made Dave furious. He was filling up the house with cigarette smoke and not even inhaling.

"One thing our clients will choose, however, is their cutlery," Dave added.

Dave knew not to react too drastically to anything Bridges was saying. Everything about the restaurant so far, everything but Dennis Rader, was all talk. It was only once they were truly setting up the place that Dave had to be ready to take a stand for what he believed in. For now, they had no lease. They had only one employee besides themselves, Dennis Rader, and they still had to figure out the near impossible task of getting Rader transferred to San Quentin, a legal battle that could take years. It was one of those moments where Dave realized that Death Row Restaurant seemed like a daydream, like something they had come up with while high.

Bridges reached into a small backpack he'd brought with him and pulled out what looked like a knife drenched in blood.

"What the fuck, Todd!" Dave screamed. "Is that the knife you killed your roommate with?"

"He wasn't really my roommate, Dave," Bridges answered, perfectly calm. "And don't call me Todd. No, this is a shiv, not the knife I used in self defense back in 1993."

Dave felt terrible for throwing that incident in Bridges' face. He didn't know why he had leapt to such a conclusion. He had knocked over the plate of Jack Mack he was picking at when he startled. Oddly, the fish Dave had so much difficulty holding together when coating and frying had become like hockey pucks. They bounced a few times on the floor making dull clunk sounds. How on earth could Dave handle working with guys like Dennis Rader, who once took erotic pictures of himself dressed in his victim's clothes and then half buried their body in a shallow grave?

"Relax," Bridges said. "It's just a shank."

"Why is it covered in blood?" Dave asked.

"It's not," Bridges coughed, putting out his cigarette. "I made this one myself — out of Jolly Ranchers."

It was true. Bridges even let Dave lick the knife, which was both tart and sweet, a nice compliment to the Jack Mack.

"Most prisons keep a 'shank museum' — a collection of all the weapons they've confiscated. Shims, shivs, coffee creamer flame throwers," Bridges said casually. "I think we can talk San Quentin officials into letting us use some of these shanks and shivs. Like this handy dandy thing —"

Bridges pulled out a huge contraption. It looked like deer antlers filed to sharp points, and the whole apparatus fit neatly over Bridges' fist, like a pair of brass knuckles. Bridges feigned a few uppercuts. "I don't think this could be useful as a utensil," Bridges admitted. "But I like this one," he said, taking the deer antler weapon off his hand and setting it on the coffee table. "This one is made out of toilet paper," Bridges added. "Prisoners make all kinds of shit out of toilet paper. As authentic as that is, I don't think we can ask our clients to cut up an aged ribeye with a toilet paper shiv after pulling up in a Rolls Royce."

"What's the difference?" Dave said. "Between a 'shank' and a 'shiv?'"

Bridges went back to his Jolly Rancher knife. He held the blade against a piece of paper from the magazine he'd been cutting his nails over earlier. The Jolly Rancher blade quickly whisked it in two.

"A shank is only for stabbing," Bridges clarified. "A shiv can stab and cut."

"Oh," Dave said. It was a weird thing to know. And even weirder, the illicit prison weapons were so clever that they set Dave at ease. "What we'll do," Bridges said, lighting another cigarette, "what we'll do is we'll have a whole shank and shiv museum at the front of the restaurant. Maybe even mount everything on a peg board. Our customers will choose their cutlery from it. It will all be authentically made by prisoners. We can even vouch for where it had been stashed — under a bunk, behind a toilet, you know. And prisoners get solitary if they are caught with something like this. Every one of these weapons led to a stretch in SHU." Bridges crossed his legs. "That's the special housing unit," he added. "Code for solitary confinement."

Dave found himself nodding. The idea struck him as radically important. You should be able to choose your own cutlery. Of course you should. There absolutely should be a giant peg board of cutlery in every goddamn cafeteria.

Bridges got up, went to the window and puffed on his cigarette. Dave couldn't tell if he was inhaling or not. He also couldn't tell if Bridges was staring out the window or admiring his own reflection in it.

"I know we've had a few conversations about personnel," Bridges began. "I know we've discussed some of our dream employees, like Manson or the Lonely Hearts Killer," he sighed in disappointment. "That was mostly marketing. Now it's time for us to get our staff together for real."

Dave felt ready. The restaurant, it was happening. And he was surprised by how ready he felt for these next, concrete steps.

"Are we just going to select from a list of dossiers?" Dave asked.

"Yes," Bridges said. "We'll review the dossiers and then conduct interviews with the most promising candidates." A haze of cigarette smoke hung in the air. Dave wanted to open a window, but he didn't want to interrupt the conversation. He didn't want to do anything that might slow the progress of the restaurant.

"One thing I need to ask, as it's bound to come up at the interviews," Dave said. "What do the prisoners get out of working for Death Row Restaurant?"

"I don't follow," Bridges said.

"What I mean is, well, what do the prisoners get out of it? What's their incentive?" Dave was hoping to find a different way to word the question, but there wasn't one.

"Nothing," Bridges shrugged. "The whole point is that they get nothing out of it, that they have no reason to cook or clean or study to be an expert bartender other than to do it."

"Yes, yes. I know that's what we talked about. But I mean, it's impossible for them to get nothing out of it. They won't be paid. I understand that. But they might get something out of it in other ways. One of these killers might think at first that they are simply choosing to do this. But, well, I've been thinking about this and I know that that's impossible."

"Dave, look. Let's just get this thing off the ground first," Bridges said. He was now seated on the edge of the couch, exactly how he'd been when he showed the dossiers to the cast of The Facts of Life, except that now Bridges was buck naked.

"Just let's think this through," Dave began again, stalling for time. He too leaned forward onto the edge of his chair. A cough or a sneeze would send him barreling to the floor. "A prisoner may think he's getting nothing out of working for Death Row Restaurant, that he's just doing it in order to do it, but then one day he will figure out that he's doing it for the sense of freedom he gets from the prison schedule. Or maybe there's a greater sense of freedom just in feeling like he made an honest choice? Or maybe, see, maybe he thinks that he's just catering to our clients, but guys like Rader, I mean, the kind of crimes he's committed, the kind of person he is. He signs his letters with just his first name, drawing 'Dennis' into the shape of a shark with these huge, imposing teeth. That's how Rader thinks of himself. As a predator with no more responsibility for what he does than a shark has. And so maybe he does get something out of working in the restaurant."

"I know all about Rader," Bridges said, sounding exhausted. "Sharks can't apologize and all that. They do what they do. And Rader did what he did. And part of that was being a loving father and family man. Rader did that. You could argue that all that was just a cover story for who he really was. But imagine if you let Rader decrumb the table for you after a meal. Don't you think it can help you figure out the answer to your question?" Bridges concluded. "I promise you, there's no contradiction here. The restaurant's authenticity doesn't depend on whether Rader gets something out of his work or not. Diners will be put in touch with the real meaning of communion. It's all right there, whether you're eating seared ahi tuna or a stack of pancakes. What you realize when someone like Dennis Rader slices your carpaccio or makes you a basket of jalapeno poppers or lights the candles on your table or is just quietly mopping up a spill a few yards away is something much deeper. In our world, everything alive has to eat to survive. And whatever you are eating was recently alive. To survive, you pretty much have to adopt the attitude that you are more important than whatever you are about to eat. That's not my rule. It's the law of the universe. The universe's basic rule is murder," Bridges concluded. "There's no way you can interact with Dennis Rader over a meal and not consider that."

"But what if these killers get some kind of satisfaction out of working in Death Row Restaurant?" Dave pressed Todd Bridges. "Let's say five years or ten years or even fifteen years of being an absolutely perfect bartender, a perfect dishwasher who never once drops a plate. What if Rader stops signing his letters with that horrible fucking shark and just sees himself as a guy who works in a kitchen?" Dave asked.

"I don't know what you're getting at, Dave," Bridges shrugged. "Whatever goes on in the restaurant itself, prisoners are legally barred from profiting from their crimes." Bridges' voice had the labored quality of an airport TSA agent, explaining over and over again that

TSA personnel don't like touching you, so please follow procedure. "The kind of people we will hire... the worst of the worst — these people have no interest in changing who they are or getting some kind of pardon for their crimes," Bridges said. "If that's what you're referring to."

Dave thought about some of the killers he'd studied with Todd Bridges. Guys like Robert Ben Rhoades, a classic sexual sadist, whom the FBI nicknamed 'The Truck Stop Killer.' Rhoades was a huge reason why the FBI started its interstate database of unsolved murders. Rhoades tortured and murdered anywhere from three to fifty or more victims. Rhoades was married, seemingly ordinary. Just an interstate trucker with an interest in bondage — only Rhoades had welded together a torture chamber in the back of his cab. He liked to take photographs of his victims as he terrorized them. He got off on their fear. And these photographs were a big part of why Rhoades was finally convicted. There was one photo in particular, a photo Dave had discovered on his own, without Todd Bridges, that terrified Dave. Fourteen year old Regina Kay Walters, Rhoades' final victim. Rhoades had picked up Regina and her boyfriend at a truck stop. He killed the young man right away, but he kept Regina for weeks. The infamous photo was taken right before he strangled Regina to death with a wire in an abandoned barn in Illinois. Rhoades used so much force that he almost decapitated her. In the photo, Regina's arms are outstretched, as if trying to hold her killer at bay. Her terror is palpable, almost unimaginable. Pure fear and profound sadness heightened by incomprehensibility. A shiver ran up Dave's spine. Just the thought of these people was almost unbearable. Dave couldn't believe how badly he smelled too. He had taken a second shower before Todd Bridges came over, but he smelled rank. There was absolutely no way Dave could work with a man like Robert Ben Rhoades.

"You have to understand something," Bridges continued. "These guys are sadists. They get off on people's fear and suffering. That's where the satisfaction is for them. And they've admitted this is who they are, sexually. Our customers, I mean, our clients. Our clients aren't submitting to some kind of negative experience. Authenticity refutes that. And these killers, it's not just that their crimes are unpardonable, that they will never get a pardon. These killers, they don't even want a pardon. How can you be pardoned for being who you are?"

"They're pure evil," Dave suggested, thinking again of the photo of Regina Kay Walters.

Bridges cupped his forehead in his hands.

"Look Dave, I get this because I kind of went through it," Bridges said. "When you are America's darling, making $30k a week and all, and you fall from grace and lose everything as a celebrity, you realize that you aren't making a comeback. It's not just that I am the last surviving cast member of Diff'rent Strokes. It's not just that you owe people you've hurt or stolen from. I apologized. I paid off every cent I owed. I went to rehab. I went to prison. I asked the public to pardon me, to allow me to go back on television and to just be Willis again. And at first, they wouldn't do it. They wouldn't pardon me. But then something even worse happened. I wrote my memoir. I went on Oprah and told my story. I received hundreds of letters of support, even some offers to act again. And I could tell, I could feel it, I was getting a pass, a pardon. And a pardon just meant that I had a new debt to pay. A pardon just meant converting my old debt to society into something that lasts forever. Oprah told me she understood me. She said she understood that drug addiction is a powerful thing. She said she understood that I was abused by a family friend when I was a kid. But even as Oprah told me she was glad I survived all of it, I could feel it. I owed her for this. It's one of those things that drives a person to tell the public to go fuck themselves," Bridges concluded. "Like Richard Ramirez did."

"Is that why your memoir spreads the blame for what happened to you around to everyone but you?"

Dave had never admitted it before, but he had finally gotten around to reading Todd Bridges' memoir. He hadn't bought a copy. For some reason Dave didn't want to own Bridges' memoir. But he'd found a consignment copy laying around in Bridges' car.

"It's not important," Bridges said, waving his left hand back and forth in a cut-off gesture. "The point is, these prisoners don't want a pardon. They won't view their work in Death Row Restaurant as a means to an end. These killers, they have finally stopped pretending. Dennis Rader broke down every detail of his murders in an open court room. This took hours. They had to take a bathroom break halfway through the testimony. And that was the end of Dennis Rader being able to do anything. Signing your name like a shark is one thing. But Rader is still a thinking being. He doesn't want to just sit in a tank. I interviewed Rader for the job. Trust me, he wants the chance to do something again. But that's not the same thing as getting satisfaction. Death Row Restaurant won't be some big redemptive act. Rader can't get satisfaction that way. None of these guys can."

Bridges was standing now, completely naked. He was shuffling from side to side on the other side of the coffee table like he was trying to avoid being tackled by police. "No one gets a pardon," Bridges reiterated, "that's in the DNA of Death Row Restaurant." Bridges smiled, like he had just nailed an audition. And Dave realized that he was going to work this material into his sales pitches. "All of this will be intuitive once the restaurant opens and you are operating in your role as general manager," Bridges concluded.

"Do you think so?" Dave asked. He had visited Lancaster prison less than a week ago to meet Jack Pierce and none of this shit had been obvious to him.

"Yes," Bridges reiterated. "Our clients will know all about everyone's crimes. They'll know all about me, all about our staff — even all about your crimes, Dave. They'll know about that slide and the reckless endangerment charge. And those few who don't know the exact story, they'll know that you've done something inexcusable, something you just had to apologize for — and they'll know that you were required to say in court that what you did doesn't reflect who you really are. And they will understand that serial killers are free from all that. That they are unpardonable."

Bridges came around from the other side of the coffee table.

"Trust me," Bridges said, putting his hand on Dave's shoulder. "I didn't choose you as the general manager of Death Row Restaurant for nothing. You understand this stuff. And managing a kitchen full of serial killers will be the easiest, most intuitive job in the world."

It was a bizarre thing to say. Dave wondered if anyone in human history had ever uttered that sentence before. Dave's gut instinct was to tell Todd Bridges what he had read about Bridges' trial. That the whole reason Bridges had been put on trial in the first place was because he was too fucking high to remember whether or not he'd actually shot someone. That to this day, Bridges doesn't remember. That not everything is as cut and dry as Bridges makes it out to be.

But then again, Dave didn't know why he had deployed that emergency slide instead of waiting five more minutes for the plane to taxi. So he was no better. What Dave did know, perhaps the only thing he knew, was that he wanted to be around people who did things because they wanted to do them. And for the moment, this was a unique group, just serial killers, perhaps Yiannis, perhaps Jack Pierce — and Todd Bridges. After all, Bridges had no logical reason to even open Death Row Restaurant.

"Okay," Dave said. "I get it."

"My man," Bridges clapped Dave on the back. "Just remember, none of that 'stinger' Jack Mack bullshit," Bridges added, picking an errant bone or gizzard out of his teeth. "We're a high end restaurant. If you want to cook, you'll need to start impressing me with something more than a fried egg and Jack Mack."

"Got it," Dave agreed.

"We've got one or two seatings per night. Perhaps eight or ten guests at most in that gas chamber. We can't have any misses. Everything has to hit home."

"Of course," Dave nodded.

Bridges smiled.

"It takes different strokes," Bridges said, flashing that goofy grin of Willis. "Different strokes to rule the world, man."

Then Todd Bridges and Dave sat back down on the sofa and began looking through a thick file of dossiers, potential employees for Death Row Restaurant. These men weren't dead. They really could work in the restaurant. And they were some of the worst men Dave had ever heard about.

———

Months passed. Dave threw himself into his work, cooking school by day and meetings to review serial killer dossiers with Todd Bridges in the evenings. Going over potential employees with Bridges was always rather strange, always bookended by Bridges' odd routines, like getting undressed and then dressed again every time he came to the Sun Valley house to work on personnel. Or the way Bridges phoned ahead to be sure the door to his Sun Valley house would be unlocked so that he could come right in and check out the refrigerator. There was just one night when Bridges broke this routine, where instead of going straight to the refrigerator as soon as he entered the house, Bridges kicked off a pair of expensive looking sneakers and announced: "We're going to put leather bunting inside the gas chamber at Death Row Restaurant. I just picked out the leather."

Bridges' process for selecting staff was curious. He didn't just go for the most infamous men he could find. For instance, although

Bridges was dead set on hiring the recently captured Joseph DeAngelo, 'The Golden State Killer,' a man who had raped at least fifty women — and murdered at least thirteen people, Bridges categorically rejected hiring Wayne Williams. Convicted of killing two men, Williams is suspected of killing nearly thirty children during the infamous Atlanta 'child murders' from 1979-1981.

"The problem is that Williams claims he's innocent," Bridges had said. "We can't have someone like that at Death Row Restaurant."

"You mean you think he might not have done it?" Dave had asked. He could only handle about forty five minutes of dossiers in a single evening. They had just passed that mark.

"No," Bridges elaborated, slamming shut the dossier and reaching for his pants. As usual Bridges had to be completely naked in his Sun Valley house. "Williams' actual innocence or guilt is irrelevant." Bridges slipped into a pair of joggers. "We don't want any killers who don't admit to and fully own what they did," Bridges said. "If Ted Bundy were still alive, if he had continued to maintain his innocence instead of confessing his murders to gain more time before being executed, Death Row Restaurant wouldn't hire him, even with his staggering level of infamy," Bridges stated, pulling on his shoes. He had been wearing these all black sneakers that Dave looked up online. Turned out they were limited edition, Nike blackout SB Blazer Supremes from a 2006 collaboration with Gucci. They cost around $3,000 a pair.

———

The routine of cooking school by day and dossiers by night went on for more than a month, before dwindling away to almost nothing. All that was left was for Todd Bridges to finagle the interviews, complete the financing and behind the scenes political work. This had given Dave a few months to really and finally settle in.

It was on one of these more relaxed weekends that Dave finally felt like he'd built a new life for himself. Dave had spent most of the day lounging around Todd Bridges' house in Sun Valley. Dave felt comfortable, despite having several nicks and cuts on his hands from this week's cooking at The Henderson Culinary Institute. And Dave had a party to go to, a party hosted by one of his culinary school friends. Most of Dave's culinary school cohort was a lot younger than he was, and Dave envisioned cramming into someone's tiny, LA apartment for some kind of coke and hard liquor binge. But since these people were inexorably a part of his new life, Dave would absolutely attend this party.

In fact, Dave even thought about inviting everyone over to Todd Bridges' house instead.

The Sun Valley house had plenty of space and even a bunch of rowdy, drug addled, would-be line cooks would undoubtedly be the lamest party ever held at Todd Bridges' house in Sun Valley. Plus, something told Dave that Todd Bridges wouldn't mind.

But in the end, Dave didn't want to have to explain to any of his classmates why he was living in such a fabulous house in Sun Valley — let alone explain the concept of Death Row Restaurant. For one thing, not a single person in his culinary school class would be qualified to work at Death Row Restaurant. Hosting the party felt antithetical not just to cooking but to the whole fraternity of the industry. So although Dave still felt kind of like an outsider, he also kept noting how comfortable he was feeling, how he had woken up feeling especially well rested and lucid. And despite the continued barrage of Yiannis' often brutal chicken history lessons, Dave wasn't concerned about serial killers or the world's brutality in general.

What Dave was concerned with this morning was carrot cake. He had decided to make carrot cake muffins for breakfast — and then for lunch, maybe some kind of chicken salad. Only Dave was going to elevate the chicken salad by massaging the cut up chicken breasts until they were plump and plush, ready to absorb the mayonnaise. And the mayo, Dave would make it himself to avoid the acid and preservatives that store bought mayonnaise contains, which firms up the chicken by cooking it in the same way that acid cooks ceviche. Dave would also add a touch of creme fraiche to his mayonnaise, to fluff up its texture, followed by celery, black pepper, toasted pine nuts — and in a surprise and avant garde move, a bit of tarragon, which Dave had come to think of as a natural partner for chicken, the yin to chicken's yang, the Laurel to its Hardy, the Arnold to its Willis.

And that was exactly what Dave did with his Sunday, even as text messages from his culinary school cohorts, many of them blasting Yiannis for his chicken centric curriculum, his line ups, his relentless criticism of their inability to cook faster, to cook cleaner, to cook better, to cook dishes before being asked to cook them —lit up his phone. Dave's carrot cake muffins came out positively medieval, just as he had planned. No giant reservoir of sugar or mantle of cheese icing.

Dave had crafted his carrot cake muffins in the wartime style when sugar was sparse. He used rum and ground almonds and lemon zest and a box of sultanas he found at the back of Bridges' pantry. And Dave knew as he was microplaning the lemon zest, that Bridges really didn't give a shit about food. That Bridges would consider Dave's carrot cake muffins (their tantalizingly slim crust of mascarpone rum frosting, as perfect as half frozen late fall puddles that kids absent-mindedly break with their boots while walking to school) that Bridges would consider the dish, just carrot cake.

Now the texts were really coming in. Warnings to start their liver exercises, as the punch will be positively lethal, the snacks both dainty and hearty, both rustic and refined. The party will be beach attire only, which Dave did not even own. And there will be cooking contests, no chicken of any kind, in fact, no discussions of chicken. Except for the losers of each contest who will have to stand around with their arms crossed over their chests and speak of nothing but chickens — as Yiannis does.

We should invite him, Dave texted the group. Receiving back a series of devastating memes — Will Smith in Bad Boys II pointing at the screen and saying, "That's some funny shit" over and over again.

Dave needed a ride to the party. He texted Todd Bridges who he hadn't seen in a while. Bridges immediately agreed.

That evening, around the time Dave needed to leave for the party, Dave unlocked the front door to the Sun Valley house, not knowing if Bridges would want to come inside to update him on Death Row Restaurant. But Bridges merely honked from the driveway when he arrived. Yet as Dave got his wallet and some leftover carrot cake muffins to bring to the party, Bridges came to the door. Only instead of going to the kitchen to check out the refrigerator, Bridges just walked around his living room like he was visiting a museum. He kept picking things up and then putting them down again, as if studying them. It was weird. And then, without a word, Bridges opened the front door and got back into his Chevy Malibu. Dave trailed after him.

"I'll try to get someone to give me a ride back," Dave suggested, while strapping his seatbelt. "Unless, that is… uh…you'd like to join?"

Other than a pair of flip flops he'd found in Bridges' closet (and an old pair of sunglasses), Dave hadn't done much to accommodate the beach theme of the party. Bridges on the other hand, was perfectly dressed for a beach themed party. He wore comfortable looking linen pants, a light blue linen shirt (partially buttoned),

Hawaiian style boat shoes, and a blue and white linen hat. He was right out of a beach catalog. Bridges' hat was especially nice. It didn't have a hatband, which minimized the size of Bridges' large head.

"Thanks, but I can't party anymore," Bridges said, as if ordering a cheeseburger without pickles at a drive through. "I mean, I go to bars sometimes. But a full on party? In LA? I might go right back to being a crackhead." They came to a red light and Bridges turned and looked at him. "Can you guarantee there won't be any coke or meth?"

"From what I've heard, cooks generally like their coke and heroin," Dave said. "I don't know about meth. A lot of the cooks I'm meeting at culinary school have awful looking teeth, though. For their age at least." Dave trailed off. He felt he had more to say, but wasn't sure what it was. There was something frighteningly true about Bridges' statement that he could just go right back to being a crackhead. Despite how an addict's true identity was a sober one, the scenario of a relapse felt a lot like serial killers who went dormant for months, years, or like Dennis Rader — for whole decades. Yet could always go right back to murder.

"I'm still in therapy," Bridges confessed. "Even after all of these years, even after having a daughter." Bridges made a series of turns paying a lot of attention to the road all of a sudden. "Even now that I have a daughter," Bridges continued, "I still have trouble imagining a relationship with a woman that doesn't involve stringing her out on dope," Bridges admitted.

"Oh," Dave said. He was momentarily unsure if Bridges had told him about his daughter before or if Dave had read about Bridges' daughter in a news story. Regardless, Dave was struggling with the conversation. He was used to participating in conversations by commiserating with people, by agreeing with and validating their feelings. But with Todd Bridges, Dave often found that impossible. It was one of the things that made it hard to hang out with Todd Bridges if they weren't discussing Death Row Restaurant. Dave dug a slip of paper out of his pocket and handed it to Bridges. It had the party's address on it.

"Victor Heights? You're going to a party in Victor Heights?"

"I guess so," Dave said. He didn't know anything about the neighborhood. Dave was starting to slip into a strange mood. His perfect lunch, the elevated chicken salad contrasted by the wartime carrot cake had given Dave the feeling that he was living a good life. Not his best life. But at least a decent one. And now that feeling was deflating like a balloon animal from the county fair.

"I used to party in Victor Heights all the time," Bridges insisted. "It was great. In the 90's, Victor Heights was called the 'forgotten edge.' Everyone joked that the police had forgotten where it was. You could do just about anything in Victor Heights." Bridges tilted his head back slightly, as if reliving a slew of coked out memories.

Dave wondered what Bridges thought of all the drugs and pimping he'd done in the 1990's. Not everyone who does coke and meth ends up committing the kinds of callous and even criminal acts Bridges had participated in, like forcing women who worked for him to eat out one another's assholes if they were short money from a drop. Serial killers, Dave had read, were unusually adept at compartmentalizing. Dennis Rader had boxes within boxes within boxes. He was a law abiding family man, a compliance officer and the president of his church. And yet he spent years casing victims. And on a few dozen days of his life, Rader had committed atrocious murders. For Dave, it was the murder of Shirley Vian that stuck in his memory. Rader had planned to murder a woman named Cheryl, whom he'd met at a bar earlier. But Cheryl wasn't home when he got there. And Rader — was all keyed up. Almost desperate. Like a cokehead. Rader started walking around the neighborhood, until he saw a little boy and followed him home. After forcing his way into the house with a gun, Rader tied up Shirley Vian, barricaded her three kids in the bathroom and strangled her. He would've killed the kids, too, Rader later confessed, if a phone hadn't rang, making him wonder if someone wasn't coming over to check on them.

In court, Rader described the whole encounter very matter of fact like. In court, Rader had to own up to what he did. But what was so chilling about it was that he didn't just own up to it. He owned it.

Bridges was driving like he had just gotten his learner's permit, hands at nine and three, the newly adopted standard position (so the airbag doesn't slam your fists into your face in an accident). And Dave again wondered what kind of responsibility Bridges accepted for his own actions back in the 1990's. At the moment, Bridges was putting all of his concentration into driving. Dave assumed his concentration was due to Bridges unconsciously sorting through a flood of coked out memories and meth binges brought on by the fact that they were driving to Victor Heights. Will Rader have this same look of blank concentration while washing dishes in Death Row

Restaurant? Will Rader use the force of his will to block off the torrent of his darkest urges by giving outsized attention to scrubbing glass-ware? Given how few tables San Quentin's gas chamber would fit, how few people would clear security and make it all the way out to the prison for dinner, how many dishes would Rader even have to wash in a night?

And would Rader plot another murder while he worked in the restaurant? It seemed unlikely. Rader had always attacked weak victims in their homes. Never at work. Although Dave had read an article about plans Rader had confessed to in prison, plans for an eleventh murder that did involve a coworker. This murder was to be Rader's magnum opus, stringing up a co-worker from the ceiling and then setting the whole house ablaze.

Dave shook his head, trying to clear out thoughts about people like Dennis Rader.

But he knew that once such thoughts began, they would pop in and out his mind all night. He'd experienced the same thing with Todd Bridges on many occasions, as they reviewed dossiers for the staff at Death Row Restaurant. In San Quentin, death row inmates get a two guard escort anywhere they go. No doubt, the restaurant will be heavily guarded. Plus, with Rader at least, his whole persona was that no one would ever suspect someone like him of murder. Unlike Richard Ramirez, an avowed Satanist, Rader was a relatively normal, boring person nearly all of the time. He could probably wash dishes for decades without incident. At the El Dorado Correctional Center, Rader had been a model prisoner for fifteen years. He even compli-mented his guards and slipped them homemade cards during the holidays.

Bridges pulled up to the curb and re-read the address he'd been given.

"See that park over there?" Bridges pointed. "That's Teardrop Park. I used to get high as fuck there all the time. I would make drops for the Teardrop Locos who ran this area back in the 90's. I would get super fucking high just to do the drop. Then, I'd get even more high afterwards, especially if there were women in the park looking to cop. Sometimes I wound up buying my own drugs back from the dealers in Teardrop Park." Bridges paused, sort of in disbelief. "I wonder if the Teardrop Locos are still around?"

"Thanks. I'll see if I can find a ride back from the party," Dave reit-erated, hopping out into the street, slamming the door and then leaning in the open window. Dave realized, he probably looked like he was buying dope, leaning into a car like that.

Bridges' eyes darted around like mad.

"Nothing makes you high quite like meth, Dave" Bridges asserted. He seemed strangely desperate to talk about it. So much so that Dave resolved to hang around the car until he was finished. "Meth makes you feel legitimately happy," Bridges insisted. "It's a lie. I know it's a lie. But snort some meth and you'll feel lucky to be alive in such an interesting world." Bridges inhaled deeply, held it in almost like he was smoking meth, then exhaled, this peaceful grin on his face.

Dave was no longer worried about seventy five year old Dennis Rader flying off the handle during one of his shifts. It seemed far more likely that Todd Bridges might park his car, get out, toss the keys into a lagoon and disappear into Teardrop Park — never to be seen again. He could probably stay high in there for years. Ultimately, all the planning for Death Row Restaurant, the restaurant's philosophical necessity, their deep commitment to authenticity, was just as vulnerable to getting tossed out the window for a different plan as any other kind of plan people make for their lives. And if Bridges did decide to bail on Death Row Restaurant, it would be Dave's fault for going to this chef party in Victor Heights.

"Todd," Dave said, just to piss Bridges off and recenter him. "You okay?"

"Just text me when you're ready and I'll pick you up," Bridges said. "And who knows?" Bridges added, without looking at Dave, his eyes glued on Teardrop Park. "You might end up meeting someone. I never went home alone from Victor Heights." Bridges took off his hat and placed it on Dave's head. Then he gave Dave's head a pat, as if Dave were a dog. Dave felt like this might be the last time he would ever see Todd Bridges.

———

The party was on the third floor. Aggressive club music tore down the stairs as Dave huffed and puffed his way up to the party. Dave wasn't sure if he should just open the door or knock first. He suddenly appreciated Todd Bridges' routine at the Sun Valley house. Dave felt exhausted and hoped that Yiannis might be at the party so he would have someone to talk to. As tired he was, Dave also yearned for human interaction. For Dave, the most difficult and draining part of being a flight attendant was the social contact with so many people in a single day. Yet now, Dave missed even that incidental contact with other people.

Dave knocked, then opened the door without waiting for a response.

There weren't as many people inside as Dave had expected. The people who were in attendance were evenly distributed around the room, which made a very nice impression on Dave. Someone even turned down the music a little, and looking around, Dave recognized a lot of faces from culinary school. They were chatting and clutching drinks. A burst of laughter came from the hallway. Dave found the host, a Colombian sous chef named Augustine who had confessed while they were spatchcocking chickens for a Jamaican grill lesson that on weekends he made furniture.

"If you ever need a bookshelf," Auggie had insisted, "— you just give me a call and I'll hook you up."

"Auggie, hey," Dave called. He handed over some leftover carrot cake and half a chicken salad sandwich. "These are worth a try. A nice, wartime lunch," Dave whispered, feeling like a complete fucking idiot. Who could make sense of a line like that? Then again, with the loud music Auggie probably didn't even notice. Plus, the sentence had been perfectly timed. Dave had uttered it just as he had handed off the package with his leftover food to Augustine. So maybe he wasn't a fucking moron. Sometimes even the corniest things you say to a person at a party can seem perfectly natural.

"Thanks, man," Augustine said. "Glad you could make it." Augustine ran his hand through his hair a few times. "I don't know about you, but I really needed this party," Augustine said. He clapped Dave on the shoulder. "Bar is over there."

If there was one thing Dave had learned in all his bizarre and often abrupt conversations with Todd Bridges, it was that real connections with people don't require longevity. In fact, Dave had learned this even before meeting Todd Bridges. Dave could still recall all sorts of people he'd briefly interacted with on planes while he was a flight attendant. Often, he had no idea why he remembered these people, the contents of their interactions being entirely routine. It wasn't, Dave knew, all that different from how Dennis Rader had selected his victims. More or less by accident, by some small thing about them that made them memorable to him. That was one of the things so terrifying about Rader. Dave's relationship with Todd Bridges sometimes had a similar quality. Todd Bridges sometimes peppered their conversations with fragments of plot lines or dialogue from various episodes of Diff'rent Strokes, which made even banal interactions far more memorable.

Dave wondered if Bridges was getting high in Teardrop Park right now while prattling on about how nice his house in Northridge used to be. If he was, it could just be a relapse. Or it could be that Bridges would fully return to his old life, inhale some meth and instantly feel his heart soar, feel the world transform into a place that is inherently fascinating, so much so that it strips Bridges of all his pesky needs — even food and water — granting him total possession of his faculties. It was hard not to want that feeling, Dave admitted, before forcing himself to mingle.

———

Dave drank two cocktails. It was like dunking in a pool. His mood lightened considerably and he was glad he hadn't overdressed. Dave had expected gaudy beach attire, Budweiser shorts and loud Hawaiian shirts with pineapples wearing sunglasses. But most of his fellow chefs in training sported old shorts, flip flops and the joy of wearing sunglasses indoors. Dave received numerous compliments on the hat Todd Bridges had given him as he made his way around the party, listening in on conversations and now and then participating. Todd Bridges would've been a hit at the party, which was not at all a coked out, high octane affair. And Dave was aware of something else. Auggie's party was one of those rare parties that cultivated the feeling that you could be a truer version of yourself while you were there. And Dave wondered if Dennis Rader or Robert Ben Rhoades or Rodney Alcala had a similar feeling when they planned to kill.

Dave had mostly aged out of parties like this after he turned forty. And the months Dave spent dating Kate had primarily consisted of cloistering up in queasy hotels. Unlike a lot of people in their twenties who wanted to feel that powerful sensation of being young and heading out into the night to party, Kate's unusual and physically demanding hatred of Wichita, Kansas, her deep seated fear of people like Dennis Rader, of their ordinariness, pushed Kate to seek experiences she imagined were extraordinary. That was how she viewed travel. And although Dave knew what a misconception this was, that even the most exotic locales could be aggressively boring and ordinary, the very thing that led Anthony Bourdain to travel the world twenty six times, Kate's desire to travel was still one of the things about her that Dave missed the most. Although Kate suffered in Wichita, she also demonstrated a willingness to embrace her symptoms, to see them as an indelible part of who she was, rather than just something she wanted to eradicate.

Dave, too, had felt that powerful sensation of being young and striding out of his apartment to party all night. Some parties were effortless, with flowing conversations and just the right balance of laughter, solemnity, drinking and drugs. There was an ease, a balance to these parties. Every decision came quickly and without regret at such parties. Yet other, parties (and at a certain point, the majority of parties) had absolutely sucked. Sometimes everything Dave had wanted to say felt so urgent that it came out too early or too late or just plain wrong. Sometimes, Dave spent half his time trying to remember something he wanted to say, while missing the entire conversation actually going on. Sometimes Dave couldn't help but regurgitate lines he had heard in movies that he'd always wanted to say in real life, or things Dave had heard someone else say earlier in the day or week that he'd rather liked the sound of. He repurposed the phrases at parties, never quite fitting them in to the context of the conversation. Parties had been places where Dave finally felt grounded and part of the world at large. And parties had also been sites of pure desperation. Occasionally, both experiences were part of the same night. On those nights, Dave became acutely aware of the terrible loneliness of being unable to interact with other people at a party without feeling deeply humiliated. And the excessive drunkenness and drugs that followed such feelings often intensified Dave's loneliness rather than relieving it.

At one party, back when Dave was still a college chemistry major, a course of study that he wasted two full years on, his party hosts served 'apple pies,' a shot of vodka with a splash of apple juice and then dusted with a healthy dose of cinnamon. They went down as smoothly as apple pie. Dave was so nervous at this party that he got absolutely hammered. Then he insinuated himself into a slew of conversations, declared his love for people he barely knew before sneaking out of the party feeling misunderstood and completely unlovable. Dave was so trashed that he couldn't fit his key in the lock of the apartment he shared with a roommate who spent every night at his girlfriend's dorm. So Dave went back to the party. He lost his shirt somewhere and wandered around the party shirtless and unable to speak until the wee hours of the morning. Friends had already left. Couples had already splintered off. It was hard not to feel that human connection was the norm rather than the exception; that everyone at the party had returned to lives filled with effortless bonding and inner richness.

Dave did even more shots of vodka at that party, drinking straight from the bottle. He kept thinking that he would quit studying chemistry and perhaps pick up a major in Eastern religions. "I'm an Eastern religion major now…" he imagined himself saying at the next party. The room began to spin. Is that the best version of myself, Dave thought. With only pockets of laughter left in the corners of the room, he slouched against the bar, gripping a bottle of vodka. Dave woke up hours later on the sticky bar floor, freezing. Later, his friends produced pictures of him passed out on the floor, a rat parked on his face.

But Dave's bad party experiences were mild compared to Todd Bridges, who had been strapped to a metal table in a diaper while he detoxed from meth and crack cocaine. And there was something in Bridges' quirkiness, in the way he had accepted his need to be naked when high, for instance (probably the real reason Bridges couldn't accompany Dave to the party), that Dave admired. Bridges knew that he could only party with people who either wanted to have sex with him or who wouldn't mind his nudity. Dave found that admirable for some reason. What after all, were Dave's non-negotiables at a party? Nothing came to mind. And the only thing worse than negative personality traits had to be no personality traits.

Dave wandered into the kitchen. His mood was plummeting fast. After what had been such a good day, the carrot cake and chicken salad, puttering around the house, Bridges giving him his hat — now things felt absolutely miserable and Dave felt certain he would end up freezing and shirtless, rooting around for hard liquor.

In the kitchen, a young woman was shucking a tray of oysters with a screwdriver.

"Auggie doesn't own an oyster knife," the woman shrugged. "I'm Louise. I've seen you at Henderson and all."

"I've seen you at Henderson as well," Dave said, "although I don't think we've ever formally introduced ourselves. I'm Dave," he said, shaking her hand. It came out smooth and nice, not at all like someone who was about to get hammered and embarrass himself. At culinary school, Louise strung up her hair in a hairnet. Dave had assumed

Louise's hair was dark, straight, and unkempt. But in actuality, her hair was chestnut brown and curled in a single wave across her exceptionally large forehead, a feature Dave found striking and ultimately attractive.

Louise shoved the screwdriver into the valve of an oyster, pried it open and then handed the oyster to Dave. He had had bad experiences with oysters, especially with women for some reason, but like when someone hands you a baby, Dave didn't feel he could do anything other than take the oyster. "To Yiannis," Louise declared, crashing the oyster in her hand into Dave's as a toast. "Oh, wait. I forgot the Mignonette."

Louise turned and Dave scanned her figure. She was curvy, unlike Kate whose beauty consisted of stark lines and wispiness. Louise smiled as she poured the mignonette over Dave's oyster, then her own. The minced shallots clumped atop the oyster while the vinegar pooled in the crevices.

"To Yiannis," Dave repeated, clinking oysters again. Perhaps, Dave thought as he slurped down the oyster, here was a woman who wouldn't flush him out of her life.

The oyster was perfect. The sweetness from the shallots provided ideal resistance to the acid from the vinegar, which in turn proved a formidable counterpoint to the richness of the oyster. Behind the mignonette, rose a subtle but beautiful essence of the ocean which surged across Dave's palette. "My tongue is numb," he mumbled. He sounded drunk, though he certainly felt very clear headed and he was sharing his thoughts rather openly.

"Auggie had no white pepper," Louis shrugged. "So I used Szechuan peppercorns."

Nice improvisation, Dave thought. Then he reminded himself to say it aloud.

"Nice improvisation," he said.

And out of nowhere, Dave thought about Death Row Restaurant.

He wanted to tell someone about it.

He didn't want it to sound like some big plan, like he had designs on changing the world. But factually speaking, the world had never seen anything quite like Death Row Restaurant. Dave opened his mouth to speak, but nothing came out. The reality was that he had never spoken to anyone other than Todd Bridges about Death Row Restaurant. In part, this silence over what had become Dave's life defining endeavor generated from how difficult Death Row Restaurant was to bring up and explain. The best thing to do was probably just to come right out with the idea, like Bridges usually did. But Dave was also vaguely aware that laying some groundwork, that some preparation and timing were necessary if the idea was to be considered at all seriously.

Luckily, Louise was busily preparing another pair of oysters. It was one of the nice things about chefs — they often kept themselves busy in kitchens — and this gave Dave time to think. He'd had never had more than one oyster in a single sitting before. At pivotal moments, the oyster had proven for Dave (as it had for Anthony Bourdain), too symbolic to be repeated.

"Another?" Louise asked, which was interesting because Dave had watched her prepare the oyster for him before he'd even asked for another, what Yiannis believed a true chef should do — prepare a dish even before the customer realizes he wants it.

"Sure," Dave said. His tongue was still numb from the Szechuan pepper, which made him feel a little unhinged. He often got a similar feeling while studying serial killers, their history, their genealogy. Studying serial killers made Dave numb and out of control. And it made him wonder if there wasn't some path he (or anyone) could set themselves on that would lead to something like killing another human being.

Louise tossed the screwdriver she had used to open their oysters into the sink. Then, she bumped Dave's oyster with hers and they slurped them down in unison. A wave of sea foam and contentment washed over Dave, followed by the numbness of the Szechuan, and it was so perfect that he couldn't help but feel closer to Louise, who had just experienced the same thing he had. Dave lifted his gin and tonic to his lips. It was all ice, though he didn't recall finishing the drink.

"Too spicy?" Louise asked.

He shook his head.

"Absolute perfection," Dave smacked his lips. He had grown attached to this moment, to being alone in a kitchen with Louise while they each worked a numb tongue inside their mouths.

Before Dave could think of something to say, he thought of the worst possible thing — Dennis Nilsen, the Scottish 'Jeffrey Dahmer.' Nilsen had murdered at least twelve young men simply because he couldn't bear the thought of them leaving his apartment. After each murder, Nilsen would bathe the victim and dress him in clean clothes and position him around the apartment for companionship. Nilsen had worked as a public servant and was a staunch union activist. It was quite odd to Dave, but lurking below the surface of what seemed at first glance to be the serial killer's propensity for power and domination was a twisted form of democracy. It was why Ted Bundy had worked on a presidential campaign. Serial killers don't see their murders as individual acts. What they see in the act of murder is the assimilation of one individual — into something greater. "Dead people," serial killer Charles Starkweather once said, "are all on the same level."

"Sorry, what did you say?" Louise asked. She had plugged one ear against the music from the living room. As she leaned towards Dave, the swooshing curl of her bangs hugged her forehead perfectly. Louise smelled a little like cucumbers, he thought. A bolt of laughter rose above the din of shuffling feet and indistinct conversation.

"Why did you choose culinary school?" Dave repeated. "You know, instead of just working in a restaurant?" he practically shouted the question this time. The kitchen was getting hot. Auggie must have something in the oven.

Louise set her wine down on the counter.

"You mean why am I paying tens of thousands of dollars in tuition for the privilege of ruining my waistline and overall well being?"

"Don't forget the nightmares about chicken history," Dave joked. In reality, nothing Louise had said was true for Dave. Dave had lost weight since moving to California. He didn't worry about the costs of culinary school because he was a kept man. Todd Bridges was paying for everything. Bridges even left cash on the counter each Monday for sundries and Bridges had selected and purchased Dave's set of culinary knives. And when it came to chicken history, Dave finally felt connected to a culture that mattered, to a culture that hadn't been politicized. If anything, his sense of well being had grown since starting culinary school.

But then Dave began thinking about another serial killer, possibly the worst of them all, a serial killer that Todd Bridges had told Dave about over a sensational dinner of traditional Nasi Goreng Kambing — Indonesian rice with goat. Touching the dossier lightly with his fingers, as if it were blazing hot, Todd Bridges told Dave about David Parker Ray, the infamous 'Toy Box Killer.' Ray used his daughter to lure his victims to a sound proofed trailer he nicknamed 'Satan's Den.' Each victim was drugged, only to regain her consciousness while strapped to a medical table inside Satan's Den.

"In a way, I've been through part of that experience," Bridges had suggested. "I've been strapped to a metal table, anyway."

Except that what followed in the case of David Parker Ray was absolutely bananas. Victims awakened to a tape recording of David Parker Ray's voice, a forty five minute recording detailing precisely what he planned to do with his victim — which was unimaginable.

"I only made it through fifteen minutes of the recording," Todd Bridges had said, shoving a spoonful of the sweet and salty Indonesian rice into his mouth. Part of the enjoyment of Nasi Goreng, Dave discovered, was how long it took to chew. But in this instance, the chewing made their conversation about David Parker Ray even longer and more brutalizing. "I had to stop at the point where David Parker Ray described how he would strip his victim naked, tie her to a metal rack, swab her privates with animal musk — and then bring in his two German Shepherds."

"I'm joking," Louise flipped her palm at Dave, as if people like David Parker Ray didn't exist. "I'm not worried about my waistline. Though I am worried about my bank account, you know?" Louise had to shout this last part about her bank account to be heard over the noise from the living room. "Actually," she yelled. "I don't really want to cook or even work in a restaurant." She shrugged. "Don't tell Yiannis. But my goal is a food adjacent career, like food critic or a job on a cooking show like Chopped."

"Ted Allen has been hosting that show for twenty five years," Dave said. He had no idea he knew that until Louise had mentioned the show. "They've done forty seasons, so I guess it must be a pretty good job," Dave concluded. "But I don't think Ted Allen gets to taste any of the food."

"What about the fourth plate?" Louise asked. "Contestants always cook four plates of food. There are only three judges." Louise drew a breath. Yelling to be heard made it hard to finish more than short sentences. "That fourth plate must go to the host."

"I saw an interview once where Ted Allen talked about how the fourth plate was for the reveal, for when they reveal who got chopped. In fact, Allen said that there is so much photographing of the food that goes on behind the scenes, that the judges almost always have to eat the food cold," Dave said.

"Oh," Louise seemed deflated.

"And you know that hallway?" Dave continued, "The hallway contestants walk down when they get chopped? That's a reproduction. It's a reproduction of the hallway in the original studio in New York. Can you believe that? When they moved the show to Hollywood, they built an exact replica of the chopped hallway from Queens, New York."

Dave felt terrible, like he was shitting all over Louise's future plans. He wasn't. Such facts about the show really did interest him. But it felt shitty just the same. Dave was very glad that Death Row Restaurant, whatever it would be like, would not be a competition.

"Food critics are definitely pretentious," Louise admitted. "But that's also what I like about the job," she said. "It's like it's so pretentious that it crosses over and becomes genuine." She had moved closer to Dave, although he couldn't recall when this had happened.

"That's why I like culinary school," Dave began, shoving a finger into the leftover ice from his gin and tonic. "I didn't think I would like it. This all happened very fast for me," Dave indicated basically everything in the apartment. "God, the timing of it all. I still can't believe it. But absolutely, recognizing food as serious, there's something wonderful about that."

"Is that why you started culinary? You had a food epiphany?"

That had absolutely nothing to do with why Dave had started culinary school. Death Row Restaurant wasn't about food in that sense. Even after months of training as a chef and countless dinners with Todd Bridges, Dave still had no idea what kind of food the restaurant would serve. He knew they had to serve something, but he also knew that the food didn't really matter so long as serial killers cooked it and served it.

Someone in the living room was smoking a clove cigarette. Dave used to argue in college that clove cigarettes only existed to annoy other people at parties. He couldn't imagine saying that now.

"No," Dave finally said. "Starting culinary school had almost nothing to do with food, in fact."

Louise gripped Dave's elbow. Already, tonight felt like one of those nights where getting drunk would have a certain cap on it. Like one of those parties where even if Dave tried to get really drunk, he wouldn't succeed because he would be too involved in conversations.

"You want to get high and explain that?" Louise asked.

———

Dave did not in fact want to get high. But before he could answer, Auggie came up behind Louise and slipped his arm around her waist. Clearly, they were a couple.

"You guys go ahead," Dave said. "I'm going to mingle."

"Nice talking with you, Dave," Louise called over her shoulder.

"Same," Dave said.

Auggie turned down the music and a good portion of the party disappeared into the bedroom to get high. Dave wandered around the apartment, checking out Auggie's stuff. He had a nice old sofa, soft and comfortable. Dave sat on it briefly. Dave liked well used things, which was why he was such a good flight attendant, riding around on planes built in the 1970's and sleeping in hotel beds that were slept in every night of the year.

"But then again, everyone uses their bed basically every night," Dave said to himself. No one was around, really. Just a couple talking closely in a corner and occasionally sipping drinks. Auggie's apartment was sort of retro, too. A glass brick wall separated his television from the hallway, for instance. And just beyond that, vertical blinds swayed whenever someone walked past.

Someone started coughing in the other room and there was a roar of laughter.

Auggie also had a sizable metal wall sculpture. It was faux gold, which had rubbed off in spots and looked sort of like a chicken or peacock but with feathers shaped like leaves, a half plant, half fowl creature made of gold. Dave thought the sculpture lent a tropical appeal. Dave finished his drink, but he felt like he was getting more sober. Should he call it a night? It was a little too early to leave without seeming snotty or like a loser. And Dave had only really talked to one person at the party. It was only ten o'clock. Which meant that Todd Bridges could probably pick him up, if he hadn't disappeared into Teardrop Park on a massive bender. Dave could only imagine the stories he'd be subjected to on the drive home with Todd Bridges, drug binges and coked out sex parties. And here he was leaving a party by himself at 10pm.

"You left a party at ten o'clock? I once partied for five straight days on meth. I spent three of those days looking for a twenty dollar bill I was sure I had lost somewhere in my apartment. I even broke into my neighbor's house to look for it there," Dave could imagine Bridges saying, before launching into a description of how many women he'd had sex with over that five day party.

It was enough to cement Dave's resolve to get another drink and linger.

The bedroom door pitched open and about ten very high looking culinary school initiates came out squinting, their eyes moist from laughter. Dave went to the bar and fixed himself a third gin and tonic, first muddling a lime with the back of a spoon, then adding the ice, gin and finally the tonic. He came back and stood in almost the exact spot he had stood in a few minutes ago. The group of stoners was continuing an argument that had started while they were getting high.

"Dude, we already had Arnold Schwarzenegger as a governor."

"Yeah, but did you have The Terminator? No, you fucking didn't." One of the guys said this as if it was a verbal dagger. Dave didn't know the guy's name.

"Schwarzenegger was a pretty good governor," the guy said. "The Cato Institute assigned him an 'A' rating for his fiscal policies." He took an index card out of his pocket on which he'd written a quote from the Cato Institute assigning Arnold Schwarzenegger an 'A' rating for his fiscal policy. He passed the card around.

"Yeah, but imagine if you had The Terminator as your governor. Not this Arnold Schwarzenegger guy, but the fucking Terminator. Like imagine if you could do that, if you could hire an actor to do a real job, but to do it in character the whole time and never break character. Imagine getting Walter White to run a Costco? Not Bryan Cranston, the actor. But Walter fucking White. Tell me Walter White wouldn't run the best fucking Costco in America?"

"Walter White isn't a real person. You can't hire someone to be Walter White 24/7. He's really Bryan Cranston. And he needs people to write the script and tell him what to say and do. He can't just run a fucking Costco you douche."

"Of course he can. He totally fucking can. You couldn't get just any actor to play Walter White. It has to be Bryan Cranston. He occupied that character. He wasn't always just reading lines they fed him"

"That doesn't make him capable of knowing what to do and say without a script. If that were true, they wouldn't need writers on the show at all. Real people have to figure out what to do and say. "

"Except serial killers," Dave interjected.

He hadn't planned on saying anything. Everyone turned to Dave expectantly. Their foreheads were all shiny from drinking cheap beer. "Okay, look," Dave began, setting down his drink. "Look. I used to be a flight attendant. Now I'm not. But when you're a serial — when you've committed crimes like these guys have — that's who you are. Take for example, Gary Ridgway, the Green River Killer. Take him, for instance. Gary Ridgway was convicted of forty nine murders, mostly teenage girls, sex workers, runaways. He strangled them. He was the last thing forty nine women ever saw. Imagine that. Imagine you're at work in a restaurant kitchen and you fuck up a galette because your hands are sore from strangling a teenage runaway."

"Jesus, they need to catch this motherfucker."

"Are you fucking stupid? He said they convicted him of forty eight murders. They already caught him."

"Forty nine," Dave corrected them. "Gary Ridgway killed forty nine women. He even brought his kid along for one of the murders."

"That's sick."

"Yeah," Dave agreed. "It is sick. Of course it's sick. But look, if Gary Ridgway, the Green River Killer, a guy who claimed he actually killed more than ninety women, well let's say Gary Ridgway also rescued stray dogs and nursed them back to health. Let's say he did that. Let's say he rushed into a burning building and saved a toddler. Let's say he did that, too. Who is Gary Ridgway? He's the fucking Green River Killer, that's who he is." Dave was out of breath. He panted a few times.

"How did we get on that topic," Auggie announced, emerging from the bedroom with Louise draped all over him. Her big forehead curl was perfect. It nearly broke Dave's heart. "Chefs, it's time for the flambé contest," Auggie announced. Dave wondered how many other things Auggie would say in that same announcer's voice. What if a person spent a whole day just making announcements? It struck Dave that prison guards likely did exactly that, as did bus drivers and even cashiers.

Dave couldn't wait to flambe something.

In the kitchen, Auggie began setting out ingredients, everything from Kasseri cheese to apple sorbet, graham crackers, bananas, rum, cinnamon, heavy whipping cream, eggs.

"And we're starting with these," Auggie said, lining up a row of shot glasses and setting a bottle of absinthe on the counter. "The Russian root beer."

Dave had never heard of such a thing. And part of him, the part that had shot past forty five a few years ago, wasn't sure a bunch of stoned, half trained line cooks should start playing with fire. But before Dave could object, Auggie had lined up the absinthe shots in a neat row — and lit them all on fire. There was something lovely about it. It reminded Dave of holding a candle in church when he was a kid, on Christmas Eves with his father. And this memory always made Dave realize that his father was unknowable at this point, just like Conrad Bain was now unknowable to Todd Bridges. This was partly due to the hue left over from strong childhood memories and the long stretches of absence or estrangement that had intervened in these relationships in adulthood. It occurred to Dave that Gary Ridgway's unknowability (like why on earth did he take his kid along for one of his fucking murders?) wasn't all that different. The only difference was that Ridgway's unknowability became his crimes.

Dave and Todd Bridges had spent a great deal of time discussing Gary Ridgway. Part of it was that Bridges had shown a keen interest in USP Florence, the supermax prison in Colorado where Ridgway (and a host of other high profile killers) were being housed. Interestingly, USP Florence offers only one advanced occupational training program — a program in restaurant management and culinary arts. While Gary Ridgway was similar to other notorious serial killers who showed a certain pride in their murders (Ridgway boasted to investigators that "choking was what I did, and I was pretty good at it"), Ridgway was also different in how unbearably ordinary and non-descript his everyday life was. Ridgway won awards for perfect attendance at work and he hid his crimes by making them ordinary aspects of his daily life. If Gary Ridgway pulled a muscle dragging a body through the woods, he would file a workman's compensation claim for something that happened at work. Unlike Dennis Rader, who sought recognition for his crimes and kept a huge stash of trophies, Gary Ridgway kept nothing from his victims. He was, in this very pure way, all about the act. Ridgway even rejected reliving or revisiting the act through souvenirs, which Dennis Rader relished. Whereas Rader once killed one of his neighbors and John Wayne Gacy buried corpses under his house, Ridgway resisted the urge to murder anyone close to him and was meticulous about hiding the bodies of the women he strangled. If a victim scratched him during a kill, Ridgway clipped her fingernails. If Ridgway drove too close to a road where he'd murdered someone, he bought new tires. Gary Ridgway took the jewelry from his victims and left it in restrooms for others to take home with them.

While all of these things were exceedingly practical ways to elude capture, the strange truth was that no one likes to discuss Gary Ridgway. Even after his capture, Ridgway's wife and extended family refused to talk to the media. Bridges was fascinated by this, how most of what we know about Gary Ridgway comes from his co-workers at Kenworth Trucking, where Gary Ridgway worked as a journeyman painter for thirty two years.

Dave looked over the ingredients Auggie was now setting out on the counter for the flambé contest and had a sudden insight about what to cook. He was going to make a version of Baked Alaska. Crushed vanilla wafers, chocolate chips, vanilla ice cream, a quick meringue topped with flaky salt and an absinthe flambé. It was, Dave realized, exactly the kind of dessert he liked to make, both highbrow and lowbrow at the same time. As Dave gathered his ingredients, he imagined working as a line cook next to Gary Ridgway, whom co-workers had nicknamed 'steady Eddy.'

By all accounts, Ridgway liked routines. He ate lunch at the same table, sitting in the same seat for twenty four straight years. Ridgway liked to peruse swap meet catalogs, to tell jokes and always had his little coffee thermos with him. Bridges liked that. He liked that Ridgway cried at church and often watched television with a bible in his lap. He liked that Ridgway was an obsessive gardener. He liked that Ridgway played freshman football in high school, and that when police interviewed his coaches after Ridgway's capture for more than fifty murders, none of the coaches could recall what position Ridgway had played. But more than anything, Ridgway had found a job that really suited him. He painted designs on trucks. This required meticulously taping off the design, strip by strip. He had to match both halves of the design, or it wouldn't look right. A single design often took an entire day to tape off and paint. Only a certain kind of personality could do this work. And Ridgway always wanted to do quality work.

Details like this, Dave had learned, as he crushed the vanilla wafers in his hand before mixing them with the chocolate chips, were of particular importance to Todd Bridges. While Bridges was also drawn towards Dennis Rader's meticulous application of compliance officer rules (measuring the height of people's lawns with a ruler), it was clear that Rader was interested in wielding some sort of authority. Rader had tried and failed to become a police officer. Once, Rader even made a jacket for his compliance work, with POLICE on the back, and wore it around town until he was instructed not to. But Ridgway was different. He didn't instrumentalize his work towards some other end. He, perhaps more than any other killer, understood that what he did was who he was.

This isn't to say everybody was shocked when Ridgway was arrested for being the Green River Killer. Gary Ridgway had long been suspected by police. Women who worked at Kenworth Trucking hated Ridgway's habit of whispering things in their ear or sneaking up behind them and scaring the crap out of them when they turned around. But these were just quirks. And many of Ridgway's female co-workers recalled how Ridgway liked to ask a lot of questions about their lives. He was a good listener and very attentive. If they changed their appearance, Ridgway always noticed.

What would it really be like to work with someone like Gary Ridgway? Dave wondered, as Auggie lined up a second round of shots and lit them on fire. Could it be as ordinary as his colleagues at Kenworth Trucking found it?

With all his ingredients ready, Dave was about to start crafting his meringue when he got a call from Todd Bridges.

"Meet me downstairs in five minutes. We've got a meeting. Don't forget my hat. "

Before Dave could even respond, Bridges hung up. Dave's hands hovered over his ingredients. He had a very hard time walking away from them.

But Dave knew Todd Bridges. He didn't change what he was doing to accommodate others. Dave understood that although he was just a culinary school student and potential restaurant manager, he was always on call. And that Death Row Restaurant experienced near constant emergencies that had to be dealt with, the same way a cardiologist might have to run to the hospital in the middle of the night. It was eleven o'clock, though. Who could they possibly be meeting? Dave almost thought he must've misheard what Bridges had said, until Bridges sent a follow up text reminding Dave not to forget his hat. Bridges had already lost enough in Victor Heights over his years as a meth head. He didn't want his hat added to the list.

PART IV: DEATH ROW RESTAURANT

BRIDGES SNATCHED his hat as soon as Dave got in the car.

He just reached over and took it off of Dave's head. It reminded Dave of the way the police had taken his sunglasses off his face in Eisenhower airport, when he was arrested for his unauthorized use of the emergency slide. As with that moment, Dave had a gap in his life. And the hat looked so much better on Todd Bridges than it had looked on him. Dave had probably looked like a guy wearing someone else's hat the whole time at Auggie's party. In fact, nearly everything Dave was currently wearing, except for his underwear, belonged to Todd Bridges.

Bridges pulled out into traffic. The night air was crisp and invigorating and the two absinthe shots Dave had gulped on his way out of the party had mellowed him considerably. Bridges was twitchy and hunched over the steering wheel as the car cut through the night. But Bridges wasn't stoned. Dave knew that if Bridges had gotten high in Teardrop Park, he would be off on a bender that might last days, weeks, even take over the rest of his life. It must be strange to know that one hit of coke or meth could catapult you into a lost week, into lost months or even lost years.

"So what were you doing while I was at the party?" Dave asked. "Did you take a walk down memory lane in Teardrop Park?"

"No," Bridges said, failing to elaborate as he pulled onto the highway.

His abruptness surprised Dave.

"Where are we going?" Dave asked. "Who are we meeting?" But he asked this right when Bridges was passing an eighteen wheeler, so Bridges wasn't able to respond. "I said, where are we going?" Dave reiterated, once Bridges had completed the maneuver.

"Ontario," Bridges muttered, like a bus driver.

"Canada?"

"No. Ontario, California."

"Why?"

Bridges hit the brakes. The eighteen wheeler roared by them. Everything felt a little out of control to Dave.

"Are you going to question everything I do?" Bridges demanded. "It's a meeting. It's for Death Row Restaurant. This is when she could do it."

"Okay. Okay," Dave said. And somehow, he couldn't shake the idea that it was Bridges who had set up this meeting in the middle of the night without telling him about it, that in classic celebrity fashion, Bridges wanted a meeting to happen when and where no one wanted to do it.

———

Dave couldn't have been more right.

"This is where we're meeting?" he asked, jumping out of the car as soon as they pulled up in front of the Ontario Mall. From the way Todd Bridges was acting, Dave felt like they were late. Plus, it was almost midnight.

"Be nice," Bridges muttered, inexplicably.

"Why are you dropping me off?"

"Because this meeting is for you, not me," Bridges said.

"You want me to pitch the restaurant?" Dave croaked. Why did everything have to be so hard to understand? All Dave wanted was to be able to be who he was and own what he did.

"We're done pitching the restaurant," Bridges said. "That's all finished. It's all lined up." Because Bridges was in the driver's seat and Dave was standing on the sidewalk, he seemed very far away. "This is the next step. You'll do fine," Bridges said. Then he drove away.

Dave stood there for a few minutes. He thought he should wait for Todd Bridges to get back from parking the car, so they could go in together. But after several minutes, he decided to just go into the restaurant and get started. After all, it's not like Bridges was giving him any sense of what they were there to do.

Dave had been to the Rainforest Cafe once before, with his sister and his niece. He recalled robotic gorillas that beat their chests every so often, faux waterfalls, plastic trees and the piped in sounds of tropical thunderstorms. At the time, Dave had contrasted the place with many of the more authentic places he'd eaten at when he was traveling the world, roadside cafes in Ho Chi Minh City and the daily box lunches he would purchase at subway stations in Tokyo, each with a local flair.

But now that Dave no longer believed in the authenticity of those places he had traveled to, the true horror of the Rainforest Cafe hit him hard.

If Dave had been at all giddy or light headed from the flaming absinthe shots he'd drank at Auggie's party, the Rainforest Cafe quickly sobered him up. Just getting to the hostess stand required crossing a mini gift shop selling every rainforest creature imaginable (in the form of a plushie, key chain or hat). Hardly anyone made it to the actual restaurant without buying something. And right away, Dave knew that Death Row Restaurant wouldn't feel like this. Walking through the gift shop at San Quentin with its prisoner made artifacts and its museum of shanks where customers would select their silverware would be totally different from this.

"I'm meeting someone," Dave said to the hostess, trying to look around for someone sitting alone.

"Your name?" The hostess asked, clutching several menus.

"Dave Aslin," Dave said. "Or maybe Todd Bridges," he added. "And can we get a table away from the rhinos?" Dave recalled that the rhinos would occasionally turn and playfully gore certain tables while eating. He wasn't in the mood.

"I'm sorry, sir," the hostess answered. "Your party is already seated and waiting. Would you like me to check if a different table is available?"

A thunderstorm rumbled in the background. Dave eyed the sky out of habit. The ceiling was concealed by a faux tropical canopy studded with glowing tree frogs.

"No. That's fine," Dave replied. An awkward moment followed in which Dave waited for the hostess to move from behind the hostess stand to guide him to his table as she made a notation in the reservations book. As it happened, the table wasn't near the rhinos. It was behind a parade of elephants in a relatively secluded corner of the restaurant. Dave and the hostess rounded the mother elephant and her two plastic baby elephants, all frozen in playful postures and half submerged in a pool of water. And sitting at a table right next to the playful elephants — was Kate.

"Oh my god," Dave muttered. "Kate, uh, hi."

"Sit down, Dave, Mr. Aslin," Kate gestured to a chair. It was a table for two.

"Don't we need a seat for Todd?" Dave couldn't believe how calm and wonderful Kate seemed. She looked as though she might be genuinely happy. And for a second, Dave regretted that he hadn't just agreed to marry Kate in Eisenhower airport and then taken her on the trip around the world she so fancied. How hard would it have been? They could have started at Les Village in Tejakula, Bali. They could have stayed at the Amrita Salt Farm Villas, an inexpensive guest house right on a little curl of a black sand beach. Each day Dave and Kate could have watched locals fetching seawater in palm leaf buckets.

"Not tonight," Kate said. "Tonight it's just you and me." She motioned towards the seat across from her again. Her fingernails had been expertly buffed and Dave felt suddenly embarrassed by his calloused hands and the many small scars he had from chopping accidents with his knives. Dave felt incomplete without Bridges' hat and wished he was wearing more of his own clothes.

"I was at this thing earlier," Dave said, motioning to his whole body. "You know. Victor Heights. Colleagues."

"How's culinary school going?" Kate asked

"It's fine. Good. You know," Dave said. How did she know about culinary school? Bridges must have told her when he set up this date. What a guy. "Look, Kate. I'm sorry about what happened. I just—"

"I know," she said, in this voice that made her seem far older than she was. It was strange talking with Kate with fake baby elephants behind her. When they were dating, she had worn her hair in a bob, which helped when Wichita made her nauseous. But now, Kate's hair was long and fell in a side braid across her right shoulder. This made her appear to be looking at Dave a little sideways.

"Are you still with United?" Dave asked, as Kate handed him a menu.

A waiter hovered.

"I'll have a Blue Nile," Kate said.

"Do you want the souvenir glass?"

"No thank you."

"And would you like to make a donation to our 'Save the Nile River Fund? I can add it to your bill."

"I didn't know the Nile River needed saving," Dave muttered. "Seems like almost everything needs a heroic intervention these days." He thought about Yiannis, whether his teaching qualified as some sort of intervention.

"Sure," Kate said, tapping a few times on the waiter's portable credit card machine to make her selections.

"For you, sir?"

"Got any absinthe?"

"Unfortunately, no. But perhaps you'd like some anise? On the rocks or straight up?"

"You know what, I'll just take one of these Cheetah Rita's. No souvenir glass. Thanks."

They waited for the waiter to depart before speaking.

"Jesus. Why the fuck are we meeting here, Kate? This place is ridiculous."

"I thought you liked American kitsch? Down home Wichita."

"This isn't kitsch," Dave said, defensively. "And I don't like 'down home' anything. I'm not even sure if I like Wichita anymore. I don't much know what I like, but I know at least a few things about what I don't. And Jesus, this qualifies. Of course this qualifies." Dave motioned to the canopy of plastic leaves above them, and to a fake monkey dangling from one of the branches. The monkey's head swiveled from side to side whenever a fake flash of lighting lit up the canopy's underbelly. Why did Kate think he would like this place? It was like so many of Dave's past relationships, all of them, really, that had ended with this feeling that the whole thing had been a giant misunderstanding.

"Isn't that why we both ended up with Todd Bridges?" Kate suggested. She slid her chair slightly backwards and crossed one leg over the other. Dave didn't know why, but it felt like Kate was distancing herself from him. He wondered briefly if he should think more carefully about what he wanted to say, if he should try to present a version of himself that Kate might find more appealing. After all, Dave was extraordinarily lonely. And the thought of another week in Yiannis' kitchen classroom, in a room full of people he felt nothing other than a formal connection to, felt unbearable.

"What do you mean that you 'ended up' with Todd Bridges?"

Dave asked. He had hoped to be more agreeable but found himself suddenly jealous. "Are you dating him or something?" He was about to say that Bridges was way too old for Kate, but he caught himself just in time. Todd Bridges was only about five years older than Dave was.

Before Kate could answer, the waiter arrived with their drinks. He bent down. His serving tray was constructed out of plastic cobras weaved into a wicker basket. The waiter set their drinks in front of them and then adjusted a set of plastic palm fronds behind Kate's head.

"The elephants frolic in their pool at midnight. This way you won't get wet."

"Thank you," Kate whispered, smiling. Then she turned to Dave. "My relationship with Mr. Bridges is purely professional," she insisted. "I learned that from what happened in Wichita."

Dave winced. He'd never thought about whether his relationship with Kate had been inappropriate. Officially, Dave hadn't been Kate's boss. But unofficially, he had been the lead flight attendant and a sort of mentor.

"Kate, I never meant to —" Dave trailed off. He had no idea what to say. Her green eyes sparkled. She looked absolutely magnificent. Dave almost couldn't look at her. They might very easily have gotten married. And Kate wasn't only beautiful. She was sensitive on a visceral level. And Dave still thought their breakup was a misunderstanding. He lowered his eyes. The table was a plastic version of a tree stump, with large, concentric rings to indicate the tree's age. Brochures with cartoons explaining how to determine a tree's age from its rings dangled from the sides of the table. Over the years, food had gotten into the rings. A subtle vomity smell wafted from them, which made Dave strangely nostalgic for his previous relationship with Kate. It had been so easy to know what to do at that time, Dave thought. Her nausea had been entirely straightforward. In fact, he had always known what to do around Kate, until that moment in Eisenhower Airport when she asked him to marry her. Dave wanted to reach across the table and take Kate's hand.

"To old times," Dave said, holding up his Cheetah Rita. They clinked glasses. "It's wonderful to see you, Kate," Dave added. He had plenty of questions. How on earth did she get involved in this — involved with Todd Bridges and Death Row Restaurant? But it didn't seem like the right time to press Kate on this. Whatever had led her here, Dave was glad for it.

"We've got a date," Kate said. "A date for the grand opening of Death Row Restaurant. It's going to be September 16th."

"That's just a few months away," Dave gasped. He was incredulous. How could they possibly have a date for the grand opening?

"I know it's sudden," Kate began. "But the reality is that if we miss this window we would have to wait another year. Who knows what things will look like politically then?"

"Why would we have to wait another year?" Dave asked. Jesus, he still had another year of culinary school. How could they possibly open in a few months?

"It's part of the employment contract with Dennis Rader," Kate said. "He negotiated it. Rader gets to choose the restaurant's opening Day. And he wants Death Row Restaurant to open on the anniversary of the day he murdered Vicki Wegerle. September 16th." Kate picked up her Blue Nile and took a long pull from it. "The Wegerle murder," Kate continued, "is absolutely critical to Rader. For more than a decade, police suspected Vicki's husband of the murder. They didn't attribute that murder to Dennis Rader at all. It was only on the thirtieth anniversary of the Otero murders, when Rader saw a news program about it, that he decided he wanted credit for the murder of Vicki Wegerle. This was the start of his capture. Rader sent polaroids of Vicki to police, polaroids from after he'd strangled her. And he sent police a copy of Vicki's driver's license. There was just no denying it at that point. Vicki Wegerle was a victim of BTK. This incident started the game of cat and mouse between Rader and police that ended with Rader's capture. But while in prison, Rader realized that he had never wanted to be like Jack the Ripper or the Zodiac killer. They had never been captured. No one knew who they were. Rader wanted people to know he committed those murders. Rader was captured earlier than he had planned, but Rader had always wanted to be exposed. September 16th. That's the date."

"Why is that bastard calling the shots?" Dave shot at her. "What else is he demanding?"

"This was negotiated a long time ago," Kate said.

Kate had this utterly quiet and professional way of delivering her points, so that they arrived stillborn, arrived as immutable truths to be accepted rather than debated.

"Listen, Kate," Dave began. Despite all the news about Death Row

Restaurant, he wanted to talk to Kate about their breakup. "I want you to know that although I liked Wichita, although maybe I still do like Wichita, the thing is, I was going through something similar to what you were going through at that time. I mean, I was trying to wrap my head around how many things in life turn out to be dead ends or just things you have to endure," Dave admitted. "And if Death Row Restaurant is my solution then I don't see why it can't be your solution, too," he offered. "I'm not unhappy that you're involved in this. If that's what you want."

Kate was quiet for a moment.

"Thank you, Dave," Kate said. She had been sitting with her fingers laced in front of her like a judge. And after Dave made this remark, she altered her posture. "Restaurant operations questions like the menu and kitchen setup can be left for you and Todd to review at a later time," she began, turning a page on a legal pad. Dave hadn't even realized Kate was consulting a legal pad. It filled him with despair. "What Todd wanted me to get you up to speed on are the interviews with staff."

"I don't think I have time right now," Dave offered. "Cooking school is a significant commitment." Cooking school was in fact, Dave's entire life.

"That's fine," Kate said. "Todd and I have finished the interviews and we wanted to fill you in on who we've decided to hire."

"Wait. Todd did the interviews without me? The final hiring decisions? The decisions about the serial killers I will be working side by side with in a tiny kitchen? He made all of the staffing decisions without even consulting me?" Waiting in the parking lot at El Dorado Correctional Facility (while Bridges was interviewing Dennis Rader) was one thing. At that point, Dave had just come around to the whole idea of the restaurant. Back then, he felt like he was having the same conversion experience that Anthony Bourdain had had while waiting for his parents outside of La Pyramide. Back then, Dave felt like he was on the verge of discovering his life's ambition.

But since that time, Dave had been intimately involved in Death Row Restaurant. How could Bridges have made all of the hiring decisions without including him? Without even mentioning it to him? Dave felt expendable, like a temp employee, like someone who just shows up and does what he is told.

"Todd wanted you to focus on culinary school," Kate explained. "He had the impression that you were deeply invested in it."

"I am invested in it," Dave asserted. "But I had expected to be a part of the hiring process. After all, I will be running the kitchen."

Kate leaned forward as if to tell him something confidential. She was wearing a light pink blouse with white buttons and her shirt collar lifted up slightly as she leaned across the fake tree stump table.

"Don't take it personally," Kate said. "Todd is dealing with a lot. Investors, politicians, regulations. He's got all the red tape of a maximum security prison to contend with and all the red tape of the health department," she looked both ways, as if she were crossing a street. "I'm sure Todd would have liked to work more closely with you on the interviews. But it just wasn't possible," Kate concluded. "And some very important staffing decisions still need to be made. We've had to make some changes," she finally said. "That's why Todd wanted me to meet with you," Kate leaned back, reached down next to her seat and pulled several manila file folders from a briefcase. Dave hadn't even noticed the briefcase. He must have blocked it out so as to view this meeting as a date. "We need to address the over whelmingly white and male staff we've hired."

"Wait a second," Dave said. "How are you so deeply ingrained in this process, Kate? I mean, I get that Todd has hired you in some official capacity," Dave said. "But when did all this happen? Why didn't anyone tell me about it?"

"I've been working with Death Row Restaurant since our last flight to Wichita," Kate said. "Todd approached me while waiting to deplane," she took a sip of her Blue Nile, made a puzzled face, as if wondering what the bartender was even going for with the drink. "Beyond that, I don't really want to get into it. That was a weird day," Kate admitted. "A lot happened in the few days after we broke up," she added. "I don't really want to go into it all. But Todd approached me about Death Row Restaurant and like you, it was the start of something for me," Kate said. The thunderstorm that had been churning in a steady patter throughout the Rainforest Cafe tapered away with a final rumble. A few crickets began chirping. "I'm sorry I hit that flush button," Kate added. Then she shrugged.

Dave was about to say something. But before he could open his mouth, the baby elephants behind Kate began this frolicking routine. It was pathetic, a clear indication that society had gone horribly wrong, especially when it came to restaurants.

"Are you ready to order?" their waiter asked.

———

Kate ordered the Tropical Island Chicken Salad, which was basically just chicken salad with some mangos thrown into the mix, served inexplicably on a toasted croissant. Dave wondered how she came to that decision, what her proclivities were. Did she usually gravitate towards sandwiches? Towards chicken? Towards house specials? The Tropical Island Chicken Salad had a double palm frond rating on the menu, indicating 'house favorites.' It was odd, but Dave had never really ordered food with Kate in a restaurant without the guiding principle of anti-nausea.

"Do you recommend the Taste of the Islands?" Dave asked their waiter. He was one of those twenty something guys who was already balding.

"It's one of the house favorites," he shrugged.

"Yeah, but do you personally like it?"

"The waiter scratched his armpit in response, sort of like an orangutan.

"Tell you what," Dave said. "I'll have the rotisserie chicken with a side of China Island chicken salad and an order of Chicken Chimi Cha Chas." Dave turned to Kate. "I have to try two or three different chicken dishes per night. It's part of my training regimen."

"Throw an order of Hickory Chicken in on that, then," Kate said, flipping shut her menu with a flourish. "And two banana daiquiris."

Their waiter disappeared between a huge tree snail and this crocodile that suddenly released a bunch of mist from his nostrils. A Mexican janitor appeared and began scrubbing this giant tree trunk with a huge sponge, paying special attention to the fake vines. Dave wondered if some kid had barfed on it earlier in the day.

"You see," Kate said. "There's literally no rhyme or reason to a place like this. We just ordered food for six people and our waiter didn't bat an eye. It's not just the decor in here that's problematic," she added. "The whole restaurant business has just become an exercise in doing whatever they think a customer wants. It's demeaning to everyone."

Kate dropped a stack of dossiers on the table. It reminded Dave of all the dinners he had shared with Todd Bridges during Dave's first year at culinary school. For months now, Dave had wondered if Bridges was even doing anything to get Death Row Restaurant started. Until a few minutes ago, Dave had believed Bridges hadn't even started interviewing outside of Dennis Rader. And now they were just tweaking staff so as to be more diverse.

Dave chugged his Cheetah Rita. "Is Gary Ridgway on the list?" Dave asked. "What was it like to interview that guy? I hear he's boring as hell."

Kate took another sip of her Blue Nile. The drink had come in the souvenir glass after all. A mistake. Dave wondered if they would get to keep it.

"I'm not here to talk about Gary Ridgway, or Joseph DeAngelo or "

"The Golden State Killer?" Dave blurted out. Dave and Todd Bridges had talked about Joseph DeAngelo a dozen times, at least. They both felt like it was a stroke of luck that California authorities had finally captured the guy just in time to work the first shift at Death Row Restaurant. "Did you know that when the police finally arrested DeAngelo, after more than fifty rapes and a minimum of thirteen murders, he told police he had a roast in the oven? He really did, too. He had a roast in the oven when they took him into custody."

"Dave, Todd and I have discussed this and we've reached the conclusion that —"

"Or what about Scott Lee Kimball? Did you interview him? Not only did he commit a string of murders in Colorado, but the FBI let him out of prison to act as an informant. And while out of prison he may have gone on another murder spree, earning the nickname the 'West Mesa Bone Collector.'" Their daiquiris arrived, each with a full banana erection sticking out of the coconut glass. Without saying a word, their waiter set down the drinks and then scaled one of the fake trees next to the table. After releasing a latch, some faux vines with a tray attached plummeted and hung next to the table.

"Your food will be up momentarily. Anything else I can bring you folks right now?"

"No, thank you," Kate said. "I'm glad you are bringing these people up, Dave," she added. "This is exactly the problem. And it's why Todd asked me to shift my role from operations to public relations. When Todd and I interviewed Joseph DeAngelo it occurred to us both that although Todd is the principal owner, making Death Row Restaurant a black owned business, the entire staff of Death Row Restaurant was shaping up to be white and male. And that had to be a blow to the restaurant's authenticity."

"Todd said that?" Dave blurted out. He couldn't believe it.

"Well, when you visit prisons it becomes pretty obvious. Black people are only 13% of this country's population, but they make up nearly 40% of the population of prisons," Kate said. "If Death Row Restaurant is really interested in being authentic, an all white staff is, well, it doesn't reflect the reality of prison populations in America. Todd was quite certain you'd agree on this point, since you share the same concerns about the restaurant's total authenticity," Kate said.

"I wouldn't say our concerns are the same," Dave interrupted. "I mean, I don't even really know what Todd is trying to do. I live at his house and —"

"The Northridge house?" Kate asked.

"No," Dave said, a little confused. "Sun Valley. I thought Bridges lost the Northridge house. He told me his lawyer screwed him out of it."

"It doesn't matter," Kate said.

"I was saying, you know I live at his house and it's basically just like a television set to Todd. He never uses anything there. I think he likes having me live there just so he can make an entrance, like when he would burst onto the set during his sitcom." The janitor who'd been scrubbing vines this whole time sighed, wiped some sweat off his brow. He made eye contact with Dave, then went right back to scrubbing the vomity plastic vines. "One time Bridges had airpods in when he came over. He just walks right in. That's his whole thing. He arranges it in advance. And I swear I heard this faint applause from his ear buds, as if there was a studio audience and Bridges was making his entrance on a hit television show."

It was things like that which had made Dave wonder if Bridges was even serious about opening Death Row Restaurant. Even now, Dave wondered if this wasn't all some kind of documentary.

"Death Row Restaurant is black owned," Kate said, ignoring Dave's remark about Todd Bridges. "There is no logical reason for it to be operated exclusively by white men."

"Black people might be overrepresented in the overall prison population," Dave said. "But most serial killers are white men, right?"

Kate took her hair braid and tossed it over her shoulder.

"Todd thought the same thing," Kate stated. "But once you look into it, this turns out to be untrue. In fact, according to the FBI, white men make up 58% of male murderers. That's less than their 76% prevalence in the population. So while there are more white male murderers overall, the ratio at which they commit serial murder is not greater than any other group."

Dave had not seen this side of Kate. She was exceptional at delivering facts and placing them into context.

"And they're not all men," Kate opened the dossiers in front of her. "This is Beverly Allitt. She killed four children in fifty nine days and attempted to kill thirteen others. British tabloids nicknamed her 'the Angel of Death,'" Kate turned the page. "And what about Aileen Wournos? She murdered seven men, each shot at point blank range." She turned the page again. "And what about Juana Barazza? The female Mexican professional wrestler who was sentenced to seven hundred and fifty nine years in prison for beating, robbing, and strangling forty eight elderly women?" Kate closed the folder, slid it to the side and opened a second folder.

"We don't include serial killers who rob," Dave pointed out. "Todd's been really clear on that. Employees at Death Row Restaurant aren't just people on Death Row. The killers have to be invested in their act and they have to admit to what they did as who they are," he said. "While Bridges sometimes includes Charles Manson in his promotional materials, he would never actually hire the guy because Manson doesn't take responsibility for what he did. Manson always claimed to be innocent," Dave concluded.

"Manson's dead," Kate said. "And this isn't only about gender." She opened the second folder. "Have you ever heard of Anthony Sowell? The Cleveland Strangler? He raped and strangled at least eleven women on Cleveland's East side. One victim leapt out of a third story window to escape his clutches, and Sowell got in the ambulance with her and pretended to be her husband," Kate elaborated. "And as you can see, Mr. Sowell is African American."

"I'm not sure this counts as Anti-racism, Kate."

"What about Samuel Little?" Kate continued, unfazed. "Perhaps the most prolific serial killer in American history, who confessed to ninety three murders, and unlike Gary Ridgway, Little remembers every detail of his victims, all of their faces, enough to actually draw color pictures of them from memory?" Kate held up a sketch. A black woman with a high hairdo, tweezed eyebrows, mascara and a sad and bemused look on her face stared at Dave from beyond the grave. She looked young. Maybe even a teenager. It was crushingly sad.

"Jesus," muttered Dave.

"And is Samuel Little overlooked because he is black? Because his victims were black? And what about Lonnie Franklin 'The Grim Sleeper.' He was convicted of ten murders but admitted to police that his real victim count is probably closer to two hundred. The FBI found more than a thousand photos of different women in his apartment, either asleep — or dead —"

Dave was exhausted. He'd been in discussions like this with Todd Bridges, where the list of heinous killers was so long and gruesome that he became exhausted by it, both physically and spiritually.

"Look, Kate. I see what you are saying but the whole point of Death Row Restaurant is that none of that stuff matters. Other restaurants get embroiled in disputes over appropriating the food of other cultures or discrimination or exploitation claims, stealing tips and whatnot, the whole point of Death Row Restaurant is that none of that can happen there. These killers on Death Row, they can't be rehabilitated. That's the point of Death Row. Nothing a prisoner does on Death Row changes anything. They are who they are and they are never getting off Death Row. That's why San Quentin has no work or rehabilitation programs for Death Row inmates. But that's also why everything a Death Row inmate does counts as a deliberate act," Dave insisted. "Critics won't even be able to review Death Row Restaurant. Todd was working on a way to keep the restaurant completely off Tripadvisor, YELP and the Michelin Guides."

"Diversifying our staff isn't about publicity or 'cancel culture,'" Kate insisted. "This is California. A diverse staff helps give us the political clout needed to open the restaurant. California politics are central to making the restaurant a reality." Kate lifted her daiquiri to her face and took a huge bite of the banana. "Todd is working all the angles here," she insisted.

Did Bridges let Kate call him Todd?

"Did you know that Gavin Newsom had the gas chamber at San Quentin disassembled?" Kate continued. "Sections of the gas chamber were just sitting in a warehouse. It wasn't just a matter of renting it out," Kate asserted, as if Dave was totally naive. She was holding her drink in her hand but not drinking it, which bothered Dave.

"I guess I can leave the logistics up to you and Todd, then," he admitted. "Honestly, Kate, at this point I think I just want to cook," Dave stammered. "Cooking school has been something of a revelation. You see —"

"Dave, Todd has asked me to bring up something else with you," Kate interrupted. "Todd appreciates the investment you've made at Henderson Culinary. But it's time for you to get ready for the opening and Todd is, well, he's not very impressed with their program." She leaned forward, and Dave realized that this was the first time since he had sat down that Kate had turned her full attention to him. "Death Row Restaurant needs an executive chef who's been properly trained in sanitation and occupational safety. The program at Henderson, well, it seems to be mostly about chicken," Kate concluded.

"This is just the first year," Dave said defensively. "There are five semesters and —" he trailed off. He knew Yiannis' concerns when it came to chefs were more existential than practical. "Look," Dave said. "Henderson is a good school. Todd has to understand the order of operations here," he began. "To be a chef, you have to actually care about the food. That's why a chef learns about sanitation and occupational safety. It's not an extrinsic, legal or formal thing one has to do. It's part of actually being a chef."

Their waiter hovered, shoved a dangling sloth out of the way and began loading up their table with their various chicken dishes, using the hanging vine tray for the overflow.

"Is there anything else I can get you folks tonight?" the waiter asked.

———

The ride home with Todd Bridges was long. Dave was tired. He was tired of these impromptu meetings. He was tired of having to wrestle with his feelings. He was tired of bouncing back and forth between Death Row Restaurant as something he thought was absolutely necessary in the world and the idea that it was going to be awful. When Gary Ridgway is the employee you hope to work closely with, you know something is wrong, don't you?

Luckily, Bridges didn't much feel like talking. He asked Dave if he would mind riding in the back seat, as if Bridges were his driver, a bizarre reversal of the way they had started their association, with Dave catering to Bridges on that flight to Wichita, and later, driving him to El Dorado Correctional Facility. While the whole situation was ambiguous, Dave was fairly certain that he was being relegated to a backseat role with Death Row Restaurant. Kate apparently knew way more than he did about the restaurant. And she had done the job interviews with Bridges. Dave couldn't get over that. Kate had always seemed afraid of what she might uncover in the world. She seemed afraid to even leave Eisenhower Airport, as if something in Wichita was waiting for her, as if any vulnerability would immediately be pounced upon. This wasn't a weakness or character flaw. Dave understood that feeling too. Part of Dave's trips around the world came down to his attempt to find a place that felt like home, a place that could banish the floating, misunderstood feeling he'd lived with for decades. And Dave had felt better with Kate. Not because the feeling went away, but because he knew Kate was intimately acquainted with that feeling too.

He was flat out scared to open the restaurant, to actually work with guys like Gary Ridgway and Dennis Rader. Dave didn't know much about Anthony Sowell, but he knew that looking him up and reading about his horrid crimes would be exhausting. He couldn't face the prospect of it. And then, there was this part of Dave that was surprised and thrilled. Had Bridges pulled this off? Was Todd Bridges making a comeback? And if Bridges could return to the public stage with Death Row Restaurant, Dave imagined that anyone could. That even he could make a comeback and finish his life without having wasted it all.

And part of Dave was just flat out confused. Did Bridges still have his house in Northridge or not?

Dave skipped school at Henderson on Monday. He had a lot to think over. He wanted to call one of his old friends from United Airlines and tell him about Death Row Restaurant. But Dave couldn't imagine the conversation. He had never been able to tell anyone about the restaurant. It was just too bananas, too hard to explain, too personal. Dave always got this feeling that any explanation he provided would be misunderstood.

The day blew by in a haze. Dave felt queasy most of the morning. He skipped breakfast. Then he didn't eat lunch until around 3pm, which left him feeling bloated. By the time Bridges and Kate arrived at Bridges' house in Sun Valley for their executive council meeting, Dave was feeling a little unhinged. But he was kind of excited that things were moving forward. He figured the restaurant opening couldn't possibly happen by September. Even a run of the mill taco joint runs into issues, delays. Given that they were dealing with at least three maximum security prisons, they could probably count on at least ten times the obstacles. When Dave thought about it, getting serial killers transferred, trained and put to work in a restaurant kitchen, the whole thing still sounded impossible. At the very least, the September deadline would have to be pushed back, giving them at least another year to prepare, and giving Dave a chance to finish his program at Henderson.

Bridges arrived first, in his usual fashion. He called ahead to make sure the door was unlocked and then came right in. He was wearing ear buds and Dave listened for the applause. He wasn't sure if he heard it or not.

"I'm going to have a quick shower," Bridges announced, before disappearing upstairs.

Then Kate arrived with a giant tray of baklava. She set it on Bridges' coffee table, took a seat next to the couch and smoothed her skirt.

Dave wanted to tell her she looked lovely, but he thought he should be professional.

"How was your day?" Dave asked, just to make some conversation.

"Busy," Kate replied. She didn't elaborate.

Outside, the sun started to set. Something about the house in Sun Valley. It made Dave really tired at dusk. When the sunlight coming through Bridges' oddly shaped, modernist windows started to fade and give way to darkness, it always gave Dave this impression of blood draining from a wound.

"I've been meaning to ask you, Kate," Dave began, shifting in his seat. He thought the chair had popped a spring. Something was poking him from below. "Have you ever actually been to Bridges' house in Northridge?"

Kate glanced at the stairs. Her mouth fell open as Bridges turned a corner on the second floor and plodded down the steps. He was butt naked, whistling and carrying his white towel.

"Jesus. Todd. Do you have to do this?"

Kate didn't seem to care. Dave wondered if they were sleeping together. He grabbed a baklava, just for something to do.

"It's an exciting time," Bridges announced with that boyish grin of his, as he laid the white towel down on the couch before sitting. Bridges nodded to Kate, who began the meeting. It bothered Dave, the way they communicated without even speaking. That's how Kate and Dave's relationship had been as well. Dave used to know how Kate was feeling just from the sound of her breathing.

"Obviously, September 16th is coming up fast. It's just a few months away. We have a lot to organize before the opening. But before we get into specifics, Todd and I wanted to share with you some developments that you probably hadn't anticipated," Kate said.

"We had to play ball a little," Bridges elaborated. "Governor Newsom, Gavin, he had some 'asks,'" Bridges said. "It isn't enough for him that Death Row Restaurant is black owned. Newsom wanted the restaurant to have more black employees —"

"Kate told me that yesterday," Dave acknowledged. "Not a problem."

"— to have women employees, to have a Native American employee," Bridges continued, tossing Dave a few new dossiers.

"Billy Glaze? I've never heard of him."

"You can call him Jesse 'Sitting Crow,'" Bridges said. "Police used hair samples from a crowbar to convict him of three murders in 1986," Bridges continued. "He's suspected in more than fifty murders and 'Sitting Crow' bragged to police about killing at least twenty women, though he later claimed to be innocent."

"Wait," Dave began, tossing the dossier on the floor. He felt like too many things were coming at him at once. "If Billy Glaze claims innocence, how can he work at Death Row Restaurant?"

Bridges uncrossed his legs. All of a sudden, Dave couldn't stand this stupid peccadillo of Bridges needing to be naked.

"Can you just put a towel over your lap at least?" Dave blurted out. "This gets a little ridiculous." He turned to Kate, who had an expressionless look on her face, as if she was sitting in the waiting room at a dentist's office.

"Look, Dave," Bridges continued, fanning his crotch with a magazine. "We've had to make some accommodations here. This is how businesses work and you'd better get used to it. You're going to have to make accommodations in the kitchen from time to time, too. The bottom line is that Governor Newsom wouldn't agree to our business plan unless we had a Native American employee. It's part of his political platform. He wants to draw attention to the plight of Native Americans who have very high alcoholism rates, poverty rates and as a group, they are the most likely to be killed by police. Even more likely than black people. And there's no 'Native American Lives Matter' movement, so Newsom has adopted the cause."

"I understand," Dave said. "But how on earth are you going to announce this to the public?" Dave asked. He just couldn't imagine telling anyone about it. It was as if Death Row Restaurant, despite how much time and energy they had all put into it, was just a private idea, just something they all liked to muse about. "I can't picture the press release," Dave said. "I can't picture the governor giving a press conference on this. There's just no way."

"You must not be paying attention," Kate said. She handed Dave her phone, which she used to do when she was dry heaving into a Wichita toilet, and her mother was calling. Dave hit play and turned up the volume. On the screen was a reporter standing in front of San Quentin, the wind whipping his hair back.

"And the controversy over proposition 66 continues, Jane. The law was intended to speed up the appeals process of death row inmates, a process that can take in excess of twenty five years. And California leads the nation in the sheer number of inmates on Death Row, nearly eight hundred of them currently."

The report cut to footage of a burly prisoner, shackled at the ankles and waist being escorted by two correctional officers in San Quentin. The news reporter continued via voice over. Dave didn't recognize the prisoners they cut to. But he did recognize the procedure. At San Quentin, all Death Row inmates must be shackled and have a two guard escort anywhere they go.

"Proposition 66 has drawn fire from critics for a provision that allows death row inmates to transfer to other prisons in order to facilitate a quicker appeals process. These other facilities often have more lax restrictions, more privileges and some even have rehabilitation programs that Death Row inmates at San Quentin aren't allowed to participate in. Prisoners can even hold a job, with any money earned going to victims."

"Bob, are you saying that San Quentin has no rehabilitation and training programs?"

"Not exactly, Jane. San Quentin has one of the most robust rehabilitation programs in the nation." The wind had died down some, almost like a courtroom going still before a verdict. "San Quentin inmates can get their GED, take college classes and get training in auto repair, welding, and HVAC. San Quentin even has a program that trains prisoners to be firefighters and assists them with job placement after parole. But these programs are not available to Death Row inmates. A controversial position that Governor Newsom wants to change."

The program cut to footage of Gavin Newsom at a press conference. Newsom was barely fifty years old, not much older than Dave. He had a baby face and spoke slowly and confidently.

"We've been looking at some of the policies and structures for inmates of the top floor of San Quentin," Newsom began, "the unit that houses our Death Row inmates. The Adjustment Center. It's like a giant Costco, but with nothing to buy. That's not the American way," Newsom argued. The wind was positively whipping his hair, but he paid it no mind at all. "We need to reassess the status of these prisoners in terms of rehabilitation training. I'm not saying that prisoners condemned to death can be rehabilitated and released. But the state has to stop telling these people that there's no point in them doing anything. Because if that's the case, then the problem with California's Death Row isn't the time the appeals process takes. It's the fact that Death Row exists," Newsom concluded.

The program cut back to the reporter.

"When asked about the controversial practice of transferring prisoners to other facilities in order to provide rehabilitative programs, facilities where Death Row inmates get increased privileges, Newsom responded, 'We are looking into starting a rehabilitation program of our own, a program specifically geared to prisoners on Death Row. The citizens of California have spoken. They support Proposition 66.'"

"Bob, is it true that this new work program will be in culinary arts?"

"That's correct, Jane. In fact, according to the governor, there's going to be a public restaurant inside The Adjustment Center. Looks like someone will finally get to enjoy those great views of the Bay. For KTLA News, I'm Bob Johnson."

Kate took back her phone.

Dave couldn't believe it. Bridges had done it. The idea was already public.

Dave was simultaneously exhilarated and terrified. He'd resisted telling anyone about Death Row Restaurant for so long out of fear that it would sound completely insane, and now he wasn't sure how to react to its reality.

Kate began handing more documents to Dave, copies of the business license and Employer Identification Number. A certificate of occupancy, a food service license, permits needed to hang signs, a music license, a building health permit, a resale permit to allow them to buy food wholesale and resell it, so that taxes are collected when the meal is sold and not when the wholesale food is purchased. They had a seller's permit, a liquor license, a dumpster permit, a live entertainment license.

"What we still need," Kate said, "are the employee health permits."

"Dave, you need to pass a state approved HACCP program," Bridges insisted. He sounded annoyed. "Frankly, I would have thought that was the first thing you'd have learned at Henderson," Bridges added.

"This needs to be taken care of immediately," Kate reiterated. "We need a food safety hazard plan with identified control points, mitigation strategies, a monitoring procedure and a record keeping procedure. And every employee of the restaurant has to be trained in food handling."

Dave took the documents. Nodded his head.

"And Dave, we'll need your signature here and here and here."

"What's this?" Dave asked.

"It's standard for anyone visiting The Adjustment Center, which is where Death Row Restaurant is."

"I have to acknowledge that San Quentin does not negotiate if hostages are taken?"

"That's correct," Kate said. She was still sitting in the same spot in her chair. She hadn't moved at all, although a few wrinkles had reformed in her skirt.

"And nothing in San Quentin is automated. If you want a door unlocked, it has to be done by hand. And when you come to work, you will be treated like a prison guard in the sense that The Adjustment Center is a closed unit. Each day, you get locked in the unit and you will not have a set of keys that allow you to leave."

Dave didn't know what to say.

"And you'll have to use the 'Sally Port,'" Kate added. "It's the only way in or out of The Adjustment Center. There isn't going to be an employee entrance. Just the 'Sally Port.'"

"What's that?" Dave asked, taking more papers from Kate and adding them to his stack.

"It's like an airlock with a drawbridge. It helps prevent escapes. It's the only way in or out."

"And it really gives you that feeling," Bridges added, fanning his crotch again. "Once you hear the clunk of that heavy lock behind you in the Sally — you know you're in a different place. You'll know you're in Death Row Restaurant. You'll feel it in your bones. This first part, getting into The Adjustment Center, making your way to the restaurant, this is going to unnerve people. We're going to embrace that, Dave."

"Jesus," Dave muttered. "This is really happening."

"It's going to be great," Bridges responded. "Just think about everything we've talked about. You will finally work with people who are 100% genuine. And by the time you get to the roof, where the exercise yard for The Adjustment Center is, where Death Row inmates have been shooting baskets and walking in circles for decades, you'll be in a luxury setting. Just imagine the views up there, Dave. Views no one has seen for decades. Not since Warden Clinton Duffy ordered the views covered in 1952. Just imagine that. They literally put up barriers so prisoners couldn't enjoy the view. And because of us, because of Death Row Restaurant, these views will be available to all prisoners on Death Row. They'll get to see the color of the ocean, the spot where the horizon and the ocean meet and blur. You'll be up there cooking in an open air, outdoor kitchen. You'll smell the ocean, take in the sunshine. At night we'll have flickering gas lamps while waves lap the prison doorstep. We're going to get famous musicians to perform there, Dave. I still have friends in show business."

Dave immediately thought of Vanilla Ice.

"It will be elegant," Bridges continued. "And the whole time you are there, everyone will be authentic. You'll know where you are. You'll know who you are, and you'll know that you are in a place where people own their actions at the level of 'being.'"

Bridges was really on a roll.

In such moments, Dave had always felt Bridges' total commitment to what he was doing. And Dave had never had that, never had that commitment when it came to a real experience. He'd only had total commitment to the idea of doing something, never the actual experience of it. It was the difference between acting and living, and Bridges understood that difference on the level that Death Row forces a person to confront. "Just picture it with me, both of you," Bridges said. He held out his hands, with Kate on one side and Dave on the other. Dave's fingers interlaced with Kate's naturally, just as they had in all those Wichita hotel rooms. "Close your eyes," Bridges said. "Picture Death Row Restaurant. Picture a cloudless sky. Picture the endless ocean. Picture the San Rafael and Dumbarton Bridges, cars inching across them in the distance. Feel the breeze on your forehead. Taste the salt in the air — and picture a wall of barbed wire that separates Death Row Restaurant from the outside world, that separates our restaurant from every other restaurant that has ever existed."

————

For the next week, Dave prepared for his HACCP exam. The training course was online, leaving Dave no reason to attend culinary school. It felt like the end of Dave's career at Henderson Culinary Institute. Auggie and Louise had both texted Dave during the week to see where he was. Previously, Dave had never missed a class, had always shown up at Henderson well rested and with his uniform crisply pressed. Dave responded to their texts by saying something had come up. He had emailed Yiannis about his need to pass HACCP certification. Yiannis hadn't replied.

Of course, Dave also began to follow the developing news story on Governor Gavin Newsom's pilot program at San Quentin. It was incredible to Dave that he'd not seen any of the reports previously. They were on television constantly. Newsom spent half of his day talking about Death Row Restaurant. It was even more surprising because Dave still couldn't imagine talking about the restaurant with anyone who didn't already know about it. Yet, for Newsom, the restaurant was easy to talk about. For Newsom, Death Row Restaurant cut a clear path through California's complex history with capital punishment. A few years ago California had two propositions on the same ballot, one to end the death penalty and a second to speed up the appeals process. Death Row Restaurant was going to unify California's schizophrenic relationship to Capital Punishment.

"We can't get rid of Death Row," Newsom announced to a collection of reporters in Sacramento. "But we can and should get rid of the idea that Death Row inmates shouldn't be allowed to do anything. We must offer Death Row inmates a way to learn, to improve themselves and to contribute to the economy of the great state of California," Newsom added.

As soon as Dave passed his Hazard Analysis Critical Control Point exam, Bridges sent instructions for their first trip inside San Quentin.

————

At the appointed time, Bridges pulled up in front of his house in Sun Valley and honked. He had already told Dave he was not coming inside. Only instead of Bridges' Chevy Malibu, Bridges pulled up in a Pontiac Aztek.

"Where'd you get this?"

The car still had dealer stickers on it, though production of the Aztek had ended in 2005.

"Did you know that they stopped making the Pontiac Aztek the same year Dennis Rader was arrested as BTK?" Bridges asked.

Dave didn't respond. He had opened the passenger door without realizing that Kate was already riding shotgun. Dave was dressed in the same clothes he had worn when he visited Jack Pierce in the Lancaster Correctional Facility, a pair of jeans and a black t-shirt.

As it happened, this was what Bridges had asked them all to wear. Bridges tossed a black t-shirt over his shoulder to Dave and Kate took out a leather journal and began scribbling. Dave unfolded the t-shirt, which Bridges insisted was made with 100% merino wool.

"It won't hold odor at all," Bridges insisted.

"I wanted to talk to you about that," Dave said, unfolding the shirt. On the front was the Death Row Restaurant logo, a rip off of the old Death Row Records logo, only with the hooded figure in the electric chair clutching a knife and fork. Kate continued to scribble. She was like a courtroom artist, sketching this maiden journey to San Quentin. "I looked at some of Dennis Rader's mugshots. He looks absolutely awful. We're going to need some standards for appearance," Dave said. "This is something I learned all about at Henderson."

"You don't need to tell Death Row inmates to look after their appearance," Bridges insisted. "Booking photos are engineered. Law enforcement interviews these guys for ten, twelve hours at a time or more. Sometimes these interviews go on for days. Rader was interviewed for sixteen straight hours after they picked him up. Then they chained Rader to a roll out mattress. They didn't even give Rader a comb the next day. All mugshots look terrible. It's part of the process," Bridges said. Bridges had just gotten a haircut and had grown a faint goatee. Every hair on his body from the neck up was perfectly groomed with sharp lines.

"I don't know," Dave continued. "I looked at a lot of photos. Anthony Sowell wasn't much better. He looks like a crackhead."

"Sowell was a crackhead, Dave," Bridges said.

"Okay, well Ridgway always carried a comb, so he might be fine in terms of appearance. But these other guys, we'll need some guidelines," Dave reiterated, peeking over Kate's shoulder at the sketch she was creating. Kate's hair smelled exactly as Dave had remembered it from their Wichita nights. He wondered if she still used the same shampoo and beauty products.

"You don't understand," Bridges continued. "The thing about prison is, you can't do the things you would normally do to feel good. You don't get good food. You can't come and go as you please. You're in a cell all night and if there's a lockdown, you don't come out at all. You can't text your friends or anything," Bridges said. "But what you can do is learn to feel good in other ways. You'll notice this the first time you step into San Quentin. Every prisoner there takes care of his appearance, his physique. Every pair of pants is ironed with a little crease. Everyone's skin is immaculate. They cut their hair. They exercise. Guys in their sixties look like they're forty," Bridges smiled. "Prison preserves you," he insisted. "I'm not even sure what it is. Maybe because they don't get a lot of sunlight. But it's something else, too. You don't have to worry about Rader or Ridgway or Sowell showing up to work all disheveled. I promise you, taking care of your appearance is one of the few ways a person can feel good in the joint. And for Death Row convicts? Guys who really can't do what makes them feel good, guys whose families have disowned them and whom the public despises? For Death Row inmates, looking good is all they care about. Rader does one hundred pushups a day. He trims his nails with Pythagorean precision," Bridges concluded.

They drove in silence for a while, with Kate sketching and Dave fidgeting. The drive from Sun Valley to San Quentin was five hours, so they all had a lot of time to think.

"We'll relocate to San Francisco," Bridges told them after an hour or so on the road. "From there the prison is only half an hour or so. Dave nodded from the backseat, even though Bridges couldn't see him.

They stopped at Pismo's grill, near Fresno for lunch. Dave tried to talk to Kate, but it was hard with Bridges around. Bridges kept his sunglasses on even inside the restaurant. The waiter asked about their t-shirts, the Death Row Restaurant logo.

"Is that for real?" their waiter asked.

"It will be," Bridges replied, before asking about the catch of the day.

Kate was quiet. She ordered fish and chips, but mostly just picked at it. Meanwhile, Bridges had never seemed happier.

"Wait until you're inside the Adjustment Center," Bridges said for like the millionth time. "You take that walk to the yard, look out over the ocean. And the gas chamber will be right there. And pretty soon, you'll be teaching Gary Ridgway how to cook a steak."

Dave hadn't decided on steak. He was actually leaning towards curries, since so many prisoners already liked to make them. That and Mexican.

"So, Kate," Dave began. "What's it like being in a prison?" He liked asking Kate questions. When they had been together, Dave was the expert. And now, he liked that their roles had flipped.

"You'll know in about two hours," Kate replied. Then she leaned in and whispered, "I've never met Dennis Rader. He's the only one of these killers I didn't interview."

"We can ask Todd about it," Dave said. "He spent more than an hour with the guy at El Dorado." But as soon as he said this, Bridges got up to use the restroom.

"I'll be finding out soon enough," Kate said.

"I'm hoping Rader will be stuck in the back, encased in steam and buried under dishes. Hell, I might create a whole Tapas menu, all those small plates, just to keep Rader busy washing dishes," Dave said. He was surprised by his ability to crack jokes. That never seems to leave a person.

"No matter what you serve," Kate began, "I'll be working closely with Rader." Her voice sounded tight and aloof. "Todd needs someone to handle Rader's journals. And I guess that's going to be me." Kate picked up a piece of fish, thought about eating it, then tossed it back into the basket. "God, I hope I don't have to do any of his nasty draw-ings," she said. And for just a second, Dave thought he saw Kate gag.

"What are you talking about? Aren't you working on public relations?"

Kate shrugged.

"There's not much left to do," Kate said. "With Newsom behind us, everything has fallen into place. Our staff has met all of Governor Newsom's diversity requirements. And now that Newsom has this moral angle on rehabilitative services, no one is even protesting." Kate shrugged. "Bridges was right. Politically, Death Row Restaurant is a hit. Newsom is finally going to close down the correctional facility at Tracy at the same time he's opening new doors to improve life on Death Row at San Quentin. And the restaurant is the beginning of a long term plan to develop the real estate along the bay."

"Is Bridges involved in that?"

"I think so. It's weird," Kate said, "but politicians need to see someone else travel way down a road before they consider something seriously. But once they see someone has traveled that path, they are willing to put up permanent road signs. That's what Bridges did for Newsom."

"I don't understand the thing with Rader," Dave asked, in a bit of a panic. "Aren't we avoiding giving prisoners special treatment and attention? They're just employees. Giving them special attention might stir up the pain of their crimes."

"Guys like Rader," Kate said. "They keep journals all the time. Rader keeps track of everything he does, his breakfast, his exercises, his mood, what television shows he watches, the weather, whether he clips his nails or finds a hole in a sock."

"So?"

"So if Rader is busy washing dishes, someone has to record all this shit for him. And for now at least, it's going to be me."

"Are you fucking serious? That's about the worst job I can imagine."

"Part of me feels that way for sure. I mean Rader, he killed children. And he's too self centered to ever really understand the enormity of his crimes —" Kate looked over her shoulder. Bridges was talking to the hostess, pointing towards the kitchen. "But sometimes I wonder if there isn't some route to understand what he did that travels through this minutiae," she said. "But, please. No fucking drawings. I'll keep track of his hangnails, his erections. It doesn't matter. Just so long as there are none of those boob drawings, or shark signatures or those bondage drawings I've seen on the internet. There's no way I can handle that."

Kate's hand was shaking. She chugged her water like it was a martini.

"Kate, why are you doing this? I mean, why not just get a nice job somewhere in Scarsdale? Your father could set you up. How does keeping track of Rader's breakfasts and workouts and the dishes Rader washes at Death Row Restaurant help you to understand why he's so twisted?"

"It probably doesn't," Kate admitted, pushing her basket of soggy fish and chips towards Dave.

"So why put yourself through this?"

"Time to get back on the road," Bridges announced, popping his Miami Vice shades down from the top of his head.

———

Several hours slipped by in a haze. Before Dave knew it, they were crossing the Golden Gate Bridge. San Quentin was less than half an hour away. Bridges yawned. He must've been tired from driving. At one point, Bridges made idle conversation about a Chinese restaurant in San Francisco they were going to eat at later. Kate scribbled in her journal. She seemed very far away.

At the prison, the first thing Dave noticed was the bathrooms. San Quentin has outdoor bathrooms, stainless steel toilets with cement sinks attached to them like backpacks. Toilets, sinks and showers just sitting in the open. Full exposure.

"Don't worry, Dave," Bridges said, clapping him on the shoulder. "You won't have to use these. We're going to have very nice toilets installed in the yard above the Condemned Row."

"Will the killers get to use them?" Dave asked.

Bridges gulped the air, relishing the place. Dave had to admit, it was a lovely day. The bay air had a freshness to it, and there was something about outdoor bathrooms and small rec areas that made San Quentin feel rustic.

"You know. Dave," Bridges said. "There's not as much distinction between Death Row convicts and other convicts in San Quentin as you might think. I mean, yes, all of the people on Death Row are murderers," Bridges continued, gesturing towards North block, "but so are many prisoners in the mainline population," Bridges gulped the air again. Dave wanted to tell him to stop, the way one might tell a kid to slow down while eating cake.

"Todd," Dave began, choosing his words carefully. "I want to be sure of something. I want to be sure Death Row Restaurant isn't giving any of these killers special treatment. That could be, you know, problematic. Bad publicity, protests."

Bridges shook his head.

"Like Governor Newsom says, Death Row Restaurant is about prison reform. We get to revitalize the economy as a bonus," Bridges said. Dave could tell it was a speech he was practicing. The guard who was escorting them, reached the Sally Port and unlocked it, swinging open the gate. "But for me, it's not about any of that." Bridges put his hand on Dave's shoulder. "Death Row Restaurant is just a place where I can finally breathe, you know?"

Bridges held open the iron gate leading to the Sally Port. "After y'all," he said.

He had a way of making everything feel like a sitcom.

Dave, Kate and Todd were thoroughly searched and then they had their hand stamped, like at Disneyland.

"I think that thing is out of ink," Dave muttered after getting his stamp.

"It's invisible ink," the guard told them. "It changes every week. This way no one can copy the stamp. Consider it your get out of jail free card."

"Oh," Dave said, rubbing his hand, then trying to stop himself. For a guy who often felt misunderstood, prison seemed like the ultimate opportunity for a misunderstanding.

Once they got through the Sally Port, they entered a courtyard. In front of them were three, white buildings. Their windows were heavily barred.

"This is nothing like the yard where Death Row Restaurant will be," Bridges assured them both. No matter where they went, Bridges couldn't stop selling the idea. Kate clutched her journal and looked around.

"Always be closing," Dave muttered.

But no one heard him, because after a few more checkpoints, they were asked to put on green vests.

"These vests are stab proof," the guard informed them. "You'll get used to them. And if someone comes at you, protect your neck. That's all you need to protect to survive an attack."

Dave nodded.

"We'll be getting vests that have the Death Row Restaurant logo on them. Fully puncture proof," Bridges declared. "I've already ordered them."

Kate was emotionless as she slipped into her vest, still clutching her leather journal. It was striking. Whatever she was here to do, she was serious about it. She didn't want help from anyone. They walked past an exercise yard, with prisoners playing hoops, followed by a second yard filled with cages about the size of Dave's childhood bedroom. One prisoner per cage. Many of them were jumping off the cage toilet for exercise. All of the prisoners wore the same shoes, white bottomed sandals with a black strap.

"SHU shoes," Bridges said, elbowing Dave in the ribs. "If you get put back in the mainline, you get to keep the Security Housing Unit shoes," Bridges said.

He seemed to have an endless supply of one liners. He was going to make a great restaurant host.

Kate meanwhile, was robotic in her movements, like a person shuffling forward in a really long line.

"Kate, we can talk about that journaling thing with Todd. I can get you something else. You don't have to be Rader's secretary," Dave whispered.

But Kate didn't say anything. She just turned her head and looked at Dave, and then very gently touched his hair, as if confirming he was really there.

They reached another Sally Port. Then another. Each door was unlocked and opened by hand.

"What's that?" Dave asked the guard. Pointing to what looked like a small refrigerator stacked on top of a wheelchair.

"That's the prisoner telephone," the guard told them. "Prisoners can't leave their cells in North Block, so guards bring the phone to them. On phone days, we leave their food tray open and prisoners can reach through and make their calls.

"When Rader, Ridgway and Sowell call you," Bridges said, trying to scratch himself underneath his puncture proof vest, "they'll be reaching out their food tray and grabbing the Adjustment Center rolling telephone. That's the thing," Bridges insisted, his voice as pure as a mountain stream. "These killers, Rader, Ridgway, Sowell, DeAngelo — male and female —" Bridges said, gesturing to Kate to note his inclusivity, "these killers are still prisoners, are still housed in the SHU. Nothing changes. So when they come to work, it's because they truly want to work at Death Row Restaurant."

"What about Jesse Sitting Crow?" Dave asked. "You forgot about him."

"Him, too," Bridges mumbled.

They arrived at yet another Sally Port. The sheer difficulty of entering and leaving the prison was exhausting. Yet Bridges was absolutely thrilled by it.

This port had a telephone, but no buttons. The guard picked up the receiver.

"Drop the bucket," he said, then hung up. Dave raised his eyes.

Above the tiny elevator door, wrapped in wrought iron were the words 'condemned row.'

———

They made it to the roof at last. Seagulls spiraled above them. Razor wire curled atop cement walls.

And the gas chamber was there. It had been broken down into pieces brought up a few at a time in the elevator and dumped into a pile. Workers wearing the same green, puncture proof vests Dave and Kate and Todd Bridges were wearing were on their knees piecing the gas chamber back together. The dome shape, the chunky metal chairs. It was starting to take form right before Dave's eyes.

The sky was clear, but the air was hazy and salty. Water from the bay shifted and receded, the sound of its girth and age roiled just beyond the wall.

"This whole section will be replaced, opening views of the bay," Bridges waved at a patch of cement, as if he were a magician. "And over there are the rough ins. That's Rader's dishwasher. There, the stove and mezedes grill. A perfect outdoor kitchen," he concluded. "And right there," Bridges pointed again, this time towards the elevator, "that's where the host stand will be, where I will greet each customer in the most authentic way possible."

It's done, Dave thought. The whole thing is done.

"Now I just have to teach murderers to cook," Dave shrugged. It suddenly seemed like no big deal.

Bridges went over to where the host stand was being constructed. He fumbled around and Hotel California by The Eagles began playing.

"Where are the speakers?" Dave muttered, looking everywhere.

"Did you know that Hotel California is actually about prison?" Bridges asked them both.

Kate turned to face them, still clutching her journal. Dave wondered if that was the journal she would use to keep track of Rader's workouts, breakfasts and other miscellany of his day. He wondered if Ridgway or Jesse 'Sitting Crow' would want the minutiae of their days recorded in a journal, too. Or if Dave would have to hold Ridgway's comb or take over on a sauté while Ridgway obsessed about his hair.

"Listen to the lyrics," Bridges suggested, bobbing his head unconsciously to the music. "On a dark desert highway... I heard the mission bell... this could be heaven or this could be hell," Bridges sang, skipping half the lyrics. His singing voice was much deeper than his speaking voice. "Really," Bridges said, dancing lightly from side to side. "Listen to the words. 'How they dance in the courtyard...'" he sang. "I used to dance in the courtyard. In prison, sometimes you gotta fight." Bridges turned towards Kate, waved her to come closer, as if they were in a dance club where he was a VIP. "We are all just prisoners here, of our own device," Bridges sang. And Dave, knowing all the words, couldn't help but join in.

"And in the master's chambers... they gathered for the feast... they stab it with their steely knives — but they just can't kill the beast..."

Protect your neck, Dave thought. He was kind of dancing with Kate now. She shimmied alongside him. A breeze swept through the yard.

"I can't wait," Kate whispered to Dave, her nose bumping against his ear as they lightly danced to the few remaining bars.

"For what?" Dave asked.

The song ended, leaving that awkwardness one feels at having gotten wrapped up in the music, at having moved indiscriminately to it.

"You know," Bridges said, slightly out of breath. "We taped one hundred and eighty nine episodes of Diff'rent Strokes. One hundred and eighty nine. And we never had a finale. They canceled the show mid season after an episode about Arnold exposing steroid sales at his high school." Bridges scratched his nose. "I was barely even in that episode," he complained. And then Bridges sang a few lyrics from Hotel California, even though the song was over. "You can check out any time you like," Bridges sang to himself, "but you can never leave."

———

A few days later, Dave called Yiannis.

"I want to ask you something," Dave said. "What's it like being a teacher?"

It was dusk and Dave was sitting on Bridges' white couch in his Sun Valley house. Cardboard moving boxes surrounded him. Bridges had put his Sun Valley house up for sale and made a bid on a condo in San Francisco. Dave would be staying at an AirBNB until he found a suitable apartment. Dave wanted to call Kate, to see what neighborhoods in San Francisco she was looking at. But so far, he hadn't gotten up the nerve to make the call. The light draining from the sky made Dave sleepy. He had made a pot of coffee. He poured a cup, blew on it, then took a few gulps.

"There are twenty three billion chickens on the planet," Yiannis replied. "Chickens are by far the most numerous birds in our world and on our plates. Chickens achieved this feat in a remarkable way, through a single, cunning move. As chefs, restaurateurs and chickens know, the world is a competition."

Not on Death Row, Dave thought. Not if you're a serial killer cooking on the rooftop of San Quentin. Dave settled in. As usual, Yiannis was going to respond to his question in his own way. Dave gulped more coffee, burning the roof of his mouth. He wasn't sure where Yiannis was going with this point about chickens, but he didn't care. He was willing to listen to an hours long lecture. You can't talk about most things directly, anyway. Not if you wanted honest conversation.

"12,000 years ago," Yiannis continued, "pheasants traveled over a thousand miles from their native range in Gansu Province and began living closely with humans. If this seems like a perfectly ordinary event, it was not. Only a miniscule portion of the world's animals have ever made this kind of move. And in doing so, the pheasant opened itself to genetic modification through human — rather than natural — selection." A gentle rain had started outside. It came in waves and Dave knew it was the kind of storm that wouldn't last long. But it was one of those moments where the world felt carefully orchestrated. "The process that followed, the process of domestication of the pheasant, required sustained and intimate interdependence," Yiannis continued.

And although they were not at Henderson, Dave could picture Yiannis reaching the end of the row of chefs and pivoting in the opposite direction, a maneuver Yiannis had performed countless times in the fashion of an Olympic swimmer turning and pushing off the wall underwater.

"Charles Darwin believed that domestic chickens traced their lineage back to the Indus Valley in what is now Pakistan," Yiannis continued.

And despite the coffee, the rain, the intricacy of Yiannis' lecture — and the fact that tomorrow Dave would be receiving the first of his weekly calls from his employees, from Dennis Rader, Gary Ridgway, Anthony Sowell, and Jesse 'Sitting Crow' (more than one hundred murders between them), despite all of that, Dave felt as if he might just nod off to sleep. He pinched his thigh. The pain woke him up.

"Yet modern science disagrees with Darwin's assessment of the chicken's origins, and has traced domestic chicken haplotypes to Northern China," Yiannis insisted. "This retroactive historicity is available to us because of leftovers. Chickens, eaten for lunch or dinner — leave behind their bones," Yiannis said. "It's of particular interest to Westerners that the chicken traces to China. After all, Northern Chinese food forms the bulk of what Westerners find palatable in Asian cuisine — meat filled dumplings, pulled noodle soups, roasts — bold, salty flavors and generous portions. And for the chicken, their migration to Northern China put them in an area that had limited agricultural means. Yet the chicken's current status as the most populous bird on the planet, as the culinary world's most ubiquitous protein comes from this one, strange decision by pheasants, the decision to fly East and the intimate interdependence that followed."

Dave had no idea how the lineage of chickens had anything to do with his question. But he had confidence that in time, he would understand. Dave loved the feeling he got from Yiannis' lectures. They required him to concentrate intensely and also required that he let go of all his suppositions about the world. Yiannis' lectures were Dave's crystal meth — the thing that Todd Bridges claimed made the world legitimately fascinating. And Dave hoped the same might be true about Death Row Restaurant.

"So why don't we eat buckets of Kentucky Fried Pheasant?" Yiannis asked Dave. "Because humans bypassed evolution. They domesticated the pheasant and created the roasting chicken."

Yiannis sighed. Silence passed between them. Dave yawned, putting almost his entire fist inside his mouth to prevent Yiannis from hearing him.

"At their absolute best," Yiannis elaborated, "a teacher interrupts evolution. This is not the popular view of the student as an explorer and the teacher as a coach on the sidelines. But there is nothing to suggest that chickens would have played the intricate role they have played in the world without the intervention of Northern Chinese diners."

By the time they hung up, it was dark outside. As usual, Yiannis had overloaded him with history. Yet Dave worried about the future.

About the phone calls he would receive from his employees at San Quentin tomorrow. First Rader, then Ridgway, then Sowell, then Jesse 'Sitting Crow.' Dave would have to discuss every policy and instruction four times, since it was impossible for the prisoners to be on a conference call. Dave would ask each murderer about his experience in kitchens, about what he cooks in his cell, about the types of food he liked on the outside. And Dave planned, if he had time, he planned to fill each of them in, at least preliminarily, on the importance of the chicken to any real chef.

Would these killers even bother to listen to him?

Would they call at all?

Ridgway probably would. He was an incredibly reliable employee. But Rader had a spotty employment history. And some accounts of Sowell's employment history link his tendency to lose focus at work with the timing of his murder spree. Like chickens whose physiognomy had been shaped by events outside of their control, resulting in a new breed, Rader, Ridgway, Sowell, and Glaze were all serial killers who claimed a manipulated history had formed them. Rader claimed he had been dropped on his head as a child. And when Dennis Rader's mother got her wedding ring caught on a couch spring, Rader's sexualization of a woman's help-lessness awakened, parked itself in a blind spot — and began to grow. Gary Ridgway wet his bed until he was thirteen years old. Ridgway's mother used to clean his genitals afterwards, leading to intense, conflicted feelings of shame, anger and sexual attraction. Ridgway had plea bargained his way out of the death penalty, providing details on forty nine murders. He received forty eight life sentences, back to back. Sowell's childhood was hotly disputed. But late in his life, Sowell testified he suffered intense physical abuse in childhood.

Dave had no idea what such men might do in a rooftop restaurant.

For Bridges, Death Row Restaurant wasn't a comeback after having been 'canceled.' Bridges' sitcom family had been in excess of his real family. That was its greatest quality; Dave had finally come to understand about Bridges' past. The allure of Diff'rent Strokes across so many decades was not that it was more real or happier than Bridges' biological family. But that it was a surplus, an extra, like Russian nesting dolls where each compartment contains another doll, then another, and so on. And the same principle held true for Death Row Restaurant and the killers who would cook, clean and serve its customers. It was a restaurant with something extra. Bridges believed that 'extra' was its absolute authenticity. Dave wasn't so sure.

Intensely tired now, Dave's mind returned again and again to the same spot, like a bocce ball on a string. What would that first "hello" coming through the phone receiver be like? Those first pleasantries exchanged between himself and Dennis Rader or Gary Ridgway or Anthony Sowell? Would there be anything special in it? Would there be anything enduring in the killer's "hello?" Or would Dave find, like Anthony Bourdain had, that there was no meal or experience that could deliver a surplus every time?

Dave wasn't going to parse his experiences at Death Row Restaurant. He wasn't going to evaluate them constantly for this quality. He wouldn't necessarily stay at Death Row Restaurant forever. But he would stay at Death Row Restaurant as long as Kate stayed. Dave still didn't understand why she would agree to keep Rader's daily journals. The worst job in the world. Dave knew (and Kate of course knew) that Rader would fantasize about killing her while she kept track of his bowel movements and breakfasts. How could Rader return to his cell each night after a hard day of scrubbing dishes and dictating to Kate what to record in his daily journal — and not imagine her bound and helpless and begging, the way Rader had structured all of his murders? Kate's fear of Rader, which she had hurriedly detailed for Dave during one of their long stretches in the airport Hilton in Wichita, was not merely about the random way Rader had chosen his victims. That was only what she thought at first. But over time, Kate uncovered something else about her fear.

"He killed people like me," Kate had confessed to Dave at the Wichita Hilton. Although she never explained precisely what she meant by that, her sense that Rader or another serial killer would choose her was stronger than any logic. Dave argued on a number of occasions that a person's chance of being murdered by a serial killer, while not zero, was less likely than winning the Powerball, which Kate occasionally bought a ticket for when she was feeling happy.

But this made no difference to Kate's terror.

Why did she agree to be Rader's personal assistant? Why did she agree to constantly be in such close proximity to him, to be at his beck and call? And Kate wouldn't only be physically close to Rader. She would be inside his head. Would he dictate his murderous poems to her? Poems as despicable for their evil and bizarre fantasies as they were for Rader's horrible spelling and rampant plagiarism? There was just no way around it. Kate's job would up the odds of something terrible happening to her. And if San Quentin refused to negotiate if Kate or Dave or Todd Bridges were taken hostage, and if the best advice from the guards was 'protect your neck' — what would prevent Rader from doing something horrible to Kate? Strangulation was unlikely in the restaurant. As a form of killing, it required time and intimacy. But Rader had planned his murders for years before enacting them. And that was what Dave struggled with. Of course, he thought. Of course these guys, all of whom killed women, Rader, Ridgway, Sowell, Glaze — of course they would all be fantasizing about murdering Kate. And what does a guy serving one hundred and seventy five years have to lose?

"His job," Dave mumbled aloud. How emasculating would it be for Rader to get fired from Death Row Restaurant and shipped back to El Dorado Correctional Center? Rader may be the most powerful dishwasher in the world. He may be able to dictate the date for the grand opening of the first commercial enterprise on a billion dollar parcel of real estate in order to commemorate one of his heinous murders. And while every prisoner in The Adjustment Center would have Rader to thank for their newfound view of San Pablo Bay, now that the screens which had blocked it had been partially removed for Death Row Restaurant, to keep that status, Rader had to keep his job. For Rader, the job (especially because it didn't involve a salary) became something extra. It was exactly what these killers loved.

And for Newsom? The whole point of Death Row Restaurant was to provide something other prisons didn't provide. The whole point was innovation. Politicians thrived on this kind of bonus enjoyment, the kind that comes from publicly boasting about the size and scope of your vision. While mainline San Quentin inmates could take college classes, auto repair, computer programming, firefighting —Death Row inmates had no rehabilitation services. Giving Death Row inmates the chance to learn and to work was perfect for Newsom's political ambitions. Newsom had seized upon this as though it were an insight. Authorizing rehabilitation services to irredeemable serial killers meant that Newsom didn't care about their utility. It meant that he did care about something greater, doing the right thing. Newsom would get behind Death Row Restaurant precisely because it provided no tangible benefit at all. Which meant that the only reason to do it was — because it is the right thing to do. Opening up prime land on the bay for economic development was just an extra benefit of Newsom's moral commitment.

While Rader had certainly reveled in the excesses of his murders, it was in comparing them with his picture perfect family life, his election as president of his church, his work with the boy scouts, that he felt the greatest thrill. Yet as remarkable as Rader was for his compartmentalization, it was soft spoken and plain Gary Ridgway who most exemplified the principle of excess. This wasn't because of his startling murder count. Dave had read that during Ridgway's extensive questioning by law enforcement, Ridgway, unlike Rader, made the extraordinary claim that he never intended to murder any of his victims. Over and over again, Ridgway lured prostitutes onto remote roadways. And over and over again, Ridgway strangled them. And in Ridgway's explanation, something distinct had happened each time to set him off.

Police interviewers pressed Ridgway.

"But you knew. You knew you had strangled women before under these circumstances, dozens of times in fact. You knew that during sex with these women, they might end up dead. So how could you take women to these remote locations and have sex with them knowing how many times before it had led to strangulation?"

Ridgway only shrugged and continued to insist he had never intended to murder anyone. Always, something extra happened that drove him to kill. It was never intentional.

And Dave and Kate and Bridges, they all needed to remember this principle. Something extra. Don't just put on the stab proof vest. Protect your neck.

Dave shifted his thoughts to Anthony Sowell. Sowell had stored severed heads in buckets. His childhood. My god. Dave didn't have the energy to consider it, let alone to dive into Jesse 'Sitting Crow.'

Dave adjusted the couch cushions. The thought of climbing the stairs had become too much. He would sleep on the couch. Dave wished he was not alone. He wished Kate would call him. He wished it felt right for him to reach out to her. But it didn't. And Dave was sure that Kate was busy with Todd Bridges and Death Row Restaurant. And those two things had a way of filling all your time, without any excess.

Dave still believed in the principle behind Death Row Restaurant and its authenticity. If the restaurant proved a flop, if there was an incident or massive protests or a recall election of Newsom, or if the restaurant just fizzled out (as eighty percent of restaurants do in the first five years) Dave might stay on and work inside San Quentin. Like Jack Pierce, Dave could cook last meals for condemned men. His final gesture into eternity. Or maybe Dave would organize the men who cooked in their cells with their stingers, organize weekly pot luck dinners where they could settle their beefs without violence. Everything takes an exceedingly long time in prison, food most of all. A guy might work all day to make a single burrito. And they would split that burrito eight or ten different ways at a gathering. Dave loved that.

At the start of Death Row Restaurant, Dave had read Kitchen Confidential, Anthony Bourdain's memoir. The book may even have inspired Bridges' idea for Death Row Restaurant. That was the starting line. And now Dave was on the verge of a second starting line. And he would begin by imagining the ending, as serial killers do.

At the end of Kitchen Confidential, Bourdain details how the pastry chef in the New York Restaurant he ran kept calling in sick. The guy would yell through the receiver, "feed the bitch!" Bourdain's pastry chef was an absolute mess, a guy who had been fired from every restaurant in New York City, a guy serially incapable of coming into work, a guy on cocaine bender after cocaine bender, a guy drinking vodka from a gallon jug, a guy with every excuse in the world for why he can't make it in to work. And every employee at the restaurant had to carry this guy by feeding his bread starter, a concoction of grapes and yeast and sugars and flour and water in a fifty gallon bucket. And feeding the starter was a pain in the ass. Scraping it all out and mixing in fresh yeast and flour and water and grape must and then scraping it all back in. And nobody could fucking stand this guy. And half the time they all wanted him dead.

But Bourdain testified to this guy's unparalleled pizza crust, which could stretch insanely thin while maintaining a tensile strength greater than most top end luggage. It baked light and crisp and could be weighted down with every imaginable topping from earthy shitake mushrooms to tangy pulled pork without losing its crunch. His fougasse was like stem cell research, miraculous and blasphemous at the same time. His pain complet, and on and on. One whiff of anything coming out of this guy's oven combined the nightmare of working with him with the magnificence of childbirth. Bourdain had fired him at least half a dozen times. But he always hired the guy back.

Because at a certain point, Bourdain argued, you don't search for 'why' anymore. Why was this pastry chef's bread so fucking good?

Why did Rader get sexual gratification on a meteoric scale from causing and teasing out and taking to the absolute limit another human being's helplessness? Why couldn't Gary Ridgway deal with his 'mother issues' in a normal way? Why did a heart attack set Anthony Sowell off on a murderous rampage? Whatever it was that allowed this pastry chef to produce godlike breads, whatever it was that brought a person to tears over a perfectly cooked steak au poivre — Bourdain didn't need to know. He understood the food, and that was enough.

Just protect your neck.

Protect your neck when you walk by San Quentin's outdoor shitters. Protect your neck while trying to explain to a fuck like Gary Ridgway why the chicken conquered the world.

Protect your neck while trying to sleep on Bridges' stupid white couch, a couch Dave had avoided even sitting on for the nearly ten months he had lived in Bridges' Sun Valley house. Whether Death Row Restaurant worked out or not, all Dave had to do was protect his neck. Or at least, that's what he told himself as he drifted off to sleep on his final night in Sun Valley.

———

On Kate's final night in Los Angeles, she was staying in The Palihouse, a European style boutique hotel. The chairs in Kate's room were embroidered with lemons. Windows stretched from floor to ceiling, with airy drapes that swayed in the breeze. In one corner sat an easel with a half completed oil painting of a Saint Bernard. Above her bed was the word 'HOTEL' in a gilded frame. Kate had just eaten banana bread from the hotel's all day menu. And now she wandered around the room, wringing her hands, certain that she would be unable to sleep. Kate had already done everything she needed to do for tomorrow. She had triple checked the itinerary with Todd Bridges. Her bags were packed. Tomorrow she would move to her sublet in San Francisco. And it was the fact that she had nothing at all left to do that made her so nervous. Kate had believed that a suite at the Palihouse would put her at ease for the night. She put her stay on her credit card, knowing she would have to call her father to pay it off. But the penthouse was not working. If anything, being in a fantastic, European style hotel with a full croquet field, plush robes and slippers, and 'palivibes' playlists to match any mood — was making Kate feel worse. A desire to travel the world welled up again inside her. She understood this was a ruse now. Traveling the world would likely make her suicidal.

Outside of business trips with Todd Bridges, to prison after prison, Kate had not traveled since the day she broke up with Dave at Eisenhower Airport. On that day, Kate had thought she had regained her confidence. She thought she had taken decisive action. She thought had refused to settle. While striding purposely away from Dave in the pathetic Wichita Airport, she recalled a poem she was forced to memorize in high school: I am the master of my fate. I am the captain of my soul! Or at least, she had recalled the last two lines. And with these lines reverberating in her head, Kate marched right to the United Airlines counter and arranged to 'deadhead' herself to Dallas, Texas where her college roommate and United Airlines training partner, Tina had been inviting her to visit for months. Prior to this moment, Kate had believed herself incapable of making the trip, incapable of competing with Tina's perfect Texas life. But as soon as Kate had gotten rid of her excess baggage, she looked forward to the trip. Dallas was over three hundred square miles, more than twice the size of Wichita.

Tina met Kate at their airport in a convertible. She looked incredible. Youthful, vibrant, her hair wind styled by the cute convertible she drove. Tina laughed loud and free. They zoomed downtown. Her apartment was industrial chic. Her lover, Herman was just as Tina had described him. His charismatic smile, his plain white cotton t-shirt and stylish loafers made Herman approachable. He had the quiet confidence of the wealthy. The three of them went to dinner at an upscale steakhouse, then to a series of clubs. Herman hired a car to drive them around. They drank martinis, 'Texas Hurricanes' and 'Watermelon Crawls' with just a dash of elderberry. Tina and Kate danced hard, until they were drenched in sweat and confessing over and over again how much they loved each other. To her credit, Tina didn't press Kate about Dave, about Wichita, about anything. Tina also didn't brag. And Herman told occasional jokes and relaxed by the bar, watching them dance.

Tina seemed legitimately happy. Legitimately.

On the ride home, Kate leaned against the door thinking that she and Dave had never once gone out to a club together. And although Dave wasn't the club going type, although Wichita no doubt didn't have clubs like those in Dallas, it was hard to fault Dave. They had hung around the hotel because of Kate's Wichita illnesses. Tina was in Herman's lap now, kissing him and laughing and teasing him about his thinning gray hair. Herman was a good sport about it. And Kate wondered if Dave knew how to have a good time like this. The car hit a bump. Tina shrieked, then laughed, then started gagging.

"Oh my god," Tina said. "Oh my god. Stop the car. Stop."

They pulled over and Tina rushed out. Kate heard her retching. She wondered if that was what she had sounded like all those nights in Wichita hotel rooms. It was the most unattractive sound she had ever heard.

"She'll be fine," Herman said, pulling the car door closed to give Tina some privacy. "How do you like Dallas?"

"It's lovely," Kate replied. The seat felt suddenly narrow, felt tilted like a slide, as if gravity was pulling her towards Herman's lap.

"Texas is all about having fun," Herman said. From beyond the window, Tina retched again. "Tina never knows when to quit with those hurricanes," he added.

And then Herman's hand was on Kate's thigh. And Kate found that she wanted this. Not because she liked Herman or because she wanted to get back at Dave or because she knew Tina was utterly phony and only cared about comparing her life to Kate's. No. Kate slid down Herman's zipper because she realized something far worse than these failings of others. Kate realized that she didn't want to be who she was.

Kate flew back the next day. She was confused and hung over and spent several days brooding in her Chicago apartment. She was lonely and she hated Dave for fucking things up, for not being who she thought he was. Had she really asked Dave to marry her? Her apartment shook whenever the Clark street bus rumbled past her building. And up the street was a restaurant called the Chicken Shack. She'd always hated that place, its corny name, as if the structure was poorly built so the chicken had to be good. RadioShack, Shake Shack. Kate hated all those places.

But really, Kate hated herself. And it was such a terrible secret that she had blown Herman, almost right in front of Tina. Tina surely smelled it. Slightly metallic, salty, a touch astringent. Nothing smells like sex but sex. Tina had to have known. And Herman was confident that, barring getting caught in the middle of the act, Tina was too phony to ever say anything about the smell, about what she knew had happened. Tina labored to preserve her fantasies, not shatter them.

Maybe five years from now, when Herman was really too old for her, when Tina felt pressed to move on from whatever this was with Herman. Maybe then she would bring it up.

"She blew you, didn't she?"

And Dave. Kate hated him more than ever. Why wouldn't he travel with her? Why couldn't Dave, like that douchebag Herman, at least enjoy her youth?

Because Dave cared for her. Because Kate's youth was part of her, not some kind of bonus. Dave wasn't an asshole. And this made Kate feel even worse. How could she hate him because his worst secret was that he liked Wichita? Kate didn't even know what her worst secret was. That she had let Dennis Rader terrorize her since sophomore year in college? That she had slept with at least seven guys sophomore year, mostly because she was terrified to be alone? Dennis Rader used to break into the houses of women who lived alone. He would crouch for hours in their closets, until they were fast asleep. Then he would emerge out of the darkness, tie them up and strangle them little by little, prolonging the fear and helplessness for as long as he could. And Kate couldn't be alone.

Sitting in the lovely Palihouse Hotel, the penthouse, Kate wanted to play piano again. Not because the music would be anything other than stiff reproduction, tapping memorized keys in a pattern with no ear, no soul, nothing a killer like Rader could ever be drawn to, as he was to Vicki Wegerle's piano sonatas. Kate wouldn't play to improve herself or to persevere or to overcome her fears. If she had a piano, she would just play it.

She huddled in her bed, one eye open, hating to look at the world and terrified to close her eyes.

Kate hadn't intended to get so angry at Dave on their last flight working together. She had gone to work with the best intentions. And Kate could tell he was also upset about their breakup, that he was doing his best to respect her wishes, that the Teflon persona she had found so attractive in him only extended so far, and did not apply to his feelings for her. And at various points, Kate just wanted to melt into his arms. But she couldn't. Not because she hated Wichita or because Dave was apprehensive about marrying her. What was so crushing to Kate was that the secret that broke them apart was so mundane. Dave liked Wichita. Why was that the end of their relationship? She didn't understand herself at all, except to realize fully as Dave took over the beverage cart with his efficient movements and decades of experience — how much Kate simply wanted to be someone else.

Was that what Rader felt like?

The only way Kate could respond was with anger. She knew how to build it, how to maintain it for the whole flight. How to push Dave farther away so she wouldn't have to deal with his earnestness, with the fact that at the end of the day, he didn't hate himself. Not really. And when Kate flushed Dave in the airplane lavatory, she had wished she could flush herself away instead.

And when the flight finally landed in Wichita, it was all too much. Another night at the airport Hilton. Only this time, alone. And Dave had quit his job of twenty years, just as she had pushed him to do. Dave had given her his Wichita route, the one thing he still liked. He gave it to Kate, knowing that she wanted it, but also hated it.

And that was when Todd Bridges approached Kate to ask her if she would consider driving him to El Dorado Correctional facility, so that he could interview Dennis Rader for a job at Death Row Restaurant.

Bridges' pitch was remarkably self possessed. Just the idea of a place where people were unalterably themselves, a place where everything one did was something one didn't really have to do at all, like Kate's mom putting stickers on her bathroom mirror when she was a kid — or Dave liking Wichita.

But there was just no way Kate could drive to El Dorado, drive herself to Dennis Rader in the flesh. She declined Bridges' request. She wished Todd Bridges well.

"What was that show of yours?" she had asked, making polite conversation after declining Bridges' offer.

"Diff'rent Strokes," Bridges said.

And it seemed to tell Kate everything. Like how she might be able to stop wishing she was another person. Bridges gave Kate his business card. Todd Bridges. CEO of Death Row Restaurant. A few days later, she called Todd Bridges to ask how the interview with Dennis Rader had gone. And Bridges told her, "It went very well. Very well indeed," and he invited Kate to Los Angeles, to work public relations for Death Row Restaurant.

Kate was terrified, but she had resolved even before calling Todd Bridges to accept any job offer he made.

As she studied the Death Row Restaurant dossiers Bridges had emailed her, some of the most horrific men in the world, Kate came to understand that a serial killer isn't mysterious.

A serial killer is empty inside. A different kind of empty. Not empty from vomiting. Not the emptiness of Tina or Herman or what Kate felt in her desire to be someone else. These killers. They were for real, empty. No explanation for what they do, empty. No identity, empty. A void. And this was scarier. And this healed Kate.

"For now," Bridges insisted, as they split a glass of champagne to celebrate having set the opening day for Death Row Restaurant. "We can always get someone else to keep Rader's journals later," Bridges added. "This is just until we get up and running. Until we really get a sense of how it all works, the authenticity of it all," Bridges suggested.

"I do," Kate mumbled, thinking of Dave. "I mean, I'll do it."

And she knew she would do it. Kate knew she would never back out of this job. Because there was no better way to remind herself of the true nature of the emptiness she had wrestled with and railed against and tried to fill up for most of her life than to force herself to record Rader's stupid journals. It's not that Rader was a whole person and Kate an incomplete or broken person incapable of unifying her actions with her being. The serial killer's wholeness didn't come from fulfillment. To possess the object of their desire, serial killers must destroy it. If the masochist proves her freedom by giving it away, the serial killer proves his wholeness by becoming empty inside. And nothing would demonstrate this more clearly than seeing the actual focus of a killer's interest, documenting when he clipped his nails and what he had for lunch.

———

At exactly 10:00am, the phone rang, its shrill, strikingly familiar tone tinged with new business. On the other end was Dennis Rader. The guard in The Adjustment Center had left Rader's food slot open so he could reach out of his cell and pick up the handset of San Quentin's rolling payphone. And Rader had called Dave just like he was supposed to. Dave shuffled the pile of notes in his hand. He'd practiced this. And yet there was no way to practice this. And after Rader, the phone would ring again. It would be Gary Ridgway. And after that, Anthony Sowell. And so on. Dave's morning was booked with serial killers, just as Todd Bridges had planned.

And in her hotel room in Santa Monica was Kate, also waiting by the phone, waiting for Dave to report what it was like to talk to Dennis Rader, the one serial killer Kate had not interviewed. Dave pictured Kate in a light summer dress, her hair pulled back into a ponytail, not because she might become nauseous but because she liked occasional breezes on her neck. Dave placed his hand on the receiver. He held it there briefly, wanting to let it ring one more time before picking up. These killers, Dave thought, he couldn't call them. No one can call them. The only way to speak to them is if they call you. They are one way streets, surprise knocks on the door. But Dave could call Kate right after speaking with Rader, Ridgway and Sowell. Their relationship didn't have to be one way. It wasn't unidirectional, like railroad tracks. And Dave could talk to Kate about anything. There was nothing stopping him from doing that, and nothing stopping Kate from doing that either.

CODA: OPENING NIGHT

DAVE WAS ALREADY SWEATING underneath his Death Row Restaurant stab proof vest when the first Bentley pulled up to San Quentin.

The sun dangled low and gorgeous beyond the barbed wire of the patio. It gave the impression it would never sink below the horizon, as if the opening night of Death Row Restaurant would go on forever. Meanwhile, the gentle surf in the bay passed the evening light from ripple to ripple in a perpetual handoff. There was something hopeful in this, like a canned food drive. At the prep counter, Gary Ridgway and Dennis Rader attended to 'mise en place' tasks, dicing onions and garlic, prepping fresh greens and sauces. Kate lingered with her notebook at the ready, waiting for the serial killers to call her over in order to record their personal statistics and observations for posterity. Dave made his way around the patio, checking off items on his kitchen checklists. A few times, Dennis Rader or Gary Ridgway (or the other killers assigned to every imaginable restaurant task) signaled Kate to jot something down. Kate did this without any hint of inconvenience or distaste, which Dave found remarkable. The whole thing already functioned like clockwork.

Dave checked off that each table had been properly set with water glass, wine glass, champagne flute, salad fork, oyster fork, soup spoon, sugar spoon, fish knife and coffee spoon, and as he did this he also noted that Rader was about to finish slicing an onion. Since greeting Rader when he had arrived for his shift, Rader had buttoned the top button of his polo. Who does that? Then again, Dave thought as Bridges sat their first ever customers (the Governor himself and his party, four all totaled), the point of Death Row Restaurant wasn't to provide a consistent experience for each diner. Eating at Death Row Restaurant meant applying to be placed on the approved visitor list at San Quentin, traveling to the prison in an official vehicle and upon arrival signing waivers and donning essentially a flak jacket and practicing a forearm maneuver to protect your neck in case of an incident. Unlike other restaurants, the point wasn't the consistency of the experience, which would be different each time. For instance, the Governor and his party had already selected their utensils from the San Quentin museum of shivs and shanks. And the available selection of prisoner fashioned weapons, each constructed with a particular violent purpose in mind, would be different tomorrow and different again the next day. And there were going to be anomalies. For instance, a young woman in the Governor's party had inexplicably selected from the shiv and shank museum an athletic sock with a padlock stuffed in it, a surprise, souvenir 'sap' that could have no earthly purpose as a utensil for her meal.

"Where are their chefs' coats?" Dave asked Todd Bridges, who had just returned from seating their VIP guests. Bridges wore a breezy linen suit for opening night and had finished his look with a pair of platinum Maybach aviator sunglasses. Earlier, Bridges had explained that his sunglasses were constructed out of titanium, a metal with the strongest strength to weight ratio on earth. This titanium had been plated with platinum. Strength and beauty together. That had been the entirety of Bridges' point, as Bridges had turned and walked away immediately after this explanation. As the opening of Death Row Restaurant had drawn closer, Bridges had started using the word 'powerful' in connection with himself. For instance, towards the end of an exhausting meeting with state regulators, Bridges had turned to Dave and said, "I'm powerful hungry." And now, on opening night, Bridges was trying to combine this sense of power with beauty.

While Dave waited for a response to his question about stab proof vests for his crew, a second very practical question occurred to Dave. Where were his killer cooks supposed to take their breaks? Remarkably, the only plan they had in place was for their collection of murderers to stand around in a small rectangle painted on the roof behind an avocado tree they had brought in. But this seemed to Dave a terrible plan. Who knows what they would talk about or do on break? They needed a place out of the sightlines of diners.

"Bring the governor a 2014 Screaming Eagle Cabernet," Bridges signaled their wine sommelier. "And don't open it until I get there," he insisted.

If Bridges was wearing his Death Row Restaurant stab proof vest, he was hiding it well, Dave thought. In fact, Bridges looked exactly the same, not a millimeter thicker in his chest or stomach. Either he had gone on a starvation diet just to look good in his state mandated stab proof vest, or he wasn't wearing one.

A hundred questions popped into Dave's head. And as Dave waited for a response from Todd Bridges, he found himself inadvertently practicing how to raise his elbow and forearm to protect his neck.

"Did you know, Dave, that many famous wineries have a connection to serial killing?" Bridges said, ignoring Dave's original question. "Gilmanton, for instance, while not as notable as Screaming Eagle, has a direct connection to Herman Webster Mudget, better known as H.H. Holmes. Holmes committed his very first murder in Gilmanton and the winery is where the Mudget family used to live. Like Death Row Restaurant, the Gilmanton Winery has embraced its past. They don't celebrate the murders he committed, of course. They just recognize that the murders are a historical fact. They produce a wine called 'Jack the Ripper,' based on the theory that H.H. Holmes committed the Ripper murders before he opened his famous 'Murder Hotel.'"

"The chefs' coats," Dave repeated, already feeling exhausted. "Rader is over there chopping onions in a blue polo. And Ridgway is wearing a women's t-shirt that says 'Green River Killing, inc.'"

Dave was shocked at how stoic his own voice had sounded. These were important issues and he had sounded as if he was reporting hypertension statistics in smokers. Dave immediately understood, even without Bridges saying anything, that of course Todd Bridges already knew all about what his killer cooks were wearing.

"Dave," Bridges responded, peering in five directions at once. He was soaking up every detail of this historic evening. "You have to remember that your cooks are not 'employees.' These killers are volunteering. We aren't paying them at all and I won't have them wearing the Death Row Restaurant Enterprises logo. They are wards of the state and the only person who can adjudicate their outfits is the warden of San Quentin," Bridges elaborated.

Bridges had added the word 'enterprises' to Death Row Restaurant, indicating that they were now a for profit business, which was new. While Dave didn't accept this answer, he had lost interest in his own question, an experience he was having more and more frequently with Todd Bridges. Besides, Dave had other things to worry about. Not only were his two sous chefs notorious sexual sadists, but neither of them had any experience working in restaurants.

"They don't get to wear the logo," Bridges reiterated.

A burst of laughter came from the Governor's table. Surprisingly, the Governor's party wasn't sitting at the coveted 'gas chamber table.' Dave wondered who would have that honor.

Bridges popped his shades onto his forehead.

"Always remember that your cooks are not employees of Death Row Restaurant Enterprises."

Dave nodded. He glanced at the bay, which was filled with windsurfers, private boats and commuter ferries. From the looks of it, one of the ferries was headed to the San Francisco Giants game.

"Don't the cooks have to wear stab proof vests, like everyone else here?" Dave asked, before Todd Bridges could walk away. Dave's vest, one of the official high end Death Row Restaurant vests, was ungodly uncomfortable, worse than the one San Quentin had given him when they got their initial tour of The Adjustment Center. In fact, Dave's stab proof vest was the hottest garment he had ever worn. His chest and back were drenched in sweat, which had started to pool in his ass crack. And the material of the vest felt like burlap. The only nice thing about the vests was the logo, which Bridges had taken care to get exactly right. The letters DRR were organized to create a hood slipped over the head of a condemned man. It was subtle, but definitely there. And the whole logo was smooth and precise. Bridges had bragged to Dave that he had the logo thermoprinted rather than embroidered, so it would have the raised, flowing letters of a business card without being on paper.

"No," Bridges insisted. "Your cooks do not have to wear the stab proof vests, not unless the warden orders them to wear one. And in that case, it will be a regular San Quentin version. Now if you'll excuse me, I'm going to help the Governor enjoy his Screaming Eagle Cabernet." Bridges sauntered off.

Dave went back to the kitchen. It was only a few paces away. The gas chamber, its tiny door propped open and intimately lit by tea candles was visible from every part of their patio. Dave had kept the menu for opening night simple to save everyone's sanity. But simple dishes leave nowhere to hide. Everything now depended on cooking the food properly. This was exactly what Todd Bridges wanted. He wanted every diner to be able to feel the fact that a serial killer had taken time out of his day, had taken extraordinary care to cook her meal properly while getting no compensation whatsoever.

Dave hovered near Gary Ridgway who was busy squaring ribs with a twelve inch Granton blade. Ribs tend to be odd looking and oval. Squaring them off makes them exponentially more appealing. The Granton blade was huge, a stunning knife and Dave couldn't help but fear for his life watching Ridgway wield it. He had to remind himself that when Ridgway killed women he didn't use knives. He was a strangler. But what demanded Dave's attention was Ridgway's focus and precision. Ridgway squared ribs with the soft, vacant expression of a monk. And yet Dave kept coming back to what Gary Ridgway had done, what had landed him in prison, the murders, minimum forty eight of them. Standing on the roof of The Adjustment Center on opening night, itching himself under his sweaty, stab proof vest, listening to the rise and fall of the bay in the background, and watching Gary Ridgway square off ribs, Dave felt all that Death Row Restaurant had to offer.

For instance, it was clear to Dave that Death Row Restaurant upends the way goods and services come to their customers. When you open your laptop, the persons who labored to produce it are invisible. When a waiter takes your order, he is a shell of his full self. The economy of goods and services, like serial criminals, harbors a secret history. Dave's scratchy Death Row Restaurant stab proof vest, for instance — who had made it? And under what conditions? No one at Death Row Restaurant knew. No one knew who had made the tables customers propped their elbows on, the chairs they sat in, even their undergarments or the gas chamber itself. And yet, every customer at Death Row Restaurant would know intimate details about the true desires and identity defining crimes of their waiter and their cook. Customers choose which killer cooks their meal and which confiscated weapon from the San Quentin shank museum they will eat with. It was a kind of personalization that Walmart greeters and Starbucks employees who print the customer's name on their disposable Starbucks cup could never match. Personalization at Death Row

Restaurant meant actual persons who owned what they did as who they are and the unimaginable personal cost of this process for the victims and the families of victims. At Death Row Restaurant, personalization meant knowing that Gary Ridgway has no separate work persona. He is a killer, through and through, yet he cooked your steak and dredged it in garlic butter and herbs. At Death Row Restaurant, commodities have no secrets. The transparency of it all really was remarkable.

Dave felt relief every time he thought about how Death Row Restaurant Enterprises would never have signage or slogans attesting to the level at which the amorphous corporate 'we' cares about their customers or to how much their employees love their jobs. After twenty years at United Airlines, this was, Dave thought, a liberation. When Dave thought about this aspect of the restaurant he literally pictured a lion being released from captivity into the Serengeti. Dave especially liked that having Gary Ridgway cook a steak to exacting customer specifications in no way implied empathy or caring about the experience of the person who placed the order. If the patron was a woman, Ridgway would no doubt enjoy strangling her, enjoy meticulously scrubbing away all evidence of his crime and enjoy planting select personal items from the victim in gas stations across the state, to mislead police. If it was Dennis Rader who cooked that meal, the same would be true, except that Rader kept huge troves of souvenirs from his victims, so he could revisit his crimes.

Dave fell into watching Ridgway's soft concentration as he pulled the razor sharp Granton blade through the meat, emulating the precise pattern Dave had demonstrated to him about a week ago.

"If you score the meat in several directions, almost like an accordion," Dave had explained, with Ridgway looking on, "it will cook perfectly in minutes. No braising needed." At the time, Ridgway merely nodded and then pulled out his pocket comb and ran it through his thinning hair a few times. Later, Dave couldn't help wondering why Ridgway was agreeing to work in the restaurant, just as federal agents had wondered why Ted Bundy agreed to help them catch The Green River Killer, who turned out to be Gary Ridgway.

———

The first seating was extremely limited. Just a few celebrity tables to get the restaurant started and to allow staff to practice their roles.

Dave didn't have much to do so he bounced around the dining room, greeting their few customers and occasionally supervising food preparation — and he kept checking in and rechecking in with Kate. The night flowed smoothly, smoke rising from the grill and mixing with the salt air of the bay, meat sizzling and plates clacking on the prep counter. Occasionally, a staccato chopping cut through the chatter of the dining room. The kitchen and its killers were that close. The moonlight and the undertow of the tides and the tiki torches and the soft salt breeze were perfect. It was absolutely possible, Dave thought at such moments — even as he continued to sweat bullets underneath his stab proof vest — to forget that they were inside San Quentin prison and surrounded by some of the world's worst serial murderers. Or more precisely, once the actual restaurant service began, such things didn't matter as much as Dave thought they would. That was Dave's impression as he listened in on server interactions.

"Good evening. I'm Lonnie Franklin and I'll be your server this evening."

The Governor and his party flipped the menu over to read Lonnie's bio. The list of potential staff had grown exponentially. Organized alphabetically, Lonnie wasn't even on the first page.

"So which item on the menu is yours?" the Governor's niece asked.

"Chicken tacos with strawberry salsa," Lonnie Franklin bent at the waist. His mouth hung open as he pointed at the menu. The teenager gripped the athletic sock stuffed with a padlock, which rested on the rooftop near her right foot and gold laced sandals.

"Are you part Latino?" she asked tentatively.

"Naw."

"A fan of tacos?"

"Naw. 'A strawberry,' see that's what we used to call a woman who exchanges sex for drugs. Back, you know, 1983 or so, I was mixed up in all that back then, taking photos of women and all that," Lonnie Franklin stood up from his crouch near the table. He was a large man, though it was hard to be intimidated by someone in his late sixties and wearing an apron.

"So you would drug women and then kill them in their sleep?" the teenager asked.

The Governor leaned in between them.

"Aria," the Governor began. "Lonnie's case was very complicated. Mr. Franklin wasn't nicknamed the 'Grim Sleeper' because he drugged women or attacked them while sleeping. He got his nickname because of his long periods of inactivity, although some speculate that he was just dumping bodies at the landfill he worked at, that the bodies have never been discovered." The Governor leaned back, held his Screaming Eagle Cabernet up to the fading evening light, then took a swallow. "Try the tacos. I'll bet they will be delicious."

"That comes with a jicama and mango slaw," The Grim Sleeper added, jotting down the order on his notepad.

"So you're on Death Row?"

"I am," Lonnie answered.

"It's a great story," the Governor began, as a backwaiter refilled their water glasses.

"Thank you," the two ladies mumbled.

"That was Joseph DeAngelo, the Golden State Killer who just filled your water glass," the Governor added. "But Mr. Franklin's case, it's still very controversial because like with Joe DeAngelo, Mr. Franklin was captured through CODIS, the FBI's DNA evidence bank. It was your son, right? His weapons charge?"

Lonnie sighed. He shifted his entire weight onto his right side. The gesture was inscrutable.

"Chris got dropped on a felony. Weapons," The Grim Sleeper began. "They did a familial search for cold case DNA. Chris came back a hit."

"I think I'll have the Tomahawk steak," the Governor stated, "just past rare, if you can. And I'd like Gary Ridgway to cook it for me."

"Yes, sir," Lonnie Franklin said, jotting this in his notepad.

"It's very controversial what happened with Mr. Franklin," The Governor continued. "The CODIS database, there's just no question, it's disproportionately African American."

"Miss, I need to know who you'd like to cook your strawberry tacos?" Lonnie Franklin asked.

The Governor's niece appeared lost in her menu.

"Why don't you go ahead and choose for her, Lonnie?"

"That's against the rules, sir." Lonnie replied. "Customers have to choose. We can't do that for 'em."

"Ah, yes. Well how about you just ask who'd genuinely like to cook these strawberry tacos, then? Surely, that meets with Death Row Restaurant standards."

"Yes, sir."

A breeze lifted the tablecloth, which fluttered as if there was nothing more natural in the world than eating a meal on top of a building exclusively reserved for murderers and sexual sadists.

"Excuse me everyone. Since the young lady is wearing such a lovely black dress, I wanted to drop off this black napkin so that she will be sure not to get white lint on her lovely outfit."

"You must be Juanna," the Governor added.

"Sí señor. Señor Gobernador. My professional wrestling belt gave me away."

"Well, that and the giant butterfly mask."

"Estas son las firmas de mi acto."

———

Dave had long wondered whether the overall hum of dinner conversations and pace of bodies in a restaurant, the rote chewing and clang of silverware and clink of glasses — would feel any different at Death Row Restaurant. Now that the first three tables were enjoying drinks and even digging into appetizers on their patio, he once again took stock of how Death Row Restaurant felt. But his impression was incomplete. Things were not yet up to speed. The coveted gas chamber table, for instance, hadn't hosted any diners. Who would be the first to eat there, to eat their meal in a space convicts had to force one foot in front of the other, prodded by guards, to step into, a place that instead of providing a meal was where convicts last meals went undigested in their guts. The gas chamber meant finality, meant stoppage, meant the irreversible, like a guillotine whose halt in space is emphatic. And soon, someone would be privileged to eat a meal there for the first time in history.

———

Kate was jotting something down for Dennis Rader. More than any other employee, Rader was dominating her time. And Kate took down Rader's notes with no judgment. Who was to say, Dave thought to himself, what was ultimately worth writing down and what wasn't? When authenticity is your guide, any impulse, any detail becomes as worthy as any other. For all Dave knew, Rader could be starting a novel during his first shift.

When Kate took notes for these killers, she did something entirely natural for her. She lowered her shoulders. When Kate engages in a conversation, she leans in ever so slightly. This had always struck Dave as a mark of how nice she is. She probably didn't even realize she did this, just as Dave hadn't realized until he met Kate how much he valued little things people do without thinking: a last minute lunge to hold a door open for someone you don't even know or giving your dog a few extra nuggets of food at breakfast even though you know the dog doesn't understand this as a special gesture.

So as Rader dictated his notes to Kate, leaning casually on a stainless steel countertop, his murderous hands inches from a flutter of Kate's hair that had escaped the neat bun she had tied it back in, inches from her delicate neck, from her carotid artery, which Rader would no doubt love to compress and restrict. The image of Kate and BTK had this surprising softness to it, all because of the way Kate leaned forward and lowered her shoulders just the tiniest bit to make sure she had heard Rader correctly.

———

The second seating was mostly philanthropists.

"For contrast," Bridges insisted. "A philanthropist cares about the cause, not about himself. Though of course, the more he negates himself, the more proof he has of his dedication to the cause. It's not without a certain violence, don't you agree?"

Dave shrugged.

"Did you know that of the top fifty philanthropists in the US, thirteen live in California?" Bridges asked. "In fact, seven live in the Bay Area, not far from San Quentin."

So they had tables of philanthropists surrounded by killers pushing in their chairs as they sat and filling their water glasses with care before going over a list of aperitifs.

———

"Did you know that Gary Ridgway might be able to apply for parole in 2028?" Bridges said from behind his Maybach sunglasses. "If SB 5036 passes, that is. You see, Washington State got rid of the death penalty by arguing that you could just have life in prison without the possibility of parole." Bridges pushed his sunglasses back over the bridge of his nose. "And now the state senate is debating SB 5036, arguing that life in prison without a chance for parole is inhumane. SB 5036 is about opportunity, is about how people can change."

Dave wondered who Death Row Restaurant would replace Gary Ridgway with if he got paroled. It was opening night and Ridgway was already a superstar. Everyone wanted Ridgway to cook for them.

"Wouldn't it be fantastic if Ridgway got paroled and then kept working here anyway?" Bridges insisted. "Imagine that. Imagine Ridgway squaring off ribs inside San Quentin for no salary or benefits. Imagine him sleeping in our kitchen and never leaving San Quentin just so he could properly prepare those ribs." Bridges seemed ecstatic at the possibility. "Ridgway's real career will always be his murders," Bridges continued. "That's how I convinced the warden at San Quentin that he had nothing to worry about with Gary Ridgway and Dennis Rader being around all these knives. They're both stranglers. They don't kill with knives. It's who they are."

Dave glanced at Kate who was leaning against the avocado tree they had brought in for opening night. It was one of the few plants that Death Row Restaurant's interior design team had trouble placing on the rooftop patio. They had even asked Dave where he thought the avocado tree should go.

"Excuse me," Dave said. "I have something that needs my attention," he barely got the words out of his mouth. He was anxious to talk to Kate all of a sudden. And yet after one step towards her, Dave had trouble continuing. He had no idea what their relationship had been or where they stood.

"How is it going?" Dave asked.

She stifled a yawn.

"Just fine," Kate said. She sounded exhausted.

"It's weird, isn't it?" Dave asked.

"What?"

"Well, everything." Dave shrugged. The sentence had come out with too much wingspan. He didn't want Kate to think of their relationship as weird. "I always thought getting the most authentic restaurant in history going would be energizing." Dave moved alongside her and leaned against the avocado tree. It swayed backwards, barely remaining upright. If they pushed the tree over it would probably land in the Governor's lap. But Dave didn't care. He lit a cigarette.

"You smoke?" Kate asked, surprised.

"Not really," Dave replied, hauling on the cigarette and exhaling for what seemed like a year. "Just tonight."

Kate held up two fingers and Dave passed her the cigarette.

"I never told you about my first real love," Kate said. "This guy named Brad."

"Brad?" Dave didn't know why, but it surprised him that she could love a guy named Brad.

"We were both very immature," Kate confessed. "Brad was a sports guy but he had a lot of potential. That's what I thought, anyway. This one time I forced Brad to go to a play with me. He wasn't the type to be going to plays, but he agreed to go because of me," Kate took another long pull off the cigarette. She tried to pass it back to Dave, but he held up his hand and Kate kept smoking. "We were watching the play and Brad kept fidgeting. He was just so immature. I was about to touch his leg and tell him to knock it off when Brad leaned over and I thought he was going to insist that we leave. But instead, he whispered in my ear 'that guy Oedipus, why doesn't he just explain how this shit wasn't his fault?' And I opened my mouth to clarify it all for him, that this was about destiny and that a Greek play wasn't about finding out what happened and so on. And realized instead, quite suddenly actually, that Brad understood the play better than I did. Oedipus. Why didn't Oedipus just say, 'look, I did everything I could possibly do to avoid killing my father and marrying my mother.'" Kate tossed the cigarette and ground it out with her heel. Then she exhaled a final plume of smoke. "Brad just kept saying it. 'Jesus, if there was ever a guy who could argue that this shit wasn't his fault it's this guy Oedipus.' Brad wasn't complaining. He was explaining. Oedipus wanted to do it, wanted to kill his father and marry his mother. It wasn't fate. It was desire."

Kate seemed close to tears.

Dave wanted to say something. Oedipus was another example of someone who owned what he had done. But Dave didn't know what to say, so he just stood there with Kate, leaning on the avocado tree.

———

By 8:00pm, things started to pick up. Dave wasn't sure who would show up opening night. Dave expected several of the restaurant's guests on opening night to be politicians since they, too, have a substantial investment in owning what they do. Being a leader doesn't equate to just enforcing laws or referring to a playbook for decision making. A leader has to know when to make exceptions to the usual ways of doing things, even exceptions to how laws are enforced like Barack Obama's DACA program. These are the decisions politicians own at the deepest level. Dave thought celebrities might show up too, but he wasn't entirely sure. Celebrities might avoid Death Row Restaurant thinking that it was disrespectful to victims. Or just as plausibly, celebrities might see the restaurant as engaging a forgotten community, as engaging in prison reform efforts. Squeaky clean, careful celebrities like LeBron James probably wouldn't have dinner in the restaurant until reaction to it had been codified. But on opening night, maybe Charles Barkley or even Tiger Woods would drop by, guys whose scandals and refusal to be a role model were now part of their personal brand. Perhaps Matt Damon or Angelina Jolie or Mark Ruffalo would seize the moment, drop by for an appetizer and make a few statements about fracking or school to prison pipelines or restorative justice.

But it was Floyd Mayweather who became the first person to eat inside the gas chamber.

"I want to see what all this gas chamber shit is about," Mayweather declared, putting his feet up on the handle of the little door that grants entry to the gas chamber as a small gaggle of reporters sweating maniacally under stab proof vests snapped photos.

"Mr. Mayweather, do you support Death Row Restaurant? Are you a principal investor?"

Dave distinctly heard the soft lapping of waves in the bay and a few seagulls squawk before Mayweather responded.

"I been to jail. For a black man, being in jail don't matter. Malcolm X and Martin Luther King been to jail. But I want to try that baseball steak cooked by that motherfucker Gary Ridgway. He ain't shit by the way."

Mayweather wore the Death Row Restaurant stab proof vest, only he had made some alterations so that his vest opened in front, showing off his impressive abs. Small, metal had been sewn into his vest. To each ring Mayweather had attached a Rolex watch. He had five or six diamond laden watches on either side. Mayweather was even wearing his most expensive watch, Jacob & Co's 'The Billionaire,' a watch with a deconstructed face full of clockwork and gears contrasted by diamonds encrusting every other inch.

"Get that Ridgway motherfucker over here," Mayweather called from behind $45,000 Bentley shades.

And Mayweather wasn't the only fighter to sit in the coveted gas chamber table that night. Mayweather was followed by Khabib Nurmagomedov, undefeated (retired) UFC Champion.

"In Sil'dih we eat Kurnick — chicken pie." Khabib told reporters. "Steak only on rare occasion in Russia. But if I'm having a steak in American prison, I want it cooked by Dennis Rader. He thinks he's a strangler, that he's 'good at it,'" Khabib said. Dennis Rader was of course a strangler, but Khabib was confusing Dennis Rader with Gary Ridgway, who famously dismissed his thirty one year painting career by explaining to the media that strangulation was his real career. "Dennis Rader doesn't last ten seconds in the Octagon. Rear naked choke. That's it," Khabib asserted. "It's about respect. Tell him I want chicken pie. He makes it for me."

And Todd Bridges could only tell Khabib that Dennis Rader is making ribs tonight and that he can only ask Chef Rader if he wants to make chicken pie. And he will only cook this if he wants to.

Although the kitchen was well stocked, Dave's small staff was not prepared to cook these special requests. But Ridgway and Rader, they were oddly into pleasing others. The special orders kept Dave scrambling.

"We can't keep doing this," Dave complained to Todd Bridges a few hours later. "These one off meals, sometimes we don't even have the ingredients. I just spent half an hour making pie crust out of crushed madeleines. I can't vouch for the quality of this food." Dave was panting, he was so busy. Not only did Dave have to come up with recipes off the cuff for these celebrity requests, but he couldn't even prepare the food himself. Ridgway and Rader and Franklin and Sowell had to do all the actual cooking. Dave wound up demonstrating the cook, then putting his meal off to the side so that the meal served was the one cooked by the serial killer. Dozens of these extra meals were lined up next to the avocado tree.

"What are you talking about?" Bridges demanded. "This is fantastic. These special requests are like last meal requests. Totally genuine," Bridges bragged. "But only honor these requests if the cooks want to make these special meals. Make sure they know this," Bridges insisted, and then began circulating the now crowded dining room.

Kate, too, was extraordinarily busy. It was that bastard Rader. He was recording his whole fucking existence. Even a sneeze meant calling Kate over. And Dave watched Rader's hands every time he called Kate to him.

"Dave," Bridges ran up and grabbed him. "Can you take care of table six? I can't deal with this woman anymore."

What now, Dave thought. And at table six was his old boss from United Airlines.

"What the hell is she doing here?" Dave demanded, but Bridges was already gone.

Dave gave Rader a lengthy list of instructions for chicken pie. He went over every step slowly and carefully. Rader nodded his head, but Dave felt certain the gesture was just for show and the second Dave turned around he would call Kate to him — and that he was plotting a way to strangle her.

"You see sir, Mr. Mayweather, Mr. Pretty Boy, Mr. TBE..." Bridges knew all of Floyd Mayweather's nicknames. Mayweather had finished his steak an hour ago but was still hanging around at the bar. "All of our serial killers are stranglers. Giving them knives isn't dangerous. That's not what they do. It'd be like giving you a pair of nunchucks in the ring."

"I don't need fucking nunchucks!" Mayweather shot back.

"Of course not," Bridges agreed.

"All I need is these knuckles."

"Just like my fight with Vanilla Ice," Bridges reminisced.

"Who?"

Table six was Death Row Restaurant's romance table. It was off the main dining area and away from the string lights that illuminated the patio. A single candle fluttered on the table where Dave's previous boss, Dana sipped a martini and smoked a cigarette. Though it had been less than a year since Dave had left United Airlines, his previous life centered around United Airlines seemed far away and unlikely.

"I had Anthony Sowell make this martini, Dave," Dana began. "That was Sowell's thing, right? He would lure women to his house of horrors by promising them alcohol or drugs, right?" Dana tapped her ash into a large fern next to the table. Dave slid her an ashtray. In all his previous interactions, Dana had wanted to be somewhere else, wanted to get whatever she was doing over with as quickly as possible. But Dana appeared to want to be at this table in Death row Restaurant. Dave, on the other hand, wanted his interaction with Dana to be over as quickly as possible. He wanted this whole night to be over.

"What're you doing here, Dana?"

"I'm here to discuss a business plan," Dana gestured with her cigarette that he should sit.

Dave sat down urgently, as if the chair might be snatched away for another purpose at any minute. He hadn't sat down once since the night began. "Remember, Dave. If I hadn't assigned you to the Wichita route you wouldn't even be here," Dana insisted.

Dave opened his mouth, then closed it without saying anything. While it was ridiculous for Dana to take credit for where Dave had ended up in life, the assertion was, factually speaking, true.

"I'm very busy tonight with the kitchen," Dave stated, although he couldn't help but ask, "Why are you wearing a flight attendant uniform?" It was true. Dana was wearing the same uniform that Kate had worn on all those nauseating flights from ORD to ICT.

"United Airlines wants to do something about a major issue in the skies. Remember all those times when you stood in front of the airport bridge and thanked everyone for flying United?"

"Of course I do," Dave said.

"Good. Well, think about the inevitably wooden goodbyes," Dana waved her hand robotically. "Thank you for flying United. Bye now. Thank you for flying United, bye now. Watch your step." Dana took a sip of her martini as if clearing a foul taste from her mouth. "How can we 'unite the world' when we are asking people to fly with attendants and pilots that don't even want to be there?"

Dana waved her cigarette like it was a magic wand and spouted a golden nugget from some leadership seminar, "'To do better, just do better,' right Dave?"

The idea of serial killers as flight attendants was ridiculous. Dave searched for something to say.

"This is just one restaurant, Dana. A few dozen killers. United must have 15,000 flight attendants. The logistical concerns alone are impossible."

"20,000," Dana corrected him, "not to mention airline associates, mechanics, etc. United has been promoting its staff as a 'big family' for the last three quarters. It was all Ross' idea," Dana insisted, though Dave knew this meant she had been heavily involved in designing whatever this program had been and that she was now distancing herself from it to avoid responsibility. "Ross had us alter the schedule, had us strategically separate the routes of staff who had worked together for years, even decades. Instead of tight knit teams who knew one another well, Ross put thousands of miles between our most seasoned staff. Ross even developed a 'time-off matrix' so he could insure such staff physically wouldn't be able to see one another on layovers. Then, United Airlines hosted a series of 'family reunions' in Michigan, Saturday picnics at a big house Ross had purchased in bumblefuck Michigan, a big house where staff would grill out and sit around a bonfire all evening." Dana sipped her martini.

"Are you fucking serious?" Dave laughed.

"It was not successful," Dana admitted. "And now that I've replaced Ross as the Midwest Regional Manager, I have assured the board that we will be taking a different track. That as I had told Ross on many occasions and using numerous visual aids — authentic staff interactions had to come from someplace deeper. That's why I want to apprentice here at Death Row Restaurant. I want to learn firsthand how this place works, what it feels like to work with staff that are totally genuine in everything they do. Then I can bring this revolutionary knowledge back to United Airlines. If we end up using serial killers, that's fine. But if not, well there must be dozens of ways to create that same feeling that United Airlines employees are doing their work because they love to do it," Dana speculated.

Dave strained sideways to get a glimpse of his kitchen. Ridgway was grilling an octopus. He wondered if Ridgway knew that the grill was only for charring an octopus. You never cook an octopus entirely on the grill.

"You'll have to talk to Todd," Dave said, pushing back his chair.

"He's resistant," Dana informed him. "I need you to explain the connection to him, the connection between travel and food and owning one's actions, the very things that brought you to this rooftop."

Dave was going to say something like "I'll do my best," which of course he wouldn't mean at all. It was just something he could say to get away from Dana. But Dave didn't say anything at all to her. He just walked away. It felt good. Maybe he was finding himself at Death Row Restaurant. Or maybe it was the fact that Rader was spatchcocking a chicken with a giant pair of razor sharp kitchen shears while Kate leaned across his prep station to take down his dumb fucking notes.

———

By midnight, things had gotten a little out of control. The kitchen was destroyed. Thankfully, they were out of everything but ribs. No more special requests. If you wanted to eat, you got ribs. Apparently, Dennis Rader had gone back to his cell. Anthony Sowell was still shaking martinis behind the bar. He was a marvelous bartender.

"Dave?"

Dave turned to see Nancy McKeon in a sleek black gown.

"You look fantastic," Dave said, his mood instantly improving. It was just like when he was a teenager. He'd be feeling lonely and awful and just seeing a girl he liked changed everything. Nancy's soft features and hardscrabble personality were an incredible relief to him. "Are you enjoying your evening?" Dave asked. This came out too formal, he thought. But it really mattered to him that Nancy enjoyed her evening.

"That bartender makes a wicked Bloody Mary," Nancy said.

Dave nodded, admiring Nancy's jet black, straight hair, which had been cut in an 80's style bob, but slightly longer and sleeker, updated to make its location in cultural time ambiguous.

"How long have you been here?" Dave asked.

"A couple of hours," Nancy shrugged. She looked over her shoulder as if whatever crew she came here with was likely to be leaving soon and she didn't want to be left behind.

"I thought you might eat in the gas chamber," Dave said. "Wasn't that what you said you wanted?"

"I did," Nancy replied. "I did eat in the gas chamber. Not a full meal, but I had some crab cakes in there."

Dave turned and looked. The gas chamber was now an hors d'oeuvres bar. Diners were stepping past the small, hermetically sealable door clutching cocktail napkins and miniature foods impaled by toothpicks. Toothpicks littered the floor of the gas chamber. Dave felt incredibly small all of a sudden, like a crab toiling away on a small hole at the bottom of an ocean.

The restaurant was packed, as full as it had been all night. Diners at Death Row Restaurant didn't want to eat and leave quickly after everything it took to get inside the prison.

"We must be at capacity," Dave mumbled to Nancy. Yet looking around, Dave couldn't spot a single one of his killer cooks. Rader, Ridgway, Franklin, Sowell, DeAngelo, Charles Ng — where had they all gone? No one stood behind the bar. No one was manning the grill or washing dishes. No one seemed to be waiting tables anymore. Their entire staff — had disappeared without a word. Dave expected the house lights to flash accompanied by a siren indicating an escape attempt or riot.

Instead, a microphone dropped from the pergola, the house lights dimmed and a little runway of LED strip lighting blossomed across the patio floor. Bridges took the microphone.

"Thank you all for coming," Bridges began as applause rose and then sustained itself.

Dave yawned massively while Bridges, humbled by the standing ovation, acknowledged the crowd. But Dave knew better. At this moment, Bridges was recouping decades of personal irrelevance. "Thank you," he reiterated. "Thank you all very much for coming." The applause died down and Bridges' smile gave way to a solemn, inscrutable expression. "As you know, Death Row Restaurant is more than just a dining experience. The idea was never easy to explain." The audience laughed. "You wouldn't believe the tactics I tried to explain this to investors," Bridges shook his head. "But Governor Newsom, he understood it right away. All I did was show the Governor a video of Bernie Sanders." A screen lit up behind Bridges, showing Bernie Sanders seated at a small table, flanked by talk show hosts Desus and Mero. Bernie's bald head, pinched lips and out of style rectangular glasses were unmistakable. The video began to play. Desus placed a pair of off white, Nike Air Jordan Retro #1's on the table between the hosts and Bernie Sanders.

"Looks like a nice sneaker," Bernie said.

"What do you think the resale value on this is?" Desus and Mero asked Bernie.

"$250," Bernie guessed.

"What's the resale value on these? $4500," Desus told Bernie, whose forehead pinched as he recoiled from the sneakers, half shaking his head.

"This is a status thing?" Bernie asked.

"It's a flex. You're not a big flexer?"

"No," Bernie said, shaking his head again.

"Are you familiar with Kanye West?" The interviewers asked Bernie, placing a red sneaker on the table. "This is Kanye's sneaker. The last sneaker he released when he was still under contract with Nike."

"I'm going to go big on this one," Bernie said. "It's weird to say it... $1000."

The interviewers broke down laughing.

"What's the resale on this one? $11,000," they told Bernie, who again shook his head in anguish.

Bridges paused the video perfectly, with Bernie holding his hand up in a stop gesture.

"The next question Bernie Sanders asks," Bridges explained, "is whether anyone pays that much for a pair of sneakers. And the answer is, sadly, yes they do."

Dave had been watching intently. He had no idea what this was about.

"Bridges is wearing Maybach Sunglasses," Dave whispered to Nancy McKeon, which probably didn't make sense because Bridges wasn't wearing his sunglasses anymore. "They cost like $20k."

"Death Row Restaurant is more than a dining experience," Bridges insisted, the words gaining power in their repetition. "That's why we are launching our own product line, the BalenSHUaga. A shoe based on the SHU — the Special Housing Unit here in San Quentin."

The whole dining room leaned in to see the BalenSHUaga, phones at the ready. Bridges pulled out a white sneaker with classic Adidas striping on the side and an excessively large and ornate sole and was met with a deluge of iPhone camera sounds. "Hold, on," Bridges said. "This is not the BalenSHUaga. This is the Balenciaga Triple S Adidas. These sell for upwards of two grand. The experience begins with a box that is different from the typical Adidas or Balenciaga box. The lid has a special logo combining the Adidas and Balenciaga logos and the box states that this shoe is a 'collaborazione'— a collaboration. The first thing customers remove from the box is not the shoes, but a complementary Balenciaga runner backpack and a pair of extra shoelaces." Bridges reached into his pockets, fumbling with the microphone to remove and display these items. The crowd hushed. It was like Bridges was performing a magic trick. "And finally, the shoes," Bridges brought the sneaker down to chest height and held it near his face like it was a precious infant. A church gospel began lightly in the background. "This may not be as floral in its design as the Balenciaga/Gucci collaboration," Bridges offered, "But the white and black together in the 'Triple S' is smooth, slick," he added. "The upper half looks like it could be an Adidas shoe. But Balenciaga always prints the shoe size on the toe," Bridges pointed out, "that and the elaborate sole are the markings of Balenciaga," he insisted, turning the shoe over in his hands. "The black and gray combination channels both the Los

Angeles Raiders NFL team and the extremely successful San Antonio Spurs NBA team. And if you want to buy a Balenciaga, as everyone knows, you have to size down. Like most luxury brands, they have nonstandard sizes," Bridges concluded, passing the shoe to an assistant. His assistant then passed Bridges another shoe, this one red. "Just the other day a fan asked Kanye West to sign a pair of Yeezy Red October sneakers," Bridges began, holding up the shoe. "But Kanye saw that the logo was slightly too large. And instead of saying 'Made in China,' these Yeezys said 'Sample Made in China.'" Bridges pointed to various aspects of the shoe. "A real Yeezy, West communicated later through his publicist, has exactly nine red dots inside the embroidered rectangle on the heel. This one had more. Kanye had spotted a fake and told the fan, 'That ain't no Nike, though.' Was the fan upset? Had the fan paid $11,000 for a fake pair of Yeezys? No, the fan knew he had a fake, but wanted to get the sneaker signed by Kanye anyway. This consumer chose to buy a fake because why pay $11,000 for something you can get for $200 when only an expert like Kanye knows the difference?"

At this, Bridges reached behind him and turned back around with a different sneaker in his hand. He held this sneaker aloft to the crowd.

"This looks like a regular old PUMA Clyde," Bridges began. "But it's not. This is the BalenSHUaga, a shoe worn by a Death Row serial killer here in the Special Housing Unit at San Quentin. If you take this shoe and put it next to any other PUMA Clyde, no one can tell the difference," Bridges asserted.

An avalanche of fake shutter noises from iPhones ensued, the first public photos of the BalenSHUaga.

"But this shoe is different. Maybe not materially different, sure, but this shoe was worn by a killer on Death Row. It has something — something that a regular PUMA Clyde doesn't have, something abstract and intrinsic, a secret life," Bridges paused, took a deep breath. "Like a serial killer, this shoe has an identity. Not an ever shifting, metaphysical identity like I had when I was Willis, when I was making $30,000 a week on Diff'rent Strokes, which was a ton of money in the 1980's. That would be around $100,000 a week today," Bridges interjected. "And that was my identity until the late 1980's, until my show got canceled and I did meth all day. I would go off on a bender and then pass out for days without eating, shitting or pissing, and later when I was strapped to a metal bed in a diaper, when I was in jail and accused of murder and warding off threats from Richard Ramirez who was in the cell next to me," Bridges took a sip of water, hearing perhaps the applause or laughter of a live studio audience in his mind. "And here I am today," he declared without elaborating. "The Balen-SHUaga, like the serial killer, has a stable, whole identity. At once unique, but not special, just like serial killers," Bridges concluded.

The air felt electric with anticipation and yet it was dead silent. No one coughed or even shuffled their feet. Dave could hear the waves gently lapping the shoreline in the billion dollar bay. "Shoes," Bridges continued, "regular shoes have always been definitive markers of identity. Back in 1989, when I was arrested for the murder of Tex Clay," Bridges admitted, "it was common practice for gangs in Los Angeles to adopt a sneaker. The Bloods adopted REEBOK because to them REEBOK stood for Respect Each and Every Blood OK? And they weren't the only gang to do this. Back then, every cop in Los Angeles knew that the MS-13 gang had adopted NIKE's Cortez sneaker. Because to an MS-13 gangbanger, NIKE stands for 'Niggas Insane Killin' Everybody.'"

Bridges' explanation was met with total silence to the point where Dave could now hear the slight sucking of air from the restaurant's tiki torches.

"The point I'm trying to make," Bridges continued, undaunted, "isn't that we should all be lucky enough to make $30,000 a week in 1980 or to buy a pair of sneakers for $11,000 or to find our identity in some group of likeminded people or through a luxury purchase. Identity is — well, take a lesson from a serial killer on this, it's what you do, it's owning what you do. That's the lesson of the serial killer who is in San Quentin for life. These killers, they are nothing special. But they are of course totally unique. You can't lump Gary Ridgway together with John Wayne Gacy because every detail of their crimes, every single thing they did fulfilled a different need for them, fulfilled a need rather than a desire. A serial killer could never find his identity in a luxury shoe purchase."

Bridges turned towards the bar, where Anthony Sowell, the Cleveland Strangler, a man who kept the heads of his victims in buckets in his house, handed Bridges a glass of water. Bridges took a small sip. "Come on out here, Anthony."

Sowell set the glass he was polishing on the bar and strutted down the little runway of LED lights. He paused, flexed his calf muscles to show off the sneakers. "These are the BalenSHUagas," Bridges declared to another round of applause. "The first honest commodity in the world," he stated. "The first commodity that declares it has a secret. This is a luxury shoe that will always be affordable because there will be no tangible difference between a genuine BalenSHUaga and a fake."

Sowell went to the end of the runway, pivoted and then flexed his calves again. An avalanche of fake shutter sounds from iPhones ensued. Bridges handed the microphone to Governor Newsom.

"Thank you, Todd," the Governor began. "And you know what else is great about these shoes?" He paused. "As the Governor of California, the Governor of an economy that would rank fifth in the world if we were a sovereign state, I want to point out something else about the BalenSHUaga sneakers. Rikers Island was the first prison to start using PUMA Clydes, and they didn't use them because PUMAs are vulcanized and provide no cavities or spaces in the shoe to hide contraband." Newsom strutted to the end of the runway himself, then came back to the center of the patio. "No, Rikers uses PUMA Clydes for the simple reason that no one is getting their ass kicked over a pair of PUMAs." Laughter rose from the dining room, then quickly made its way out to sea. "You've got hardened gangbangers walking around Rikers in shoes repped by professional golfers like Ricky Fowler," the Governor added, to more laughter. "And I think the point is clear. This isn't some kind of 'flex.' This SHU isn't for Hollywood elites. The essence of the BalenSHUaga is owning what you do. And that's a very different concept than accepting the consequences of your actions."

The Governor gestured towards the bar and a line of killers made their way through the runway, all wearing PUMA Clydes. "We are all paying way too much, not for gas, groceries or electricity — for our identities," Governor Newsom declared. "Calling a pair of sneakers 'Yeezy Red Octobers' and selling them for $11,000 isn't inflation. It's the wrong kind of identity and it's clear how costly this practice has become for society." Newsom let the microphone fall from his hands, he began applauding, applauding himself, sure, but also the whole enterprise. The entire restaurant joined in.

Newsom recovered the microphone.

"As Governor of the world's fifth largest economy, I've signed hundreds of bills into law. I signed a bill requiring the Department of Justice to investigate police killings of unarmed civilians. I signed a bill creating a task force to investigate reparations for the descendants of slaves in the United States. I strengthened coverage for fire insurance and prevented corporations from buying foreclosed homes in bulk. I signed SB 145, a controversial law allowing judges to decide who must register as a sex offender in cases of statutory rape. I sanctioned same sex marriages before they were legal. I legalized recreational marijuana. I issued a moratorium on state executions." The Governor took a deep breath. A low applause began near the bar, then petered out.

"But I don't want to dwell on signature legislation. It's time for politicians to do more than that. Back in 2007 I apologized for an affair I had with Ruby Rippey-Tourk. While I am sorry for the pain this affair caused, it's time for me to admit that with Ruby I found a way to stop apologizing for what I wanted. It took many years for me to understand that lesson. In fact, it wasn't until Todd showed me that video of Bernie Sanders, until we sat down and hammered out a historic redevelopment plan for San Pablo Bay that I realized what it truly means to take ownership of what you do." Newsom paused. He looked around the room, making massive eye contact. "I'm here to tell you that politicians need to change. I'm no longer going to propose legislation with the argument that it's the right thing to do. What's 'right' and moral isn't up for grabs. What's 'right' applies to everyone. And being a politician isn't about what's right. Being a politician is about making decisions, about deciding things that can't be decided by universal principles like doing what's 'right.' So I'm dropping that playbook. And going forward, I'm going to be as upfront as possible that I'm making decisions because that's what leaders do. And these decisions will have nothing to do with right and wrong and will have everything to do with owning what I do. That's what it means to be a California dreamer," Newsom concluded. "These killers," he added. "I fucking hate these guys. But I get why the public is fascinated by them. They are what they do. The rest of us just pretend."

Governor Newsom spoke these final words while standing in a sea of serial murderers.

"When Todd first told me about Death Row Restaurant I tried to think through where this thing would get us, what it would do for the state of California. And I tried to figure out how this venture would end. And just about every one of my advisors came out against it. They thought the public would hate the restaurant. They thought it would look like I was celebrating serial murder. They were sure these killers would stage a riot. And I fired every damn one of my advisors," Newsom bragged. "I fired them because that kind of thinking is what's wrong with the state of California. If there's one thing we can learn from the serial killer, it's that they have no endgame. These guys killed because they wanted to, sure. But it was more than that. Obviously, I despise these killers. But some good can come of their crimes. The restaurant exists in order to honor the tragic loss of the victims, the innocent souls who not only never got to achieve their dreams, they never even got the chance to try because their lives were foreclosed. To honor them we need to recognize that serial murder isn't the only thing stopping people from owning their actions as their identities. The other reason people don't do what they want to do is because we are taught to give up on desire. Ruby showed me how wrong this is. You can't be a person without desire. Politicians don't need to be in hiding about this. You can't trust a politican who hides behind his duty to do the right thing. Politicians who act out of duty are not substantially different from serial killers who act out of their duty — to kill. This is the kind of thing you realize when you eat Lonnie Franklin's strawberry tacos in The Adjustment Center of San Quentin."

The Governor was really on a roll. Dave had never heard a politician talk in such abstract terms and with such obvious commitment. Not a sound bite in sight. Newsom had found something inside himself that wedded him to the logic of the universe.

"This is wild," Nancy McKeon declared, threading her arm through Dave's elbow. "Maybe I should have ordered the tacos."

Then all of their serial killers, even the killers who weren't on the schedule to work that night, stopped milling around and strutted down the LED runway in their BalenSHUagas. Gary Ridgway and Lonnie Franklin (likely hundreds of murders between them). And they were followed by Joseph DeAngelo, 'The Golden State Killer,' by Wayne Williams, 'The Atlanta Child Murderer,' by Charles Cullen, the 'Kindness Killer,' by the infamous 'Truck Stop Killer,' Robert Ben Rhoades, by Karla Homolka, Paul Bernardo, Rosemary West, by 'The Pig Farmer Killer,' 'The Bible John Killer,' 'The Suffolk Killer' and on and on. Bridges had arranged for an astonishing number of killers to be transferred to San Quentin to work in Death Row Restaurant.

"Rader," Dave whispered, barely able to stand up anymore in his exhaustion. "Kate," Dave choked out.

"Kate took a cell for the night," Bridges said, smiling his golden smile from the 1980's. "She was too tired to go through all the Sally Ports, to drive back to the city. So she took a cell. It's perfectly safe."

A cell for the night? In the Adjustment Center? How did they possibly have room? How were they even fitting all these killers from other prisons, from all over the globe in San Quentin and still finding room for Kate?

"We've got a lot more killers coming," Bridges declared. This is only the beginning. "We're working on Ted Kaczynsky," Bridges said. The restaurant was packed with men Dave had winced reading about in the official profile folders Bridges had created, all of them strutting around in BalenSHUagas — to continued applause. And Bridges was absolutely correct, Dave thought. The idea of going through all those ports, of getting all that authorization and then driving back to the city. It was unfathomable to Dave in his exhaustion.

"You look like you're about to take a nosedive," Nancy McKeon said, shooting an arm around Dave's waist.

"Do you think you can give me a ride?" he mumbled. "I can barely stand up. But first, we have to check on Kate," Dave choked out, coughing dryly.

"I'm staying the night," Nancy replied. "Newsom got me my own cell."

How on earth could there be room? Dave thought. Dave recognized Peter Moore strutting down the LED lit runway of the Death Row Restaurant patio to raucous applause. Moore stopped to flex his calves and show off his BalenSHUagas, the same exact shoes as every other killer.

"The media dubbed Moore 'the man in black,'" Dave whispered to Nancy. "Moore terrorized North Wales for twenty years, mutilating at least four men and committing dozens of sex attacks. He blamed his crimes on a fictional lover named 'Jason,' whom Moore later admitted to inventing based on the killer in the Friday the 13th series," Dave elaborated. The whole thing was true and yet it was ridiculous. Dave was burning up in his stab proof vest.

"We're going to get you a cell," Nancy said. "Pronto. You need to lie down." She began loosening his chef's coat. But that did almost nothing. It was the stab proof vest. It was suffocating the life out of him.

Dave wanted to respond but was too exhausted to move or speak. He felt helpless, like his limbs had been tightly bound with ropes by Dennis Rader, like Rader had strangled him until he blacked out, then brought him back to consciousness only to strangle him again in a drawn out and merciless process that he couldn't escape, that he could only try to teach himself to embrace. He felt like Kate was suffering this exact fate too, right at this second, and yet Dave had almost no will of his own left to do anything about it. Bridges was going to make a fortune, Dave thought. And Newsom was on a political bullet train. As long as these killers don't pick up a knife.

ACKNOWLEDGMENTS

Quite a few people knowingly helped this novel come to life. Thank you Cristoph Paul and Leza Cantoral. I am grateful to Cris Mazza, Garnett Kilberg Cohen, Chris Grimes, Dan Magers, Brooks Sterritt, Katrina Washington, Travis Mandell, John Goldbach, Justin Raden, Corbin Hiday, Justin Allen and Brett Polivka who were early readers of the novel and/or put up with my theoretical obsession with serial killers and Capitalism. Thank you to Sylvia Rosman, Anna Kornbluh, Walter Benn Michaels and Todd McGowan whose theoretical work inspires one to write. Love and thanks to Darcie, Maeve and Alice who put up with years of me obsessively thinking about this book and injecting its ideas into otherwise innocent conversations. Special thanks to Robin Winer, Stacey Margolis, and Brian Evenson. As with any novel, quite a few people unknowingly played a key role through their art and scholarship. Thank you.

ABOUT THE AUTHOR

Daniel Gonzalez is the author of *Death Row Restaurant*.

His work has appeared in *The Lifted Brow, Hobart, The Fiddleback, Defenestration, Pravic, The American Book Review, Nonsite* and other places. He lives in Evanston, Illinois and can be contacted on Twitter @DRRmarch2024.